ABOUT THE AUTHOR

Lexie Winston has been an astronaut, rock star, princess, and time traveller. In her dreams. But none of the dreams have lived up to what becoming an author has been like. She gets to live in a world of pure imagination, and her heroines get to do the things she's always wished she could.

When not writing books, Lexie is a mother of two gorgeous teenagers and the wife to a patient and understanding man. They live in Western Australia and are lorded over by a black toy poodle. She loves camping, reading and if her iPad was stolen, her world would explode. (It has the kindle app on.)

Follow Lexie on

ALSO BY LEXIE WINSTON

The Collectors Division

(Reverse Harem Series)

Guardian

Guardian's Blood

Guardian Ascending

Arbor Vitae Coven

(Paranormal Romance Series)

Candy Conniptions

Dreamy Delights

Fangtastic Fireworks

Neighpalm Industries Collective

(Adult Bully Reverse Harem)

Abandoned Girl

Broken Girl

Cherished Girl

Seductive Sins Collection

(Reverse Harem Series)

Glorious Gluttony

Gangs, Guns, and Glory

GUARDIAN ASCENDING

The Collector's Division Book Three

LEXIE WINSTON

Guardian Ascending : Collectors Division

Mobi format: 978-0-6487933-6-6

Print: 978-0-6487933-7-3

Cover design by Infinty Book Covers

Edited by Inked Imagination

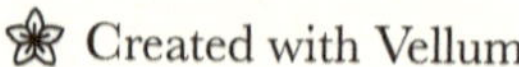 Created with Vellum

The author's husband has asked for her to say that no marriages were harmed in the making of this novel. Also, much to the author's disappointment, nor do any of the situations reflect real-life experiences.

To all the readers who like to be surprised in their books and do not require trigger warnings or cliff-hanger warnings, please skip the next page and continue to chapter one. To all the special snowflakes who need a heads up, continue onto the next page.

AUTHOR'S NOTE

(Snowflake Edition)

This book is a Reverse Harem. The main female character will end up with more than one partner. There will be multiple sex scenes throughout the series that have more than two people participating.

There will be MM, FF, MMF, MFM, and MMFMMMM. There may even be demon tails involved in the sex scenes.

There are scenes in this book that may trigger you. There is dub-con and what can possibly be seen as rape. I apologize for none of it.

Now that I have given you this warning, if this is not your thing, read no further. But if this still interests you, read away, but please don't then turn around and give me negative reviews because you don't like any of the things I have mentioned. If you don't like the story, that's cool, but complaining about things I have warned you about isn't.

Saying that, I hope you all give the story a chance and just skip past the things you don't like, because I really think it's awesome.

To Hope and Madeline.
I would have been lost without you two. Love you both more
than a fat kid loves cake.

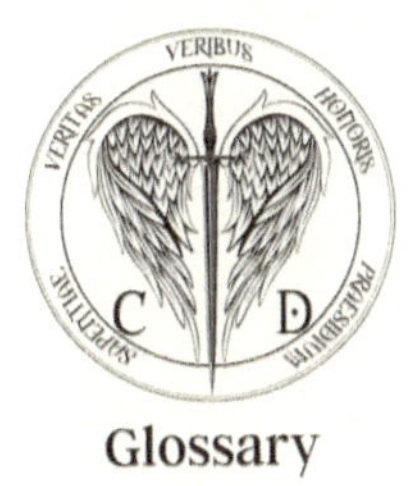

Glossary

Five Worlds

Reath Home-world to the Collectors Division. A mish-mash world of steampunk, magic, and some advanced technology. This world is surrounded by nine realms. **Mylea, goddess of Magic**, is their god.

Earth No Magic, no advanced technology but incredibly creative minds and talents. Earth's creativity clashed with Reath's magic and created the beings that inhabit the nine realms. **Eagi, god of Freewill**, is their god.

Minzeon An advanced civilization of high IQs and innovative minds. **Matoz, god of Technology,** is their god.

Amilles Angel home-world. **Azeyr i**s their god.

Habbalea Destroyed Demon realm. **Hammus is their god.**

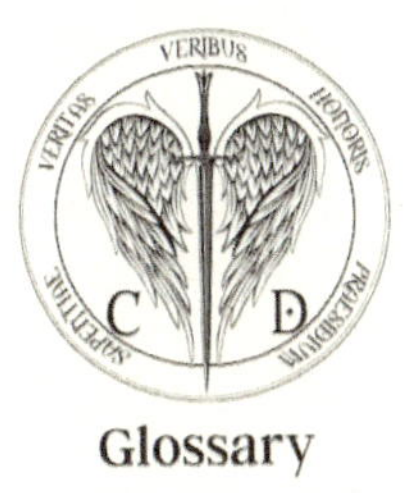

Glossary

Nine Realms

Zeli Gods of the European continent
Lyneon Gods of Africa, India, and the
Middle East
Kolekin Gods of Asia
Resnea Gods of South and Mesoamerica
Neadna Gods of Australia and the Pacific Islands
Elkly Mythical figures realm, e.g. Santa,
Tooth Fairy, Easter Bunny
Ferijen Halloween and mythical monster realm
Glieh Fairy-tale realm
Dikan Fictional character realm

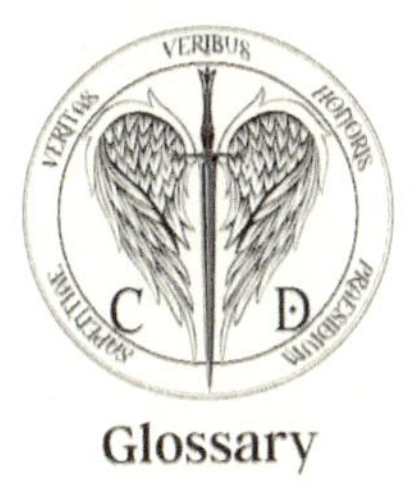

Glossary

Characters

Jessamina Michaels Daughter of **Lucifer and Michael**

Zephaniah Aldridge Son of Archangels **Jophial and Zadkiel**

Lysander Caldwell Son of Archangels **Uriel and Haniel**

Drusilla Caldwell Daughter of Archangels **Uriel and Haniel**

Samuel Mason Son of Archangels **Chamuel and Sofiel**

Mavromichali Atwater Son of Archangels **Azrael and Gadriel**

Patrick Longhurst Son of Archangels **Raphael and Ariel**

Jagger Archdemon Son of **Asmodeus**

Malakai Archdemon Son of **Belphegor**

Grayson Son of Archangel **Tiberion**

Prologue

Samuel

When I'd woken after they'd injected me, I found myself confused and disoriented. My senses were giving me so much conflicting information. My eyesight distorted, my ears and nose picking up sounds and scents at a level of sensitivity I'd never experienced even with my already heightened senses. The sound of a nearby heartbeat thudding frantically and the sour smell of fear made my jaw ache and my stomach rumble with hunger—my predatory instinct kicking in after detecting nearby prey. The sensory explosion was so invasive I almost found myself passing out again, but before I could succumb to the darkness, a familiar voice, dripping with disdain, and a rough hand on my neck drew my attention.

"Don't you dare pass out on me, boy. I thought you were made of stronger stuff." His words were short and exasperated. "Get up and move around! You're no use to me if you can't handle the gift I've given you."

My head felt heavy, my face itchy, and I desperately shook to try and clear the fog from my mind. I wonder if it's from the drugs they gave me. *Slowly, I looked around the room, trying to find something for my mind to focus on. Across the other side, my eyes locked onto an unexpected reflection in a mirror. A huge white tiger, fur bristling, tail whipping back and forth in an agitated manner, and teeth bared, Sabboath holding the scruff of its neck.* Holy Shit! Is that me? What the fuck have they done?

Watching carefully, the tiger's reflection corresponded with what I was feeling, and the horrifying truth was confirmed in my mind. Suddenly, he let go of my neck and gave me a shove. "Get moving," he demanded as I stumbled slightly, my four legs not quite coordinating. Instinctually, they regained balance, and I slowly started pacing back and forth in front of the mirror, closely watching each step. My tail swished back and forth in agitation, my motions sleek and predatory, as so many questions ran through my mind. How have they done this? Am I going to be stuck like this now? God, am I going to go crazy like Connie? What if I'm never normal again? What if Mina thinks I'm a freak?

Mylea did warn me of the hard choices I was going to have to make and promised she had protected me from the consequences. So hopefully, I would come out of this mentally intact. My thoughts turned to now, and I cataloged all the emotions my tiger was feeling. Or is it me that's feeling these things? It's all so confusing. I'm agitated, annoyed, scared, and aggressive all at once. It's like I'm me, but there's also an animal instinct that's urging me to turn around and rip Sabboath to shreds no matter how disgusting he might taste. *A* chuffing sound came out of my mouth as I continued to pace up and down, the animal having no other way to express its frustration to me.

"Good, very good. You're picking this up quicker than any I've given it to yet. Usually, they're down for days and then stumble around for hours once they first wake up. The pain is too much for them to do anything." He sounded pleased, and when I glanced at him through the mirror, he looked smug as fuck, a predatory glint in his eyes to rival that of my tiger.

"You are going to be a very welcome addition to my arsenal. Now see if you can change back," he commanded, and I stopped pacing.

Well, how the fuck am I supposed to do that? My confusion must have been evident as he rolled his eyes, no wariness in mocking the giant predator before him. "Shift!" he snarled, and a wave of magic rolled over my body, followed by another round of excruciating pain. Muscles tore and bones popped, my body rearranging itself into its original configuration. As my body agonizingly twisted to mold itself back into my humanoid shape, I could only pray that my wings decided to stay inside; otherwise, my status as an Archangel would be announced to the world with just a peek at the color of my wings.

Finally, the pain subsided, and I found myself crouched at Sabboath's feet, naked, panting, and sweaty, unable to care about being so exposed. With a huff of annoyance, he waved his hand, instantly covering me in clothes.

"Get up." His voice left no room for argument, and I staggered to my feet as he watched on in bored amusement.

"Once you get the hang of shifting, you'll be able to do it

by yourself, but I built in an override; both Connie and myself can command the shift of all of our followers who have been made better thanks to our cause. But you, my boy, you are special. I gave you every advancement I could think of. You are my ultimate masterpiece and the wave of the future. With an army of soldiers like you at my disposal, the world will bow down at my feet." His fervent declaration made my suspicions rise as my interest piqued. *Bow down to him? What happened to Hammus?*

Lost in thought and delusions of his own grandeur, he didn't seem to notice my frown at his revelations. That's if he even noticed himself speaking out loud... *His rapid pacing back and forth looked slightly unhinged, and the thought crossed my mind that he might be just as nuts as his daughter. In fact, the more I thought on it, the more likely it seemed. "I wonder what it is about you that made this possible," he mused out loud like he had expected it to fail.* Crap, there must have been a high chance that it would go wrong. *He kept talking to himself as he circled, eyeing me carefully.*

"I wonder if there's something different about you? And if there is, maybe the rest of your team is the same. You all managed to survive that solar flare that Hugh sent you into a couple of years ago. Maybe that mutated your body in ways that are beneficial to me." His eyes took on a manic gleam, and he came to a sudden stop like he'd reached some decision.

"We need to get a hold of other members of your team, so we can try the new formula on them! Maybe run some tests before we inject them so that we can compare before and after results. I wish I'd thought to do that to you; we'd be closer to

isolating the thing that makes you recover so much quicker. Even your change is smoother than all the others'."

I shuddered at his words, a wave of nausea hitting me. God, if my transformation is smooth, I dread even thinking what their pain must be. It's no wonder Connie's brain has fractured if she experiences that every time she changes.

My mind drifted from Connie to my teammates. I couldn't imagine their reactions when they found out about all this. Loyalty was everything to them; this would destroy the bond we've built during our years together as friends and teammates. Will finding out this is a goddess-sanctioned mission make a difference? Can a little divine intervention heal the betrayal I know they feel? I can only hope so.

"Bring the girl; she may come in handy." Startling me back to the present, Sabboath's words raise a chill through my fur-clad body as he stalks through the open portal. We're still on Minzeon, waiting to return back to the compound. My paws are heavy on Mina's chest, pinning her to the ground, my claws retracted so as not to damage her more than necessary. Her lavender eyes are fogged over with panic as they meet mine, her struggles stopping as she seems to look into my soul, her brows wrinkling in confusion as though she recognizes me. *Anything but that. I can't handle that right now.*

I watch in horror as Connie's booted foot comes down hard on Mina's head, knocking her out.

"Get off her and shift; I want them all to see

that you've picked me over them. I want them all to feel the pain of rejection," she orders, the gleeful malice in her voice obvious as she triggers my shift. Unable to fight it, my body shudders in pain as I shift from tiger to human again, my mind echoing the screams that my inhuman vocal cords aren't capable of making. After only doing it two times, the transformation is still freaking slow, not that Connie or her father give a shit. Getting to my feet, I stand over the woman I care so much for, a wave of impotent fury eclipsing my other emotions as I find myself unable to help her.

Mylea had told me I was going to have to be strong. I'd had no clue what she meant at the time, but she obviously had. *How is it that nobody else had any idea that AoA had been experimenting with magic?* Her inability to interfere or maybe her conscious choice not to interfere is really becoming a problem. Because let's face it, she could have warned us about all of this.

Connie's shouted orders to the rest of our team has my attention returning to now. They start pouring through the portal after Sabboath as Team Alpha and Raphael batter ineffectively at the force field that has conveniently appeared between them and us.

"Bring that bitch, Sammy. Daddy wants to use her for something." The disgust in Connie's voice is evident, and I school my features into a look of disdain, trying desperately to disguise my fury, as I bend down and carefully throw Mina over my shoulder.

It's now up to me to look after Mina and make sure she doesn't come to too much harm. If I can get her free without incriminating myself, I will, Mylea help me.

Turning my gaze toward my team, my eyes skim over Jagger and Kai. I don't know either of them all that well, but I can tell that they're angry from the snarls on their faces. When I get to Sander, Trick, Mav, and Zeph, I'm met with such furious looks of disgust and disappointment that my knees almost buckle. Nausea rolls through my stomach, acid rising to the back of my throat.

I have no idea what conclusions their minds have drawn. Well, I know they must think that I asked for this. Why else would they stare me down like I'm the next villain they need to purge? I can only hope and pray that they'll forgive me when they find out the truth.

I have so much explaining to do when this is all done.

Taking that last step through to a place where we'll be cut off from them all, I've got to hold on to the belief that they will absolve me of my wrongdoings, or I may crumble to dust on the spot.

The portal shuts down behind me, and with a deep breath, I say a little prayer to Mylea to look after us as I follow Connie into the madness that is now my future.

I can only hope that my team forgives me for what I'll have to do next.

Chapter One

Drusilla

(Earlier in the evening before the mission.)

Kissing Mina goodbye and watching her and my brothers leave on a mission has never felt so difficult before. Feelings of déjà vu and dread plague me, causing my stomach to roll with anxiety as I take my seat at my command desk and start running diagnostics on the wrist guards and earpieces. My fingers fly across my keyboard, checking and rechecking that everything is functioning as it should before pulling up the schematics of the building they're infiltrating this evening. With that done, I tap into all the surrounding cameras and overhead satellites to give myself a clear idea of what we are working with.

The pressure to make sure a job goes off without a hitch is huge. A communications officer can make all the difference in whether a team returns home in one piece or not. If I have all the intel available to us, it makes the assignment run smoothly, so it's easier for everyone involved. Over the years, I've developed my little rituals to make sure I have everything literally at my fingertips should the need arise. "All set, Drusilla?" Clementine's voice behind me has me turning to find her eyes filled with the same anxiousness I'm feeling, which doesn't help me at all. Her partner Riarliel is standing close, giving her comfort through touch. The two women are usually pretty reserved in front of others, so even that small show of affection emphasizes how much we all feel is riding on this mission.

"Yeah, I think we're mission-ready. From what I can decipher, they're just waiting on one more Archangel." The chatter from the portal room fills the communications center where Clementine, Riarliel, and I are the only ones in attendance. The revelation of the CD being infiltrated by traitors has thrown us all for a loop, and everyone else has been confined to the portal room until they can be interrogated and their loyalties confirmed.

"I'm not sure I'm going to be able to run this on my own," I tell her, worried that something will be overlooked, putting my team in danger. Having to be responsible for two different teams is giving me a lot of people to watch over. I also don't know how I'm going to cope with having Mina in the thick of things. I've always been pretty good at compartmentalizing my emotions, having had my brother on the team and out in the field, but this is now a whole other feeling of worry.

"No, and you shouldn't have to, which is why I'm here." A musical voice has me looking toward the door where a smiling, chestnut-headed Archangel stands, her own worry clear in her whiskey brown eyes.

"Jophial." The word leaves my mouth like a benediction and probably much too familiarly for the mixed company, but the sight of the woman close enough to be my aunt is a huge reassurance. *With her help, we might just be able to do this.*

Zephaniah's mother glides into the room, her elegance far surpassing anything I've ever been able to achieve, and settles in the seat at the console next to mine. Watching her take control of the system as she activates the station and connects to the earpieces the teams wear makes relief flow through me, chasing away the biting edge of the panic that had been growing before her arrival. My bad feeling about this mission was weighing me down, and I was worried I was going to put them all in danger if my focus was split in too many ways.

"I'll take the crusty old angels, and you take the young sprightly Alpha Team." She winks in my direction, and I snort at her description of the dads. Old though they might be, they've definitely still got sharp enough looks to make most of the recruits swoon when they're anywhere in the Collectors Division building.

"Better not let them hear you say that," I warn

her, but a flood of complaints are already flying over the speakers as they bite at her dig one by one.

She, too, brings up all the relevant details and starts com checking her team, and I bring my focus back to my team and finish doing the same.

Feeling a lot better, I set my mind to the task, studying the compound schematic as I listen in to what's happening in the portal room. Now that we've covered communications, there's nothing I can do until they go through the portal and start the mission.

As I listen, a jolt of what feels like surprise, followed by a feeling of wonder flows through my bond with Mina, and the next thing I hear is my dad's joyful chuckles.

"Yes! *Now* we're ready to bring the pain."

"Archangel Michael, good to see you again," Zeph says with confidence, his voice full of respect. I nearly snort; for all that he can be super casual with us at home, Zeph is the perfect team leader when the right ears are listening.

Ah, that explains Mina's surprise. She hasn't met Michael before, and he really is an awe-inspiring sight.

Although he was never around all that often, I'm not ashamed to admit I've always been his favorite. He was always bringing me treats or presents and making me feel special. I guess I was a substitute for the daughter he never had. I'm not sure why he was the only one of the group that didn't try to have his own children, but I'm not upset about the attention he gave me. I feel good that I could fill that void for him.

There are some manly slapping sounds, and I exchange a glance with Jophial as she rolls her eyes, knowing the usual performance the six of them put on. They really are the best of friends, a bond forged through many years of being together and the responsibility of overseeing the Collectors Division.

"Let's go," Michael orders, and Mina's emotions change from gentle feelings of amazement to alert determination as the mission commences.

I watch on my screen as they portal from Reath to Minzeon. The uniforms they wear contain a built-in camera, and I activate them once they're through the portal and away from our building's in-house surveillance setup.

I have the screen split into eight sections so that I can monitor the live streaming from each uniform's camera. Right now, the feeds from their uniforms show a wooded area with a compound in the background. Looking over, I see Jophial has the same thing on her screen. The eighth square shows the most-recently updated schematic for the building. Between the schematics and tracking chips in my team's suits, I'll be able to give them directions if needed. I try to focus on one screen at a time as it tends to get a bit nauseating if I try and watch all at once. I designated Mina as the pink dot in honor of her new second form, and I keep my eye on her camera, needing to know that she's safe for as long as possible. While they discuss their mission, I think of my mate's sexy demon form as they make their way over the wall of the compound, Mav grumbling about not being able to use their wings when Jagger, Kai, and the dads sail over.

I feel a brush against my mind and open my walls, and Jophial's voice is suddenly there.

"What are you smiling about? You look like you have a secret. And a fun one at that."

I look at her quickly, realizing I've been caught. Her eyebrows are raised, her eyes wide in question. I blush slightly, having been daydreaming about Mina, but I quickly brush it off and smile at her, excited that I can actually talk to someone about this. I haven't had a chance to talk to my mom yet.

"So much has happened to Team Alpha in the last week or so, and it must be exhausting keeping up with it all," she probes a little further as my eyes quickly jerk back to the screen in front of me, Mina's screen having gone blank.

"What the hell happened? What happened to Mina? She disappeared off the screen!" Did the tech malfunction? I try inputting some new instructions, but it stays blank.

Before I can ask them again, I hear Zeph grumble, "Mina, stay on our six. You being invisible is all well and good, but we won't know if something happens to you." My heartbeat returns to normal.

Her being invisible must be affecting the camera as well. That's something I'll have to keep in mind for future missions, or I'll end up with gray hair before the end of all this. Figuring the demons will be wherever Mina goes, I turn my eyes to Kai's feed. I don't get to answer Jophial's question as we both get busy directing each of the teams through the building.

I hear Kai reassure Zeph that they can feel her even if they can't see her and watch as Jagger puts his boot through the entryway.

"Guns on lower stun?" Zeph asks our teammates.

"Okay, stay alert, and if you meet one of the Five, don't forget to adjust the intensity. Trick and Sander, you go right, and Mav and I'll go left. Kai, Jagger, and Mina, you go straight ahead."

Taking a deep breath, I start to issue instructions.

"Alright, the compound is like a labyrinth, corridors weaving back and forth. It's an ingenious design, easy to get lost and trapped. I've got a lock on your locations, and I'm ready to guide you if you run into trouble," I reassure them, my focus entirely on my task now. I slipped up and let a little of my nerves show when Mina disappeared, but now I have to try and stay calm and collected. I have to be here to "catch" them if need be, and they need my head in the game.

"Roger that," Zeph replies. My mind whirls

with possibilities as I map out three routes for the groups our team has split into, blocking off paths that would draw them straight into bigger enemy forces than their smaller numbers should have to handle.

Watching closely, adrenaline running through my veins, part mine, and part Mina's, I think, I get them through the compound. Jagger, Kai, and Mina make it to the central room first. The others were held up longer, having met more workers on their way through.

As they get to the room, I watch the dads battle the Five and wince when Dad's blast hits Zadkiel. *That's gotta hurt.* Although I don't have their comms in my ears, I can read Dad's lips. Jophial gasps in shock seeing her partner go down but starts to snort with laughter at my dad's outburst.

"Uriel's going to pay for that. Zad's going to make him his bitch. I wonder how long he'll drag it out for."

Suddenly, Jagger's focus moves away from the fight with the Five and the Archangels, and movement on my screen draws my attention. Anansi is on the wall behind them, and Mina's emotions scream at me with anxiety and panic, her breathing getting faster. She's a riotous mix of confusion and horror that threatens to overwhelm me.

Watching, I see Kai fire his blaster at the spider. With a loud thunderous noise, it crashes at his feet,

Jagger quickly conjuring up some restraints and binding him tightly.

"Mina, are you okay? You sort of blanked on us for a moment, and all we could feel was terror and sadness," Jagger asks, his calm voice tinged with the edge of concern for our mate.

"Yeah, I'm okay. I just got my memories back in a rush," Mina replies, her voice shaky as I feel her emotions settle and her focus return. "I'll tell you everything when this is over."

Finally, they get the Five immobilized and secured. Clementine and Riarliel cheer behind us, making me jump. I'd forgotten they were there, totally absorbed in my team's mission.

Suddenly, the rest of Alpha appear in the room from different directions, and I can't help but snort at the disgusted look on my brother's face as he realizes the action is all done. *Always wanting a chance to show off, Sander.*

"Well, that was kind of anticlimactic," he complains, looking around the room. Team Alpha relaxes and holsters their guns, and Dad tries to rouse the still-unconscious Zadkiel, his lips twitching as he holds back his laughter the whole while.

Jophial, on the other hand, is holding her sides as hers breaks free and fills the room with amusement. I join in as Dad slaps Zadkiel hard a couple of times before he regains consciousness and stumbles to his feet, bitching at my black-winged father.

Mina must be watching because her amusement

matches mine and Jophial's, and it brings me a moment of joy to feel something positive coming from her. In this crazy life, you have to appreciate every moment of levity, especially something like one Archangel bitchslapping another's unconscious face.

We both relax back in our seats as they clean up the scene and interrogate the scientist. The hardest part of our job is done until they want to leave and need directing out of the compound. For now, while they focus on what's happening inside, they rely on us to watch everything else. I keep an eye on the cameras we've hacked into around the compound, but nothing looks suspicious. Clementine and Riarliel congratulate us and head out to their apartment, clearly feeling like this mission was a success. Jophial and I will finish up then head down to the portal room to meet everyone upon their return.

"So, now that we're alone, what was that smile about?" she pushes again, and another grin breaks out across my face. I knew she'd tucked the question away in that vault of a brain.

"I assume you know all about Mina?" I start, excited to be able to share this with someone. I've wanted to shout it from the rooftops, but I hadn't even been able to talk to the boys about it yet, not wanting to freak any of them out. Jophial's smile bursts wide at my words.

"Oh yes, I'd had my suspicions, but when Zad confirmed it, I was thrilled. We haven't seen Siffa in years, and I can't wait to reconnect with her!" Her smile slips from her face, replaced with a frown and a glint of a tear in her eye. The switch between feelings is so rapid that I almost can't believe it, but there's so much history between all of them that I don't think our team will ever fully know what happened when we were all newborns.

"Such an awful thing that happened to them. It was bad enough for us to have to give you guys up, but at least we could be a part of your lives. They had to sever all ties with her, worried that her precious life would be at stake if anyone found out."

"I don't understand," I admit to her. "What was so bad about Mina's parents being together that they had to hide her like that?"

Before she can respond, I hear Jagger's voice, his words taking away the calm that's built in my few moments with my "aunt.".

"Fuck."

Instantly, I'm on alert. I hadn't been paying attention to the feelings through our bond, but now that I focus, I can feel Mina's nerves and her adrenaline pumping again.

"Damn it, what's she doing?" I press a few buttons until I find her dot on the screen following a path I hadn't noticed before.

"Mina, Mina, can you hear me? What are you doing?" There's no response, and I can't get to her through our mental bond either. It's just too new to be that reliable over that distance. Feelings, being more primitive and instinctive than sending thoughts, seem to have a longer range of access. Thoughts require a stronger connection and take more overall effort to send if you're not in semi-close proximity to the intended recipient.

Raphael's voice is now in my ear as well as Team Alpha. "Let's go," he commands. "How was this missed?" he barks. *Well, that's both useful and annoying all at once. Why'd we even have to arrange their comms if they could just use magic to talk to the comm center?*

Responding, I insist, "It's not on the schematics of the building."

My heart races as the guys run after her, but they're met with an outpouring of animals blocking their way through the corridor, and as I watch them fight, my bond with Mina is severed. A pounding pain in my chest, agonizing in strength, has me buckling while a scream escapes my mouth, but as quickly as it comes, it disappears.

Feeling nothing but a void where my bond with Mina used to be, horror freezes my system as they desperately struggle to reach my mate.

Chapter Two

Zephaniah

My heart is pounding a million miles an hour, both anxiety and annoyance clamoring for the forefront. I can't believe she didn't tell us she was following Hugh! Even if she wanted to stay hidden and not let on that she was following him, she could have said something to Jagger or Kai before taking off.

Cursing under my breath, we follow Raphael down a corridor as he barks accusations at Drusilla before trying to get in touch with our missing teammate.

"Mina, talk to us," Raphael demands. "What's happening?" She doesn't respond, and before we get much further, an abundance of animals pours from every corridor. The Archangel lifts his gun and aims at the wolf that bounds in his direction. With the weapon still set to stun, it falls to the ground, shifting shape and turning into Brock, Team Bravo's former leader. For a minute, we're all stunned stupid, frozen.

"Holy shit," whispers Sander.

"Don't kill them, just stun," Raphael orders, the usually unflappable Archangel showing some of the same confusion mirrored on my teammates' faces. "Who knows how many of them are here voluntarily or not." They just keep coming, domesticated pets, wild animals, and even insects, all swarming the corridors, our path to the outside slowing dramatically. We set about taking down the animals one by one, each shifting back into the human bodies of former academy classmates. Students who hadn't made the cut into the active teams and opted not to take on other roles in the CD. When that happens, the student can choose to leave the CD and pursue other paths... It's clear now what those avenues were. I also see ex-CD team members besides Brock, ones that had been declared missing or dead over the years. *Holy shit. How far does this all go back?*

The unconscious bodies are piling up, but at least our way is getting clearer.

Finally, it's just one or two stragglers, and we quickly stun them before we move forward and out into the courtyard. Quick, harsh pants shake my chest as we run down the corridors, following the path Mina took. Bursting through another door, we arrive outside.

A screeching sound overhead draws our attention, and we all look up just in time to see a stunning red and silver dragon dive bomb Asmodeus, who looks to be fighting with Sabboath in the air. The screeching is followed by a ribbon of flames rushing from the reptile's mouth, hitting Asmodeus in the side and sending him careening into the thick canopy of the surrounding forest.

"Dad!" Jagger's broken cry echoes across the clearing as his father falls into the trees, spinning wildly out of control. Before we can get any further, we're surrounded by another wave of animals. Raphael takes aim in an attempt to stun them, but this time, he's met with resistance. His shot hits a barrier and bounces back, narrowly missing Mav as he jumps quickly out of the way. Some sort of force field is stopping us from getting through.

Fuck, where's Mina? I can't see her anywhere. *Is she still invisible, or is she hidden somewhere?* Scanning the area, my eye catches on Hugh's body, not far from the portal, and my heart skips a beat. *Damn, Mina, where are you?* My eyes keep scanning the area, looking for the slight haze her invisibility gives off, but apart from the fallen briefcase, I see nothing else. My heart races as sweat drips down the back of my neck. Jagger and Kai are both frantic with fear, bashing against the force field. Jagger doubly worried, with his dad now down as well.

Taking a deep breath in an attempt to calm myself enough to think, I put my hands up and try to feel how far the force field extends, but before I can get a real idea, Sabboath lands and opens a portal. I can see him speaking but can't hear him from this side. After issuing his orders, he steps through, the animals following until the area clears, revealing a body pinned to the ground by a great white tiger.

Fuck, that's Mina. The team's banging against the barrier intensifies, blood dripping down the invisible wall from Mav's hands. He's split them open in his attempt to get through, his eyes wild enough that I doubt he's even registered the pain he should be feeling.

"Mina!" I shout as I bang my hands against the barriers, but it's no use; nothing can penetrate it. Raphael even tries his sword, but it bounces off with an arc of sparks.

The barrier is restricting teleportation too, so I go nowhere. With horror, I watch as the tiger moves from her body and Connie's booted foot comes up and she pauses, looking at us, a wicked grin crossing her face before she stomps on Mina's head.

I sink to my knees in shame; we've failed her again. *What kind of team leader am I that this keeps happening?*

In disbelief, my eyes follow the scene in front of me. Connie's mouth moves again, and this time my shame turns to disgust as the tiger standing next to Mina starts to contort, shifting fluidly into a different shape.

"Fuck me," Sander rasps, his eyes wide with disbelief and throat tired from yelling. Samuel now stands where the tiger had been. My eyes shift to

Connie, and the smile on her face is smug as she throws her head back, laughing in delight at our anguish. Despite the barrier blocking out sound, I swear I can hear her cackling, the hair on my arm raising with every shake of her laughing body. I guess they decided to give up the subterfuge now that they have Sam on their side.

With a wink, she waves a hand at Mina's body. Our ex-teammate's head turns toward us, and a frown crosses his face, regret shining in his eyes.

"Fucking traitor," Mav screams as he continues pounding at the force field. Samuel shakes his head subtly and then turns back around, bending down to throw Mina over his shoulder quite forcefully. As he does, her magic wand falls out of her hair, landing on the ground below her, unnoticed. With a wink of his own, his smile turns smug, and he follows Connie through the portal. It closes, leaving the magic wand and our broken team behind.

"Nooooo!" Mav's tortured scream sends shudders of despair down my spine. I just pray that this doesn't break him, that my friend's mind doesn't shatter from the turmoil of his thoughts. Staggering up, I go over to him and wrap him in a tight hug, pulling him close to my chest in the hope the pressure will calm him some.

As he rests, my eyes dart around the clearing. The minute the portal closed, the barrier disappeared, and Dru's voice came through the comms, loud and clear, like a chainsaw in my ear, but I just don't have the presence of mind to respond at this moment. Kai and Jagger rub at their chests, Trick and Sander echoing the motion.

Shaking my head, I can't think about that now either. Mav's body shudders in my arms, his breath sawing in and out much too quickly. As I start to whisper to him, encouraging him to calm his breathing, Jagger gets himself together and rushes into the trees. Kai's eyes follow as his partner hurries away, showing no sign of getting up to join him, and Sander is still frozen in shock. Trick shakes his head to clear it and trudges after our teammate to help, but Raphael reaches out and stops him. I can't hear what they say, but he hugs his son close, and Trick's body starts to shake like Mav's. Raphael pulls away and starts to follow after Jagger, but before he can get far, a flash lights up the area, and Michael and the other dads appear.

The leader of the Archangel's eyes are wide and hopeful as he scans the scene, taking in all that is in front of him and obviously looking for something. When he seems to come up empty, his brow furrows and his eyes blaze as a scowl crosses his lips. The words booming out of his mouth next nearly have us dropping to our knees from the sheer power of his rage.

"Where the fuck is my daughter?"

Thunder crashes across the sky, and lightning arcs down into the trees, hitting a branch nearby with a crack that echoes through the clearing.

Michael's words have everyone pausing, and the silence that follows is like the calm before the storm. Even Mav has stopped at these words like they've shocked the chaos into submission, his mind quieting in an instant. He pulls away, looking at me with wide eyes that ask for answers I can't provide.

"Did he say what I think he just said?" His disbelief slams into my mind.

"Well, that explains a lot," I reply, and suddenly everything makes sense. All of her exceptional and unexpected abilities explained in an instant. She's the daughter of two of the most powerful beings in all the worlds.

"Oh fuck, I call dibs on not telling him." Sander quickly jumps into our conversation, and Trick echoes rapidly behind.

"Let Dad tell him. Maybe we should just move out of the line of fire." He waves Kai over to where we're now all gathered. I help Mav to his feet, his hands slippery with blood, though at least the splits have closed over. We need to regroup and make a plan to get her back. I rush over to the spot where I'd seen Mina lying, searching for her magic wand. Catching a sparkle out of the corner of my eye, I turn and find it lying not far from me. I pick it up and stab it into my own ponytail, promising I'll look after it until I can get it back to her. I head back toward the guys, who are still watching the dads, nervous expectation on their faces.

Raphael grabs Chamuel first and whispers in

his ear, likely telling him about Samuel's defection. I can't hear what he's saying, but Chamuel shoots a quick look in our direction before he shakes his head in denial. "*No!* Fuck no, my son is not a traitor. No, I don't believe it." His words come out stilted, showing none of the emotions I thought he would.

"Did that reaction seem a little contrived to you?" I ask everyone through the link, seeing the doubt I'm feeling mirrored by the furrowed brows and frowns on their faces.

"Do you think that they knew he was a traitor before this?" Mav's inner voice sounds broken, and I know before long we're going to have to deal with him to get him back on track. God, I don't have time for that at the moment.

I shrug in reply as we watch as Raphael move from Chamuel to Michael, taking his friend by the arm and gently breaking the news to him. Michael's anguish immediately has more thunder rolling across the sky and several bolts of lightning arcing through the air. My skin prickles with all the charged electricity.

"Oh, for fuck's sake, will you calm down? You're going to end up setting something on fire," a voice growls in annoyance, and we turn to watch Jagger helping his dad out of the copse of trees. Asmodeus' deep blue wings have a scorch mark on one side, and he's looking a little disheveled, with a few leaves in his hair and a couple of scratches on his face. They'll be gone within the next few minutes.

"That's it! Your dad's dead," Sander says wryly to Jagger through the team link, and Jagger snorts almost imperceptibly. His face is a picture of concentration, one arm wrapped around his dad, trying to help, but Asmodeus pushes him away and approaches the other fathers, only a slight limp in his step. Archangel and Archdemons heal very quickly, but it's not instant, and his body was likely healing the open wounds first.

"Why was I not informed of this?" Michael bellows, looking to each of our fathers. "How did she end up in the Collectors Division? She was supposed to be safe and far away from anything or anyone that might find out her heritage. When we said she had to attend the academy, we thought she would end up in the archives, not an active member of Team fucking Alpha!" His words are tinged with desperation by the time he finishes, the final words quieter than the first though holding no less vitriol. The dads all jump in, trying to offer explanations, their words tumbling out and over each other, but at his next question, they all stop suddenly.

"Has anyone seen Lucifer? Does *she* know about this?" Now, they all start to edge away from him slowly. *Shit, that's not a good sign.*

"Everyone prepare to teleport on my command," I warn them all as Michael's face turns thunderous at his friends' movements.

"Zeph, get your team back to headquarters and have Teams Dragon and Charlie called to collect the traitors in the

hallways, please. They're all out, but who knows for how long," Raphael directs in my mind, his voice betraying an urgency that he's cleared from his face.

"Tell me!" Michael orders, his voice like God commanding the heavens, and the weight behind those two words is suffocating. I can feel it pushing in on every molecule of my body like it could actually crush me beneath its weight.

Before any of my team can give in to it, I give my own order. "Teleport now!"

As one, we all dematerialize away from the confrontational scene, leaving our dads to sort out Mina's.

Huh, it's like she was made for this team, her father rounding out the posse of best friends. I'd overheard Dad complaining to Mom about how distant Michael had been since we were born. He's been so busy with all manner of tasks, basically becoming the gods' right-hand man for dealing with the beings of the four remaining planets and the nine realms, that he hadn't had time for anything or anyone else.

We rematerialize in the command center of the Collectors Division, finding my mom comforting a distraught Drusilla.

"What happened?" she wails the minute we appear. "She's gone, and I can't feel her anymore." She rubs a hand over her chest in the same spot where Jagger, Kai, Trick, and Sander had all been rubbing theirs. *Okay, I guess I need to ask about that as well.* I have a fair idea of what this means, but my stomach rolls at the thought that all but three of Team Alpha are Mina's mates. I want my chance too, and now I might not get it.

Sander walks over and extracts Drusilla from Mom's arms, pulling her close and whispering in her ear. Trick joins the cuddle, wrapping his arms around her too. Mom moves to my side and pulls me in close, her familiar scent soothing. She then moves around the group, hugging first Mav and then, to their surprise, Jagger and Kai. She laughs at Kai's stunned expression as she steps away from him.

"Don't be so surprised, boy; your parents were once a part of our circle before Hammus blew that all to shit. Don't forget we've all been around a long time," she scolds him, earning a sheepish apology.

"I'm sorry. I forgot about it because you're so radiantly beautiful; it really doesn't show your age at all."

Jagger snorts next to him, the roll of his eyes showing exasperated amusement with his mate. "Smooth, man, real smooth." Instead of being embarrassed, Kai's looking rather pleased with himself, and the little bit of levity changes the feeling in the room.

"Right, so Mina's been taken, we saw that much, and Samuel's turned traitor." Mom blows out a deep breath, her head hanging down as she seems to take it all in.

"God, Sofiel is going to be so upset, and we

need to let Lucifer know." She starts to pace back and forth, but she stops suddenly. "Fuck, that means Lucifer and Michael will be in the same room for the first time in over twenty years." Her eyes are creased in worry at the thought, and she pales a little.

"But aren't they mates?" Drusilla's voice is quiet and shaky as she asks the question. "How could Lucifer have been apart from him for so long?"

"Their bond broke down not long after they left Mina with the nuns. Neither of them could cope with the decision, and they both blamed fate and the gods and Mylea for putting them in the situation. How could they make them mates when relationships between demons and angels were forbidden? Well, they still are, technically, but once upon a time, Mina would have been put to death. Same as why you guys were given to foster parents to raise and told to hide your Archangel abilities. But Mina was doubly in danger, so they put a spell on her to hide her powers and left her with the nuns, with the instruction that she attend the academy. They never thought that she would be mistreated, that the nuns had certain prejudices, or that the orphanage was associated with AoA. No one did."

Mom stops and waves at the nearby console, conjuring up bottles of water for everyone. Grabbing one for herself, she uncaps it and takes a deep drink before continuing.

"They decided to go their separate ways, both angry with each other and the world. Eternal Damnation came about due to the split and Lucifer's need to feed. Michael doesn't actually know that she owns that club or even of its existence in the city. Where he thought she went, I have no idea, but he went feral for a while. Took every mission assigned to any team in the CD and slaughtered his way through the fictional realms. Mylea finally put a stop to it and conscripted him to her service. He's been at her beck and call ever since, and now we have to have them in the same room together while we break the news to Lucifer that her daughter has been kidnapped and is in danger once more."

"Fuck me, that's going to be bad," Sander grumbles over Drusilla's shoulder.

"Yeah, she had the whole worried momma thing happening when Mina was just injured and unconscious. What's she going to be like now?" Kai's unfortunate but important question has us all cringing at the thought.

"Look, we'll worry about it when it happens," Mom redirects, all business-like again. "One thing at a time. First things first, they have to be interrogated to see if they were coerced or there voluntarily, and the ones that were there under their own steam need to be put into the cells in the Menagerie." She smiles sympathetically at us. "I'll organize the cleanup crew, with Charlie and

Dragon as support. Why don't you go home and get cleaned up? You can head back here when you're done. I'm sure the dads will have calmed Michael by then, and he'll want to strategize. I'll contact Siffa and get her here."

"Someone needs to tell Maggie and Peter," Mav says quietly, his voice devoid of emotion.

"Not it," Sander calls out quickly, and Drusilla starts to chuckle. Before long, we're all laughing at Sander's words; even Mom is giggling, the mood in the room easing again.

"We'll make Michael do it," she decides when she finally gets herself together. "That should keep him busy, and Maggie might be too star-struck to kick up too much of a fuss."

There's a brief pause as we take in what she said, and although we're all worried about Mina, this is enough to bring smiles to our faces.

"Not likely to happen, but it's worth a try."

Chapter Three

Jessamina

My mouth is dry, and my brain feels like it's been split in two when I finally manage to open my eyes. I've been conscious for a while, but the effort to open my eyes was too much to begin with.

When I first regained consciousness, it took my mind a little bit to clear away the fuzz. I couldn't hold onto a thought or a memory for long before it slipped away. Once I was able to hold onto them, I realized that I wasn't able to move, so to keep myself calm, I ran through my senses. I couldn't smell anything that stood out; it was just a musty dampness that penetrated my nose, and as much as I strained, all I could hear were some snuffling sounds. They didn't sound too close, so it wasn't anything I was particularly concerned about yet.

The temperature didn't feel any different than Minzeon, but I wasn't really subject to temperature fluctuations anymore, so I could be anywhere. My arms ached, and when my brain started to catalogue feelings and sensations, I realized I was chained against a wall. My arms were stretched out wide, abrasive metal cuffs at my wrists and feet, the burn in my shoulders finally registering to my confused mind.

I breathe in and out through my nose and wriggle my hands, trying not to panic when neither they nor my feet budge. Willing my eyes to finally open, I raise my head, a clanking sound ringing out through the cell. A metal cuff is clamped around my neck, biting into the skin and pulling on another chain as I move. My stomach rolls as my heartbeat races, because now that my eyes are open, I can see I'm chained up in a dark and barren cell, with metal bars across from me and a dirt floor. In the corner, a wooden bucket sits, and I shudder to think about what that's there for. Wanting to look further, I try to turn, but the cuff around my neck stops my head. There's light in the room, so I can only assume there's a window somewhere.

When I assess my body further to catalogue any injuries I might have, I suddenly realize there's a gaping metaphorical hole in my chest where my mates used to be. A hollow desolate wave flows over my body as I try to reach them through our mental connection, but I get nothing. *Absolute silence.* No words, no emotions, nothing. A keening sound echoes through the cell, and my body jerks at the noise before I realize it's coming from me. Wetness on my face also registers, and I recognize I'm crying, sobbing, in fact. Being cut off from my mates is agony, a pain even worse than what my physical body is feeling, and I don't know if I'm going to survive it. *How did Mom do this?*

I'm not sure how long I hang there, sobbing, but I can't seem to stop. Eventually, clanking sounds outside the cell draw my attention. Slowly raising my exhausted head, I see Connie entering the cell, followed by a massive black wolf and two people that I can't say I'm surprised to see, though at the same time, I am.

I hadn't thought about Silas and Beatrice since we were all summoned when the Five were first causing havoc on Minzeon. They'd just faded into the background, not worth remembering. But here they are in full technicolor, with smug smirks, standing behind Connie and the wolf, arms crossed like bodyguards, and my mind catches on a small fragment of memory. That explains the sludge on the bottom of Silas' wing that day! I knew it had looked familiar when I'd been searching for survivors to evacuate. He must have been there prior to us all being called in. *How long has he been a part of AoA? How far do their poisonous tentacles reach? How are the Archangels going to be able to stamp this all out?*

"Oh, poor Mina," Connie coos as she runs her hand through the wolf's fur. It turns and snaps at her, and she quickly moves her hand, not hiding the shock she feels before facing me once more. I'm so exhausted I giggle at the action.

"Not sure your pet likes you, Connie." My voice is raspy and hurts my throat as I taunt her, but it's so worth it nonetheless.

Crack! Connie's hand connects with my cheek, the force so great my head flops to the side, and I scream when the metal collar bites deeper into my skin.

"Shut up, bitch! You're really in no position to be laughing at me now." The sweetness and light has disappeared from her voice, leaving behind the biting venom that tells me how she really feels. "If it were up to me, I'd get rid of you permanently, but Dad wants to use you as a test subject. See how well you take the new serum before we start distributing it through our network."

Serum? Testing? Her words have me frowning in confusion, my ears still ringing from her hit.

"But for now, we're going to test you to see how durable demons really are." Silas and Beatrice snicker behind her. "Thanks to Hammus convincing them to fight amongst themselves, it's been so long since we've been able to get our hands on a demon. Demons are ruled by their emotions; that's why they were so easy to manipulate," she spits out, her disgust as clear as her prejudice. "Angels are a *much* different creature. Maybe if we can work out how a demon's emotions are triggered, we can work out a way to infect angels with the same responses, and then after the whole population has been infected, they'll tear themselves apart too! Nothing will stand in the way of us ruling over the Earth, Reath, and Minzeon after that. Especially with all the magic disappearing from the Reath people; they're practically human."

Fuck me! Her crazy is being served with a small side of megalomaniac war-mongerer. My eyes slide from one to the other, realizing all three of them have a feverish look in their eyes, almost like they're under some sort of spell. *Maybe it's the serum they keep mentioning.*

My eyes drop lower, and I find the wolf staring at me, his blue eyes seeming so sad. Maybe it's just because he doesn't have the same maniacal light the others do, but as I stare into the deep depths of his eyes, something starts to happen. My fangs drop, and my mouth starts to water. My hungers are beginning to rear their ugly heads at the worst time possible, locked away from all potential food sources. *What am I going to do?* I'm going to go feral and start projecting pheromones to attract every Tom, Dick, and Harry. A tear rolls down my cheek, its path nearly scalding, at the thought that I'm going to end up betraying my mates. Unless they keep me chained here... then I'll probably just go crazy and die.

Connie's peals of laughter draw my unseeing eyes away from the wolf and back to her. "Crying? Do you cry blood from those demon eyes, all red and ugly? Come now, Mina, I thought you were tougher than that." I ignore the bitch, focusing on the two standing behind her. Beatrice looks bored, rolling her eyes and studying her nails like she'd rather be anywhere else. Silas, on the other hand, is practically salivating, the manic light in his eyes causing me more concern as I measure who's really a threat in this room. My eyes move back to Connie.

"Come closer and look, unless you're scared," I spit back, but she ignores me and keeps rambling.

"And don't count on getting rescued anytime soon. We've destroyed your wrist guard and removed your world chip. The collar around your neck also protects us against anyone, namely those asshole Archangels, trying to locate you. You're at my mercy until you either decide to change sides or die, and I'm sure you can guess which option I prefer."

I start to chuckle before it changes to hacking coughs as my lungs burn. "Please, my team will find me, and then it's you who'll need to be worried."

The wolf starts to pace back and forth in front of her, a quiet rumble deep in his chest echoing around the cell. Connie's laughter drops, and she shoots a look of annoyance and calculation at the wolf before waving a hand at me.

"Oh, is *that* how you want to play it?" she growls at the wolf before fixing on me. "Oh, Mina, I wouldn't be so sure about your team. I mean, who knows where AoA has infiltrated. We're everywhere, maybe even within your precious Team Alpha."

I try to shake my head back and forth, but it's

just too much work. "No, not my team, they would never."

Her eyes narrow, and she purses her lips. "Don't be so sure. Shift!" she demands, and before my very eyes, the wolf's form starts to shimmer. It's slow, like perhaps he's fighting it, but eventually, his body contorts, limbs reshaping and fur receding. It's not long before my eyes see something that horrifies me and tempts the tears to start again.

Moving from a crouching position, he stands and runs a hand through his hair, a cold glint in his eye.

"Samuel!" The name falls from my mouth in surprise. He doesn't say anything, his ice blue eyes scanning my body before turning to a smug as fuck Connie. Peals of laughter explode from Silas and Beatrice at my exclamation of horror.

"Are we done here?" he asks, his voice flat and emotionless like the sight of me like this doesn't bother him in the least, and my heart dies a little inside. My friend, my oldest friend, is not who I thought he was— was he ever?

"Silas, Beatrice, I'll leave you in charge of testing her limits. You know what needs to be done." Both of them stop laughing, and the wicked gleam that enters their eyes makes my stomach sink. *How did the Collectors Division not know the depth of AoA's infiltration? How did they become so complacent?*

"Come," Connie orders Samuel, and she stalks away, leaving behind a chilling silence.

They both stare at me with dead eyes. I always knew there was something off about these two, but I never thought they would be traitors.

"Still someone's bitch, Silas?" I rasp out, coughing a little, my throat dry from thirst. I don't even get the chance to blink before his fist connects with my face, the pain nowhere near as bad as the collar digging into my neck.

"You hit like a pussy and still have no impulse control, I see." I spit out blood at his feet and laugh, causing a growl similar to the wolf's to escape his mouth. I think I'm starting to get a little loopy. How long have I been here?

"Go and get the equipment," he snaps at Beatrice, and when I crack my eye open again, she's gone, leaving the two of us alone. His eyes flash with intense anger, and his fists are clenched by his side as he stares at me with hatred. I knew that he had a problem with me, but I didn't think it went as far as *this*.

My eyes float away from his, still a little disoriented and unable to focus, but they quickly find his throbbing carotid artery, my hearing zooming in on the sound of his heartbeat thudding faster than average. I wonder if that's from excitement or nervousness; regardless, it's an enticing sound, and a thrill of excitement flows through me. It must be similar to what a predator feels when it spots its prey, and the anticipation for the hunt throbs in my fangs.

I must have been hanging here for a while to be this thirsty. It's so bad that when I get free, it's not going to be a delicate, sensual exchange of blood between two mates but a gory feeding frenzy as I guzzle their lifeblood down. My skin prickles with goosebumps at the thought, this time not in excitement but fear. *I don't want to be a monster.* The first person I come across once I get down from here is not going to survive, and I don't think there's anything I can do to stop that. God, I dread to think of what will happen if the need for sex gets too bad. At the moment, it's fine, nothing I can't handle, but I'm not sure how long that's going to last.

My mind must drift again because the next thing I know, I'm being shaken by the shoulders. My armpits are screaming with pain as my blood flow becomes less sluggish, waking up limbs that had long gone numb.

"Argghhhh." The screams bounce around the cell, and I realize it's me, but it peters out as my throat closes up. In the silence that follows, I register the hand wrapped around my throat, blocking off my airways.

Opening my eyes, Silas' blazing ones meet mine as he spits out, "How do you control it even when you're unconscious? Nothing we use can penetrate it." Spittle flies into my face as confusion settles in. I have no clue what he's talking about.

"Stop it, Silas," Beatrice begs. "She's no good to us if you kill her before we figure anything out.

Sabboath will kill you if his precious test dummy gets damaged before he can use it, and I don't intend to let you drag me down with you!" She's pulling on his hand against my throat, and my head flops forward. I don't have the strength to hold it up anymore.

He releases his grip and steps back, but the collar is still digging into my throat, and I'm still hanging from the wall. *So, not much of an improvement.* The numbness has returned to my limbs, and my body feels heavy and useless.

"What is it?" he screams at me. "What are you? No one has ever mentioned demons having a second skin like that before. It's like your mother fucked a dragon. Was your mother a dirty animal fucker?" he rages, and I crack my eyes open to watch his meltdown, a small bit of entertainment in an otherwise horrific moment. He paces back and forth across the cell while Beatrice tries to placate him with soothing words. My lips crack in pain as I smile at his tirade, but I finally process what he's ranting about. My scales look dull and lifeless in the low light, but they're undoubtedly there; they must have subconsciously triggered to protect me while I was unconscious. Good to know they can stand up to torture.

I start to laugh, uncontrollable hysterical giggles escaping my dry and cracked lips, dragging Silas and Beatrice's attention back to me. Her eyes widen, and she smacks him on the arm before throwing her arms up in disgust.

"That's it! You've broken her, and we're not going to get anything out of her now."

"But how? We didn't do anything except for a couple of hits to the face. What's wrong with her?" he complains as he stops and frowns at me before a smile twists his lips in a hideous display. "Oh, Mina," he sing-songs, "are you starting to feel a little thirsty?"

He turns and walks back to a small cart covered in what I can only think are torture devices, picking up a bottle of water before casually strolling back to me. All signs of his temper tantrum are gone, and the deceptive switch has me steeling myself for what might happen next. Stopping in front of me again, he holds up the water. "Is this what you need?" he taunts, unscrewing the lid and taking a long sip of it. His throat muscles work as he swallows down the water, my eye brought back to that delicious throbbing vein in his neck, and I lick my dry lips once more, using a precious bit of the moisture in my mouth to try and soothe them.

Noticing where I'm looking, Beatrice gasps and stutters out, "Ah, I don't think it's water she's thirsty for." He stops what he's doing, another gleam entering his eye, this one cool and calculating. Turning back to the trolley, he grabs a knife and moves back to me once again.

"No, water's definitely not what she's thirsty for. She wants *this*." He draws a thin line across his palm, and a small amount of blood wells to the surface before he holds it up to me. Quickly closing my mouth, I grit my teeth as he smears his blood all over my lips before laughing sadistically. The smell reaches my nostrils, and they flare in excitement, but I clench down hard, refusing to swipe my tongue over it.

"Stop it, you idiot. You don't want her to get a taste for your blood," Beatrice scolds him, and I can't help but smile at the way he pales slightly. I must look a sight, my wicked grin with his blood smeared all over my lips, because he takes a step back.

"Why don't we drop her down and leave her to recover a little? Like I said, she's useless to us if she dies before Sabboath can inject the new formula into her. Connie might be fine with her dying, but we know she's not the one who really makes the rules," Beatrice points out, and he huffs before jerking his head.

"Okay," he agrees, "it's no fun with her just hanging here like this anyway, and it's not like she can go anywhere. We've disabled all the tracking, and the collar stops portaling even if someone could get to her."

Crap, that's not good. I was hoping if I could get free, I could create a portal and leave, but that's out of the question now.

"We also need to clean up around that collar; it's

digging too deep, and it's likely to kill her too," Beatrice whines a little more.

"Yeah, and I like a little more life and a lot less smell in the girls that I fuck," he says, running his thick tongue up my cheek before cackling his amusement, and my skin chills as my stomach rolls with nausea. *Does he mean what I think he does?*

"Yeah, yeah, he said you could have her once he was done with her. Maybe he'll find a use for her, and you'll miss out," Beatrice snaps, her face turning red.

They both move to either side of me and start to fiddle with the manacles holding my legs and then my arms, but the returning blood flow to my limbs must be too much for me because I pass out again before I can even hit the floor.

Chapter Four

Samuel

My footsteps are silent on the jail floor as I follow Connie from Mina's cell up the stairs to the central part of the complex. Fucking hell, I can't believe she just did that. I'd chosen my wolf just in case Mina had connected the tiger form to me, hoping to delay the moment that I had to see her recognize me as a traitor. Not that Connie let me have that little bit of dignity. The look on Mina's face felt like a knife to the chest, and there wasn't even any doubt or argument, just pure acceptance in her eyes. I can't believe she wasn't even skeptical. Sure, we want them all to believe I'm a traitor, and it certainly helped my position with Connie, but shit, it hurt that she believed it so quickly.

As I think back to the look in her eyes and the too strong scent of blood and damp dirt in her cell, my wolf howls inside my mind. The tiger is quieter now, perhaps because the wolf was the one most recently let out, but his presence is still there as well, awake and very unhappy with me. They don't understand or agree with me following Connie's orders and standing beside Beatrice and Silas. When my animals see that sadistic trio, their instincts scream *prey*. Even louder than that, when they see Mina, the word *mate* echoes through every fiber of my being, my wolf howling and the tiger snarling when I allowed her to stay chained up to that wall.

It was all I could do to keep the wolf from making us lunge at Connie to rip out her throat. Right now, the wolf very much wants to do the same to me, considering me a failure. I allowed our prey to hurt our mate. In his eyes, I'm not fit to live, and I'm starting to think it might be better for my own chances of survival if I give him some time to cool down before I reassume his form. Shaking my head to clear away some of the animals' grasp on my mind, I focus back in on Connie, staying close behind her.

She slams through a door at the top of the stairs, her silence a frosty chasm between us, as I try to keep up with her furious pace. I'm sure I'm about to cop some kind of tirade when we get to where we're going; she was already unhappy that I'd gone with the wolf instead of the tiger. The noise of the complex is a background hum as we make our way through it, my mind still so stuck on Mina's reaction that I don't take in anything around me.

It doesn't really matter anyway; after I woke from my transformation, Sabboath gleefully showed me his secret lair, and I've made a point to memorize as many of the paths around the building as I can. He has an entire complex hidden in Ferijen, the realm of Halloween and mythical monsters. Because it's stereotypically gloomy and covered in a thick fog, it's easy for him to hide here, and I believe that Hammus has helped shield it from the naked eye as well. That's why any patrol from the CD doesn't see it. The mystical creatures from this realm don't say anything because, to them, the CD *is* the boogeyman.

Now that crazy Connie and her equally manic father think I'm on their side, or at least under their control, I've been able to scope out more of the AoA members, though I couldn't believe how many people I recognized. The extent of their infiltration is astronomical, but nobody trusts me yet, sending skeptical side eyes my way whenever Connie isn't looking. I guess I can't blame them, but I'm also not going to be able to get any information out of them until they start to open up.

I follow Connie into Sabboath's thankfully empty office, and before I can do anything, she whirls on me and screeches, "How dare you threaten me! What is your problem? Growling at me like that when I put that bitch in her place. It seems to me that you're a little protective of her. Hiding something, Samuel?" She starts to pace back and forth across the room, her hands ripping at her hair with jerky movements.

"Are you reconsidering which side of this war you want to be on? Don't make Daddy regret trusting you. Don't make him punish us, *please*." By the time she's finished her tirade, she's gone from superior to begging me. I guess Sabboath would hold her responsible if I did anything he didn't like. A slight pang of guilt hits me, but I quickly shake it off. Connie made her own informed decision when she chose to take up her father's cause, and *she* volunteered for the serum. I can't say for sure that anyone else has. I can't even be sure those two idiots we left behind are here voluntarily. They seem different from the day I saw them when we chose Mina for our team. There's a manic sort of energy within them that wasn't there before. From what I've seen, all of Team Echo is dirty, and Brock from Bravo was around somewhere too, but he didn't return from Minzeon, so I assume he was captured. Sabboath has been ranting about all the captured AoA members since we returned two days ago. I've managed to avoid him all this time, but today was the first time I'd been able to get to see Mina. Connie has been especially vigilant, no matter what form I'm in.

I hold my hands up and attempt to placate her. "I'm sorry, Connie, the wolf was feeling edgy, like he wanted to maim and kill, and that was the only way I could keep him under control. You must know what it's like when you're in a different form and the natural instincts of the animal take over..."

My tone is quiet and soothing, trying to make it seem like we have something in common, and I feel sick about the fact that I continue to play games with this poor, crazy, mixed up girl, but I repeat my new motto: she made her choice. I need to harden my heart against her because she's not the Connie that I knew anymore, and if the others are to be believed, maybe she never was the girl I'd thought.

But I guess my words don't have the effect that I hoped for because she starts screaming. "I should know?! Well, I *don't* because my shift is fucked up, and I don't have an animal in my head. It's just me, fucked up, ugly spider me. Daddy offered to fix me, but it didn't work. He says my DNA is broken, and he can't rewrite it." She picks a pretty glass paperweight up off the desk and hurls it at the wall, where it shatters on impact. Her form starts to shimmer and contort, and my heart rate increases, worrying that she's going to shift involuntarily. She's right; it didn't fix her. In fact, it's made her even more unstable. Tears are streaming down her face, but I feel nothing. Any pity or sadness I once felt for her disappeared the minute she ordered Mina to be tortured. "So I'm going to be a monster forever. Can you love a monster, Sammy?"

I swallow around the anger in my throat. *How am I going to answer this question without giving myself away?* "Who couldn't love you, Connie?" I avoid the question like a pro and appeal to her vanity all in one, and it somehow works, earning a smile that's not much more appealing than her spider form. With that settled, she starts to rant about Mina again, and I turn my back on her so she can't see my face as she describes precisely what she would like to do to her.

I tune it out, thinking about Mina and how she looked when I saw her in the cell. Strung up and chained against the wall, her uniform ragged and ripped, her body listless and unresponsive. The red glow of her pupils gave away how hungry she is, and the light perfume of her pheromones was beginning to drift in the air. It won't be long before that gets out of control as well. I need to convince them to feed her blood, at least; otherwise, she's not going to survive.

All of my instincts are riding me hard to fix this, the animals' needs melding with my own Shifting is weird. You're yourself, but you have so many of the animal instincts too, and my wolf was practically screaming at me to protect Mina, while my human brain said I couldn't without jeopardizing her safety and my position. I haven't learned enough yet. I need to know what their plans are, and I need a location on Hammus. Then I might be able to get us both out of here.

Connie's still ranting wildly when Sabboath enters the room, a frown on his face. "What is all this noise? What is the problem, Connie?" he snaps, his patience with her even more nonexistent since the serum failed to fix her. He's been in the lab since we've returned with Mina, trying to work out what it is that has kept me sane when all of the others seem to be losing their minds day by day. He's taken blood samples and DNA, and it's only a matter of time before he works out that I'm an Archangel instead of the regular AB he thinks I am, so I need to find out everything I can about his plan before that. Luckily, he's the only one who trusts me. I think he's <u>so desperate</u> for his plan to work that he let his wariness drop after I voluntarily took the serum. I can't say for sure whether it's the Archangel status or the divine intervention that has kept me sane anyway, and Sabboath hasn't treated himself in case it has negative effects, so it's possible that there is no actual way for him to perfect his experiment. Not that I'm going to point that out to him. Once he's perfected it and fixed all the kinks, I think he plans on taking it. Or, now that I think back to the other day, perhaps he has another plan for himself.

I had been in his lab so he could draw my blood again, and I snuck a good look around while he was distracted. There was vial after vial in a fridge, ready to be given to the AoA troops as needed, but that wasn't what sent my pulse skyrocketing. Set aside from the bulk collection of serum were a couple of small vials that looked to be filled with liquid gold, a word written on the side that nearly made me gasp: Matoz. My mind whirled; when he captured the god, he must have taken some samples of his blood. It's all speculation, but I think he may be planning to add it to his serum so that he can become a god.

I tune back in to find Connie still whining about Mina and Sabboath rolling his eyes at her from behind his desk. "No, you can't kill her. I want to inject my serum into her. Who knows what interesting results might come from experimenting on a demon."

A snort escapes my mouth, and they both turn to look at me. "You're not going to be able to do anything with her if they continue to torture her; she's barely hanging on as it is."

Sabboath jumps up from where he's been sitting, fists already clenched in dissatisfaction. "She's being tortured? Who ordered that?" he shouts at us both, and Connie hunches her shoulders, trying to make herself smaller as she takes a step back. His hand flings violently in her direction, and she flies backward, ending up pinned against the same wall she threw the paperweight at, the shards sparkling on the carpet underneath her. She tries to speak, but with another wave of his hand, a gag appears across her mouth, secured tightly enough that she'd likely have bruises if it weren't for her accelerated healing. It's easy to forget because he's so weasily, but this man is an Archangel and possesses all the same abilities as my dad and his friends.

"Silence!" he bellows. "I have had enough of

you! You've let me down time and time again." His lip turns up into a sneer, eyes practically glowing with the heat of his anger. "It must be your pathetic mother's inferior blood running through you." *Ouch*, that's a direct hit. Tears are welling in her eyes, but he just ignores her and turns to me, pinning me with his cold glare.

"Talk to me," he commands. "What do you mean?"

"I don't know everything; today is the first time I've seen her since we bought her here, but she's not in good condition," I admit, unable to hide the disdain in my voice, but thankfully, he doesn't seem to notice who it's really directed at.

He sits back down, a worried look on his face. "Go on." He rubs a hand across his weak chin, eyes narrowed in suspicion.

"Well, she's hanging against a wall, shackled, and she looks like she's been roughed up. There's a bucket full of human waste in the corner of the cell, and from the look in her eyes, she hasn't been fed or given any water. Can't say I'm impressed, Sabboath. I thought you wanted her to join our side; there's no way she's going to do that if you mistreat her."

"How do you know she hasn't been fed?" he asks, ignoring the rest for some reason.

"Come on, you're not stupid. You know she's a..." Before I can finish the sentence, my vocal chords seize. The harder I push to say the word, the louder I begin barking, the geas still preventing me from saying anything.

Sabboath rolls his eyes. "Yes, yes, she's a demon, get on with it."

"Has it been so long since you've had anything to do with them that you've forgotten what they need? There are still a few in the CD; there are still some around."

He shudders, his disgust obvious. "Yes, I know there are, but I avoid them at all costs, filthy creatures." His snide superior tone is grating on my nerves, and my animals snarl inside my head, pushing for me to kill him.

"They need blood," I tell him flatly, and his eyes widen as he comprehends.

"Oh yes, and they also have *other* needs too. What do you know of her specific breed?" All the while we've been talking, Connie has remained against the wall, gagged. Suddenly, she starts wiggling furiously, shouting beneath her gag until he must get sick of it. Suddenly, the gag disappears, and she drops to the floor, landing in all that glass. She screams her discomfort, but he ignores it. With another wave, the glass disappears, including the bits that cut her, and the gashes close up. *Holy shit, he's more powerful than I thought. I'd always assumed because I've never seen him use these kinds of powers that he couldn't.* My surprise must show because he winks at me with a knowing look on his face. "We all have our secrets, boy." *Crap, what does he mean by that?*

Before I get the chance to try and finesse some answers out of him, Connie's on her feet, demanding answers of her own.

"They drink blood?" Her nose is screwed up in disgust, and she looks a little green at this information, totally unjustified since the woman turns into a giant spider creature. But then she raises an eyebrow. "And what do you mean *other* needs?" She looks between us both, waiting, but he ignores her.

"What is she?" he asks cautiously, as though he's not sure if he wants to know.

"She's a lust ……," I break off again but he seems to understand, and his face pales considerably as he blanches and swallows deeply.

"Shit."

Chapter Five

Samuel

"What's wrong, Daddy? What's her being a walking cum bucket got to do with anything?" Her clueless question has my anger rising to the surface, my wolf and tiger snarling in my mind, but before I can say anything, Sabboath is in front of Connie, backhanding her.

"Shut up, you stupid girl. You know nothing." The only sound that leaves her mouth is a grunt. It's like it's happened so many times she's used to it now. Her hand comes up to cradle her cheek, tears welling in her eyes, but they don't spill over.

"If her pheromones get out of control, we'll be in trouble. They'll infect the whole compound, sending everyone into an uncontrollable orgy. No one will be able to help themselves, and if they can't get at her, they'll take the next available thing. It's one of the reasons succubus demons often have multiple partners." He's started pacing again and yanking on his hair. The dude isn't going to have any left if he keeps going the way he is now.

"Why do we even need to keep her, Daddy? We've got Sammy, and I'm sure we could capture the rest of Alpha if we tried." Her eyes light up at the thought, but Sabboath is still scowling.

"Fuck, you're dumb! There's no way we could convince them to join our cause, and you had enough of a hard time controlling this one. Imagine having to control four others as strong as him." He gestures to me, confirming that my behavior had been manipulated, and my temper surges, pulsing in waves. I clench my fists to keep it together, but I can't help the growl that escapes, my wolf making itself known. He doesn't like the thought that we've been manipulated, been someone's prey. They both raise their eyebrows at me, but neither say anything about the challenge. Instead, Connie just keeps whining.

"Yes, but look at him now that you've given him the new formula. There's no resistance, and we have him fully in check. He's not even a little crazy! Not like any of the others you have to keep injecting. God, I wish all of them were as compliant." She reaches up, twirling a strand of hair around a finger. Her movement draws my eyes to the pink handprint on her cheek, a stark contrast to the rest of her pale, sickly tone. "Half our forces are here through no choice of their own, and they're going more and more crazy every time you inject them." The information just keeps rolling out as she puts forward her argument. "If there's something special about Sammy and Team Alpha, well, we wouldn't need any of the others. We could get rid of them or use them as cannon fodder, much like the ones we used at the compound. At least that gave them some kind of purpose in the end."

Shit, I need to update Jophial on all of this. They need to find a way to reverse the effects of the serum, or we're going to lose a bunch of ABs who are nothing more than pawns in Sabboath's game.

"No, we're going to stick with using her first; see if she has anything special about her. We don't know who her parents are, but maybe she has some higher-level demon blood in her which might make the serum more stable." He breathes out a big sigh, the stress getting to him. "So I need her alive, well, and functioning to be able to do that. Maybe if it works, we can use her for breeding more soldiers for our army. I was going to breed you and Samuel, but that's not going to work now that the new serum hasn't worked on you."

Her face falls, and she hunches in on herself at his scathing words, but he pays her no mind. Every interaction between the two of them makes it clearer and clearer that any love he might have ever had for his daughter has disappeared in the interest of his twisted experimentation and mission to take down the CD. His head swings to me all of a sudden, and my heart skips a beat as his eyebrows turn in and he stares, deep in thought.

"Well, let's just throw another prisoner in with

her and let her fuck and drain him?" Connie suggests, the whine in her voice like scratching nails across a chalkboard.

My blood starts to boil at her suggestion, but before I can say anything, he shouts at her.

"We haven't got any prisoners at the moment because I turned them all and used them on Minzeon, so they're all sitting in a holding cell at the CD because Hugh fucked up and failed to get us that device. All we have left for grunt work are the troops that are here voluntarily." He takes another deep breath and lowers his voice, seeming more like he's trying to keep his cool in front of me rather than out of respect for his daughter.

"There *is* the dragon, though. He's become combative and unruly lately, questioning everything I tell him to do, no longer the obedient and reliable soldier I taught him to be. Ungrateful brat. He's proving more difficult to contain than I thought, so he may be a good option." He looks at me, his eyes narrowing with a calculating glint. "Though I don't think we need it anymore. Samuel, let's talk a little bit more about the serum I gave you." My anger recedes at his casual change of subject, but my heart rate increases. *Shit, what now?*

"You know all about the shapeshifting, but I used the essence of all the magical creatures that I'd captured in that new formula," he starts to explain.

"Does that mean that it won't last? That the magic will fade just like it does when the human realm moves on to something new?" I interrupt, my curiosity winning.

He frowns at my interruption but answers the question. "No, it shouldn't, because I've now infused that magic into your very makeup, and you are a real living and breathing being. It's infused into your DNA, so it's very much a part of you now. It won't matter what happens to your... donor."

"If I'm such a success, why did you need the DNA device from Minzeon?" I ask. I'm both confused and curious, but he seems to like any chance to show off his intelligence and experimenting, so it's worth a shot.

"Ah, yes, that's for something else, something more powerful than mere magical essence." My mind instantly goes to the golden blood, and I breathe a small sigh of relief that he's stalled on the project, at least for now. "We'll have to come up with another plan to get our hands on it. If we're able to get Mina over to our side, maybe we can get her to retrieve it for us. They'll never suspect her of being a double agent." He rubs his hands together, his mention of her bringing me back to our current and more pressing issue.

"If she's still alive, remember she needs blood *and* sex," I remind him, and he shakes his head before continuing.

"Yes, anyway, I gave you the ability to shapeshift into any creature I could find, including a mermaid and dragon, but more importantly, I gave you demon essence. I just need to activate that with a little demon blood, and you should transition and find your demon form," he says, his eyes lit up with mad scientist fervor. A shiver of concern runs down my spine, but I hold myself steady, not wanting him to see it.

Connie gasps at this information and looks at me with wide-eyed wonder. "Wow, Daddy, he really *is* a great asset to our cause." *God, she really is stupid.*

"Yes, and since Mina won't recognize you in your demon form, we can throw you into her cell, a little roughed up, and you can be her next meal."

"NOOO!" Connie screams, her wide-eyed awe gone, but Sabboath waves his hand and gags her again, not taking an eye away from me. My heart races at the thought of getting close to Mina, but I know he's watching for my reaction, so I screw my nose up in disgust. *Come on, Sam, just pretend you need to get close to Connie instead and channel that feeling.*

"Do I have to? I don't want a demon form, nor do I want to touch *her*." I pretend to shudder with disgust, like doing that would be revolting. "Ask anything else of me but that, please," I beg, laying it on thick. My reaction seems to satisfy him as he walks toward the door, gesturing for me to follow.

"Yes, my boy, you do. You'll do this for our cause, and you may just be the one to get her on our side. If you don't, well, maybe you'll just knock her up and get me the start of my new army." My stomach rolls with nausea at that last little bit, and I nearly drop the mask of indifference I've been trying to maintain. Before I can even come up with a response, the warmth of Connie's hand grips my arm, and even though she's gagged, her eyes are imploring me not to do it.

"What about the transition?" I remind him. "Demons go through a big change with the transition. I don't know the specific details of Mina's, but it involved a lot of blood and sex. What kind of demon was I injected with?"

He enters his lab, one that I've become so familiar with, but I hadn't even noticed where we were headed, my mind whirling with too much information. He goes to a fridge and pulls out some vials of blood.

His grin stretches wide in excitement as he loads them into one bag. "That's the best thing! I didn't want you to just be any *one* kind of demon; they're so limited by only being able to feed on one thing. You, my masterpiece, were injected with lust, wrath, pride, and envy demons' essences, and I'll put a mixture of their blood into you, activating all of their traits at once. You'll be much more formidable than the average demon, able to adapt and feed no matter where you go. I'm pretty sure that there will be no transition for you, except to assume your demon form, and you'll need blood, obviously, but you can just drink Connie's." He offers his daughter up without a blink of his eye, and the sound that escapes her mouth from around the gag is heartbreaking. I can see in her eyes that as much as she wants me, she can't get over her prejudice against demons, but I can't spare a thought for her. I need to worry about myself.

What am I going to do? Will the goddess' protection allow this to happen, or will it block it? I don't see that I have any choice but to go through with it and hope that I won't hate this newest creature I'll become.

He loads all the blood into one bag and pats a nearby examination bed. "Come on, boy, let's make this happen."

After sitting on the bed and rolling up my sleeve, he starts to clean the skin. "Do you think it might be a good idea to stop…" Before I can suggest halting Mina's torture, Silas and Beatrice walk into the room, making my words unneeded.

Silas walks over to the table to see what Sabboath is doing, eyes alight with curiosity and envy.

"That stupid bitch has some sort of outer body armor that's fused to her skin," Beatrice announces, flopping down in a chair next to a still gagged Connie. She raises an eyebrow before laughing at her predicament, and Connie gives her the middle finger.

Sabboath stops what he's doing and raises his eyebrows. "Body armor?"

"Yeah, it's like her mom fucked a dragon or something." Silas lifts the bag of blood and peers at it in the light, seemingly unbothered by the frown Sabboath is sporting after his flippant words.

"That's not possible; magical creatures can't breed with real ones. Otherwise, that would've solved my problem years ago. There would've been no need for all my experiments," he snaps, snatching the bag away from Silas and hanging it from a metal pole. Taking the needle, he places it into one of my veins, causing a sharp pinch as it pierces the skin. He then tapes it in place. "Right, we'll just let it run its course."

He turns to the other three and waves his hand at Connie, ungagging her once again. "You three stay here and provide him with blood. There's plenty in the fridge, and well, if you run out, he can feed on you."

The three of them turn pale, and Silas shouts, "Fuck no! No dirty demon is going to feed on me."

Sabboath smirks at him, coldness leaking into his eyes. "You *will* let him feed on you; just be glad he isn't going to get any other urges; otherwise, you would be letting him do more than just drink your blood." Silas blanches and quickly moves away from me, sitting down with the two girls.

"Dude, don't look so frightened. You're not my type." I smirk at him, and he puffs up his chest, braver now that he's facing me and not his "boss."

"What, male?" he sneers, and I shake my head.

"No, I don't discriminate when it comes to sex." Connie's eyebrows shoot up at this, her surprise evident. She clearly hadn't realized I swing both ways. I wonder if that will change her mind about wanting to be with me. I don't think she realized Mav and Zeph did either when she was chasing after them at first. She was always so rude to Trick, Sander, and Dru, to the extent of being homophobic. Strange, because our society has always been so fluid and accepting.

"Nah, I discriminate when it comes to assholes, and even besides that, you're just pathetic." He jumps to his feet to charge me, but Sabboath just rolls his eyes and uses his power to push Silas back into his seat.

"God, you're like children," he complains before continuing. "Once you get through this, if your demon form doesn't look too much like human you, then we'll move on to the next half of the plan: get you into the dungeons and work on getting her to trust you. Saving her life with your blood and maybe your cock will be a good start. I'll go and throw the dragon in with her now. If I punish him like this, he may come to see reason again and fall back into line. Hopefully, he can keep her alive until you can work your magic. The siren in you might come in handy as well."

"Dragon? What dragon?" I know he mentioned one before, and I'd seen one during the battle on Minzeon, but I thought that was just a creature he'd kidnapped from one of the realms.

"I had one other success before you, my own

special creation. A child that I managed to acquire at a young age and bring up as my own. A very special child. I didn't inject him until I had perfected the formula; he was far too valuable to waste on my earlier tries." My eyes whip to Connie, fury glistening in her eyes at his slight, but he doesn't seem to notice. *Or likely doesn't care that the lesser child hates him.*

"No, he got the perfected formula, but unlike you, he only has one creature attached to his DNA. My thinking hadn't quite developed to adding them all at that stage. I think I might upgrade him though, give him the same as you. If he proves his loyalty to me and feeds Mina to keep her alive, anyway. For now, this will be his punishment. He is proving to be rebellious, and I can only control him for small windows of time. His will is strong, and he doesn't want to be here, so he'll have to earn the upgrade." He sighs with disappointment, unlike the annoyance he shows toward Connie. It seems whatever genuine feeling he's capable of has been strictly reserved for this golden child of his.

"Maybe I can use the same collar that's on Jessamina to keep him in line. But then he couldn't access his powers, and he'd be useless to me." He seems to be talking to himself, his eyes glazed over in thought. As he pauses, I take a moment to inspect the IV. The blood slowly drips down the plastic tube into my body, but I don't feel anything as of yet, so I force my mind back to the topic at hand. *What's so special about the dragon guy? And where did he come from?* Another bit of information I must tell Jophial, but I guess all of that is going to have to wait. Hopefully, I can get five minutes alone soon, so I can pop outside of the barrier and send her a telepathic message.

"Alright, I'll be back in a little while to check on you. Try not to kill them, please. They do come in handy occasionally." His words are flippant and uncaring as he walks out the door without a backward glance. It swings shut with a loud clang and the ominous click of the lock as heat starts to flow through my body. My eyes dart to the blood bag, which is now nearly empty.

"Ah, guys, you may want to get a hold of a couple of those blood bags," I tell them as that heat is followed by blinding pain, and my body starts to contort. "Now!" I scream, and before my eyes close against the agony, I see them scramble into action.

Chapter Six

Lysander

It's not until the following day that we all finally get to sit down and discuss another failed mission. Fuck, it feels like déjà vu. My head is hammering due to last night's binge drinking, but instead of turning on my team like I did last time around, we all got drunk together, not wanting to accept that Mina had been taken.

We're all sitting around a huge conference table at the Collectors Division, the only ones here so far. The apartment had seemed empty without Mina, and none of us had wanted to be there. My hand rubs at the ache in my chest, the missing mate bond causing a dull pain to throb throughout my body. All five of us who have sealed the bond with Mina have gotten sick since she's been gone. Looking around the table, I study the others.

Drusilla looks pale and clammy, her eyes barely open against her exhaustion. She'd climbed into bed between Trick and me and proceeded to toss and turn all night. Whimpers filled the moments when she'd managed to fall asleep, only to wake back up, screaming, from nightmares. Trick and I were keenly feeling the lack of sleep ourselves. Trick, once he finally fell asleep, spent all night tossing and turning like my sister, so between the two of them I'm running on basically no rest at all. Jagger and Kai also look like they hadn't gotten much shut-eye either. Neither of them has been able to hold their form this morning, and there's an almost sickly quality about them that I'd only seen when Jagger's old team had starved him. Even though they've been able to feed off of each other, they still look like they're struggling.

My eyes drift to the other two members of our team, realizing they look just as bad as we do, proof of how much Mina means to all of us. Mav has withdrawn into his chaos-filled mind, and Zeph looks like he didn't even go to bed, still wearing the same clothes as yesterday, his eyes bloodshot. Not to mention that the smell of whiskey emanating from him is enough to make the eyes water. We're sitting in heavy silence when Clementine and Riarliel enter the room, both having been thoroughly checked for interaction with the AoA and cleared of any suspicion. With that done, the Archangels had briefed the pair on some of our team's secrets, and now they officially have more information than Hugh ever had. They walk behind us, taking their seats further down the large conference table, and Zeph's face suddenly becomes animated now that there's a chance we might get some answers.

"What's going on? Is there any news? Why was this meeting called?" He fires the questions at her, one after the other, before she even has a chance to sit down. We all watch, nearly holding our breath in anticipation, as she settles herself in her chair, placing a tablet on the table and murmuring to Riarliel before she bothers to answer. Steam's practically pouring out of Zeph's ears by the time she finally responds, but she *is* our boss, so he keeps it together... mostly.

Riarliel doesn't sit, instead moving to a side cabinet where a coffee spread has been set up and proceeding to make them both a cup. That actually looks pretty good to me, so I push back my chair and join her, figuring it will at least be something to do while we're all waiting. Riarliel smiles at me when I approach but doesn't say anything as I start to turn over seven cups and go about making some for my team. Everyone looks like they could do with a cup or five.

"Now, Zeph, I know this is hard for you," she starts, and I flinch internally as Riarliel takes a small glance back like even she knows that was a terrible way to start.

"Fuck, here we go," Trick says to me through our link. Turning quickly to look, I catch Zeph throwing his chair back as he jumps to his feet, his palm slamming down on the table.

"You don't know shit," he barks back.

"Stop him, Mav; she doesn't deserve this," Drusilla pleads, and Mav actually listens, his eyes becoming more focused now that he has a job. *Hmm, we're going to have to keep him distracted.* Mav stands up and rights Zeph's chair before murmuring some words into his ear which have him taking a deep breath and sitting down again. Turning back to the coffee, I continue with the task now that Zeph's settled down.

Softly, he mumbles an apology to Clementine, his eyes downcast. It's not like Zeph to lose his shit, but I guess what might be worse than being mated to Mina and losing her might be losing her without the chance to ever see if they were also meant for one another.

"I'm sorry, I really am, but I didn't call this meeting. The Archangel council did, and they should be here shortly. This AoA situation is out of control, and I'm handing it over to them to deal with. I can't run the CD and deal with all of that as well." She sounds tired as she pushes a strand of hair back from her face, smiling gratefully at Riarliel when she puts a cup down in front of her. I start to distribute the mugs I'd made amongst my team and get grateful smiles and grunts of appreciation before taking my own and sitting down. Taking a long sip of the milky, sugary drink, I finally start to feel a little better.

"You'll now be working directly for them until

this is handled. You will follow their orders, and when we get Mina back and snuff out the menace that is the AoA, you can then return to being Team Alpha. God knows we're going to have to overhaul all the elite teams. And we have so many people to interrogate down in the cells, I just don't know where to start." She blows out another tired breath and slouches in her seat, not the polished perfectionist I usually know, and my heart sinks.

Her words also remind me that I need to fill Livie and James in on all that's been going on. I'm confident they're not traitors. Before I can give Clementine any words of encouragement, blinding light fills the room, and when it finally clears, our fathers, Mina's included, are standing there. They make their way quietly to their seats and sit down. They, too, are all looking unusually tired and worn. When I checked in with Dad, he'd told me it had taken them well into the night to make Michael see reason. He'd been determined to burn down the worlds in search of Sabboath. I guess Heaven hath no fury like a dad separated from his daughter.

Michael looks around the room, nodding to us all, his eyes stopping on Drusilla. She'd always been his favorite when we were children; I guess now I know the reason why. A small smile lights up his face as he sees her, the first sign that he's capable of feeling something other than rage right now. Seeing his look, she jumps to her feet and races around to him. Before anyone can say anything, she throws her arms around him and sobs into his shoulder.

"I miss her so much," she cries, and he looks around at us awkwardly, not quite sure what to do with the crying woman in his arms. Dad just snorts with laughter, his shoulders shaking, but he offers no help. Michael shoots him a glare that promises payback as he gently pats my sobbing sister's back.

"Ah, um, there, there, Silly." His childhood nickname for her flows off his tongue, low and soothing. "We'll get her back, I promise." With that reassurance, the tears slow down and she stops shaking.

"She's my mate," she announces, and that has me freezing, waiting for her next words. "In fact, she's mated a few of us already." *Fuck, there it is.* His head shoots up, and he eyes the rest of the team with a cold stare as if he's trying to work out which of us he has to kill.

Raphael, ever the sensible one, stands up and extracts Drusilla from Michael's arm before walking her back to her chair. Michael, in the meantime, smooths out his tear-stained shirt before sitting down, his glare still moving from one person to the next.

"Let's worry about getting her back before we worry about who she's mated with." Raphael's voice of reason cools the tension in the room, and I breathe a sigh of relief after Michael nods. *He's not going to be as easy to charm as Lucifer was.* We earned significant brownie points with her when we all stepped up before we knew we were her mates, but it's not going to be like that with him.

"Way to go announcing that at the wrong time. We're lucky he didn't smite us there and then," I grumble in my sister's head, and she at least has the grace to blush in embarrassment.

"Sorry," she mumbles back, *"I got carried away."*

"Fuck yes, you did."

"We're just waiting on the rest of the council, and then we'll get started," Raphael tells everyone before stepping over to the coffee bar, holding up the empty pot in disgust. "Damn it." Before he can do anything, Michael waves his hand in its direction, and the container is full again.

"I could've done that," Raphael grumbles, pouring himself a cup, his lips turning down in a childish pout.

"I'll have one too, please," Michael says quite politely as he smirks at the frown on his friend's face when the other dads place their orders as well. Again, my dad snorts with laughter. He's happy today, but I guess having your best friend around for the first time in a long while is reason enough to make the grumpiest Archangel smile.

Looking around the room, I notice the four empty chairs. "Who else is on the Archangel council? I know Sabboath was." My words bring disgruntled mumbles and hisses from the other members, but I ignore them. "But I don't think I know the other four Archangels. Why don't I know this?" Our dads exchange glances, and I can tell they're having a telepathic conversation between themselves. They're good at hiding any expression from their faces, but the total silence is enough of a giveaway. There's nothing we can do but wait for them to finish.

"The Archangel council is made up of eleven angels, an odd number so that there is never a tied vote. Obviously, the six of us and Sabboath are members, but the three others have kept a lower profile over the years. They keep up to date on everything, and they attend our meetings, but they don't have anything to do with the CD. Having too many of us involved would lead to headaches, and the six of us always worked well as a team. It was decided that we would oversee it and all the angel affairs, with the others only weighing in on important issues," Chamuel explains, but I do the math in my head, and it doesn't add up.

Before I can say anything, Jagger speaks up, his voice gravelly and weary. "That's only ten. What about the eleventh?"

Azrael rubs a hand over his face before picking up where Chamuel left off. "We're not sure about him. He was a part of our group, the first of us to have a child, actually, and he and his wife were so happy."

"It was their happiness that convinced us to go against all the others and have children of our own, even if we did have to hide them," Zadkiel chimes in.

"They didn't hide their child?" Kai asks, his eyebrows turned in confusion.

"No, they were the first Archangel couple to ever have a child. After he was born, it was discovered he was born an Archangel. The normal angels kicked up such a fuss about it and were *furious* at us. I mean, how were we to know they would be born Archangel instead of just angel like we all were? It was then we were forced into an agreement that we wouldn't have children with each other, all to appease all the others."

"It got so bad that Mylea actually had to oversee the negotiations. As Archangels, we're inherently powerful in our own right, but they had us in numbers. Angels can be such petty, jealous creatures." Though Michael's words are sad, they're also tinged with a hint of annoyance. Even after all this time, there's some bitterness lurking there. I'm sure it has a lot to do with all the years that he missed sharing with Mina while watching his fellow Archangels bond with their children.

"Anyway, we agreed, and everything was okay for a while. But it didn't last. Tiberion and his family, found themselves persecuted by all of those who were jealous of their happiness and his son's skills even though he was just a small child. Mylea had told us as a born Archangel his major magic wouldn't come in before he turned ten, but he'd already exhibited telekinesis by the time he was five. To keep the peace, it was decided that Tiberion and his family would leave Amilles and come and live here on Reath, but before they could, their house was set on fire, and his wife and child were stuck inside. No one is sure how it happened, or why she couldn't teleport out or even stop the flames, but she perished in the fire, and there was no sign of their son. When her body was retrieved, she was wearing a collar that we think had restricted her from using her powers. It was too badly damaged for us to do any tests to figure out its composition or what magic might have been laid upon it."

All of them blanch at Zadkiel's words, and I remind myself that for us, this is a cautionary tale, but for them, this is a real memory of what their friend went through. The thought of not being able to access my power causes goosebumps to erupt on my skin.

"Oh my god, that's horrible," Dru whispers, sadness and a bit of fear trickling down the link. *"No wonder they were so adamant about keeping us a secret."*

"Anyway, Tiberion cracked a little after that. Although we don't have mates like demons do, Archangel couples have the same kind of bond with their partners. Part mental, physical, and emotional, and without it he just shut down and disappeared, not wanting to have anything to do with the race that pleaded their innocence. After all these years, we still can't think of who else it could have been."

Raphael finishes the story, and the room is filled with somber silence as everyone becomes lost in their own thoughts.

"How old was his son when this happened?" Trick asks, breaking the mood.

"Grayson was only five," Chamuel explains, "and it was another ten years before we finally decided to defy the rulings, so he would have been sixteen or so years older than you all."

"And no one ever found out what happened to him?" Mav's voice is low and rough, his eyes blazing with anger.

"No, it's like he just disappeared. No body has ever been found. And Tiberion, we haven't seen since. Who knows if he's even alive?"

God, could the room get any more depressing than it already is? Before anyone can say anything else, there's another blinding flash of light, and when it clears, two more Archangels are standing in the room. What's most surprising, though, is how they look. Both of them show signs of aging, unlike our parents. The one on the left is tall and slim, his long gray hair and beard making it easy for him to be mistaken for someone's elderly grandfather; his wings are a mottled brown, and they too have streaks of gray through them. The other on the right is shorter and, dare I say, plump and going bald. His wings are a sickly shade of green that I've never seen before. Neither of them is what I've come to expect Archangels to look like, but then again, neither is Sabboath.

Turning my head, I notice the shocked looks on our dad's faces, like this wasn't what they'd been expecting either.

"Reorniel, Sainsiel, thank you for coming so quickly." Raphael shakes off his surprise the quickest, hiding it with a mild smile for the couple who do not look happy to be here at all.

"It's not like we had a choice," grumbles the tall, slender man before he takes one of the remaining seats.

"I'd like to say you both look well, but I'd be lying," Michael snaps, his voice holding obvious suspicion as he eyes the one who remains standing. *He's definitely not pulling any punches today.* "What the fuck has happened to the two of you? Sainsiel, you both look like old men! We don't age unless we choose to."

"As you said, we chose to. Life has become boring, and both of us have decided we have had enough. We're going to let nature take over." He looks down at his age spot-covered hands, not meeting anyone's eyes before taking a seat next to Reorniel.

"Did that seem like the weirdest explanation ever?" Kai skeptically asks, and all of us nod our heads slightly, Zeph narrowing his eyes as he looks them both over. I can see that none of our dads quite believe the excuse either.

"Do they look like they have that same funny skin tone that Sabboath has?" At Trick's question I focus my attention on the two newcomers, trying to subtly check them out, but before I can answer him, another two people appear in the room.

These people have everyone but Team Alpha leaving their seats and dropping into deep bows. My eyes move from the prostrating elders to the first being. A large bulky male who must be close to seven feet tall with short-cropped hair and opaline eyes that seem to change color every time he blinks. His forehead is set in a disapproving frown, his arms folded across his chest. He gives off *don't fuck with me* vibes, even more so than my dad, which is both impressive and slightly terrifying. Azyer, the god of angels, is someone you don't want to fuck with.

The other one is a female, dwarfed by the giant beside her. She has gorgeous curves that would've once made my mouth water, with long silver hair and a pert nose. Her mouth is lush and made for sin, and as I get to her eyes, the same color-changing shade as the man, they're looking at me. As they twinkle with amusement at my perusal, I realize I've just checked out a goddess and feel my cheeks pinking with embarrassment and guilt. *How could I do that? There's a gaping hole in my chest where Mina is supposed to be, and I'm checking this woman out?!*

"Don't be embarrassed. I'm quite flattered; it's not often I get eye fucked quite like that." Her voice is musical, as is the laughter that flows from her mouth.

Fuck, now I just want to curl up and die as everyone's heads turn to me. Trick snorts in my head, the first sign of amusement I've heard from him since Mina was taken, but Drusilla elbows me violently. "Seriously, Sander?" Her scathing tone makes my cheeks burn even hotter.

My dad's looking at me like he wants to put his hands around my neck and squeeze, and the weight of my embarrassment nearly doubles. But Mylea waves her hands. "Oh, relax and get back into your seats; we've got more important things to worry about."

Everyone follows her directive except Michael, who heads to the woman and pulls her into a tight hug. "Thank you for coming, Mylea."

She reaches up and pats him on the cheek. "Of course, there's nothing I wouldn't do for my favorite Archangel." The chemistry between them is affectionate, but it's not sexual; it's like a sister talking to her brother. He sits back down, gazing at her with the same small smile on his face as when he looks at Dru.

"Right then, who wants to tell me all about this clusterfuck?"

Chapter Seven

Jessamina

My breathing sounds wet and raspy as I regain consciousness. This time, my face is pressed against a hard surface, but the agony in my limbs has disappeared, blessed numbness saving me from that bit of torture. There's a coppery taste in my mouth that I know is from my own blood, and it does nothing to assuage the ravenous hunger I feel. God help the first person I come across if I survive this; there's no way I'll be able to keep from draining them. I might feel guilty later, but right now, I don't have the energy to care. I just hope someone comes along soon.

I can also feel the burn of my desire and know that my body is going to go into overdrive soon, pulsing out those pheromones in the hope of attracting someone to sexually feed from. My stomach rolls at the thought of taking away some-one's choice, practically rape, really, since he or she would have no defenses against the succubus lure.

There's a dripping sound somewhere, *drip, drip drip*, a soothing beat in time with my rattling breath, and the foul smell of waste emanating from nearby. I have a vague recollection of being unshackled to use the bucket by unrecognizable guards, but my mind can't retain how many times this has happened or how often. I do vividly know that the guards didn't hesitate to drop me or give me a punch to the kidney if I didn't behave. Without any of my powers or strength, I'm reduced to the weakness of an Earth human. With no possible way to fight back, I stopped trying, resigning myself to my fate until I either die or someone takes pity on me and feeds me.

I'm not sure how long I lie there, but the small shaft of light coming into the cell has moved every time I manage to open my eyes. The sound of a rodent or something scratching around in the dirt has my sluggish pulse speeding up slightly at the thought of being nibbled on, but it soon moves away, looking for a more appetizing meal. Next time I manage to open my eyes, the light is draped in shadows, and I watch as it slowly disappears altogether, plunging the cell into darkness. As I drift off again, the hole in my chest where my mates used to be seems to throb with longing, an empty ache that will never be filled again.

I must fall asleep again because the clanging of my cell door is the next thing I'm aware of. There's not enough energy even to raise my head now, let alone try and feed on someone, so maybe I'm just going to die. That throb comes even harder, the pain turning torturous, as thoughts of my mates and the fact that I may never see them again becomes a very real possibility.

Footsteps stop near my ear, and I can hear someone tutting. "God, what a mess." The words are spat out coldly, almost clinically. "Get her cleaned up! I need her; she can't die. How did this happen?" The voice is raging now, and my ears finally recognize it as Sabboath, but hope kindles with his words.

Hands under both armpits lift me up, and I can't help the scream of agony that escapes my mouth as the pressure of their grips unfortunately awakens feelings in my limbs. When I open my eyes, I'm dangling between the two guards who helped me into this condition, though neither admits it to him. As I gingerly turn my head, I can see that they're both eyeing me salaciously, my pheromones already at work. I shudder, unable to control the fear that rolls through me. I'm going to end up raped because I have no strength to defend myself, and my damn body can't control its pheromone output.

My eyes come back to Sabboath. He's glaring at me in disgust, the flush of anger still on his cheeks and nose turned up as he quite literally looks down on me. "I want you to take her and wash her. Be careful. She's dangerous."

The one to the left of me snorts. "She's not dangerous; you could knock her over with a feather." Sabboath's eyes narrow, and even my muddled mind knows the guard is a fool for talking back to his boss.

"Don't say I didn't warn you," he tells them both before walking out. "Oh, and return her to the cell in the same condition. If she's worse when I get back with her lunch, I will make both of you her meal as well," he threatens over his shoulder, but they just laugh like it's a joke.

Lifting me, they drag me to a room at the end of the corridor of cells, my senses overwhelmed by their closeness and lack of cleanliness. The one on the right smells like cheese, and the one on the left smells like stale cigarette smoke; both make me feel like gagging. We stop, Cheesy pushing a door open, and we enter a glaringly bright white bathroom. My eyes recoil from the light and slam shut as the two of them continue to drag me forward. My ass smarts as they drop me down onto a hard wooden bench and proceed to strip me down, removing my ratty clothes as they chuckle and throw nasty comments about my body to each other.

"Look at all that weird pink skin! She's definitely a dirty demon, but why doesn't she have any of the other bits? I wanted to cut off a horn or something for my collection. I haven't got a pink one yet." Smoky's voice sounds exactly like he smells, all phlegmy and gross with a rasp like his vocal cords have been abused by two packs a day. I thank the goddess that I'm not in full demon form, and that even in my weakened state, I've been able to stop the transformation. Goosebumps rise at the thought of him having tortured other demons to stock his collection of parts, and my fangs click into place, anger simmering just below the surface.

I'm unable to hold myself up, so Cheesy supports me as Smoky gets rid of my shirt and pants, leaving me in just my underwear. My armor must have receded while I was unconscious, and I can all too clearly feel his clammy hands dragging up the inside of my thigh.

"Are you sure you want to be doing that?" Cheesy asks, sounding unsure. "Sabboath will kill us if anything happens to her, and I'm not sure she'll go along with that without a fight."

"What he doesn't know isn't going to hurt." Smoky chuckles as his hand moves up over my waist and across my stomach to grope at my breast through the bra cup. I try to struggle, but Cheesy holds me tight. Smoky's finger pinches at my nipple, and another chuckle escapes his mouth, his foul breath washing over my face.

"Let's get her in the shower; I want to wash off the filth before I touch anything else." He releases my breast, and they haul me up between them, Smoky thrusting his tiny cock against my panty-clad ass as they lead me over to a row of showers. My skin crawls at the feeling, and I gag slightly at the violation, but the lust he's giving off brings me a slight pulse of power as I start to absorb it. I just about vomit at the taste of it, but right now, I can't be too fussy.

They turn on the water, and it starts off freezing cold, the bite of it painful against my already sensitive skin, but it soon warms up after they both get a blast of it on them as well. *They might not care about how I feel, but they certainly don't enjoy their own discomfort.* They hold me under the flowing water for about five minutes, just letting the grime caking my body slide down before circling the drain. Smoky then leaves me to Cheesy and steps away, grabbing a block of soap from somewhere. He rubs it all over my body, his fingers caressing and pinching as he goes, his lust building into a fever and feeding me even more.

Although Cheesy is only holding me and initially disagreed with Smoky, I can feel his desire ramping up as well. Small bursts of power trickle in, bit by bit, and as he releases the clip to my bra and lets it fall to the ground, my breasts now exposed to his naked eye, that trickle turns into a deluge. His hands come up to grab both, the soap now forgotten, and I'm still unable to control my limbs, so I stand there, helpless to resist. A sob escapes my mouth at the feeling of violation while my body continues to feed, not caring for what my mind is going through. After tweaking my nipples a couple of times, hard enough to hurt, his hands leave my breasts and find the edge of my panties. "No, please, no, don't!" I shake my head back and forth in denial, but he just ignores me. Energy starts to flow back into my body quicker and quicker as their lust ramps higher at my struggles.

He starts to drag my panties down, exposing my pussy to his leering eyes, and anger surges through me. As they drop to the floor and one of his thick fingers heads toward my folds, my armor snaps into place, the pink and gold scales glittering in the harsh bathroom light. Suddenly, feeling returns to my limbs in force, and I rip myself from Cheesy's grip and throw myself at Smoky, my claws popping out. All I see is his eyes widening in surprise, a shout escaping his mouth before I grab hold of him.

Wrenching him toward me, my teeth sink into the thick juicy vein in his neck, tearing through the skin like it's tissue paper. Pulling back, I open a gaping wound and watch with detached interest as a crimson waterfall of life-giving liquid starts to spurt out of his body in time to his beating heart. He tries to struggle, but it's no use. Their greed has fueled me enough to fight back, and as I attach my mouth to the warm flow of much-needed suste-nance, his struggles weaken until he's limp in my arms. Cheesy finally comes to his senses behind me and starts battering on my back, but it's too late. My scales are protecting me, and my strength is slowly beginning to return. Even with the slow trickle of energy, they're not a match for me. It's officially too late for Smoky, and if Cheesy's not careful, he'll be next.

He gives up on the assault on my back and runs from the room, screaming, "Help! Help me!" I'm too enthralled with my meal to stop him. I can hear and feel as Smoky's life drains away from him, but still, I keep my mouth attached. This meal hasn't even touched the tip of the iceberg that is my hunger. A shadow falls over me, and I rip my mouth away from his warm flesh to snarl at the person interrupting my feeding. Before I can get out a sound, a bolt of power slams into my body as the collar around my neck sends electricity coursing through me. Unable to control myself, I convulse with the onslaught of pain and find myself on the ground twitching in a puddle of water as the power starts to fade, my eyes in line with familiar black boots.

"Sloppy, I warned you she was dangerous." Sabboath's voice remains clinically detached as he crouches down next to me, and I find myself wondering if he'd actually been planning on this outcome to begin with. "Well, look at this. That idiot was right," he says quietly, almost to himself. A finger runs over my scale-covered back, and this time, my body wants to convulse for an entirely different reason. "They really are quite fascinating, very similar to a dragon's hide. Miss Michaels, you are *quite* a find. I can't wait to see what you can do with my new formula."

His words echo around the now quiet bathroom. Someone must have turned off the water as the puddle surrounding me slowly drains away, along with all the energy I'd gained with my unexpected meal. My eyes meet Smoky's wide-eyed death stare not far from me, his neck ripped open like a fierce predator attacked him, but I don't feel any ounce of remorse. He wasn't going to stop, and whether my pheromones encouraged it or not, I wasn't interested and had clearly told him so. No means no, whether you're a demon or any other species!

"Well, don't just stand there! Get her back to her cell and give her something to cover up with. I don't want her getting sick on top of all the other damage." His words could almost be misconstrued as kind if I weren't so worried about this formula he mentioned. Cheesy has been joined by a couple of extra guards, and I'm once again dragged to my feet. I watch, detached, as one of them lifts Smoky's corpse, throws him over his shoulder, and disappears out the door. Cheesy and the new one who smells like cabbage help me back down the corridor, my legs actually working this time, though that doesn't do me any good. The pair quickly open up my cell, shoving me back in before slamming it closed behind me. I stumble over a hard lump in the middle of the floor and fall to my knees on the other side of it, its groan of pain loud in the quiet cell. *Hang on, that wasn't from me....* Before I can assess the situation, something made of fabric hits me in the back.

"Here, put these on," Cheesy snaps at me. "Don't want you getting sick." Then he starts to cackle loudly. "Good luck with your new cellmate. I hope he does to you what you did to Phil." His words end in a sob, and I snicker lightly at his slip of weakness. *Oh, so that lust coming from Cheesy wasn't just for me.* His footsteps are loud as he stomps away, but he's left a flickering torch in a ring on the wall outside the cell so I can actually see. Gingerly, my body still aching from the electric shock, I turn around to see what he's thrown at me.

There's a pair of black sweatpants and a black t-shirt, no underwear or anything else. I don't want to put the clean, dry clothes on over my wet panties, so, keeping an eye on the bundle of what I now think is a person, I quickly strip off the wet underwear before pulling the sweats on, commando. Before I pull the t-shirt on, I will the scales away, taking on my normal appearance. My body sags slightly once they're gone; it's like the armor was holding me together, and now my body wants to fall apart, but I can't yet. No, now I need to assess whether that lump is friend or foe.

Crawling over to it, I roll the large mass over

and discover that it's a man. A semi-conscious man with a large bruise blooming over one cheek. A very handsome cheek from what I can see in the pale light. He has long shoulder-length hair that looks black, but it might be a little lighter, and it has a large patch of streaked hair running through it, a mix of red and silver. His skin is a deep mocha color, and he has a wide nose over plump lips and defined cheekbones. His eyes are closed beneath thick black eyebrows, and as I watch, his chest rises and falls with each breath. He's wearing sweats and a t-shirt, similar to mine, and I can see the outline of his broad shoulders and defined pecs that taper down into a slim waist. He also looks really tall. Altogether, he's very handsome, and while I sit there studying him, his scent reaches my nose. Something smoky, but unlike the guy I just killed, this is seductive, like a warm fire on a winter's day, and my stomach clenches, followed quickly by my core. I don't know whether I want to eat him or fuck him, but I know we're both in trouble.

"Hey, hey, wake up." I shake him a little, the exertion causing me to breathe deeper, sucking in more of his delicious scent. A little more urgently, I repeat the motion. "Hey, *please* wake up."

Suddenly, a hand is on my wrist, and as I look at his face, I gasp in shock. His eyes are now wide open, and they're elongated like a reptile's. He has a set of inner vertical eyelids that flick quickly across his silver pupil when he takes a deep breath inward, his nostrils flaring slightly before exhaling again. *What is he?* He has the same kind of eyes as that dragon I met when I did my first jump, and he's staring straight at me; his head slightly cocked to the side as if he's trying to figure something out about me just as much as I'm trying to figure out him.

I shuffle back, somewhat giving him some space, but he sits up and abruptly lunges toward me. Grabbing hold of me, fangs shining in his open mouth, he wrenches me against him and buries his nose into my neck, inhaling deeply. I think about invoking my scales, but I don't actually feel like I'm in danger. In fact, I feel quite the opposite, and in my current state, that safety is pleasantly over-whelming. My fangs drop down again, and I too draw in deep gulps of his intoxicating scent before pushing him away in panic.

"No, no, you can't! Don't come near me." I quickly move to the other side of the room, some-thing inside of me repulsed by the idea of seeing his eyes locked in a lifeless stare. Holding my hands up to keep him away, he watches me as he follows my movement with his keen gaze.

"Who are you?" His voice is deep but raspy like it's been unused for a long time. "How did I get here?" He looks around my cell, confused, shaking his head as if trying to make sense of everything. When our eyes meet again, they're back to normal, a smoky gray color, and his fangs have disappeared.

"I'm Jessamina, and I don't know how you got here. You were here when they threw me back in, but you need to stay back, please," I beg, a sob escaping my mouth. "Please stay back. Otherwise, I won't be able to control what happens."

Chapter Eight

Mavromichali

Hearing that language come out of the goddess' mouth cleared the last of the fog I'd been living in since Mina had been taken. It had started to lessen when Dru gave me something to do, helping me find some solid footing in the chaos swirling within me. It by no means settled all of it, but at least I could focus. For Mylea and Azyer to get involved, shit is about to get real.

I look around the room, taking in the Archangels then Team Alpha, Clementine, and Riarliel, doing the math in my head. There's supposed to be eleven on the Archangel council, but I've only counted ten if I add in Sabboath and the missing Tiberion.

"Who else are we missing?" My words have the table all turning to look at me, my dad raising his eyebrows in question.

"What do you mean, Mav?" he asks gently, shooting a worried look at the gods in the room; after all, I had interrupted.

"Well, I count eight Archangels in the room, and we all know where Sabboath is, and you explained about Tiberion."

"Is he *still* hiding?" Mylea huffs, sounding annoyed. "I think he needs to be here. Things are happening, and we need everyone to be involved. It's time he moved on from that. It was tragic, but he has more to live for than he knows." Her words are cryptic, the last said with an obvious air of mystery that guarantees the goddess is keeping secrets, and Michael shoots her a sharp look before they both look back to me.

"That's only ten. Aren't we missing one more?" Team Alpha nod their heads, backing me up, and Sander looks relieved that I'm participating, shooting me an encouraging smile.

"Yes, we are, but to be honest, the last one's a complete waste of space," Azyer the god of angels says, speaking for the first time. His voice is deep and his disappointment in his creation clear. "Lesterial spends all of his time in a euphoric haze, indulging in whatever he can to avoid his responsibilities. Who knows where he is? Probably in that den of iniquity, Eternal Damnation..." Mylea puts a hand up to her mouth, hiding a small smile at the grumpy god's words.

Raphael is shaking his head, a smirk on his face. "No, he was kicked out of Eternal Damnation and told never to set foot in it again. He tried to hit on the demoness proprietor and didn't want to take no for an answer. He's lucky she didn't take his head for the offense."

"To be honest, he's been useless for so long, I'd kind of forgotten about him," Chamuel admits.

"He's an asshole, always has been, always will be," Uriel adds, his words gruff. "I don't miss him at all."

"Actually, now that you bring him up, weren't he and Sabboath tight for a while?" Zadkiel muses, rubbing his chin. "Do you think that he could be a part of AoA?"

"Anything is possible," Dad adds, "but until we have confirmation, we need to give him the benefit of the doubt."

"Like hell we do! Guilty until proven innocent," Uriel growls. The remaining members of the council all add in their own two cents, and the table becomes a riotous clamor as they argue with one another. Azyer has the same steely glare on his face, but Mylea looks amused at the whole thing.

"Will you shut up?!" Clementine's voice projects across everyone else's, stopping them in their tracks. She's standing up, her face red with annoyance and eyes flashing with fury. "I don't have time for you to argue. The CD is a mess, and the Menagerie is full of AoA members that need interrogating. I've got to rearrange teams, and magical creatures are missing. Not only that, but Earth is having issues with a plague, volcanoes in Minzeon have suddenly started erupting, and portals keep randomly popping up on Reath. They're somehow connected to one of the realms and creatures keep escaping. My teams are being run ragged, and I could do with Alpha's help, but you're all here, moping. I don't have time for your internal squabbling. Sort it out!" The room drops into silence, everyone's eyes on the frazzled-looking director of the Collectors Division. Riarliel breaks office protocol, rubbing a soothing hand over her arm.

Before anyone can say anything, the door bursts open, and everyone turns to see who has the audacity to interrupt the meeting. Standing in the doorway, chest heaving, eyes flashing with anger, is the big brute of a man also known as Mina and Sam's foster father. Muscles upon muscles flex with his ragged breathing, the fury flashing in his brown eyes enough to have an average person wetting their pants. On an average day, he's a force of nature, a respected instructor and *very* talented former active-duty member of the CD. On a day like today, well, I'm honestly not sure whether we'll all be left standing at the end of this discussion.

"Oh, fuck! This is not going to go well." Once again, Sander has summed up the situation perfectly.

"What the fuck is going on?" he demands, anger and confusion radiating through his words. "Where is my Mina? And what the fuck did I hear about Sam? Someone needs to start explaining things right now. I've just had to have my wife sedated, and I want to know who the fuck is responsible."

"Peter, thank you for joining us. Why don't you take a seat?" Mylea reacts quicker than anyone else, smoothly defusing the situation. She calmly gestures to the last remaining seat at the table.

He blanches slightly when he sees the two gods in the room but quickly recovers, slamming the door closed.

"He has balls of steel," Sander comments, his internal commentary bringing a smile to all of our lips, which we quickly smother as his gaze moves to each of us in turn. Peter stomps over to the offered seat, stiff and inflexible as he sits in the chair at attention. Team Alpha has gotten to know Peter during our years of working and training with Sam, and this side of Peter is one that we only see when he's entirely on edge. It usually takes a lot to rattle him, but a missing daughter and a traitorous son? Yeah, that'll do it.

"Right, it has come to my attention that Hammus no longer cares whether he gets caught interfering. It was him that erected that barrier around you in Minzeon, stopping you from rescuing Mina. It's confirmed what we've long suspected, that Hammus is directly behind the terrorist organization AoA. Not only has he not been satisfied with the almost complete annihilation of his own people, he's also set his eye on taking over everywhere else his followers can help him reach. Greed and jealousy have festered inside him over the centuries, creating and feeding an insidious desire to rule over the universe, and he *must* be stopped."

The room is dead silent as everyone takes in her words, my heart racing as it realizes we're coming to a pivotal point in our fight. Our dads just looked resigned, like they knew this was coming, but Peter and the rest of my teammates look surprised. Why now? Why has she finally decided to make this stand *now*?

"Let's start at the beginning, shall we? Most of you know bits and pieces, but you may as well hear it all." She stands up and starts to pace around the room, Azyer's eyes never leaving her body for one moment.

"The annihilation of the demon race, although tragic, was his prerogative. They're his creations, and while it was truly horrific, none of us were able to step in and stop him. That's the way it's always been. When it comes to matters of our own people, they are ours and ours alone to care for. Or destroy, as the case may be. Our hands were bound, though I believe you have since discovered the one way we were able to help the survivors."

"So you're the one who's been protecting the demon stronghold." Trick's brain is working quickly despite all the information being given to us. "We thought it might have been Minzeon technology."

"It is, but Matoz is the one who acquired it and gave it to the demon rebellion. Along with the technology, I layered a spell surrounding them that repels people with dishonest intentions from discovering the stronghold," she tells him before continuing her story. My mind latches onto every word; the more she tells us, the more centered I feel.

"For many years to follow, it seemed like Hammus was happy with what he'd done, no longer having any responsibilities to tie him down. At one stage, he did consider creating another race to inhabit the world, but we were able to dissuade him from this. In time, he became distant, and decades went in between us seeing him." She breaks off, her eyes filling with tears and her breath hitching with emotion, but she composes herself and keeps going. "Please remember that Hammus is one of my mates, so I turned a blind eye to many of the things he did because I loved him."

"What a load of rubbish," Peter bites out, his scathing words making us all recoil in shock.

"Oh fuck, he's dead," Sander murmurs in our heads, and I'm not sure that he's wrong, but Mylea just stares at him blankly. Azyer growls quietly next to her, but she puts her hand on him, and he quiets.

"He should have been stopped when he tried to annihilate a complete race." Although he has a fair point, there's a bit of recklessness to him right now that is so unlike him. He's being driven to desperation, and I wonder if he's going to be more of a help or hindrance in whatever we must do to fix all of this. Kai snorts. His dissatisfaction with her response and agreement with Peter is clear, but nobody else says a word. She's still a goddess, after all, and despite our Archangel blood, our team definitely doesn't have the authority to truly defy a goddess.

"I'm a woman, first and foremost, and hoped that he'd eventually return to us, but then little things started to happen. When looked at individually, they didn't seem like much, but putting them together over the years told a *very* different story. Then came the rumors of the AoA, and I still desperately thought maybe that I was wrong, that he wasn't responsible. But as time went on, it became clear that they had many of the ideals that Hammus himself has, and things might be worse than I first guessed."

"You think?" Uriel grunts, but she ignores him as Azyer shoots him a frosty glare.

"Anyway, as this all started to happen, I realized that Hammus was not going to stop and he needs to be. This task was beyond me and the others, so I set in motion a set of events that led to my chosen champion being born."

This time, her eyes turn frosty, and she glares at each of our fathers before lingering on Michael. "But instead of being raised by a group of powerful individuals, this champion was abandoned. Left to grow up in a world without their parents and without knowing how special they were. Because those parents were manipulated and bowed down to group pressure."

"What the fuck are you talking about?" Peter is the only being in the room willing to ask the question that Mylea is hinting at. Sainsiel and Reorniel look confused as well, but everyone else knows, and I can tell by the various looks on their faces that the dads are not impressed with her dig. Azyer growls a little from where he stands behind Mylea in silent support.

"Do you think I judge you for your choices? I, who am in a relationship with four different men, at least before Hammus became a monster and left us. I was not the one who decreed that Archangels couldn't have children or that the races shouldn't mix. *You* are the ones who allowed a small minority of people to make decisions for you. Allowed them to dictate what was right or wrong with their small, narrow-minded opinions. I'd have stepped in, but Eagi stayed my hand. Told me to allow you to make your own choices of your own free will. So I did, and what happened disappointed me greatly. You allowed your fear to rule instead of letting love conquer all. If you had come to me for help, then I would have protected those children like they were my own. After all, I did put their creation into motion. But no, you chose to hide them and their powers so that one small group of individuals wouldn't be upset." She looks at the six men, her eyes glistening with tears and disappointment, and the dads start to shift uncomfortably. They're much more used to doling out the lectures than being on the receiving end of them. Combined with a woman's tears, this must be a nightmare for them.

"Let me tell you this, and perhaps this time you will listen. I will not pass judgment on these children of yours, nor will I allow anyone else to. All children are sacred, no matter what race, or races, they are. There's no need to hide them, especially now they're adults and able to protect themselves. Be proud of your children, as they have grown into capable, wonderful beings." Her gaze moves from the dads to us around the table, taking in Kai and Jagger as well with fondness softening her eyes.

"I'm so proud to see demons with us at the table; I just wish it had happened sooner. I think the worlds are in for a shake up, and I can't wait to see it happen."

"Let me see if I have this right." Michael's words are the calm before the storm, a simmering violence bringing weight to the very air around us. I can see the anger building in his eyes, the rigid way he's holding his body. The weight of his power is starting to fall on us as it did when he realized Mina had been taken. "If we'd appealed to you in the first place when our children were born, we could have raised them ourselves? My mate and I could have been together, instead of hiding our bond in shame. You would have embraced it all and protected them." His voice has gotten louder as he goes until he's shouting by the end, but Mylea stays calm in the face of his pain.

She reaches out a hand to soothe him, but he shrugs it off in his anger. "Of course, I would have, but you were all so scared after what happened with Tiberion that none of you thought to ask, and for that, I'm truly sorry. Especially because I manipulated it all into happening. Yours and Lucifer's mating was not accidental. I chose two of the strongest beings I knew to birth my champion. Instead, you asked me to protect her with a spell and willingly gave her away."

"You're saying *Jessamina* is your champion? My princess, who I saw all of fifteen minutes before she was kidnapped, is to take on a god and win?" Michael growls at Mylea.

"Oh fuck, now she's *going to die,"* Sander whispers, and I can feel all of my teammates' amusement flowing through our connection.

"Can goddesses die?" Kai muses, and Jagger responds sarcastically.

"They must be able to because it sure seems like that's the plan for Hammus."

"Hush, I'm trying to pay attention," Dru admonishes them, taking on a role she plays far too often.

"Well, not on her own." Mylea looks disgruntled at his accusations, and I'm definitely glad the goddess isn't directing that face toward me. "I made sure she has the right weapons and support to be able to do it. I gifted her the mates that I knew she would need to overcome all her obstacles. She's bonded with five, but there are still four more to go." Her gaze moves to Zeph and me before returning to Michael.

This has me sitting up straight in my chair, hope racing through my veins like adrenaline. Is she saying that we, too, are her mates? She must see the hope in my eyes because she winks very subtly at me.

"But what about my boy?" Peter demands. "It can't be true what they're whispering. Tell me." The anguish in his voice is agonizing, and I can see he doesn't want to believe what he's been told, but there's also a hint of resignation, like he knows deep down it's true.

Chamuel clears his throat, and Peter looks at him. "I'm sorry, Peter, but if you mean that Sam has turned against us, I'm afraid that's true."

Peter's head shakes in denial, some of his strong exterior seeming to crack. "No, no, not my boy; he wouldn't do that. He must be under a spell or something."

Noise breaks out over the table again.

"Do you think that's it? Could he be under a spell?" Drusilla's voice is quiet as she asks us all through the team bond, grasping onto that little snippet of hope.

"Maybe," I reply, not wanting to let her down but also knowing it's not likely, not with his superior Archangel blood.

"It doesn't matter; at the moment, we've got bigger things to worry about than a traitor," Mylea interjects, putting an end to any possible arguments. We all flinch at that word; my anger at Sam has dulled into a deep disappointment and sadness and shame. Shame that we weren't paying enough attention to notice that he was heading down that path and sadness because, despite everything else, Sam is still my teammate, my brother. If we could find a way to save him and redeem him... I don't think I'd have it in me to say no.

"Same with worrying about Mina, she's a big girl and is capable of looking after herself for the time being. We have to work at this logically. All these other things that Clementine mentioned are a distraction to keep us busy while they make more plans, and we need to stop all those before we can focus on anything else."

Peter starts to shift in his chair, likely gearing up for a fight, but Mylea holds her hand out to stop him before issuing instructions. "Here's what's going to happen. Zeph and Mav, you're going to jump back in and help Clementine. Peter, you're going to join them and become an active member in the CD once again."

"What! She can't be saying we can't look for Mina," Kai practically screams in our minds, his fury almost scalding, and I can see him getting ready to argue, but Jagger places a hand on him, stopping him.

"Hang on. Let's just hear her out," he cautions, a calm voice of reason that buys us at least a few more moments before Kai's possible explosion.

She looks at Mina's five mates, lips twisting down in a frown. "I'm afraid you guys aren't going to be able to help much. Your connection with Mina has been cut off, and right now, that's a huge distraction to you all."

"Is the damage permanent?" Drusilla interrupts, sounding like she doesn't really want the answer. Mylea looks at her with sympathetic eyes and shakes her head.

"No, darling, it's not permanent." The sighs of relief from them all are loud throughout the room. "But I'm afraid it is going to be extremely debilitating for you now that you've bonded." She looks apologetically at Michael. It's a true testament to his and Lucifer's powers that they survived and thrived without being around each other for over twenty years. Their bond was still intact so that must have been worse, being able to feel what each other was feeling while being so distant from their mate.

He squirms at the knowledge of his daughter having bonded five mates, obviously aware of what that entails, and I struggle to keep a smile off my face. Looking around the room, the other dads are having similar reactions, especially Uriel. I bite my lip, and the struggle to control the laughter is the hardest thing I've had to do today, especially with my teammates' amusement echoing through my mind.

Before any of us can break, there's a bright flash of light throughout the room. We all shield our eyes from it, and when it finally clears, Lucifer is standing there in full demon form. In a case of déjà vu, her thunderous voice echoes around the room when she growls, "Where is my daughter?"

All our amusement dissolves like the hounds of hell are after it, and the room is filled with a harrowing sense of dread.

Chapter Nine

Patrick

"Lucy?" Michael's voice is the smallest I've ever heard as he stands up where he is, his eyes wide with surprise.

Her eyes just about bug out of their sockets when she turns toward the sound of his voice. "Mikey?"

They stare at each other like two piranhas ready to devour each other. It's like the rest of the room has faded away, their attraction to one another practically sending sparks flying through the room.

"Well, this is awkward," Sander deadpans, snickering as nobody quite knows what to say, nor do they want to interrupt this reunion.

They both start to slowly move toward each other, and I hear Dru's breath hitch in anticipation. Moving steadily faster until their bodies are a blur of movement, they crash against one another in a flurry of hands and mouths, moans escaping both their mouths as Lucifer's tail tries to press between them both. Lost in a world of passion, not seeing anything else around them. Uncomfortable rumblings are heard around the table, and before they can get much further, Mylea thankfully stands up. "I don't think we need to watch this," she announces to the relief of ninety percent of the room. Pretty sure only the twins are disappointed. Dru's such a romantic she would have loved seeing everything unfold, and, well, Sander's just a perv. Waving her hand at them, they both disappear. "We'll get them up to speed when they're done."

"They might be a while," Uriel grunts, trying to put annoyance into his voice, but we all see through it. He might be a grouch, but at heart he's as much of a romantic as Dru. Though no one is brave enough to say that to his face.

"That reunion is well and truly overdue," Dad adds in. "Cut them some slack. I'm sure Mina's situation will bring them back quicker than you think."

Sander grabs at my hand at the mention of Mina's name, and I give it a reassuring squeeze. I mean, what else can I do? I'm just as worried as he is. Since she's been gone, I feel like I've been run over by a pack of charging wildebeest, achy and tired, and in the space where Mina used to be is a gaping hole. It's a struggle not to fall into a yawning pit of despair, and I need to make sure that Sander doesn't fall in also. It's exhausting, but I know I'm not the only one struggling; we all are, even those of us who haven't mated her yet.

Mylea starts to talk again, drawing my attention back to the room.

"Shall we continue with what we were talking about before hurricane Lucy joined us?" She smiles around the room; despite the circumstances, she looks happy at what just happened.

We all agree and focus back on her, and I can't help but notice the frown that crosses her face as the room fills with a whole shitload of power. Bearing down on all of us, causing everyone at the table to fidget with the force. "Before we go any further, let's take out the trash. Especially because they just heard a world of information, they can bring to Sabboath and Hammus." She turns toward the two Archangels that I don't know well—the ones who don't quite look right.

"Sainsiel and Reorniel, you've been very naughty boys. I can tell by looking at you that your deterioration is not natural, that you have been messing with things you shouldn't. Did you think I wouldn't notice or find out? You're both relieved of your positions on the Archangel council and will be charged with treason." Both of them jump to their feet, and a wave of magic ricochets through the room as they unsuccessfully try to teleport away.

Azyer pulls a great big flaming sword out of thin air and points it at them. "Don't move," he commands. Mylea waves a hand, and they're both wrapped up in chains.

"Uh uh, can't have you teleporting away and

exposing all our secrets. You'll be housed in confinement in the Menagerie until we can decide what to do with you, but for now, I'm demoting you from Archangel." We all watch in surprise as he draws magic out of both of them, their wings fading to a dull white. Their shouts of surprise and pain are loud as they try to fight the chains binding them, but they're no match for the goddess, and their struggles cease as the power leaches out of them. Their bodies showing even more signs of aging until they're nothing but old and wrinkled, even their wings drooping behind them like the angels are no longer strong enough to hold them upright.

A look of resignation crosses Reorniel's face, but there's a spark of defiance in his eyes that you'd think would've disappeared along with his vitality. "It was worth it," he sneers. "Anything we can do to help the one true god is worth the sacrifice."

"That's right." Sainsiel's voice is shaky yet still superior and condescending as he looks down his nose as us. "When he kills you all and takes over as supreme ruler, we will be rewarded, and we will get our status back. We may even get an upgrade. He did say he would need a few new gods by the time he's done." As one, they begin to laugh, the diabolical sound echoing through the room, but it's Mylea's look of astonishment that has me pausing. It must be shocking to hear your former lover is plotting to kill you. She collapses in her seat, unable to move after their words, so Azyer takes over, waving his big sword at them. In a flash of light, they're gone, sent behind bars to await their punishment.

There's an uneasy quiet around the table as Azyer moves toward Mylea and puts his arm around her, whispering in her ear at a level we can't hear. Even if she had suspected the depths Hammus had sunk to, I think it's an entirely different kind of pain to hear it confirmed.

"How did they end up looking like that?" Jagger asks, waving at where they'd just been, trying to break the awkward silence.

"Dark magic," Uriel sneers. "Going against the forces of nature. It requires a price, and if you don't use a blood sacrifice, then it takes it from you."

"So, you're saying they haven't killed anyone to get what they want?" Zeph asks quietly, his skepticism coming through despite the softness of his question.

"No, but it wouldn't have been long before they did. Their bodies couldn't take much more," Samuel's dad chimes in, the sadness in his voice getting my attention.

"Is this what will happen to Sam?" I ask, not sure I want to hear the answer but needing to know nonetheless.

"Yes, I want to hear the answer to that, too," Peter adds in. "I know he's your boy, but we care for him very much. Maggie was so upset when she heard about both our children. I know my wife has a flair for the dramatic, but I've never seen her so genuinely heartbroken as she was today." Tears well in Drusilla's eyes at his words. She gets up and goes over and hugs him, which he accepts kind of awkwardly, before returning to her seat. Maggie has always been in the background of our lives since we've known Sam. She can be ridiculous, a bit extra, and gods know the woman can mother anyone to death, but she's well-loved by each of us, and anything that causes her pain hurts us too. Especially in this case.

The remaining council members squirm, and it's Mylea who ends up answering, the question drawing her out of her own misery. "If he goes the way of dark magic, yes." Her words have a sobering effect, as if it were possible for us to get any more serious, and the room falls into silence.

She rolls her eyes at everyone, her mood breaking. "For fuck's sake, it's not the end of the world, at least not yet, and if I have anything to do with it, not ever. So get over it! Everything happens for a reason, and here's what's going to happen now."

After giving everyone a verbal spanking, the goddess outlines a plan that has everyone on Team Alpha, excluding Zeph and Mav, grumbling. Clementine and the dads all seem to be on board and pleased.

Mylea calls the meeting to a close, issuing orders to get moving. Zeph and Mav are to go with Peter. They're gearing up and heading to Earth to deal with their problems. The rest of our team is on leave until we can figure out a way to get Mina back. We all protested vigorously, but in the end, Mylea overruled us, and the dads were hesitant to take our side against the goddess. I think the loss of Mina and Samuel has gotten to them more than they might want to admit, and it's put the idea in their minds that they could lose their own children too if they're not careful.

It's with grumbles and grunts that Zeph and Mav shepherd us toward the door to get us moving, but before we can get very far, Drusilla stops. "Are you okay?" I ask her, putting my hand on her back. Before she can respond, her eyes roll back into her head, and she collapses to the ground, convulsing.

Shouts sound out through the room as everyone realizes what's happening. Uriel and Sander push their way through and throw themselves to the ground, Uriel reaching out to stop the shaking.

"No, don't!" Dad shouts at him. "With your strength, you might accidentally break something if you try to hold her still.

We stand around, helpless to do anything. "What's wrong with her? Why is this happening?" The anguish in Sander's voice is heartbreaking as he watches his twin foam at the mouth. My stomach rolls at seeing my lover's sister like this, unable to help either of them.

"I'm afraid it's the lost bond," Mylea says, crouching down next to them and putting a hand over Drusilla's forehead. It glows golden for a moment, and Dru stops convulsing though she remains unconscious. Uriel breathes a ragged sigh of relief, and Sander watches silently, a tear running down his cheek. Bending down, I wrap an arm around him and help him to his feet, holding him tight.

Mylea stands up, eyeing the rest of us. "I was afraid this would happen. I made you Mina's perfect mates, and when you bonded with her, your power levels doubled. You don't feel it because you haven't needed it. I did this knowing she was going to have to draw from your power and your strength and vice versa. When you're around each other, it's like your bodies subconsciously equalize, an instinctual, smooth push and pull of energy that's so subtle you haven't actually noticed it. Cut off from each other, your bodies are not able to cope with the overload of power because Mina isn't here. Think of it like a closed circuit suddenly being snipped; where the electricity once flowed in a continuous and balanced loop, now it's flowing to a raw end that can't channel the power. For now, I've put Drusilla into a spelled sleep that will help keep her power levels even until you can reconnect with Mina."

"What about the rest of them?" my dad asks, clamping a firm hand on my shoulder in support.

"It would probably be best if they were all put into a sleep. Sooner or later, they will all end up like

Dru here, and if I'm not around when that happens, they may die."

Jumping to his feet, Uriel bellows, "What the fuck? Did you know this could happen?"

"How could you not warn them all of the consequences of this mating bond?" Dad chimes in, his worry uncharacteristically clear on his face.

The others start to argue, but Peter holds up a hand. "You will do this," he growls at them. "You will do this and keep yourselves safe for Mina. She needs every weapon in her arsenal when it comes to defeating Hammus, you included." This one simple order shuts down the arguments, and Jagger, Kai, Sander, and I all nod our agreement.

"We'll get them set up in the clinic so that they can be monitored," Dad tells the goddess.

She nods her agreement, frowning before issuing a warning. "Yes, but guard them carefully; we still don't know who is and isn't with the AoA."

"Don't worry, I know the perfect people for the job, and I will make sure there are two of them there at all times."

"Who?" Mylea asks, wanting to know for sure.

"Their mothers, of course." Dad's grin is a little bit cheeky as Sander groans out loud.

"Thank god we'll be unconscious. Their fussing will be unbearable," Sander mumbles, but if the resulting smiles are any indication, everyone hears.

"Leave them be," Mylea admonishes him. "They missed out on a lot of that when you were children, so let them have this. Alright, gather round. I'll take you there and get you settled and protected. The rest of you, you know what to do."

We wish Mav and Zeph good luck, and in a flash of light, Mylea brings us, Dad, and the sleeping Dru to Mina's apartment in the palace of the demon realm.

"This is probably the safest place at the moment. The CD certainly isn't." She levitates Drusilla into one of the rooms, and Dad follows quickly after. The remaining four of us throw ourselves down onto the plush couch in the living room. Running a hand through my hair, I blow out a deep breath and pull Sander toward me. He snuggles into my chest and closes his eyes. Jagger and Kai take up a similar pose not far down from us on the sectional.

"What a nightmare," Kai growls. "I want to be helping Mav and Zeph and everyone else, but to be honest, I think if I had to fight someone right now, I'd end up badly beaten at the least if not dead."

Jagger nods his head. Both of them have only been in demon form since Mina went missing. I don't know if they chose to or they just couldn't hold it anymore, but based on Kai's words, I'm thinking it's the latter.

"Do you need to feed?" I ask them, my words having both of their eyes glowing. "You're not getting enough without Mina, are you? And the missing bond is zapping all that you give each other?" My question has them both nodding, wide-eyed surprise on both of them. Kai, probably because he's just not used to what it's like being on a team, and Jagger because, well, his old team definitely wasn't a good example of how we should look out for each other.

"Yes, how did you know?" Jagger looks down in his lap like he's ashamed, though I'm not sure why.

"I can feel it," I tell them, and my admission has Sander struggling to sit up, so I help him.

"Is that what that is?" he asks, surprised. "The hunger that sits just next to Mina's bond, the one that feels like it's starving at the moment. It almost seems far away, like an echo of a feeling, so I figured it wasn't mine, but I'd thought it was from Mina." He rubs at his chest, and I look down, finding myself doing the same thing.

Kai and Jagger both sit up straight at our words, looking between each other. "Do you think?" he starts to say, but Mylea bustles into the room without Dad and quickly answers the question.

"Yes, yes, you're basically all mated to each other, even Drusilla, although she obviously won't partake in the sex side of things with you all." Sander turns a little green at her words, gagging dramatically, which gives us at least a moment of comedic relief that is sorely needed. "But yes, if the four of you were to fuck and they bit you, they would be counted as your mates as well as Mina's. I made it a tidy little circle. Sander and Dru being twins was unexpected and messed up my plans slightly. Then Drusilla being gay complicated it a little more, but I think I adapted beautifully. So later, when we have a little more time, you guys can explore that, but right now, feed them quickly, and then I'll get you all in stasis like Dru. We need to make sure you're well fed now, so you're healthy and able to help care for Mina when we get her back; depending on what condition she might be in, those few moments could be life or death."

The four of us are dumbfounded, and no one makes a move. Given the sexual nature of being bitten, it's also kind of weird to have the goddess as an audience, though she seems totally unfazed. She claps her hands then flicks them at us with an insistent motion. "Well, chop-chop." I stand up and walk toward Jagger and Kai. After exchanging a glance, Jagger gets up and goes and sits next to Sander. Both of us have fed Jagger before, so feeding either of them doesn't really bother me, but I can't say my cock doesn't twitch slightly with the thought of the handsome Asian demon sinking his fangs and other things into me.

"Don't think I can't hear your thoughts," Sander whispers into my mind, and even though his voice is amused, I turn back to look at him, feeling slightly guilty. Adding Mina into our relationship was one thing; I mean, we were both aching to have her be a part of what we share together, but we'd never even thought of, let alone discussed, the other demons.

"Sorry," I apologize, but he just smirks and winks at me, affection traveling down our connection, before Jagger's big body blocks his face from my sight.

Blowing out a breath, I sink down on the couch next to the purple demon; his almond-shaped eyes are on my every move, trying to gauge my reaction, I think. Before he can say anything, I grab him by the shirt and pull him toward me, molding my lips over his deliciously plump ones and thrusting my tongue into his mouth. I must take him by surprise because he gasps slightly, and just when I think he's going to pull away, he becomes pliant and sinks into the kiss, his hands coming up to weave his fingers into my hair. Our tongues dance, twining in and out of each other's mouths as we explore. My tongue catches on one of his fangs, and there's a prick of sharp pain before I feel the blood start to well up. Our mouths are filled with a coppery tang, but he just pulls me in tighter and sips and slurps at the wound. Pulling away, my eyes go to his face. He looks surprised, but there's a heat in his eyes that can't hide his interest.

"What was that for?" His breathing is still a little ragged as he asks the question.

"Just thought we get it out of the way, shouldn't be awkward anymore," I tell him, pulling my shirt over my head, partly so that he doesn't get any blood on it if he misses but also to tease him. When I look at him again, his gaze has dropped to my naked chest, and when it does return to my face, that interest has increased. He runs his tongue over his bottom lip, flashing a little bit of fang as I ease into his embrace.

A moan comes from behind me as Jagger drinks from Sander, the sound only increasing the echo of Kai's hunger in my chest. My new partner pulls me so that he's now lying down on the sofa with me on top. He uses my hair to drag my head back, my neck stretching to give him plenty of access. "No, not awkward at all," he agrees, a gleam in his eye. "In fact, I think I'm going to enjoy this a lot."

His fangs pierce my skin, and he thrusts his now hard cock against my own, his tail running up and down my naked back, caressing me. As the languid, delicious feeling of a building orgasm starts to creep up and through my body, I can't help but thrust my own hips, and as he drinks his fill, we dry hump each other into a blissful explosive orgasm.

Somewhere behind me I hear a shout of alarm from my dad, but Mylea's voice is calm and reassuring as I slowly black out.

Chapter Ten

Jessamina

The *drip, drip, drip* sound echoing through the cell is the only other noise I can hear apart from the two of us breathing. Mine labored and shaky as I beg the gorgeous man-creature not to come any closer and his deep as he takes even more lungfuls, trying to taste the pheromones around him.

"I mean it, if you come any closer, I can't be held responsible for my actions, and you may end up doing things you really don't want to do," I beg him, holding my hands up in front of me.

A chuckle fills the air that has us both turning to see where it's coming from. Peering through the gathered shadows, I can finally make out a shape. "Oh, Mina, don't be like that. After all, Grayson here has been a naughty boy, and, well, being thrown in with you is his punishment. I'm sure you can't quite be full with only your impromptu meal in the bathroom, especially after such an electrifying time." Sabboath chuckles, the sound as slimy as he is, as he steps into the light, illuminating his whole being. "Why don't you indulge a little more, and if he doesn't survive, then I guess it wasn't meant to be."

"You know very well blood is not the only thing I need," I growl at him, flashing a fang that has dropped into place. It's taking all my strength to hold my form, but I know it's not going to be long before my full demon comes out to play, and then the guy, Grayson? is in a lot of trouble.

My unexpected cellmate struggles to his feet, stumbling over to the edge of the cell and grabbing hold of the bars. He's so tall, I have to strain my neck to look up at him from where I am. "What did I do, Dad?" Holy crap, *Dad?* This is Sabboath's son, and he's feeding him to me. Whatever happened to family loyalty? *Though I guess this isn't that surprising considering he's okay with his daughter being completely crazy.* "I fought that demon for you."

A scowl crosses Sabboath's face before it clears and he looks more than annoyed. Dare I say he's disappointed and upset? "Yes, Grayson, you did, and I appreciate it, but don't think I haven't heard about all the questions you've been asking. Nothing escapes my notice in my compound. You're starting to question your loyalty to me and my cause, and I just so happen to have found someone who might make an excellent replacement for you. Someone whose loyalty is unwavering." His eyes dart to me, and he smiles that smarmy grin again. "Sam's making an excellent addition to the team."

My stomach rolls at his words, and the ache in my chest where my mates used to be gapes even wider. *What I wouldn't give to have them here with me.*

"Let's see if you survive being in there with Mina, a demon with some very interesting appetites. If you're alive when I come back, I'll consider this punishment done and welcome you back into the fold," he replies with a bland smile on his face. Grayson, on the other hand, shares none of his father's satisfaction. His eyes are wide with horror, so I think it's safe to say that whatever happens between us might not go easily.

"A demon, you've thrown me in with a *demon?*" The disgust in his voice has me flinching again, making it harder for me to hold back my urges, and I'm afraid it's too late. Closing my eyes so I don't have to see his grimace, I let go of my form and embrace the demon. Wings erupt out of my body, and my tail stretches out, shaking back and forth in agitation. My claws pierce through the skin of my palms, where I had them clenched, the delicate scent of my blood filling the air around me. Slowly releasing my hands, I feel the skin knit back together as I open my eyes, watching the man in front of me. Sabboath's peals of laughter fill the room.

"Oh, Mina, you do not disappoint; for a dirty demon, you certainly are sexy. Who did you say your parents were, again? If Grayson isn't enough to fill you up, I might have a go myself. Would you like that?"

"Actually, I hadn't said who my parents are." My eyes leave the man in front of me, and I turn to face the Archangel. "But I'll make sure to tell Lucifer just how much you admire my demon form since I inherited it from her." His already pasty face pales even further, and his mouth drops open in what I could only describe as horror.

"L… L... Lucifer? Your mother's Lucifer?" He's stuttering slightly, and now it's my turn for the wicked grin.

"Yes, she certainly is."

"Ah, well..." He glances between the two of us, looking resigned but no less satisfied with his plan. "Yes, good luck," he says to Grayson before turning to leave.

"You would take away his choice? Leave your son to be mauled by a demon?" I ask before he can leave. He turns back around, face blank again.

"I see it as paying the price; if he's a good soldier like I think he is, he'll do this for me and prove his worth. Let's hope there's something left of him when you're done." And with that, he hurries away.

"What an asshole," I breathe out as I watch the slimeball scurry away like a rat.

Turning back to face the man in front of me, I shrug. "Don't look so worried; I'm pretty sure I can't even stand up on my own without help. I'm certainly not able to attack you."

He stumbles away from the bars of the cell, moving to the opposite side of the room from me. "Who are you, and where did you come from? I thought demons were extinct, and now not only did I fight a powerful one the other day, here you are as well." The disgust is still there, but there's also curiosity in his tone. Smoke drifts from his nose as he breathes in and out, a steady sign that he's no more in control of himself than I am right now. "And what is that delicious smell? My dragon is riding me hard."

"Ah, you must be the dragon who fought Asmodeus the other day at the compound." I shuffle my body over to a wall and prop my shoulder against it, putting more distance between myself and this intoxicating man dragon. His own scent is making my mouth water, and if I had more energy, I'd probably pounce on him. Lucky for me, my pheromones are doing their job. I can feel the little trickle of desire starting to emanate from the guy, and my energy slowly starts to return. Good for me, not so good for him.

I can feel all the conflicting emotions flowing off of him, confusion, lust, frustration, anger and sadness, all mix together in a miasma of feelings. I have to admit I feel a little bit sorry for the guy. His dad just threw him to the preverbal wolves.

"Oh, ah, the rumors of the demons' extinction

have been highly exaggerated. They," I emphasized, waving vaguely toward the direction Sabboath had gone, "just wish they were. Daddy dearest is a little deluded, but we'll take care of that problem soon."

He snorts again, more smoke exploding from his nostrils. Little puffs of grey smoke which could be cute if we weren't in the situation we're in. "You and whose army? From what I can see, you're well and truly in trouble." He smirks at me, condescension coloring his words, and for the first time in our short connection to one another, I see the vaguest resemblance to Sabboath. Much like his father, he has no clue that a predator bigger than himself is stalking him, his ego doing him absolutely zero favors.

I just have to keep him talking a little longer; he obviously has no clue about demons, which is going to work in my benefit. I stretch my aching arms, pushing my tits against the thin t-shirt, my nipples puckered in the cold air. *I might as well use everything I've got in my arsenal.* And it works, his eyes roaming my figure as more of his desire laces the air, my body sucking it in like a desert in a freak storm. My tail wraps around me, running its blunt tip across my body like it's assessing the damage, and his eyes track it, widening a little at its slow caress of my body. While he's distracted, I take note of my injuries, but I can feel everything starting to heal except for where the collar sits around my neck. Running my finger between it and my throat, I pull on the metal in the hope of loosening it, but there's absolutely no give. Its rough edges cut into my skin, small drops of warm blood weeping from where it's digging in.

A grunt draws my attention, and I find Grayson eyeing my neck, brow wrinkled in confusion. My eyes drop lower to see that his neck is unadorned. He's here by his own free will, or at least he was before our unfortunate introduction.

"So..." I run my tongue across my lips, drawing his steadily hungering eyes to the slight movement. "Sabboath's your father, making you Connie's brother. How come you never came to the academy?"

His eyes cloud in confusion, and he runs a hand through his shoulder-length locks, the dim light of our cell shining off his colored streak. "Um no, I'm adopted. Dad found me when I was about five and brought me home. I'd been abandoned by my parents, I guess." In the moment after that confession, he seems to be lost in his thoughts, but he quickly gets himself together and hardens his face with a sneer. "And I didn't go to the academy because it's a place for pathetic individuals who don't know how to think outside of the box. A place where the sheep blindly follow each other, not fit for a dragon unless he wants an easy meal."

"Or maybe you just couldn't cut it," I suggest, "and Daddy didn't want to be embarrassed. I mean, it's bad enough that Connie is how she is."

"Shut up!" he screams, yanking on his hair and rocking back and forth, though I'm not sure if he was offended by the insult I'd directed at him or if he has some misplaced sense of loyalty to his horrible sister. The dramatic reaction also does nothing to make me feel more comfortable with him. *Oh goody, he's as bat shit crazy as Connie. Sabboath really excels at fucking up his children.* He stops shaking, and his head pops up. This time, his eyes are reptilian again, focusing on me like a predator hunting its next meal. My heart rate accelerates, and being the dirty girl that I am, my core clenches in excitement. A thrill runs through me at the thought of being chased by this beast-man, and I groan as my body floods the cell with more pheromones, instantly feeling guilty about it within my next breath. How can I think about betraying my mates? God, I hope they're okay, that nothing happened to them, that they're not aching for me as much as I'm aching for them. I know I still have mates to find, but I had been holding out hope that Mav and Zeph and even Sam would be the ones to make my mark finally darken. My attraction to Grayson just seems too much like cheating even though they all understood and were on board with it. I just hope they forgive me for what I'm about to do. I can't control it any longer; the succubus in me is officially deciding to take charge.

A rustling movement draws my attention back to the present. Grayson has gotten to his feet and started pacing back and forth across the cell, his eyes not leaving my body.

"What is wrong with me?" His breathing is ragged, and I can see a bulge in his sweatpants. A delicious, long, and hard bulge that has my fangs dropping down and my own breath increasing. I start to giggle with delight, the delirium of my hunger finally getting to me.

"Oh, Grayson, have they taught you nothing about demons? Did Daddy's delusion about their extinction blind him into teaching you nothing about our needs?" I'm taunting him now, and scales ripple across his forearm before they disappear just as quickly. Fuck, I hope he doesn't shift, then I might as well say goodbye, Mina.

I've got enough energy now that I pull myself up the wall to a standing position. Maybe if he starts to shift, I can stop him by drinking his blood, but I would have to be quick to latch on before he can really begin the process. I'm not sure my fangs could pierce through his scales if they're as hard as mine.

I track him back and forth across the cell as he shakes his head, waving his arms in agitation. "No, nothing! I know nothing, okay?" he shouts at me, and I take pity on him. It doesn't seem fair that his dad has dumped him in here with me with very little knowledge of what's about to happen to him. His dad might be a douche, but it doesn't mean I need to be as well. I feel guilty because he really isn't going to get much choice in the matter.

"Well, to start with, demons need blood to survive." He stops his pacing, those lips of his turning up in disgust once more.

"Blood? You drink it? Like a vampire?"

"Hey, don't knock it until you try it," I spit at him. "Believe me, you'd end up begging for more." He starts pacing back and forth again, still keeping an eagle eye on me as I take small sideways steps, maintaining my position against the wall. I have to get closer to him as I'm pretty sure I'm only going to get one shot at this.

"You said blood *to start with*. What else do you need?" He gestures widely for me to continue my explanation. *How magnanimous of him.*

"Well, it depends on the type of demon. Some need violence, some need acquisitions, some need lots of sleep. Each one of them can feed on those things."

"But what about you?" he asks, not even noticing how close he is to me as he continues his back and forth across the cell. "What do you need?"

"Me? I like to fuck." My words are like a slap across the face for him, and he stops inches from me, an almost stricken look on his face. Stepping into his space, his delicious smoky scent swirls around me, and I run a finger over his hard chest and down his stomach, feeling the ridges of his muscles flexing with my touch until I get to the top of his sweatpants. "My favorite thing to do is feed while I'm being ridden by a hard fat cock, having my hair pulled and my ass slapped while I've got another one fucking my mouth like they hate me." I whisper these dirty words into his ear, and his reptile pupils dilate, his hips thrusting forward just a little, just enough. That impressive cock pushes against my stomach, and my inner whore purrs with delight.

I see when he finally gets himself together. He starts to step away, but I hang on to his shirt, not allowing him to move. The dragon could if he wanted to, but I know he really doesn't. He just needs to put up a good show now and act like he doesn't want to be here, but he can't hide his reactions, and he *certainly* can't hide that erection. My tail snakes out and pulls him even closer so that our chests are rubbing together. He opens his mouth to speak, and I manage to hide the threatening flinch when his words might as well be straight from Sabboath's mouth. "So you're a slut demon. I've heard all about those, how they would take as many men as they could whenever they wanted. Unfaithful whores, each and every one of them."

I shrug as my tail creeps around to the front of his pants, rubbing against the very obvious large bulge. His skin is heated against mine, his breathing getting erratic. "And so what? Nobody is making any promises, just a night of fun. Different when mated, of course, but then there's no need to stray."

His eyebrows wrinkle in confusion even as his breathing continues to rasp unevenly. My eyes lock onto the throbbing vein in his neck, my mouth watering. "Mated? Demons have mates?"

"Oh, poor Grayson, so much you don't know. But right now, I really don't want to talk." I have him right where I want him, and he still has no clue. "You know, I've never wanted to take away someone's choice, and I'm sorry for this, but a girl has to survive to get out of here."

He looks at me like I'm losing it, my words nonsense to him—poor boy.

With lightning-quick moves, my fangs are puncturing that vein, and before he can shift, I'm drawing deep mouthfuls, his blood rich and smoky like a fine red wine. He struggles, but they soon cease. Waves of lust and desire start to overwhelm him, his breathing increasing and his hips beginning to thrust against me. I keep swallowing, remembering the first time I fed Jagger and the orgasm he gave me. No one had given me one like that during sex, let alone without penetration, so although I feel guilty, he's getting something out of this too. As my stomach finally starts to feel better, I ease back on the sucking, but he grabs hold of my arms, trapping me in place with a loud groan and throwing back his head, his hips flush against me. His cock throbs as a wetness seeps through my clothes.

Running a tongue over the puncture holes, I step away from him. He collapses to his knees in front of me, his eyes wide with orgasmic bliss, albeit a little dazed from blood loss. I kneel down next to him and drag my tongue up his neck to catch some of the blood I missed before running it across my lips, cleaning myself up, and to be honest, I don't want to waste any of it.

Unlike Smoky, who tasted disgusting, Grayson was delicious, and I wouldn't mind another taste of his blood and something else. With that thought, I look down, noticing cum on his stomach; his sweats must have started to fall as he thrust against me. *Waste not, want not, I suppose, and the power can't hurt.* Kneeling down, I run my tongue over the mess, licking and sucking and slurping, moans escaping him as he thrusts his hips before stopping himself. Like his blood, his cum is delicious, and a zing runs through my body at the taste. A burst of energy I'd been missing pumps through my veins, and a spark fires around my collar, shocking me. Slapping a hand to it, it quickly fizzles out, so I put it down to a malfunction. Moving away from Grayson, I lean against the wall again as he stays in place, too shocked by my actions to do much more than blink and breathe.

"Well, if you thought that was good, you should see what I can do with a cock."

My words must finally knock some sense back into him because he shudders. I'm not sure if it's from desire or disgust since he quickly scrambles away from me.

"How dare you!" he stammers out, and I roll my eyes. *What? Like I had any real say in the matter?*

"I dare because Daddy gave you to me for just that reason. But don't worry, your virtue is safe now. After what you just provided, I'm all filled up. But come on, tell the truth. Admit you liked it, even just a little." My words have definitely crossed the line into antagonism, but I can't for the life of me figure out why I want to get a rise out of him so badly. This taunting and teasing is something I'd expect from Kai, but there's just something about Grayson that brings it out in me. Maybe it's his relationship to Sabboath, or maybe he simply has the misfortune of being my attitude's only target at the moment.

He just growls and turns his back to me before striding forward and grabbing the bars of the cell, shouting for help.

I start to chuckle to myself, not bothering to stifle the sound. I really am a twisted bitch for laughing at how poorly Sabboath prepared his son. Who knows? Maybe someone will hear him before I'm hungry again.

Chapter Eleven

Zephaniah

I watch in dismay as the rest of my team disappears with Mylea and Raphael, one of them already unconscious and the others not far from it. Shaking off my worry, I head toward the exit behind Mav and Peter, but before I can get far, a hand clamps down on my shoulder. Looking up, I come face to face with a god. The power that crackles through his palm circulates my body like an electrical current, but it seems to have a calming effect on my mind, and I relax slightly.

"I think I'll tag along with you if you don't mind." I nod. I mean, what can I say? He's a god. "It's been a while since I got to kick some ass, and, well, I think you're going to need some help." With that, he strolls ahead of me, the big sword from before lodged in a sheath on his back. I follow quickly after him, my excitement and nervousness at the prospect of working with a god overshadowing the worry I feel for my team and Mina. *Maybe that was his whole point.*

We make our way through the deserted halls of the Collectors Division. At the moment, all teams have been recalled and will be going through evaluation to root out any remaining traitors in our ranks. That's what the dads are going to be doing, along with interrogating all the captives from Minzeon. While this is happening, Mav and I will be partnering with both Peter, and apparently Azyer, and heading first to Earth, then Minzeon, and then into the realms to try and put out all the fires.

Quietly, we approach the elevator, lost in our heads. Between thoughts of Mina, my team, our mission, and keeping an eye on Mav, I've got a lot on my mind. He seems to be okay now that we have something to focus on, and Azyer must have done the same thing to him as he did to me, which appears to have helped.

Stepping into the elevator, I lean against a wall, running my hand through my hair. I'm already exhausted from thinking about all of it. Before the doors can close, a hand shoots in between, stopping them, and they reopen to reveal Clementine. She steps in, a clipboard in hand and her forehead lined with worry. "Thank you for this. You're all I've got at the moment, though I'm pretty sure Team Dragon will be cleared soon too, and I'll have them join you for backup." She taps on the clipboard with a pen, her eyes scanning the sheet of paper on it.

"Okay, this is what's happening. Earth has an outbreak of some kind of flu; it's spreading quickly, and the rate of mortality is high. This is *not* natural. Before we recalled all the teams, we had one on Earth investigating it, and they'd reported that a realm being had been spotted at all the epicenters of the outbreaks. The being was caught on CCTV throughout the world. We have since identified him as a Chinese plague god, Wen Shen, and he will need to be captured and returned to the Menagerie."

"Hang on," I interrupt her, "I didn't think realm beings were able to use their magic on other worlds."

"They shouldn't be able to. We're not sure how he was able to do this, but his power is continuing to grow as the plague spreads. It may be because the balance of power throughout the universe is out of whack; that's how the realm beings came to exist in the first place, so this could be just another evolution. It's why Mylea is finally acting and why Hammus needs to be taken care of." Azyer's voice is deep, and his eyes cloud with sadness as he speaks. It must be hard knowing that your teammate or bondmate has gone rogue. Team Alpha is getting a taste of that heartbreak from this situation with Sam, and I can't imagine how much worse it would be if the traitor were my bondmate of centuries.

Clementine breaks the quiet that falls after Azyer interjects, looking no less worried than when she first joined us. "We also need a sample of the disease taken to a laboratory in Minzeon so that a vaccine can be created. We think he's there on his own, and we just took out the two beings that could have put him there by detaining Sainsiel and Reorniel. There are a few more Archangels whose loyalties we are unsure of, but at least those two are taken care of."

Azyer nods his head, the grim set to his lips giving the god an all-business vibe that just demands to be obeyed. "I think we should also try to lock down Lesterial's whereabouts. Sabboath could be using him in exchange for whatever his latest addiction is. Until we know where his loyalties lie and if anyone is pulling his strings, we should keep him locked up." Between Azyer's gruff voice and continually changing eyes, it's hard to look at him for too long; the power emanating from him is breath-stealing. The whole elevator pulses with it, and even Clementine and Peter look mildly nauseous. Suddenly, it cuts off, Azyer likely realizing that ABs and Archangels are no match for his undiluted presence, and both let out a sigh of relief.

"Okay, I'll get one of the others to track him," she agrees, making a note on her clipboard. "According to our sources, most of the world is infected, but there are a few South Pacific countries that claim not to have the virus, so I would start the search there. He's been moving rapidly enough that we assume he'll be heading to those 'clean' areas."

She turns back to Azyer again, a steely look in her eyes. "Will you be able to track him?"

He gives her a short nod. "Yes, I think so. Once I've got a lock, I'll leave you three to deal with him while I grab a sample from somewhere and rush it to Minzeon. With their tech, they should have a vaccine within days."

"Isn't that something you can do?" Mav asks him, no judgment in his voice, just curiosity. "Cure them, I mean."

Azyer shakes his head and rolls his eyes, though his irritation doesn't seem to be directed at Mav. "Yes, but no. Eagi can be a real asshole, and he has his panties in a twist about allowing his creations free will and having them solve their own problems. Unfortunately, Earth is full of idiots who either believe the disease isn't real or just can't comprehend the severity of the situation, and it's gotten out of control. Without a vaccine, more than half of the world's population could eventually die. We can't let it get that far, and they're not going to help themselves, so we'll give some scientist our vaccine and make him a very popular man."

"So, interfering but from a distance," Mav summarizes, his forehead wrinkled in confusion, but when Azyer slowly winks at him, it clears.

"Yes, sometimes people need a push."

"What do you want us to do with him? Return him to the realms or bind him?" Peter finally joins in the conversation, having shaken off some of the rage that accompanied his frightening entrance into the conference room. His unhappiness with the situations surrounding his children is still leaking off him like an ominous aura, but he's managed to regain some of his focused confidence that makes him a great operative and instructor.

"We'll place him in the Menagerie for now, in the same block as the Five. Their holding cells have all been re-warded, and nobody should be helping them escape," Clementine tells him, and he nods his head.

The elevator is nearly to the portal room, Clementine takes a close look at Mav and me, her eyes suddenly blazing as though she's either come to or has finally steeled herself to make a decision. "Oh, and no more hiding your Archangel status." My heart skips a beat, and Mav and I exchange an excited glance. "You're adults, now. What are they going to do about it? With your parents as backup and some even higher support, I dare say it'll be a challenge for anyone to try and penalize you simply for being what you are." Smiles cross my and Mav's faces, and as we step out into the portal room, we allow our wings to emerge. The wash of relief as they're able to stretch free is immense, my body instantly feeling lighter. Always having to hide them was becoming tedious and more irritating than helpful, and I'm stoked that we no longer have to.

The portal room is a hive of activity, and as we start to walk through it, everyone stops to stare. The number of open-mouthed looks of shock is amusing, but as we move forward, those looks turn to whispers, and soon, the crowd is speculating and tossing around reasons for our Archangel wings. A small smile crosses my mouth before I can stop it as I hear some of the more ridiculous ideas.

"Why are there so many people here?" Mav asks, looking around the crowded cavernous room. "I've never seen it so full of people before. It looks like every team in the CD is here."

"That's because they are," Clementine ruefully answers as she scans the crowd. "This was the most secure place to have everyone gather while waiting for evaluation. We can keep it locked down while we shuffle through their minds looking for info which will tell us whether they're traitors or not. But that's all on me. You guys just worry about fixing Earth, and then we'll move on to Minzeon."

The whispers and a crowd of people follow us until we get to the world jump point. "Why are they only talking about us? How haven't they noticed the god in the room?" Mav asks quietly as we stop.

"I've masked my power. Their brains acknowledge my presence but not who I am, so they would recount that four people entered with Clementine, but they'd be hard-pressed to describe me with any detail. There's no point in scaring them, because that's all my presence would do," he replies in a quiet tone. I try to figure out what it is in his eyes, but he's holding back some feeling that I'm unable to name. Does it bother him that his power makes him so intimidating to others? Mylea didn't seem to have any hesitation about showing herself, but maybe the life of a god is lonelier and less glamorous than one might think.

"Alright, let's get Earth queued up," Clementine tells the operators, but I hold up a hand, figuring we've already thrown ourselves to the wolves so why try to look ordinary now.

"Actually, if you don't mind, I'll do it since we no longer have to hide who we are." My voice is pitched for only her to hear me, and she gives me an encouraging smile.

"Of course, if the wings aren't enough to tell them what you are, that will be. Especially because you're not wearing your wrist guard." I look down at my left wrist, finally realizing the familiar weight is missing. While loosening my wings felt freeing, I almost feel... naked without the accessory I've worn for so long. *Lots of things to get used to.* "Now, you'll be on your own since I haven't got a communication officer who's been cleared yet, but I figure with him on the team you won't need one." She nods respectfully at Azyer, the god solemnly returning the motion.

"Okay then, I'll leave you to it. Just report back in when it's done, and I'll give you the next assignment." She starts to walk away, but Peter grabs her by the arm.

"Will you move my Maggie to the same room as

the rest of Alpha? That way, they can keep an eye on her as well, and I won't need to worry. I want to put all my focus on this assignment."

She grabs him by both hands, their years as co-workers giving them an easy familiarity now that he's not in a rage. "Of course I will. We'll look after her, don't you worry."

His small sigh of relief is audible, and a grateful smile crosses his face. "Thank you."

With that, I turn and point at the open space, weaving the portal for Earth before opening it directly in front of us. The crowd around us bursts into noise.

Did you see that?

He just opened a portal on his own.

They really are Archangels! How did that happen?

Pride flows through my body as well as an immense sense of relief. There was always that cloud hanging over us, our actions tempered by the pressure of keeping our heritage under wraps. It put a significant strain on us all, and there was more than one situation where we almost had to choose between our secret and our safety. With that weight off our backs, I can only imagine how much better Alpha will be when we're reunited.

Leaving the noise and speculation behind, the four of us step through the portal and onto a tropical beach with white sand and crystal blue water lapping at the shore. The temperature is balmy and humid, the warm breeze gently caressing the tips of my feathers.

"Where did you bring us?" Mav asks, looking around as a frown grows on his face. "You know I hate beach sand." I just give him a feral grin. I *do* know this, which is partly why I chose this spot. *If I can bug the shit out of him, that's even less time for him to get stuck in his head.*

"Samoa," grunts the god next to me, and I nod my head.

"Yes, this is one of the places not to be infected yet, according to Clementine. Can you do your thing and track him now?" I ask Azyer, and he rolls his eyes like I asked a stupid question before closing them. He starts to shine, his eyeballs moving under his closed lids as he tracks the foreign entity.

"Okay, so what's the plan once we catch up with him? What do we know about Wen Shen, and how do we capture him?" I look around the group, feeling a little lost. Now that we don't have Drusilla in our head as our on-mission researcher, that wrist guard would have really come in handy. *Okay, so maybe we have some kinks to work out first, and then we'll see how much better Alpha gets.*

"Fuck, we didn't think about bringing our wrist guards," Mav groans, and I know the guy is already preparing to beat himself up if we can't fix this mistake. "Can we conjure them from this far? We haven't pushed those powers over this distance in a long time."

A smug smile crosses Peter's face, and he pushes back the long sleeve of his CD uniform. "I don't go anywhere without mine."

"Yeah, you've made your point," I grumble, and Mav rolls his eyes.

"Do you wear it to bed too?" He jokes, "It could help tell you where Maggie's..." He doesn't get to finish his sentence before Peter cuffs him around the ear.

"Shut it; you're not too old for me to teach you some manners." Mav rubs at his ear, but he's still laughing as he apologizes. The little moment of normalcy, Peter stepping back into instructor/surrogate dad mode, is nice, and it helps to center us before we get into the action of our mission.

Peter nods and inputs Wen Shen into his wrist guard. The information quickly returns, a hologram projecting around us as a voice narrates the results of his search.

"Wen Shen is not an individual god in Chinese mythology but a name given to the Five Commissioners of Pestilence who governed Heaven's Ministry of Epidemics."

I hold up a hand and pause the narration. "Fuck, does that mean we're dealing with more than one being?"

"Just listen to the information, you impatient asshole," Peter gruffly chastises, a hint of affection still underlying his words. He swipes a hand through the hologram for it to continue.

"They are Zhang Yuanbo, Liu Yuanda, Zhao Gongming, Zhong Shigui. They were said to be associated with Spring, Summer, Autumn, and Winter, respectively. The fifth is Shi Wenye, who is the Central and Superior God of Pestilence.

Chinese folk belief says that the Wen Shen was responsible for releasing plagues and pestilence in punishment for the misdeeds of humanity. Prayers or offerings were necessary to placate them. Another alternative solution says if you call their name three times, the gods can be exorcised."

The recording cuts off and leaves a picture of five stern-looking Asian warriors, each one fiercer than the other.

"Crap! Five gods, not one," Mav quietly curses in my head, waves of anxiety coming through our connection. *"Are we going to be able to beat them with just us two and Peter? Is Azyer even allowed to interfere?"*

"No, I think he can track them, but then he has to leave and handle the vaccine part of the mission. It'll just be the three of us." His anxiety ramps higher, the waves of it becoming sharper, more pointed. *That's not like him.* Usually, he's willing to tackle anything, so the chaos in his mind must be bothering him, and since Azyer gave him some relief in the elevator, his worries must be piling up faster than usual. We need to do something about that, but getting Mina back should really be at the top of the list. It's hard to think of anything else that would be as successful as having our team whole again.

"Five of them." Peters humphs. "Well, this should be interesting."

Azyer's eyes pop open. "No, not five, just the one. Shi Wenye! He's currently located on one of the little uninhabited islands off the coast of Upolu. His power is low, so he must be waiting for an infected human to bring the plague to the island, but he'll be waiting a while. It's in complete lockdown, no travel in or out. And with no one to transport him anywhere now that those two rogue Archangels are in the Menagerie, he's really in a pickle."

Mav and Peter crack bemused grins at the all mighty powerful god's word choice, and I guess I probably look the same.

"He must have only had enough juice for the initial infection, and now he's basically useless. He should be no trouble for you three; you're all very talented fighters. I will take us to him and leave you there while I get a sample."

Before we can blink, he has us in a dense jungle with tropical trees, a white lighthouse visible in the distance. "He's in there. Subdue him and take him back to the CD. I'll meet you there shortly. The lighthouse is automated, so there's no reason for humans to be in the vicinity." I raise a brow at him, not sure where he's going with that point, but he conjures up three guns and holsters, with extra clips for each of us, before I can ask. We grab the shoulder holsters, pulling them on before shoving the guns and clips in. "These are set to maximum stun, so they should be powerful enough."

"Thank you," I tell him, and with those words, the stoic god disappears to take on his part of this mission.

"And now we need to trek through this jungle," grumbles Peter, but I grab his arm, stopping him before he can head into the jungle.

"Ah, no, we don't." Keeping my arm on him, I teleport us directly to the lighthouse, Mav quickly following my lead. We all appear at the base of the tall structure, and I let Peter go. The smell of the sea is that much stronger now that we're right on the edge of a cliff overlooking pounding waves. His nose wrinkles at the smell, and he has a slightly bewildered look before he shakes his head back to clarity. Sometimes it can be a little disorienting to be teleported, especially if you don't have a moment to prepare.

"Thanks. I got so used to treating you like normal ABs, I forgot that you're actually so much more." He rubs a hand across tired eyes, the strain of everything getting to him once more, but before I can say anything, Mav does.

"Peter, you need to sit the next one out. You are no good to Maggie, or Mina, or even Sam, if you don't look after yourself, and this has to be taking a mental toll on you." Peter starts to argue, but I add in my two cents.

"He's right. I hate to say it, but who knows what

condition Mina's going to return to us in, and she'll need her family the most then." I'm laying on the guilt a bit thick, but at this stage, if he doesn't rest, he'll be a hindrance rather than a help.

Peter nods, the worry that lights his eyes causing wrinkles to form. "All right, let's get this done, and I'll go home and watch over my wife and help with your teammates; it's the least I can do."

We both agree, knowing how hard it is for the formidable man to be benched like that.

"So what's the plan? Shall we just storm the place? There's only one entry and exit; there's nowhere for him to go," I suggest, brushing my sweaty hands on my palms, the anticipation of this fight getting my adrenaline running.

"Yeah, let's do this." Mav sounds hyped but focused on the following task which, like Peter's agreement to take a break, is another small weight lifted from my shoulders. Thank fuck this mission has been good for one thing.

Removing our guns, I take point, carefully pushing open the door to the lighthouse. The three of us look up the long circular staircase that winds its way upward.

"I vote we teleport." Peter snorts at Mav's words but agrees, so I grab his shoulder this time, allowing his gun hand free movement, and focus on our destination. "Get ready for an attack when we get up there," I warn them both before moving us through space. But when we arrive, the situation becomes clear. Not only is he low on power, but he also seems to be suffering from the same symptoms of the plague he created. *This is just a tad pathetic.* Curled up in the fetal position on the single cot in the room, his breathing is labored and his body is covered with a fine sheen of sweat.

"What the hell? How is he sick?" Mav sounds concerned, and I can't say that he's wrong even though it works in our favor.

"His mythology is a human construct, so maybe that makes him susceptible to human viruses. We don't know much because they're kept away from the other worlds as much as possible. This was one of the reasons the CD was initially created. We didn't know how these magical beings would cope with various illnesses and diseases that are throughout each of the worlds, and we wanted to protect them as much as we could by giving them their own realms." Peter's lecturer voice is in full effect as I move over to the sickly Chinese god. I don't even have to subdue him or contain him with any shackles; he's unconscious. *Well, this is the easiest mission we've ever had,* I say to Mav, and he shrugs, the corner of his mouth tilting up in an almost smile.

Putting my gun back in my holster, I look to Mav. "Can you bring Peter? I'm going to take this one to an isolation cell in the Menagerie. When Minzeon has the vaccine, this one's going to need it too."

"Yeah, man, of course. I just hope we don't

catch it in the meantime." Oh man, not another worry to add to the swirl in his mind.

"We shouldn't; our physiological makeup is different from humans," Peter reminds us. Putting my hand on the sick man, I leave Mav and Peter behind and head back to the CD.

One mission down. Only the most important one to go.

Chapter Twelve

Samuel

The pain from changing into a demon is even more excruciating than learning to shift, and I'm not sure how much time has passed when I finally become aware again. Before opening my eyes, I consider the changes in my body. Much like a shifter, I have heightened senses, and I've grown a few new appendages. My nails are super sharp, and running my tongue along my teeth, I discover how sharp my new fangs are too. They cut through it like a knife through butter, and my mouth fills with the tangy taste of my own blood. There's a coppery scent in the air, but it's older and unappetizing, with a hint of plastic. Opening my eyes, I slowly sit up, taking in my surroundings. I'm sitting on the floor in the middle of a sea of empty plastic blood bags, which I guess explains the smell.

It seems that my clothes haven't survived my shift, and with a hard swallow, I realize neither has my skin color. Holding out my hands, I flip them back and forth, taking in their new color. It's a chromatic black, shimmery like an oil slick with purples and golds in it when the light hits it right. Scanning my body, I see all of it is the same color, even my cock. Struggling to my feet, I find a mirror on the other wall and get a really good look at my new form. Where Jagger, Kai, and Mina all resemble their human form, I don't look like me at all. *Maybe it's because that asshole gave me so many different kinds of demon essence.*

I think it's partly to do with the color, but my facial structure has changed too. My irises are no longer blue, but a black similar to my skin, and they have that cat's eye look like Kai's. My cheekbones are sharper, and my hair is longer and an emerald green color. My eyes move to the horns now on my head. They're pointing backward and are quite long, longer than the other demons that I know, and they're so pointy and sharp that I have no doubt they could shred flesh if I needed them too.

I'm probably about the same height, but as I run my hands over my stomach, the muscles there are rigid and defined, and I have a prominent v down toward my cock. I've always been fit but never had this kind of muscle definition before; it's other-worldly. A movement in the mirror draws my eye downward, and my heart skips a beat at the tail that's waggling behind me. Unlike Mina's blunt tip, mine is very much like a cartoon demon's tail with a triangular shape on the end. *Hmm, that's going to hurt if I sit on it.* Those thoughts must trigger something, because as I watch, the triangle morphs into a blunt tip before changing back. *Well, that's handy as fuck.* The tail gives a jaunty wave like it's happy with my approval, moving in sinuous waves like a cat's. *Crap, that is going to take some getting used to.* It wraps around my body and caresses my skin in an affectionate way, and I laugh for the first time in a long time.

My eyes drift back down my body, still marveling at the change. Nobody will recognize me like this, and that gives me some comfort. I conjure up some clothes to cover my body, the tail wiggling to get out, so I modify my pants to allow for that. I know there's a way to go back to my human form, but I have no clue how to do that at the moment.

I may have to ask to convince Mina to teach me, but I have a feeling she's not going to be too interested in that. Suddenly, a rumble echoes in my stomach, a pulsing need to feed reverberating through my body. I remember overhearing Mav and Zeph at breakfast the other day talking about Mina's feeding schedule and how she would need so much blood every day. *With such a cocktail of demon blood inside me, what will I feed on?*

Flashbacks of my transition suddenly pop into my mind, and turning, I survey the room. My mind was so focused on me that I forgot about the three that had been locked in here with me. I scan the room, taking in all the empty blood bags, and remember that horrible taste before I see a pair of feet behind the couch. Hurrying over, I find

Connie's unconscious, limp body sprawled like she was running and was tackled from behind. More memories flash like a movie reel in my mind. I had grabbed her, she'd run, and the predator in me had been thrilled at the chase then disappointed when it ended almost instantly.

Leaning down, I feel for a pulse, kind of relieved when I find one. To be honest, I wouldn't have cared too much if I hadn't, but it might have pissed off Sabboath, and that would've made my life a bit more difficult. Remembering the taste of her blood and the way it slid down the back of my throat with the feel of swallowing oil has me wrinkling my nose. I will *not* be taking a drink from her again. Straightening up, I check the room for the others.

One of them had tasted like that too, and when my eyes catch sight of a limp hand on the other side of the exam table I'd first been lying on, I head over to check on them. As I approach, Silas's wide-eyed blank look tells me everything I need to know. He didn't survive, and from the way his throat has been torn open, it isn't a surprise. Again, flashes of memory assault my brain. My inner predator had seen red the minute it opened its eyes. It knew that this man was responsible for torturing Mina, and it was going to make him pay. I'd torn his throat out before he could even run and guzzled down that foul blood, spilling more than I drank thanks to it being tainted by Sabboath's corruption.

Now, where is the other one? With that question, one last memory comes to mind of a terrified yet quiet Beatrice.

I had sunk my fangs into her flesh, but I was so surprised at her fresh and tangy taste after the rot of the other two, I stopped and looked at her. She hadn't begged or tried to run; she'd just stood there and accepted her fate.

"What's different about you? Why do you taste so much better than the others?"

"Because like you, I have divine protection," she whispers, though there isn't any need to. One's dead, and one's unconscious, but I guess there could be cameras. I'm not sure whether to believe her words or not, but her blood certainly seems to support her claim.

"Please don't blow my cover! You need to finish drinking," she frantically insists. Her eyes plead with every word, so with a quick nod, I drink a little more.

"There are plenty of blood bags in the fridge. Drink until you can drink no more. I'll pretend to go limp, and you can just drag me to the fridge and drop me like you've lost interest," she instructs, keeping a surprisingly clear head considering I'm using her as a juicebox.

Heading over toward the bank of fridges on the far wall, I find her propped up against one, limp head to one side, but I can hear a steady and strong heartbeat along with the rise and fall of her chest. Leaving her there, I pull open the fridge that she's not leaning against, pulling out one of the few remaining blood bags. I use my fangs to rip a hole in the plastic and tip it back, swallowing the cold, thick coppery blood with a grimace.

"Maybe warming it up might make it taste better." The voice has me flinching and looking up at the doorway to find Sabboath standing there with a wry smile on his face. Crap, I was so intent on the blood I hadn't even heard him open the door.

I finish the bag and let it drop to the ground with a shrug as he surveys the room. "I think I prefer it from the source," I answer, nearly startling myself when I hear myself, deeper and more gravely than my normal voice.

He moves into the room, his eyes alight with both interest and thinly veiled disgust as he takes in my new form.

"Well, well, well, look at you. You don't look a thing like yourself anymore! You are going to make the perfect double agent." He's rubbing his hands together in glee, looking like some cheesy tv villain. *Crap, does that now make me a triple agent?*

A moan behind the couch has both of our eyes turning to the source. Connie staggers to her feet, her hand clasped across where I had drunk from. There's no wound, so I must have instinctually healed it, not like Silas. *Why would my demon spare her?*

She's looking at me with horror now, something I've never seen her do before. "Sammy?" Her voice is quiet as if she can't quite believe her eyes, and I shoot her a smug smile. *I guess there's no need to keep sucking up to this bitch now.* I've secured my spot here, and I'm pretty sure her dreams of happily ever after just went up in a puff of smoke.

She swallows visibly and then starts to edge away from me as both her father and I observe her.

"Hmm, I see she survived," he notes, clinical detachment back in place. He might as well be talking about a lab rat instead of his daughter. "What about the others?" Before I can answer, Connie's screams echo throughout the room. "I guess that's a no." He laughs callously at his daughter's distress. She's thrown herself at Silas's body and pulled him into her arms, rocking back and forth.

"No, I can't believe you did this!" she screams at me, tears streaming down her face. *Hmm, that's a pretty extreme reaction. I guess I wasn't the only one she's been sniffing around.*

"Sorry, babe, nature of the beast." I shrug my shoulders in response, and Sabboath laughs again like it's the funniest thing he's ever heard, holding out a fist. Huh? Oh, he wants a fist bump? *What a cunt.* I indulge him despite the eye roll dying to break out since I've got to keep on his good side.

"What about the other one?"

"Nope, she's over there." I point toward the fridges where her body is just out of sight. "The anger was gone by then, and I didn't feel the need to rip her throat out. It was just pure hunger, and she let me into the fridges, so I let her live," I explain, and he nods his head, not one bit of suspicion to see.

"Yes, that was smart of her. If she's got some brains to her, maybe there's a bigger role in our cause for her. I could do with someone who can think on their feet," he muses while rolling his eyes at his still distraught daughter.

"Oh, for fuck's sake, will you stop with that hideous noise? He's dead, get over it! He was a waste of space anyhow." Walking over to an intercom, he presses a button before stepping away from it again.

"Alright, Sam. Let's make a plan to get you down into Mina's cell and work on getting you on her good side." He eyes me up and down, more happiness shining through his face than I've ever seen before. "Yes, there is no way she's going to see the connection between you and her traitorous teammate Sam."

After a couple people in white coats walk into the room, he dismissively waves in Connie's direction. "Can you deal with that, please?" I guess he means Silas' body. "There's another one over by the fridge that's still alive, and I'd like her to stay that way." They nod their heads, and one moves Connie out of the way, dragging the body out by one leg. It warms my heart to see the asshole treated so badly. Connie hurries after him, hurling threats and pummeling him on the back, but he ignores her. The other one gently picks Beatrice up, and I watch with a careful eye so I can note who I'll need to eat next if she's mistreated.

"I'll just take her to the hospital wing for recovery," he tells Sabboath, who nods.

"Yes, good idea, she may need a blood transfusion as well," he tells the white-coated figure, who looks at me before swallowing nervously and hurrying away.

"Would it be alright for me to have a shower before we move on with the plan?" I ask, knowing I need to pop outside the barrier and message someone regarding all the prisoners from Minzeon.

Sabboath looks at me a little skeptically, so I quickly give him another reason.

"Look, you said the dragon is down there at the moment, so another couple of hours isn't going to matter, and I think I need to eat some real food and possibly grab some sleep. Who knows when I'll be able to next?" Before he can answer, another person enters the room, this one looking more like a soldier in black fatigues, which are similar to the CD ones.

"Sir, we have a problem. Rumors are coming out of the CD of a complete cleansing. They're having the Archangel council scan everyone's minds for signs of AoA information. The rest of Echo has been detained, except their leader, who has just reported in. He's trying to find a way into the realm, but the transport room has been deactivated, and he can't get in contact with our Archangel contacts."

"Fuck!" Sabboath's eyes blaze with anger and a little terror as his shout reverberates around the room. "Fine, I'll come and deal with it. Three hours, Samuel. Then we're moving on with the plan." He storms out, followed by the soldier, leaving me to myself. Not wanting to wait for him to change his mind, I hurry back to my quarters.

The rooms are nothing fancy for the soldiers of the AoA, but the bed is comfortable, and I don't have to share a bathroom, nor are there any cameras. Sabboath thinks too highly of his medical skills to think we could really sneak around after he's scrambled our brains and DNA. Closing the door behind me, I finally take five minutes to breathe, running my hands through my hair and taking big deep cleansing breaths as I sit on the bed.

Coming into this, I knew it was going to be tough, Mylea had warned me it would be, and although my emotions have been a lot more stable without Connie's interference, this certainly hasn't been a smooth ride. I've felt off-kilter the entire time. Seeing Mina and being unable to kill them all and escape with her was brutal. Then add in all the changes to my body, and it's no wonder I'm exhausted and hungry. But I have no time to dwell on that. I need to teleport out of the barrier and send a message. That's the only way in or out, and someone has to bring you if you don't have the skills. Which, realistically, is ninety-nine percent of the AoA members. To say I was surprised when I'd heard that there was more than one Archangel in AoA was an understatement, though based on the report Sabboath received, they're likely short a few now.

Hopefully, I still have that ability even in my demon form since it's a skill that Archdemons have as well. Standing up, I concentrate, landing in a room somewhere with Jophial bending over my sleeping teammate's body, running her hands through Drusilla's hair.

"Whoops." My voice has her looking up quickly as I scan the room. No one else is in here, thankfully.

"Who the fuck are you?" A blazing pair of daggers appears in her hand as she steps up to protect my sleeping friend, and I quickly hold up my hands.

"Whoa, whoa, it's me, Sam!" I try to convince her, and her daggers drop slightly as a confused look crosses her face.

"Sam?"

"Yes, this is just part of what Sabboath has done to me." I gesture to my body. "It's not even the half of it."

"If you're Sam, tell me what animal you were shifted in when you took Mina," she orders, not ready to trust me yet. Jophial has always been very sharp. If she wasn't busy with the Menagerie, she'd be a kickass addition to the Archangel council.

"A tiger, a white tiger," I quickly reply, and she

lets the daggers go and hurries toward me, pulling me into a tight hug.

"Oh my god, what has he done to you?" Her shock and concern aren't easy for me to hear.

"I'm okay," I assure her. "It's an adjustment, but I would do anything to keep Mina and the rest of the world safe from Hammus." She squeezes me even tighter before letting me go, and I'm filled with the first bit of warmth I've experienced in days. It's been easy to forget what actual care feels like, being stuck with Connie and Sabboath. The softness in how she regards me is almost enough to make me crack.

"Look, I only meant to pop outside the barrier to telepath to you, but I'm afraid this demon change is messing with my abilities, and it brought me straight here. I think Mylea may have made it possible for me to even though no one else can teleport directly here." I explain to her, and she nods but looks toward the doorway.

"We need to be quick. Your mom is here along with a couple of the others, and they don't know about any of this. They all think you've gone rogue too." My heart sinks at my mom thinking I'm a traitor, and it must show on my face.

"She doesn't believe it and is sticking by you, but she shouldn't see you. She'll want you to stay." Knowing she's right even though I don't want her to be, I quickly update her.

"You need to examine each of the prisoners one

by one; not all of them were there voluntarily. A lot were, but there are some that were coerced too, and whatever he did to them to change their structure, it's making them all sick and compliant. We need to work on changing them back or, if we can, healing them at least." Her face pales in understanding. "Also, his base is located in Ferijen. I'm not sure where, and it's a pocket of space that I don't think you can see with the naked eye. You'll need to search for it. I'm sorry I can't help anymore, but I have to get back and keep an eye on Mina."

"Thank you for doing this, Sam. I promise we'll make it right when it's over," she reassures me, but it doesn't make me feel any better.

Just as I'm about to reply, the door handle rattles. "Quick, go!" she harshly whispers, and as I leave, I watch my mother's shocked face appear in the doorway.

Chapter Thirteen

Grayson

After shouting for help for a while, I realize no one is coming to get me out, least of all my father. He knew that Mina would want to feed off of me and had hoped it would bring me into line. Just recently, I pissed him off by questioning the AoA's values, especially now that the plan of worlds domination is coming to fruition. The couple of times I'd met Hammus brought chills of fear to my body; his dark, predatory eyes feel like they're looking into your soul and have the ability to leave you nothing but a shell. The last time I was in his presence, I'd decided I didn't want anything to do with a creature like him, and when I discovered the extent of the cleansing that had happened to the demon race, there was no way I wanted to inflict that on anyone else.

Refusing my adopted father's requests is difficult. When I first arrived, he conditioned me well, to fear and obey him. For many years, I have unquestionably, and it's only now that I see him for what he really is, a delusional megalomaniac.

Sliding down the wall opposite Mina, I observe her. My dragon was useless when she pounced on me. He has different forms of breath that can be used as a defense, fire obviously, but he also has a poison that will kill within a second and a sedative, which will make the victim docile and compliant. I tried to use that one, but he flat out refused, even when I was screaming at him in my head. He let her drink from us, and enjoyed it.

The silence of the cell is only broken up by my ragged breathing and the pink demon's funny purring sound. She sits in the corner sounding like a happy, contented kitten, a blissed-out look on her face. I can't quite believe what just happened. She sank her fangs into my neck and drank my blood like it was her favorite meal. Not only did I stop struggling, but I also came the hardest I ever have in my life. And then she happily licked the cum off my stomach, and I just stood there and let her. I didn't push her away in disgust; I reveled in the feel of her tongue and mouth on my body. It was almost like it had direct contact with my cock. In fact, I almost shoved her down on her knees and buried myself in her. A *demon*, what am I thinking? But even as I shudder with disgust and no small amount of lust, my eyes scan her body.

She's gorgeous, there's no doubt about it, all lithe limbs and curvy body. Even her horns and tail are sexy. I'm not sure why I've always thought demons were hideous creatures because she certainly isn't. I have fragmented memories of before, of loving parents, parents who cherished me and taught me tolerance and kindness. Little flickers of light before the darkness. I have no memory of how I came to be with Sabboath, but my life certainly did change. *Just how far has my "father's" brainwashing gone?*

An intoxicating scent fills the cell, my nostrils flare, and I breathe in deeply. Desire floods my body, and my cock fills with blood again.

"How are you feeling over there?" Mina's voice is husky, and my cock throbs at the sound, my mind flooding with images of burying it deep within her. I scrub a hand across my cheek, trying to push the thoughts aside.

"What's it to you?' I snarl back, ashamed at my visceral reaction toward a being I had always been taught was inferior and lacking.

She chuckles quietly. "I'm still hungry, and I was wondering if you were interested in helping a girl out."

"Didn't you take enough blood the first time?" I spit back at her, but she just chuckles again. My dragon quivers with excitement at her suggestion; he's up for anything she'd like to do to him.

"Oh, dragon boy, it's not blood I need now, and I'd prefer not to take it by force." She purrs and starts to crawl toward me on her hands and knees, her red eyes are hooded with lust, and I catch a flash of fang when she licks her lips. "I swear I'll make it feel so good, better than anything you've had before."

I shudder as she moves my way, but this time, it's not in disgust. The scent in the air is intoxicating, and as she gets closer, she sits up on her knees and pulls her shirt over her head. Her breasts, pink like the rest of her body, are full, and her nipples are tight with desire. She shuffles nearer still, her hands coming up to massage them.

"Please, Grayson. Everything hurts, and I need you to make it feel better." This time, when her eyes meet mine, they shimmer with desperation. There's a pleading note to her voice that calls to my better nature, reaching out to the part of me that doesn't want someone to suffer. This is not the cocky demon from before; this demon needs help, and she's begging me for it. Seeing her on her knees, breasts bared and drawing me in with that seductive voice, sends all hesitation flying. Leaning forward, I wrap my arm around her waist and drag her forward into my lap. She starts to pant and squirm, trying to get my hard cock against her aching pussy.

Running my hands through her black hair, I yank her forward and plaster my mouth against hers, thrusting my tongue into it like I want to shove my cock into her wet heat.

Her tongue meets mine and tangles with it as we wrestle for dominance, but I yank on her hair and growl, my dragon asserting itself, and she softens, yielding to me. The rush of triumphant power runs through me, and my dragon grunts in approval.

Her small hands grope at my shirt before finding purchase, and as we break apart, she lifts it over my head before her mouth latches onto one of my nipples, and she bites down. *Oh, she's fighting back again.* My dragon starts to rumble in delight; he does like it when they put up a bit of a fight. Pushing her away, it's my turn, and I lean down, taking one of her nipples into my mouth. I suck and lick and bite, alternating between the two, and she moans with enjoyment, all while grinding in my lap.

"Please, Gray, I need it. Please!" Hearing her beg has my dragon roaring internally in satisfaction. Grasping her waist, I push her away, and she mewls in protest, but I stand up, pulling her with me. I get rid of our sweatpants and step back, taking in all the glorious pink curves. While I run my eyes over her delectable body, her tail wraps around her waist and sort of waves at me in a come hither motion. Shocked, my eyes meet hers, and she rolls them. "It's kind of got a mind of its own," she warns me almost bashfully, and a small smile crosses my lips. My eyes go back to scanning her gorgeous figure, my heart rate increasing as my skin tightens in excitement.

"Fuck, you're beautiful." Her eyes dilate, and

she purrs in appreciation before returning the perusal.

"Wow, I'm not sure that's going to fit," she nearly whispers, giggling a little deliriously while licking her lips, "but I'm willing to give it a go."

I pace toward her, backing her up to the rusty cot with a moldy mattress that's in the cell, but she balks in disgust. "Don't worry; we're not laying on it," I reassure, turning her around. "I just need you to brace yourself," I whisper in her ear, pushing her hands and head down as I nibble on her neck and down her naked back. Pulling her hips out a bit, I run a finger through her soft lips, finding them soaking. Circling her clit to tease her, she whimpers, the sound quickly turning into moans.

"Now, Grayson, or she'll take over."

She? What does she mean? Shaking my head, I ignore her words and run my cock back and forth through her lips, coating it with her juices before lining it up at her entrance.

Without another word, I thrust deep into her wet, tight heat, and she screams out my name. My heart pounds as her cunt grips my cock like they were made for each other. I thrust forward again and again before I'm finally seated. She moans, flinging her head back. Inhaling a deep breath, I start to take long sensual thrusts, my hands skimming up and down her body, pulling at the base of her tail, and she gasps with pleasure.

"Grab my horns," she demands breathlessly,

and I slap her on the ass, my dragon hissing at her challenge to our authority.

"Please, Gray, please." Her voice is low but more demanding, and a prickle of awareness takes over, my dragon sensing something powerful. This time, it's threatening, and when I turn her head to kiss her, her eyes are now shimmering with an ever-changing iridescent color. I pause. *What the fuck?* Before I can do anything else, she takes the lead, fucking herself backward onto my cock and shouting out dirty words.

"Yes, fuck my cunt, fuck it hard." I'm sort of speechless, but the pheromones ramp up, and I'm helpless. I start to pound into her, hard and fast. Grabbing hold of her horns, I yank her head back, biting down hard on the muscles stretched out before me. My scales ripple under my skin at the heightened emotions.

"Yes!" she screams in delight. "Harder! Faster, put your hands on my neck." Her voice is no longer hers now; it's hypnotic and enchanting, and there's nothing I can do to stop myself. I wrap my hands around her neck, just above the collar, and squeeze. Not too hard because I'm still able to control that much, and I don't want to damage the already broken skin any further. She moves one of her hands off the bed, still begging for more, and brings it up to my arm. She grabs hold, and as her pussy flutters, she groans long and low. Just as I feel her orgasm take hold, she pulls my hand off her neck and places it in front of her mouth. Screaming her pleasure, she bites down hard on my wrist, and I instantly flood her hot, spasming pussy with my cum, thrusting a couple more times before seating myself, panting with the pleasure.

Her mouth suckles on my wrist as she takes both blood and cum from me, and once again, I can't help myself, biting down on her shoulder. My teeth sink deep into her flesh, her blood filling my mouth like a decadent dessert. I swallow the mouthful and let go, licking a few swipes over the wound to heal it. As I check out the damage, my eyes widen in shock. *These aren't normal teeth marks!* I must have shifted my mouth before I bit down on her, and I haven't had a lapse in control like that since I was a child. *What is it about her that made me do this?*

There are four perfect holes where my fangs have marked her pink skin, and before my eyes, they pucker and scar. My cock has swollen, and the barb on the end sinks itself into the front wall of her pussy right in the spongy pleasure center. She lets go of my arm and screams again, grunting and groaning as I rock back and forth, locked in for the moment. My orgasm seemingly never-ending. I've never had one like it before, and my eyes just about roll back in my head, but my dragon roars triumphantly, and this time, that sound actually comes from my mouth as well while Mina shudders beneath me.

She still grips my arm, and while I continue to

rock, she laps at the holes in my wrist, her small tongue licking and sucking at the trail of blood running down my arm. The feeling translates to my cock, and it pulses inside her again, drawing another gasp from her lips. Just as she places a final lick across the puncture wounds, sealing them closed, a searing pain toward my groin has me shouting. My barb immediately retracts, allowing me to quickly pull out of Mina. *Fuck, what has she done to me?* She staggers away from me and slides down the wall, groaning in her own dose of pain.

"What the fuck have you done?" I shout at her, looking for an injury, but there's nothing there except a newly forming mark, just left of my still hard dick.

She looks at me wide-eyed with surprise then glances down at the appearing mark.

"Well, shit, it looks like you lucked out."

"What do you mean?" I ask, wanting to shake the answers out of her but refraining from doing it; I can see she's rattled too.

"Looks like you're one of my bonded mates. Who'd have guessed? I guess there was a reason for me being caught," she mumbles to herself.

"I'm sorry, what?" *There's no way I heard that right.*

"Demons have bonded mates that are completely devoted to their mating circle. No straying. It's the one thing Hammus did right for his people. The number of mates varies from demon to demon, but the more powerful the demon, the greater number of mates, usually. So far, I have five, and it looks like you're lucky number six." Her eyes are closed and head back against the wall, looking completely worn out. Even her voice has gone flat like she's waiting for rejection.

The mark has finished forming, and the pain disappears. Quickly, I pull on my pants and top again, my head clearing.

"What the fuck was that?" I shout at her before I start pacing again. My dragon rumbles at me, but this time it feels like he's telling me to shut up. *What's with that? We're usually so in sync with one another.* I stop pacing and look within myself. The smug bastard is curled up and purring, happy with everything that happened. He opens one large reptilian eye and looks at me, a hint of condescension in his eye like he can't believe how stupid I'm being.

"Mate," he grunts at me before settling down to sleep.

"No, seriously, what *was* that? I have never treated a woman like that, and no matter my dislike for demons, I wouldn't have treated you like that either." Now that we have a quieter moment, I can check in with my own feelings without letting my dragon's emotions or her power overwhelm me. There's plenty of confusion but also a healthy dose of guilt for how I handled her. Normally, even if I'm with a woman just for sex, I treat them better than I've treated Mina today.

Her eyes stay closed, but she waves a hand at

me. "Yeah, sorry about that, my succubus took the reins. I guess I was weak enough for her to break through, and she likes it rough. The rougher the better, she's a dirty bitch," Mina mumbles, sounding a little bit embarrassed, and though her eyes open, she won't meet mine.

"She was compelling you. I'm so sorry for taking away your choice." A tear rolls down her cheek, and my heart and stomach drop in disappointment. Seeing the woman that my dragon calls mate cry is disturbing. Moving over to her, I curl her small, still-naked body into mine. Instincts I never knew I had are kicking in, and when I look inside again, my dragon is ready to kill whoever upset our mate. My body heats in anger, smoke starting to puff out of my nose again.

I reassure him everything is okay before I accidentally shift in the cell. He settles, but only after I promise that I will make his mate feel better. I go back to caring for the girl in my arms, my dragon's warmth and need to give her affection stirring in my soul. Stroking her hair, I reassure her everything is going to be okay even though I'm not a hundred percent sure that it is. All I know is I've got a feeling my life is about to change. I've got my fingers crossed it's for the better, and I secretly hope that it includes this beautiful woman somehow. My feelings are completely different now from when I first entered the cell. A small sliver of me wonders if it's all a spell, but it's my dragon's turn to reassure me, and he says this bond is natural, *fated* even. Even if the bond is with a demon... if it's fated by the gods, can it be wrong? Her breathing slowly settles, and she snuggles up into me, content and asleep in my arms.

Before I can do anything, I hear footsteps approaching, so I wake Mina and get her back into her clothes.

"Quick, it might be my father; I don't want him to know what just happened." Mina's sleepy eyes flash hurt before looking sad, and she moves away from me, pretending to be asleep on the other side of the room.

My heart drops at the movement, and I know I just damaged our fragile bond, but I can't do anything about it now as the footsteps get closer.

No, I need to play along for as long as possible until Sabboath either confides in me, or I can work a way of getting us out of here. I hope she will forgive me once this is all over.

Chapter Fourteen

Jessamina

Grayson carefully shaking me awake and helping me into my clothes has my mind-clearing, and my heart sinks in my chest as I comprehend what I've just done. I've just bonded a man to me against his will. A man who was so disgusted by demons he couldn't even look me in the eye. Basically, what I just did was tantamount with rape, and I have no idea how to redeem myself from this.

I couldn't control the succubus inside. She took the driver's seat and my body out for a joyride, and although it felt fucking fantastic, I'm so ashamed that she activated the mate bond by biting him during the process. I mean, I know it would have happened regardless, but he had no warning that it was a possibility and no choice as to whether I would fuck and feed at the same time. My stomach twists with guilt as he moves away from me quickly, footsteps alerting us to someone's presence. Hurt rolls through my body, but I close my eyes, pretending to be asleep as the steps come to a stop.

"Oh, my boy, you're still in one piece?" Sabboath sounds pleased, but there's a cautious note in his question that says he's still not convinced he should trust his son. "Did she not feed on you?"

"If you mean did she drink my blood, then yes, she held me down and took her fill. I feel degraded and dirty now. Was that what you wanted, Dad?" Grayson's voice is petulant and annoyed as he replies to his adopted father.

He chuckles his amusement at the sound of his angry son, satisfied and likely patting himself on the back for choosing such a "successful" punishment. "And was that all that happened?" he probes a little more. "The smell of her pheromones is quite intoxicating but doesn't seem to be as strong. Are you sure nothing else happened?"

"Are you asking if I fucked the beast? Fuck no! But I wasn't able to control myself when she was feeding on me, and I'm afraid something happened then." He sounds ashamed, and opening my eyes slightly, I can see he has his head bent in embarrassment. "The scent seemed to ease after that," he admits, words mumbled.

"Ah, yes. Don't be ashamed, son. It would have happened to anyone. I'm just pleased you were able to resist the lure to do more. I know how strong her mother's can be, so it shows me how powerful you are. Well done. At least that's another thing that has gone right today. Between you and Samuel, you're going to be the generals in my… *Hammus'* army as we march against the rest of the worlds. You will be feared and fawned over by the masses."

"So, are you going to leave me in here, or are you done punishing me?" Grayson snaps, his eyes blazing with fury. "I think I've been here long enough, and the thought of feeding her again makes me feel ill."

"I suppose you can come out. I'm having another prisoner brought down, so he can be her food, but I also want to run some tests on her. I need her docile and compliant. Can you dose her up for me, please?"

My head turns to where Sabboath is standing, and his look of hunger scares me. *Dose me up, what the hell does he mean?*

Grayson pushes away from the wall and walks toward me. I scramble to my feet, prepared to fight back, my scales sliding into place across my body. This has him pausing as his nostrils flare and eyes widen before heating with lust, but he shakes his head and keeps coming. Before I can try anything, he opens his mouth and breathes a huge gust of air in my direction. It's sweet and sugary, smelling like strawberries, and the minute I draw it into my lungs, my body relaxes. I drop my hands, eyelids drooping, head hanging. He wraps his arms around me to stop me from falling to the ground.

"Yes, good job, Grayson," Sabboath compliments as he turns a key in the cell door, opening it wide. "Carry her to my lab, will you?"

Grayson lifts me bridal style into his arms and follows obediently behind his dad. I try to struggle, but my body is non-compliant, so I stare at him, but he won't meet my gaze. How could fate, or Mylea, or whoever the fuck is responsible, give me this man as a mate? He loathes me, and to be honest, I'm not all that impressed myself. I mean, the package is super pretty, but I'm not really liking the inside so far.

We make our way up a flight of stairs and through some corridors, the drab interior blending together until I'm honestly not sure how many turns we might have made or floors we might have climbed. I'm unable to move my head, so I can't learn the way out even if I do find a way to escape. I'm going to have to wing it. Before long, we enter a bright white lab, and Grayson places me down on an examination table. My scales are still in place, so I'm not sure what Sabboath hopes to achieve, test-wise, but I'm pretty sure that needles won't penetrate the skin. In any case, I can't even ask questions or demand answers. My tongue feels big in my mouth, and my lips can't form the words. I'm essentially paralyzed, and my heart rate is through the roof, panic surging at the thought of not being able to fight back.

"What are you going to do?" Grayson asks, his

voice not really all that interested. It's like he's just filling the empty space.

"I'm going to draw some blood, so I can compare it to yours and Samuel's. I was also going to harvest some eggs." His words have me freaking out, and I feel a finger twitch as the paralytic starts to wear off. "But I don't think I'm going to be able to penetrate those scales. Before he met his demise, Silas told me they were impenetrable."

My ears pick up on his words. Silas is dead. *Good, hope he fucking suffered.*

"Why would you want them, anyway?" Again, he sounds disinterested as he stands looming over the top of me, poking his finger into the scales on my arm. But I do start to wonder... if he truly doesn't care, why ask? "Huh, they feel very much like my dragon scales."

"Well, she can only carry one or two fetuses at a time to stay optimally healthy, but we can have surrogates carry more. I need my army, and I wanted to experiment in fetal growth acceleration so I can have them sooner, but I refuse to permanently damage what might be my best donor. I guess I can always harvest Connie's eggs. Mina's are too valuable to waste on experimentation, and that's probably all Connie's are good for."

Holy fuck, this guy truly is a sick freak. I start to feel sorry for Connie but quickly put a halt to those feelings. Bitch deserves it all. She tried to torture me, and she stole my friend. I hope she gets fat and has cankles if he has her impregnated.

All of a sudden, Sabboath appears above me, that smarmy smile on his face. "Hello, Mina, now this would go a lot easier if you would cooperate. I don't suppose you can make the scales go away," he coos encouragingly, and I give him the middle finger with my mind.

"I gave her a big dose; I don't think she can do anything at the moment."

"You ask her; it's your voice that triggers the compulsion part of that power. Ask her to remove the scales so that I can do what I need to do," Sabboath orders, and he steps out of eyesight. Grayson's handsome, douchebag, ball-sucking fuck face comes back. Hmm, ball-sucking, I wonder if he does that? My mind drifts off on a tangent thinking about Grayson wrapped around my other beautiful mates, his darker skin contrasting with all their paler tones. My core clenches with desire, and my pheromones start to perfume the air. Sabboath's nauseating chuckle can be heard off to the side. "Damn, boy, she really likes you. I'm not sure how you held off. Get her to remove those scales because I'm not going to resist as you did. If this keeps up, I'm going to take the whore for a spin; I figure it's the least I'm owed."

Oh fuck. I try to rein in the pheromones, but the succubus has caught sight of her prey, and while we're immobilized, she's going to use all she can to get out of here.

Grayson's dark eyes harden with Sabboath's words, but his face stays blank. He opens his mouth, and I wait with dread for his voice to compel me to remove my armor.

"Mina, retract your scales for Sabboath, please." I clench my eyes closed, the only things I can move, and wait for the order to overrule my body, but nothing happens.

"Mina, look at me." His voice is soothing and seductive, but nothing about it is compelling. "Mina, do as he's asked." He tries once more, but nothing happens.

"Fuck!" Sabboath screams, and there's a crash and a clattering of what must be instruments across the room. "How is she able to resist that?"

My eyes are still on his, and they narrow slightly in surprise before quickly flickering to reptile and back again. Abruptly, he moves out of my sight, leaving me staring at the white ceiling.

"I don't know; it's never happened before," he apologizes, and there's the sound of metal against metal. He must be picking up the things Sabboath threw. My mind whirls at his words. *Why am I able to resist? Does this have something to do with me mating him?* Jesus, maybe the accidental mating has saved me from a fate worse than death. At the thought, guilt floods my body again. I did to Grayson what

Sabboath wants to do to me. I'm no better than he is.

"Next time we dose her, we need to make sure she hasn't got time to activate those scales. How they are still able to do that I don't know. That collar should have stopped the form change," Sabboath grumps from nearby. A moment later, he appears in front of me again, a huge needle also filling my view.

"But lucky for us, they stop at the collar, which means I can still draw blood through the vein in her neck." His eyes sparkle with madness as the needle moves toward me. A sharp prick is felt, and then I hear my blood filling the vial. He fills up a couple of them before he removes the needle from my neck. "And it also means I can inject her with my new formula. That way, any children from her won't only be demons." He's disgusted but excited at the same time, torn between his desperate supremacy and love of experimentation.

"They'll be super demons. I can't wait to see how it's going to affect her. I wonder if it will be different for you and Samuel," he muses as I listen things rattling around. As much as I try, I can't move my neck, and only my pinky finger is able to move still. Nothing I can do is going to be able to stop him from injecting me. This must be the same thing that changed Connie, and from what I saw this morning, Sam. Fuck, I wonder if he's as crazy as Connie is. *Am I going to suffer the same fate?*

"Hang on." Grayson finally sounds concerned, and a spot of hope lightens up within me. "Shouldn't we wait and harvest her eggs first? I mean, what if she reacts badly to the formula because she's a demon." That cock stick. Here I was thinking he was trying to protect me.

"Hmm. Maybe you're right. Okay, I'll have someone return her to her cell, and I'll inject you with the new formula instead."

My heart skips a beat. Grayson managed to stop him from infecting me, but now he's in the firing line.

A resigned sigh follows, likely Grayson trying to buy some kind of time. "I'd prefer to return her myself. Your guards weren't exactly able to resist her lure last time; we can't really afford to lose any more loyal followers, especially after the Minzeon debacle." I can practically hear the sneer in Grayson's voice, and I almost have to admire the way he can skillfully manipulate his father. That jab to Sabboath's leadership and decision-making gets an almost instant reply.

"Watch your fucking tone with me! It's that kind of thing that got you thrown in with her in the first place. But you may be right. Fine, take her back but return here straight away. I'll go and chase down that other food source I have for her. I need the mother of my future army kept well fed."

Footsteps fade, and Grayson comes into view

again, but this time, his eyes are softer even though his face is still a mask of cold.

He scoops me up into his arms and cradles my head against his chest, his heartbeat loud in my ears. Turning, he carries me back the way we came.

He doesn't speak a word the whole time, but one of his thumbs caresses my leg, a soothing motion that has my breathing slowing. I can feel us going downstairs, and the stench of the prison block assaults my senses again before he once again places me down on the floor, leaning me back against a wall.

"That paralytic should wear off soon. I'm sorry, Mina. I had no choice in subduing you, but I was able to avoid the compulsion" he tells me, pushing my hair back off my face. His thumb brushes against one of my horns, sending a pulse of desire to my core.

He leans down, his warm breath whispering across my ear. "Be patient. I'll try to get us out of here, but I'm not sure if I will survive this next formula. I've already had it once, and that's how I got the dragon. I'm not sure if I will survive it a second time, or what I will become. But if I can come back for you, I will," he promises before standing up and walking out—the clang of the cell door behind him sounding quite final. I can feel a tear roll down my face but can't do anything to stop it. I just close my eyes and pray for the paralysis to wear off.

Chapter Fifteen

Jessamina

The numb, hopeless feeling slowly wears off. I'm not sure how much time has passed since Grayson left me here, but all the energy I got from him has gone, and that starving feeling is eating a hole in my stomach again. I must have used everything I had fighting off that damn paralytic he breathed at me. I'm just glad I was able to keep my scales in place.

Once I can move again, I stand up and stretch out all my limbs, and that painful pins and needles feeling that happens when all the blood starts circulating again has me groaning out loud.

Moving over to the bars, I try to peer out. This has started to become tedious. I need food, *real* food. How do they think I'm going to survive to breed his army of children if they starve me?

"Hey, hey! Is there anyone there?" I shout down what looks like a deserted corridor. I can't hear anyone in any of the cells nearby. *I must be the only one down here.*

"Come on, a girl has to eat; how else am I going to grow big and strong?" Waiting, I listen, but I still get no response.

Restless, I turn around and survey the cell. The window above that disgusting bed catches my eye, so I climb up and peer out the tiny barred gap, but there's not much to see. Not far from the building, there looks like a shimmering barrier that sits between us and the outside world. That must be how Sabboath keeps this place hidden because my mates surely would have found me by now if that wasn't the case. *My mates*, my mind keens, a sense of loss overtaking me. My hand rubs at the gap in my chest where everyone used to be. Only Grayson is there now, and even though that offers some kind of relief, it just doesn't feel right.

Beyond the barrier, the scenery is creepy. Old, gnarled, and misshapen trees feature widely with sad cracked and broken tombstones littered here and there. A spooky wispy mist drifts just across the ground, and to round out the cliché, a few bats flutter between the trees. If that's not a Halloween graveyard, I don't know what is. We must be in Feri-jen, the realm of monsters.

Apart from the bats, there's no life to be seen, and I watch as one of those bats flies directly into the barrier, instantly being vaporized. Fuck! I guess even if I do escape, I'm not getting out that way. I need to work out how to remove the collar so I can transport again.

Climbing back down off the bed, I start to pace back and forth. It sparked before, the collar, it sparked when I was drinking blood from Grayson and then feasted on his cum. My core clenches again at the reminder of his taste, and my pheromones start to fill the room. My damn succubus is going to use the next person to come down here if I'm not careful. God, I hope it's not Sabboath.

So what made it spark? I mean, it did nothing when I actually bonded him to me, and I got both sex and blood that time too. What was it the first time that made it spark?

I don't have any chance to think about it further because multiple footsteps approach the cell, and it sounds like they're dragging something too. What could that be? I step up to the bars, peering out as they approach. It's Cheesy and Cabbage from before, and they're dragging a black heap between them, accompanied by Sabboath.

"Step back from the bars, bitch," Cheesy jeers as Sabboath stares at me with a gleam in his eye.

"Hmm, Mina, still hungry? I can smell your delectable scent. You really need to do something about that before it wafts through the whole compound, and I can't stop my soldiers. And since you didn't make use of my offering before, I've brought you another. Maybe this one is more to your taste, being the same species and all. Now move away from the door like a good girl."

I ignore him and try to get a look at what's between the two soldiers. He doesn't like that, and before I can ask any questions, the collar around my neck fires up, and a burst of electricity flows through my body. My hands convulse on the bars before I drop to the floor, writhing around, my head banging against the hard ground. Unable to move, I'm blocking the door, but that doesn't deter Cheesy. He gives a hard push to open it, rolling my body over at the same time. I try to claw my way to my knees, but the collar pulses again, and another burst of pain flows through my body.

I grit my teeth to stop myself from biting my tongue and roll my head back. Sabboath is holding a remote of some kind that must control the collar. Fuck, one more jolt like that, and I'll piss my pants too. That would be unpleasant, so I stay still.

The soldiers drag the lump into the cell and drop it down next to me before leaving, the door banging shut behind them. Sabboath crouches down and looks me in the eye.

"Food will be brought to you, but to fill your other needs, you're going to have to use this one. It's all I can spare. Nobody else wants to fuck a dirty demon, even one as sexy as you." He stands back up, eyeing the cell in disgust. "You know what? This won't do. I can't keep the mother of my future soldiers in such filth." He waves his hand in a dramatic gesture, and the room changes completely. Rolling my head to look, I can see it's become a luxury bedroom. The rusty cot turns into a sumptuous cushion-clad bed surrounded by thick brocade curtains. The bucket in the corner disappears, and another door appears. It's open and leads to a bathroom. The hard ground I'm lying on morphs into plush carpeting. Struggling to sit up, I can see there's also a couch on one side with a coffee table. On the table lays a platter of food and what looks like a first-aid kit. *What's that for?*

A pained groan has me turning my head to look at the lump. I thought it might be Grayson when they first arrived, that maybe he hadn't made it through his change and they were throwing him to me for a mercy kill. But this lump's skin is way too dark to be Grayson, although there's a lot of bright red blood, which frankly smells delicious and has my fangs clicking into place. This being has skin the color of oil, a slick, metallic black with shimmers of color when the light hits it. I guess the first-aid kit is for him.

"Do with him what you want, but it will be your only food source, so I suggest you not allow him to die. Oh, and Mina, he's only just gone through transition, so he might not be quite with it when he wakes up." *Oh, how kind of him to give me a warning.* "I wouldn't want you to get hurt." I roll my eyes, unable to help the scoff that bursts past my lips. He shrugs before leaving, the soldiers following behind him, a trail of snickering in their wake.

"I want to watch that demon bitch get reamed, boss," one of them whines as they leave.

"You can watch it on the camera," slimy Sabboath reassures him, and I shudder, my eyes searching the room until I spot it sitting in one corner, a discreet little dome, but my eyes pick up the red light saying it's on. *God, everything we do will be recorded.* Thank god it wasn't there when Grayson was in here before.

Breathing out a sigh, I crawl over to the figure, a demon. My eyebrows raise in surprise. I wonder how he got hold of another demon, and a newly transitioned one at that. Mom had explained to me that most of them stayed in the hidden demon underground, and only ones like Jagger, who know how to fight and defend themselves, leave. Catching them is usually impossible, but here is this one.

My eyes scan his body. Wearing just a pair of sweats, like Jagger and Kai, he has a body to die for. Beautifully sculpted muscles, with long black pointy horns. Much longer than mine and wow, those points are like daggers. I go to put my finger against one to see how sharp it is, but as I get close, it becomes blunt. Pulling my finger away, it sharpens to a point again. *Huh.* I try it again, and the same thing happens. Wow, I wonder if it does that for everyone. A movement against my leg has me flinching and looking down, but it's the demon's tail wrapping around my ankle, caressing it, the movement bringing a giggle to my lips. Even though he's unconscious, the tail still has a mind of its own.

Quickly, I stand up and move over to the table to check out the first-aid kit. The demon has plenty of blood on him and some gaping wounds like he's been whipped, and he doesn't seem to be healing. He must need blood. I wonder what kind of demon he is, what else he's going to need to feed on, and my skin prickles with desire. Surely, he can't be another lust demon. What would be the odds?

Suddenly, the food on the table quickly gets my attention—steaming plates of what looks like lasagne as well as a big loaded pizza. My stomach gurgles, and I decide I need to eat before I do anything else. Especially if I'm going to have to give the big guy there some blood. So I flop down on the couch and inhale a couple of slices of pizza, making a dent in the ravenous hole in my stomach. Now that the immediate danger is gone I allow my scales to recede. Pouring myself a glass of water from the nearby jug, I hope this is all enough to kick my blood production into overdrive. Mom explained that demons produce more because everyone drinks it. Not having to feed my mates the last few days coupled with the abuse I've suffered, I'm not sure if I have enough, but we'll soon find out, I guess.

After gulping down the cold water, I slowly chew my last piece of pizza. Just in case Grayson doesn't come through as he promised, I need to come up with a plan to get out of here. I can't wait around for my mates to find me, not with that barrier or whatever it is hiding this compound. Who knows how long it may take? I could be pregnant with Sabboath's super-soldier if it takes too long. I shudder at the thought. Sure, one day I'd like kids, but not ones that were bred to be some kind of super-soldier.

I need to find a way to get the collar off so that my powers will return. There's got to be a way to short circuit it.

Finishing my food, I open up the first-aid kit, but it's empty. *Fucking Sabboath! What was the point of that?* Making my way back over to the demon, I study him again. His face is angular with sharp cheekbones, plump lips, an aristocratic nose, and long emerald hair. Looking again at his still-bleeding wounds, I think that maybe there is a way I can help him while also helping myself, but again, it feels a lot like taking away his choice. *If we don't get those wounds closed, he may not survive to make that choice,* my succubus whispers in my mind.

So I shuffle in close to his chest and lean closer, swiping my tongue over one of the wounds.

God, his blood is like liquid chocolate, warm and rich with a hint of spice, and my eyes roll back. Before I can stop myself, I'm licking his chest like he's my favorite ice cream or lollipop. Long strokes of my tongue over each of the wounds have them closing, and I clean up around each, making sure not to leave a drop of that delicious blood behind. Moving to his stomach where there looks to be a knife wound that's flowing quite freely, I can't help but seal my mouth over it, suckling, but because it's not in a vein or artery, the blood flow is sluggish. After a couple of draws, it becomes too hard to get at the blood, so I lap at it, sealing it up.

A grunt from the unconscious demon has my head turning quickly to look at him, but he doesn't seem to have regained consciousness, so I keep healing the remaining wounds. Sitting back up, I study his sweats. There is now a large bulge tenting them, so I guess something is waking up. I'm trying to decide whether I remove them to check for wounds... or that's the excuse I'm telling myself. When a scent hits my nose and travels straight to my core, my skin tingles, nipples pucker, and I start panting with want. *Holy shit, what is that smell?* Oh god, Sabboath said newly transitioned. Maybe he hasn't finished? Maybe he's only just changed shape and now needs his hungers fed? And with that kind of scent, I'm going to guess he's a lust demon.

Before I can do anything, a hand is on my wrist, the grip like a vise, tighter than I would have thought a newly transitioned demon should have. Unless he's a sloth demon and being unconscious actually fed him? My eyes meet his, black and a little glazed, and he licks his lips as an aggressive snarl crosses his face. Oh, okay, maybe not lust or sloth, perhaps it's wrath. Shit, I wish I had more experience at this.

Before I can blink, he's jumped off the ground, scooped me up in his arms, and thrown me against the wall, the rough texture biting into my back through my shirt.

Even though I struggle, he has me easily pinned, his broad chest against mine. He leans in, fangs bared, and runs his nose up my neck, his tongue coming out to test the throbbing vein there as he groans.

"You smell so good," he growls, and his voice, deep and gravelly, has me squirming.

"Please, are you sure you want to do this?" I'm trying to appeal to him, but he's not hearing me as he runs a claw through the middle of my shirt, the ripping fabric loud over the sounds of our heaving breath. The soft material gapes, exposing my breasts to him, and he groans again, running his nose over my erect nipples and inhaling deeply before circling each with his tongue. His tongue is rough, and it scrapes deliciously with each lick, and this time, even as I groan, I quickly shake my head, trying to push him away.

"You need to stop, *please*. We can't do this," I beg, but he's too far gone, and my words fall on deaf ears. Then my succubus rises up to meet this demon. Whatever he is, she's intrigued, willing, and wanting, but I'm not on board.

His mouth draws away from my now aching

nipples, and he quickly divests me of my sweat-pants, leaving me naked and panting. *God, where are my scales? Why haven't they clicked into place?* I know my body is willing, but my mind is still screaming no; why aren't they listening? He drops to a crouch in front of me, still holding me in place with a vise-like grip, hands now on my hips. This time, he runs his nose up through my dripping center, breathing deeply, his tongue cleaning up the mess in its wake.

Another moan escapes my mouth, and my hands grip his head, holding onto his thick green hair as he swallows all my juices. A pleased grunt accompanies the action, and he becomes more enthusiastic. *Okay, well, maybe he'll get all he needs like this. I'll just let him go a bit, and hopefully, he won't need anymore.* I justify my actions in my mind, but I already know there's no stopping him. There was no stopping me either. Jagger and Kai were kind enough to get me through my transition, so the least I can do is help him through his.

His tongue changes shapes as it thrusts deep into my pussy, and I scream embarrassingly loudly. It's thick, ribbed, and vibrating, and it has me panting hard, but as he brings me to the edge of orgasm and I'm about to slip over, he withdraws. I yank on his hair in frustration, but he just chuckles. Standing back up, his dark eyes meet mine, and I know I'm in trouble.

With one quick movement, he has his cock in his hand, and before I can protest, he's sheathed it deep into my pussy. Long and thick, it stretches me wide to the point of pain, and I groan loudly, but he doesn't stop. He just pulls back and thrusts deep again. It's lucky I'm so wet because by the third time, the pain has receded, and pleasure takes over. He's like a machine, pistoning into me without a care, and all I can do is hold tight to his shoulders and take it. As he moves in and out, his cock changes shape, growing ridges, and holy crap, what is that? Something has suctioned onto my clit and is now pulsing in time to each thrust. There's nothing I can do, though I'm not sure I even want to stop at this point. The orgasm overtakes me like a tidal wave, flooding me with such electrifying sensations that I come so hard I almost black out—screaming so loud my voice aches with the overuse.

The demon's movements start to become a little erratic, and finally, he throws his head back and bellows as I feel his cum pulsing into me, setting off a round of orgasmic aftershocks, the suction on my clit easing so that the feeling is not too extreme.

His release wanes, and he drops his head again, his eyes meeting mine, wide with surprise, and he quickly pulls out, tucking his cock back into his pants and stepping away from me. Finally looks like someone is at home in his brain.

Now that he's not pinning me, I scramble for the sweats at my feet and pull them on, tying the two pieces of my shredded top together to cover my breasts. Moving away from the demon, I try to give him some space. He seems to have come to his senses, but I'm not a hundred percent sure, and he still hasn't taken my blood.

He frantically glances around the room, seemingly surprised by his surroundings, before looking back at me.

"Mina?"

Chapter Sixteen

Mavromichali

I teleport Peter and I directly back to the CD's portal room. Still crowded with people, it falls silent again as we arrive, but we must not be that interesting because general chatter starts up again. I can see my father's large black-tipped, gray wings over to one side, so with a quick word to Peter, we make our way over to the dads.

When we get there, it looks like they have an interrogation area set up. Dad, Zadkiel, Uriel, and Chamuel are each facing a chair with restraints, the seats occupied by members of the CD. Each of the dads has their hands on the head of the immobile CD operative in front of them. I roll my eyes, unsurprised by their dramatics. They *could* do it without touching them, but it freaks the victim out and makes their mind easier to penetrate. Off to the side, a containment area is situated, four people currently stashed in the space.

Surrounding the area are all the remaining team members and support staff waiting to be tested. Some appear extremely nervous, while others just look bored. Even for Archangels, the process takes time. If they rip into someone's mind too quickly, they could destroy it, and no one wants to damage the mind of a loyal team member or possibly destroy evidence in a traitor's.

Silently, Peter and I observe the process; he nudges me when he loses interest. "They must be the traitors," he mutters, gesturing to the containment. Studying the four men, I recognize some of Echo's team. Missing are the two new ones, Silas and Beatrice, and their leader. The four that are there look resigned to their fate. Instead of raging and yelling, trying to plead their case or talk their way out, they're remarkably quiet. They've made bad choices and now have to live with the consequences. *Who knows if they can be redeemed? Maybe they'll spend the rest of their lives imprisoned in the Menagerie.* A shiver travels down my spine at that thought, hating the idea of being trapped, no chance to see my family or the sky ever again.

A flash of bright light draws my attention away from the containment area, and when it clears, Zeph's mom is standing there. Dad has also noticed her arrival, and he drops his hands off of his suspect and waves them, releasing the restraints. He helps the woman to her feet and pats her on the back, apologizing for the invasion, but fortunately, she's clear. She just smiles her relief and heads in the direction of the elevator. It looks like Raphael has been assigned as the guard, making sure only the tested people are allowed to leave because I see a couple of others trying to weasel their way out, but he stands firm and only lets out the girl.

Dad steps away from the area and moves over to where Peter and I are standing, Raphael leaving his post to join us as well. Not chancing anything, he secures the elevator before he does.

"How are the others?" I ask as they join us. "Any sign of them getting better?" The continuous worry for my teammates is making anything else hard to concentrate on.

She shakes her head, putting her hand on my arm. "Oh, Mav, no, I'm sorry. They're all resting peacefully, Mylea and Raph assured that, but there's no change."

"So, what are you here for then?" Dad asks, the words gentle yet impatiently curious at the same time. She gives Peter and me a sideways glance, frowning before looking back at him.

"One of our inside sources has gotten some information to me."

Inside source? We have someone inside the AOA? My face must show my surprise because Raphael confirms it. "Yes, Mav, we've got a couple of spies in there, both under deep cover, and for one of them to risk contacting us, the information must be important."

Jophial nods, seeming a little more settled now that Raphael has given us at least those crumbs of information. "It is. They told me that the AoA is not made up of just volunteers; a lot of their soldiers are there by force, compelled to stay because of the formula that Sabboath has injected into them. It's unstable, and a lot were too scared to leave, worried what would happen when they did. Our source said you need to interrogate the traitors from Minzeon much like you're doing with all of these." She gestures to the rest of the room.

"And we need to find a way to stabilize the victims. Mind reading, even though it takes more time than we'd like, is the only way to go. He doesn't trust that some of the Minzeon traitors won't try to play us if we show signs of mercy. We also need to get a team started on trying to find a cure, or at least a way to stop the side effects. He said to talk to Mylea about that, as he and the other spy seem to be okay, and that's the only thing they have in common. They each got different strains of the formula, but they both got a blessing from Mylea."

Both Dad and Raphael looked worried while she was speaking, their feelings betrayed by the subtle clench of Dad's fists and the tightness in Raphael's jaw. At least that worry seems to ease with her reassurance that both spies are okay.

"Okay, we can do that. We'll finish up here and then make our way downstairs to the prison to sort through all of them," Dad agrees, easily taking charge now that he has priorities to tackle. He and I are alike in that way. "Raphael, leave the door for now. We need you interrogating too; otherwise, this process is going to take forever."

"But we need to stop the others from trying to escape," he argues.

"Every time someone tries to escape, make them the next person in the seat. You can freeze them on the spot with your magic." Peter's ever-practical words have Dad and Raphael looking kind of sheepish.

"Thank you, Peter." Jophial smiles indulgently, shooting Dad and Raphael an amused brow raise. "For smart men, they sure can be dumb. Now, would you like to come back with me? We've got Maggie with the others, and she's resting comfortably, but I expect she should wake soon."

Relief crosses his face, and a deep sigh escapes as tightness leaves his shoulders. "Yes, please, I'm no good to these guys at the moment anyway. I'd rather be with Maggie, looking after her. Sorry, Mav."

I shake my head, my own worry for Team Alpha and especially Mina giving me an all too perfect idea of how he must be feeling right now. "No, Peter, go. I completely understand. If I could be with my teammates, I would too."

He nods his thanks, and Jophial puts her hand on him, ready to portal, but before they go, she focuses on me. "The source also said that Mina is in Ferijen Realm and that the compound is invisible.

That's all they could tell me, but they hoped it would help you."

My heart races, excitement starting to bubble up along with something much too fickle and dangerous: hope. Finally, some information about our girl. Leaning forward, I kiss her on the cheek. "Thank you." She just smiles, and they disappear.

The elevator doors opening have the three of us looking up. Clementine steps out, followed by Zeph, who must be coming from the Menagerie. They both head toward us, but no one tries to escape this time. I guess it makes it all too obvious that they've got something to hide if they try. I'm just hoping most of them are innocent, hence the tense but oddly calm scene in the area.

"Did everything go okay?" I ask my teammate when they get to our group. He nods his head, looking a little disheveled.

"Yes, he was delirious and tried to fight me, but as soon as I got him into isolation and we pumped in fresh air, he started getting better immediately. I was just saying to Clementine that I think the prolonged exposure to a place with no magic made him more susceptible to the weaknesses of humans. If he had been at full power, he would have been fine, but there is a reason the CD prohibits them from staying on any of the planets. Apart from the fact that they risk exposing people to the possibility of magic and the temptation to abuse their powers, it's that their power wanes over time. Without an

Archangel to move him around, he was stranded, and no one around him had the plague he created, so he couldn't get any juice off of that."

"I agree with Zeph. It seems to make the most sense. He'll spend some time in the Menagerie as punishment, and then we will return him to Kolekin. Hopefully, with two less Archangels on Hammus' team, we'll see a downturn in magical beings turning up in the other worlds and the CD can go back to managing the beings within their own realms," Clementine continues, sounding more pleased than I'd be if I were in her shoes. There are still many more issues to solve. "But we still have a problem on Minzeon that needs to be dealt with, so if you guys are ready, I'll give you the run down, and you can head out."

"No," I tell her flatly, and she raises an unamused eyebrow.

"What do you mean, *no*?" She crosses her arms and taps her foot, every bit of her body telegraphing her displeasure. Dad and Raphael hide small smiles but don't say a word, and I'm not sure if they're amused that she's getting ticked off or if they're waiting for me to get my ass handed to me by a very pissed off Clementine.

"Minzeon is going to have to wait. We're going after Mina first."

She tries to argue, but I stand my ground, Zeph coming to stand beside me in solidarity. With so much of our team down for the count, their survival relying on Mina's return, there's no question that she needs to be our priority. We might not be her mates yet, but we love her all the same, and we won't let her and our teammates down when they need us most.

"Respectfully, ma'am, half our team lies in an induced coma because their bond to Mina is broken. We need to fix us first so that we can help you. Two members of Team Alpha are not enough. We were lucky that Wen Shen was sick and on his own, or we likely wouldn't have stood a chance. If we come up against a full-powered being or AoA soldiers, I'd feel better to have my team by my side. Not to mention all the things they could be doing to Mina while we wait. So, no, we're going to Ferijen."

She looks confused for a moment, and it becomes clear that Jophial came straight to us. "Why there?"

"Jophial's source said that's where she's being held, in an invisible compound filled with Sabboath's troops, some willing and some not. So we're going in. Actually, I think we should dig around in Reorniel or Sainsiel's heads for the exact location; surely they would know it."

"I'll do it," a booming voice says from across the room. We turn back to the interrogation area, and Uriel is just releasing his latest suspect. The guy must be cleared because he wobbles away a little dazed, heading toward the elevator and freedom.

"Let me pry open one of their brains! I'll crack

them like a walnut." He strides over, the gold tips of his black wings shivering in agitation. "I agree with Mavromichali." He claps me on the shoulder, but I hold my ground, a feat that isn't easy when someone as big as Uriel makes contact. "Both of my children are suffering, and there's no telling what Sabboath might be able to do if he has Mina at his mercy for too long. She's our priority."

A bright flash of light fills the room, and when it clears, Lucifer and Michael are standing there, slightly apart and neither acknowledging the other. Lucifer is in full demon form, wearing a fitted black bodysuit. Everyone waiting to have their minds read bursts into whispers, questions flying around the room as no one had expected to see a demon arrive. The general vibe seems to be curious; if there's any hostility, they're holding it in while we're in earshot.

"Oh shit," mutters Dad as they come closer, warily eyeing the distance between them. "They must be over the lust segment of this program, and they've moved on to the blaming each other segment."

Both of them shoot him a look of annoyance but ignore his words.

"Yes, and we have to worry about what she's feeding on, if anything," Lucifer reminds us, having overheard the last of Uriel's words. "If her succubus takes over, the men and women of that complex won't be able to help themselves, and to be honest, neither will Mina. The defense mechanism takes over, and she will take what she can get without a care in her mind until she is finally filled again, and then the guilt and horror will kick in."

Michael pales with her words and runs a hand through his hair, looking the most unsettled we've seen him so far. "Fuck."

Clementine blows out a resigned sigh, but I don't really give a fuck what she thinks either way. It's not like she could stop us, not with the dads and Lucifer on our side.

"Okay, Uriel, head down to the Menagerie and get what you need from one of those traitors. Mav and Zeph, grab something to eat, so you can keep your strength up, and as soon as he returns with information, head to Ferijen."

"We're coming too," Michael starts to insist, but Lucifer puts a hand on him. The Archangel almost startles, clearly not expecting her to have reached out, but the contact accomplishes what she wanted. His eyes are only on her.

"No, Michael, that's not something you want to see your daughter doing if she's that far gone. Let the boys handle it. I trust them, and you should too. Pretty sure these two are going to join the ranks of son-in-laws, like the others have, as soon as they get a chance." Lucifer casually talks about us bonding with her daughter like it's not an issue, but both Zeph and I step back as all that information runs through Michael's head. Hell hath no fury like an Archangel with decades of protective dad duty to make up for. A scowl wrinkles his forehead, and the room rattles like an earthquake has struck, the waiting CD members shouting and screaming as they try to find something to hold onto, but Lucifer calmly runs her hand up and down his arm, and the shaking and rumbling stops. He nods but doesn't say a word.

"Phew, thought we were fucking dead," Zeph whispers in my head, echoing the relief that I feel.

"No shit. Thank fuck for Siffa," I reply, immeasurably grateful for Mina's very open-minded mother.

Uriel disappears with a wicked grin on his face as Michael turns in a flash of gold and white wings, storming over to the interrogation area and shouting, "Next!"

Clementine blanches and turns to Lucifer with pleading eyes. Right now, with everything Michael must be feeling, Lucifer is our ace to keeping Michael even somewhat level.

"Oh dear, I better make sure he doesn't turn anyone's brain to mush," Lucifer rushes out as she hurries after her mate.

Dad waves a hand, and a table laden with food appears in a quiet corner, two chairs set up for us. "Go and refuel," he tells us both, "and be ready for when Uriel gets back." My dad's grin changes from indulgent and encouraging into something bloodthirsty that almost makes me wince, and I know the next words out of his mouth won't be good for someone. "But don't hurry, I'm sure he's going to make the most of being allowed to play with them a while." Raphael just rolls his eyes, and they both head back to the interrogation area, discussing options for the AoA prisoners.

Moving over to the out of the way table and chairs, I retract my wings, my back aching from having them out so long. It's certainly something I need to rebuild tolerance for, and with our heritage now being public knowledge, I guess I'll get used to it quickly. Zeph does the same and blows out a relieved sigh before taking a seat.

I join him in the other seat and look at the two plates on the table. Piled onto each plate are thick slices of roast meat, vegetables, and gravy. My stomach grumbles with excitement, and Zeph laughs. We both make quick work of the food, not talking, just listening to the sounds around us. Since the initial excitement when Michael and Lucifer arrived, the crowd has stayed mostly quiet. Even the few more that have joined the others in the bubble are resigned to their fate. Plus, it doesn't hurt that Michael basically created a mini-earthquake a few minutes ago. The dads are all intimidating, but Michael's uneasy edge just exudes a sense of danger.

Zeph waves a hand, and a privacy bubble goes up around us, blocking people from sight and sound.

"How are you doing?" he asks, watching me closely for my response. I wipe my mouth with the provided napkin and lean back, picking up my untouched drink. Taking a large sip, I cough and splutter violently when it burns on the way down, and I realize it's not water but whiskey. Zeph jumps up and smacks me on the back a couple of times before returning to his seat.

Getting myself together, I think about his question. "To be honest, I'm not sure. My brain is filled with chaos and turmoil, and normally I would be asking to go to Eternal Damnation to take care of it, but now, with the thought of going after Mina and getting her back, I don't want to waste time. The importance of our mission is enough that I'm able to push it back. Not let it overtake me like it has in the past."

At this, Zeph looks slightly disappointed. Unlike me, who needs to both be in control but also sometimes be controlled, Zeph is all Dom, and I know he enjoys it when I need the pain to push my mind to calm. There's a darkness in him that I recognize, and I know he's particularly drawn to me, my relative indestructibility turning him on and reassuring him that I will be fine if he pushes it too far. He's never crossed the line, at least not without my permission, but there's a part of him that wants to, I think, and I know our sessions together give us both something we need.

"I'm pretty sure once we get Mina and the team back together, I'm going to need your help. There will be nothing to hold all of that back then, and, well, it needs to be dealt with. Maybe Mina can come with us? I can't wait to show her all the delights of Eternal Damnation. She will be such an eager student." His eyes widen with pleasure at the thought, nostrils flaring as he nods his agreement. Maybe it should feel weird that we don't know if she's even still alive and we're planning out our first sexual encounter, but I can't keep functioning in a world where I think she's been lost to us. I have to think about a future with her in it because that's what's keeping me upright and moving forward right now.

Changing the subject because my cock has started to get too interested in this conversation, I ask him about Ferijen.

"Where do you think we should start looking?" It's not a huge realm, but it's creepy as fuck, and with all that mist and darkness, Sabboath's lab would be really easy to miss, especially if it's invisible."

"Well, hopefully, we won't have to look. Hopefully, Uriel will pluck the location right out of those assholes' brains," Zeph replies, almost baring his teeth as he thinks about the traitorous Archangels.

"I can't believe you doubt me." A growly voice has us both jumping out of our skin as Uriel materializes directly into our bubble. His arms are crossed, and he looks smug as fuck... Is that a bit of blood dripping off some of his feathers?

He must see what I'm staring at because he

turns his head to look. With a grimace, he waves his hand, and it disappears before looking back at us, this time slightly sheepish. "Let's keep that blood between us, hey?" he suggests, an almost blush lightly coloring his cheeks.

"Blood? What blood?" I reply, and a wide grin crosses his face as he slaps me on the back. "You're good boys. Anyway, here's the location." He leans forward and puts a hand to each of our foreheads. An electrical sensation tingles from my head through my limbs as his power floods into my skull. A picture forms in our minds, giving us enough detail to safely teleport there. The compound can be seen, but a forcefield of some kind surrounds it. That must be the invisibility barrier, but having the Archangel's memory is allowing us to see through the illusion.

"Aim inside the barrier," he tells me, his words the voiceover to a bunny hopping into the force field and disintegrating on impact. I wrinkle my nose as the memory of the smell is also transmitted. "There are no patrols of the outside because they're confident that only an Archangel can bring someone in and out. Apparently, portals can't even be opened from the inside." He starts to grumble in disgust. "Sainsiel and Reorniel were basically glorified taxis, shuffling his troops here and there as needed. What a waste."

"Alright. Good luck. Bring our Mina back to us in one piece, or your future father-in-law might just lose his shit and kill you." He waves his hand, dropping the privacy bubble, and walks away, whistling with happiness.

"I guess torture makes him happy," Zeph says with a laugh before looking at me. "Are you ready?"

"Yes, let's do this. Let's get Mina back."

Chapter Seventeen

Samuel

The sexual fog in my mind clears, and when I focus on my surroundings, I find myself standing in front of Mina.

"Mina?" I ask in confusion, stumbling backward and away from her, and a look of surprise covers her face. Fuck, that's right; she doesn't recognize me. Looking around the room, I'm surprised to see her cell is very different from the last time I was in it. Gone is the disgusting bucket and moldy, rusty cot, replaced with sumptuous bedding and an actual bathroom. Needing five minutes to work out what happened, I stalk toward the bathroom, stopping in front of the mirror. My new reflection is still jarring, and I stare fixedly at the image that meets me. Around my neck is a collar like Mina's. *Is it strictly for show, or does Sabboath now have another way to keep me under his thumb?*

The smell of sex and blood fogs my mind as a riot of unanswered questions swirls and my stomach rolls with nausea. Confusion has me blinking my eyes and shaking my head to clear it so I can form some kind of coherent thought as my gaze takes in my naked body. The taste of her in my mouth and scent of her on my face is distracting, so, turning on the taps, I cup my hands beneath the water. Allowing them to fill for a moment, I splash my face, washing away the tantalizing smell and flavor.

The cold water is a shock to the system, helping bring some clarity to my confusion. *Did I just rape Mina?* Dread flows through my body, a shiver flowing down my spine as snippets of her begging me to stop flash into my mind. Horror comes with the realization that I had indeed taken her by force. *But how did this happen? How did I get here?* I stumble away from the sink, pacing back and forth across the small room, trying to regain more of my memories.

Flashes of scenes filter through my brain, quick moments of blinding pain, the sound of fists meeting flesh, and the whistle of a whip as it flies through the air. He'd had an older team of soldiers rough me up to make it look authentic for Mina, but they got a little carried away. Higher up in the organization with definite hate for demons, they're the ones who complained about Archangels having children and rallied to put a stop to it. Jealous and petty and perfect soldiers for AoA, just the kind of people Hammus and Sabboath needed to join their cause. Elitist snobs with a dangerous hunger for violence, they remain "untainted," unwilling to take Sabboath's serum until new, more powerful strains are created. They don't want to be inferior shapeshifters; they want the power and glory that they think the Archangels have.

As I think about what happened before now, I fuzzily remember Sabboath injecting me with something, saying, "This should guarantee his reaction to her and hopefully kick start breeding my new army." My stomach churns at that word, *breeding*. As if Mina were just some kind of animal and not a powerful being in her own right. *Just what did he make me do?*

Like a movie reel, my memories flow from flashes of violence to a completely different scene. My cock sinking into Mina's wet heat, grunts and groans escaping us both almost violently as I fill her with my seed. I lift my head, looking at my reflection in horror, the memory of her asking me to stop flaring most brightly in my mind.

"What have I done?" I practically whisper, my knees threatening to give out, to drop me to the floor. Guilt flows through me, and I shudder in disgust. *There's no way she's ever going to forgive me now.*

"Ah, are you okay?" Mina calls from back in the cell, her voice hesitant and unsure.

Turning from my reflection, I stomp back out of the bathroom, and she backs up very quickly as she sees me approach, immediately halting my movements.

I drop to my knees in devastation. *She's frightened of me.*

"God, I'm sorry. I don't know what happened; I'd never have taken you without your permission. I feel sick," I apologize, my voice breaking over the words. Her eyes widen, and she holds up her hand, shaking her head as she walks over to me. There's no recognition in her gaze, but she lowers herself, grabbing my hands.

"No, don't apologize! It's okay. I've just recently gone through transition too. It's common not to be in your right mind when it happens," she reassures softly, squeezing my hand, and my mind just boggles at this gorgeous, compassionate woman.

"But I practically raped you," I hiss at her in frustration, and she *laughs.*

"You *were* quite insistent, and there wasn't much I could do to stop you, but unlike me who had people volunteer to help me through my transition, you had no one. You had to make do with what was around, and I completely understand that. I just didn't want you to regret it after it was over. Like you are now. Plus, I like sex, and you're pretty damn good at it." She winks, trying to make me feel better, and my heart sinks even more. That's certainly not going to be her reaction when she realizes the truth.

She must see the guilt in my face because her hold tightens as though she's trying to keep my mind anchored to the present instead of falling into my self-doubt. "You said my name before; how do you know it? I'm afraid I don't recognize you, but then I don't know many demons yet," she apologizes, her curiosity taking over though her voice remains soft. It's almost like she feels bad that she doesn't know who I am.

Fuck, what should I tell her? I jump up again and pace back and forth across the room, my eye catching on the camera. I lunge at her, pulling her in close like I'm trying to bite her. She struggles but shortly stills as I start whispering.

"There's a camera, and we're being watched, but there are some things I need to tell you that they can't overhear. So, what we're going to do is have a mock fight." She pretends to struggle a little more, and I hold her tight, throwing my head back and growling, making sure the camera catches my fangs before dropping my head again.

"I'm going to throw you on the bed, where those curtains will surround us, and then they won't be able to see anything. I'm also hoping it will muffle the sound." She nods slightly in agreement and pushes me away, her lip curling in a snarl that anyone who doesn't know her might believe.

"Stop! I asked you a question," she insists, sounding annoyed. "I'd like to know your name before we go any further."

I growl and stalk toward her, pretending to be out of control again, which isn't far from the truth. Knowing what's about to happen has agitated my inner animals, the creatures finally making themselves known again now that the transition fog has cleared. Both are shouting for their mate, demanding to get a turn at biting her, but I have to tell them to settle and that now is not the time. But fuck, the angry bastards are not happy, and both are letting me know. My head pounds with their fury as they slam up against the metaphysical barriers that contain them, trying to force a shift. I grit my teeth and hold strong, my demon not willing to give up form so soon after my transition.

As I reach her, she puts her fists up and socks me in the jaw, which hurts, but that's all she can do because I'm bigger, and her collar doesn't allow her to do anything else.

I consider teleporting us out of that cell right now, but I'm not entirely sure that the collar I'm wearing is just for show, and I also have no idea how Mina's would react if I did. It could very well be programmed to blow her head off if she leaves the barrier. No, we need to figure out how to remove it before we do that.

Grabbing her around the waist, I put her over my shoulder and stomp toward the bed. She pummels my back in a show of defiance, but it doesn't really hurt. I've been struck by worse during training exercises. Flinging open the thick curtains, I throw her onto the bed and quickly pounce on her to keep her in place, the curtains flowing closed behind us. Whispering in her ear, I start talking.

"Look, we're going to have to make movements like I'm fucking you and some noises so he doesn't get suspicious and come and investigate. She nods her head, and I roll off her, shaking the bed as I do. "We'll just keep moving around; that should look authentic."

"Oh wait, please, just wait," she shouts for the camera, her eyes twinkling with the deception. My mouth lifts in a small smile, but I'm sure her mood is about to change.

Lying on my stomach, I look her in the eye as she moans again. Fuck, that's not helping my cock, who is very much enjoying how she sounds, but I ignore it.

"You asked how I knew your name," I murmur, and she nods her head while rocking back and forth, still enjoying the charade.

"You know we could just fuck again, and then we wouldn't have to pretend," she suggests. Her eyes are bright, and that scent that is uniquely Mina starts to fill the tiny space, forcing a groan past my lips.

"I really don't think you'll feel the same way when you find out who I am, so we should probably put a pin in that idea."

She frowns at my words and stops what she's doing. "Why do you say that?"

"Because I haven't been very kind to you over the years. Now explain to me how I change back to my normal form," I ask, and she sits up straight, throwing her hand over her mouth.

"Silas?" she asks in horror, and I burst out laughing.

"No, not Silas. He's dead; I killed him during my transition." A blinding smile crosses her face, and she throws her arms around me, hugging me tightly.

"I don't care who you are; you just made my day! That's awesome. Filthy pig deserved it." She sits back, a contemplative look on her face as she tries to explain something she only just learned. "Okay... so, it's like pushing your demon form down and sprinkling your other form over it. It's all in the mind, so you have to imagine the process. What I do is imagine my demon form fading and my human form appearing. That's about all there is to it."

I breathe out a big sigh and grab her hand with a gentle squeeze. "Okay, promise you won't go anywhere until we've talked?" She nods her head, and I close my eyes, trying to picture it in my mind.

First, I imagine the demon form I've recently come to possess. The big black guy from the mirror that looks nothing like the original me. Bit by bit, I make his demon features disappear. First the tail and horns disappear, and then the fangs and claws. Next, my skin color fades before being replaced by my normal tone. Once the extras are gone, I imagine what's left transitioning back to my original body and features. There's almost a tingling feeling, so I know something's happening. Hope I don't accidentally give myself a third eye or some crazy shit like that.

She jumps up and down on the bed and shouts out more sex noises while I'm doing this. *At least pretend me seems to be doing a good job.*

"Christ, Mina, can you stop? I can't concentrate when you sound like that," I hiss at her, and she complies almost immediately.

"Sorry," she quickly replies, but the apology is practically smothered by a laugh that renders the word meaningless. I hope it's not the last one I hear for a while.

My inner animals are sending me encouragement, and it's only then that I realize it's almost the same process as shifting. A wave of power flows over my body, and when I hear Mina gasp, I know I've been successful.

"Sam? *What the fuck?*" I open my eyes to find her staring at me in horror with a look that I haven't seen since we were younger. We broke Maggie's prize crystal vase when we were messing around and wrestling one another. This was before Connie came into our lives and things were still okay between us. That time, the horror had faded away into a gleam of excitement as we fought over who would take the blame and Maggie's wrath. I have the feeling that this time won't end nearly as well.

"You're a demon! *How* are you a demon?" she

babbles in shock before she makes a fist and slams it into my face, knocking me backward. I tumble across the bed and just manage to stop myself from falling through the curtains and into the camera's view. Sabboath would kill me if he knew I was showing Mina who I really was. Rubbing my jaw, I wince at the pain this time. My ears are ringing, and I'm seeing stars. *Fuck, she can pack a punch when she's motivated.* I move back on the bed carefully, hoping that a slow approach might keep her calm.

"Fine, I deserved that, and you can tell me off, but can we keep the volume to a whisper? I'm a dead man if he hears what I'm saying."

She rolls her eyes at me and growls, "Like I fucking care! You're a fucking traitor, Sam. You chose Connie over us. How could you do that to the team *and me*? We're your family; she is nothing, and watching you fucking change as I hung there in pain broke my heart, goddamn it. And what the fuck is with that? That's not something Archangels can do." She starts smacking me as tears trickle down her cheek, each blow half-hearted as though she's too upset to even focus her energy into another proper hit. "And I just fucked you! Ewww, god, I hope she hasn't given us a disease."

I grab hold of her hands to stop her from hitting me. "Quiet, for god's sake, they'll hear you. And we can't get diseases," I remind her, but I guess that wasn't the right thing to do since her eyes turn furious, a fiery glow nearly lighting up the space between us.

"Really, that's the thing you choose to focus on?" She keeps hitting me.

I swallow hard. *Ah, yeah, maybe not the smartest decision.* Figuring I need to stop her assault so that she might actually hear what I need to say, I haul her into my lap so I can whisper, "I didn't choose Connie over you, and I'm not a traitor. When I realized that Connie was influencing me, I went to the council. The dads and Mylea confirmed it, but they also said I was in a unique position to get on the inside of the AoA and asked me to continue the way things were going. Mylea did give me protection against Connie's continued influence, but that doesn't extend to Sabboath's experiments, unfortunately." She pulls away so she can look me in the eyes, her mouth wide with shock, but at least she lets me continue.

"Sabboath injected me with his latest formula, and it's given me the ability to shift into most realm beings and use their magic, but he also infected me with demonic essence, four different types, and I went through my transition. He promised that the extra hunger shouldn't affect me, but that was obviously a lie." I lower my head in shame. "I'm sorry. I wasn't able to control myself... I didn't even realize what was happening until it was over."

She's frowning and shaking her head, trying to process all that I've just told her. But before she can say anything, I finish the story, not skipping any of the important bits, though I can't hold back my grimace when I get to the part where he hopes I'll impregnate her.

She screws up her nose at my words, rolling her eyes. "Yes, he's already shared that information with me and tried with the last meal he gave me."

"Last meal?" Now it's my turn for confusion.

"Yeah, he served his pet dragon up to me on a plate." She glances down at the space between us as though she's embarrassed, and the memory of him saying that trickles into my brain. "I was so hungry from not feeding, my succubus took over, and *things* happened."

A growl escapes my mouth, her head shooting up in surprise. "That sounded like the wolf you were before."

I nod my head, a sheepish smile taking over. "Yes, he isn't happy about you fucking the dragon; he's jealous. And so is the tiger."

She frowns at my words, her eyes narrowing. "Well, tell him to shut the hell up. He has no right!" She sounds angry, and I decide not to tell her that they think she's their mate. A moment later, her eyes widen in surprise as she realizes something.

"*Tiger?*" she gasps in comprehension. "You were the one who stopped me from getting away. You can shift into more than one animal, too?"

I nod my head again, confirming both things, and she slaps me across the face this time before continuing. "Thanks a lot, asshole. That bitch's boot to the head fucking hurt, not to mention all the shit I've been through since." Her voice rises the angrier she gets, and I slap my hand over her mouth, shaking the bed back and forth with my knees. Her eyes shoot daggers at me the whole time, but she doesn't fight it. When I take my hand away, she's quieter but no less angry.

"Double agent or not, you still hurt our team. You could have told us all! We would have supported you." I shake my head sadly, the pain of hurting everyone welling up inside me once more.

"I was told not to. They said your reactions needed to be authentic and that Mav or one of the others would have wanted to help, but it would have been too suspicious." Her eyes narrow as she thinks about my words, and she reluctantly nods.

"Yeah, okay, you might be right, but that still doesn't make it any better."

I look down at my hands, clenching them into fists to stop from reaching out to her. That last statement was soft, vulnerable, and now that I'm beyond Connie's influence, my feelings for Mina are free. There's a part of me, of just Sam, that wants nothing more than to comfort her right now even though I'm the cause of her pain. "No, I know. I just hope that you will all forgive me one day."

She doesn't say anything, just changes the subject, and my heart sinks with acceptance. It's going to take more than a few words to make up for everything I've done.

She gasps out loud all of a sudden and won't meet my eyes. "I had sex with you. Really good sex with you," she chokes out, sounding a little surprised. *Well, that's a blow to the ego.*

I snort at her words but don't say anything; I don't think she was expecting me to say anything. Plus, my track record of saying the right thing definitely isn't in my favor at the moment. She makes her hands into fists and pummels my chest with them furiously. "How dare you have good sex with me while I'm so fucking angry with you!" she snarls, her lips curled back to expose her razor sharp fangs.

"We could have sex again; angry sex is hot," I suggest with an exaggerated eyebrow wiggle, trying to make light of the situation. Completely not the reaction I intended, now there's a tear running down her face. *Holy hell.* I pull her flying arms to her sides and yank her into a tight hug.

"I'm so sorry, Mina," I whisper. "That's not what I wanted our first time to be like." Before she can say anything, I hear footsteps approaching and voices yelling.

"Quick, change into demon form again!" Mina urges me. "Then take off your clothes and pull up the blankets," she instructs, quickly yanking off her own clothes. My eyes drop to her breasts, and my cock comes to full attention.

She smacks me again to get my attention, messing up the bedsheets before climbing under.

"Hurry up," she hisses, and I force the change, following her directions in record time. "You're supposed to be mindless during transition. That's what they'll be expecting, so bite me and pretend like you're fucking me." Before I can even think about her words, she shoves her ass into my cock and wraps my arms around her like I'm spooning her, exposing her neck to me. I grunt as her ass rubs deliciously against my painfully hard cock, and the thought that I could quite easily slip in between those cheeks and slide into her wet folds... Well, it doesn't make my cock situation any easier. She slaps my chest lightly, the contact meant to get my attention, not hurt.

"Get it together. Bite me before they get here, and don't seal the holes. Let them see the blood."

"I've never bitten anyone. Well, I have, but I don't remember it very well," I tell her, ashamed at the foggy memory of ripping out Silas' throat. I know she said she was glad that he was dead, but there's a part of me that is going to struggle with how brutally I ended his life.

"Well, you'll probably cum, I always do, but there's nothing we can do about it now. It'll look more authentic if you do. Now, listen to the sound of my heartbeat, and if it starts to slow, stop. We'll probably be interrupted before then because demons can feed on one another a lot before it becomes a problem." She grabs my head and forces it to her neck just as the door to our cell opens.

Without any more hesitation, I plunge my fangs into her throat before removing them and latching onto the holes I've left behind. Her blood fills my mouth, sweet and seductive, much like her, and I start to drink while my dick grinds into her ass from behind. Her moans fill my ears, and she squirms with what I know is her impending orgasm. The cell door creaks open, and she screams out loud just as my own orgasm explodes through me, covering her back with my cum. As I continue to swallow and ride out my orgasm, the brocade curtains are yanked back and Sabboath peers in with a leer. Mina screams and yanks the covers up over us as he cackles his joy, not one bit of suspicion in his eyes, thank god.

"Oh, Mina, you are a hungry beast, and I see so is your friend. Well, I brought you two more to snack on. Have fun, my dear."

He backs away, leaving the curtains open, and I watch as Mina carefully looks over the side of the bed. My cum drying on her back causes my animals to growl and chuff in delight. Their pleasure fills me upon seeing her covered with our scent and seed, warning off others.

A gasp of shock from her has me coming to my senses and moving to see what the problem is. My heart sinks when I see who the new prisoners are. *Fuck.*

Chapter Eighteen

Zephaniah

Mav and I teleport into a shaded corner of the hidden compound, Uriel's information working perfectly. Hiding behind the side of the building, we watch as a couple of soldiers patrol the perimeter just inside the barrier. Why, I'm not sure, considering nothing can get in or out, but maybe it's just to keep them busy.

I can tell they're both ABs, but I don't recognize either of them, so I'm guessing they were in a different year at the academy than us. Either that, or they're just a couple that didn't make the cut since I've never seen them on active teams.

"How about we draw their attention and knock them out then strip them of their uniforms? We can send them back to the CD, so they can't sound the alarm if they wake up before we're done," I suggest to Mav, nodding at the two not far away.

"Good idea," he replies, sounding more settled than he has in days. Bending down and picking up a rock sitting at the base of the wall, he pitches it at

them. It hits one in the back, the guard jumping as though he's been hit with a bullet and not just a pebble.

"Shit, what was that?" he shouts, looking around. We wait for them to investigate, but they both look a little freaked out, not moving from where they are.

Mav rolls his eyes at me. *"Wow, AoA has some really brave soldiers."*

"From what Mom said, I don't think a lot of them are here voluntarily," I remind him, and he nods his acknowledgment. It doesn't change what we have to do right now, but it would account for the reason they seem afraid of their own shadows. They have fear for their lives driving their participation in AoA's plot, not a diehard belief in what the organization is doing.

"Dude, this realm is so fucking spooky. Do you think something is inside the barrier with us?" the one who didn't get hit asks, his hand on the gun at his hip, which looks suspiciously identical to our CD-issued weapons. Sabboath must have stolen or copied them since he's had open access to the CD for so long.

I pull my wings back in and wave my hand, changing my uniform to look like theirs. That's easier than stripping them, especially since they're a lot more paranoid than I thought they'd be; this could potentially get messy. Mav follows my lead, and we just barely step out from the corner, letting the guys get a glimpse of us but not enough to make them feel immediately unsettled.

"Hey, have you got the time?" I shout out, waving them over to us. They both look relieved to see someone else around as they oblige, not a hint of suspicion in their eyes. Hopefully, they don't recognize Mav and me from the CD or the academy when they get a closer look. Neither of us does a lot of socializing in our downtime unless it's in the dungeon at Eternal Damnation, so I think we're probably safe. *But with the way our luck has gone lately...*

They get to us, looking much too friendly for their own good, and before either can say anything, we knock them both out with one punch to the temple. They fall to the ground, and I wave my hand, conjuring some bindings and securing them. I'm about to send them to the portal room, but Mav holds up his hand. He grabs the two access cards they have hanging on their belts, giving me one before attaching the other to his belt.

"Hang on, let me see if I can do what Uriel did and get a location for Mina or any kind of information that may be useful."

I agree and watch as he puts a hand on one of their heads. He closes his eyes, and his hand starts to glow. His forehead wrinkles as I feel him struggle with the power. There's a fine line between sifting through a mind or barreling through like a mac truck. None of us have tried this sort of thing before since it's one of those Archangel powers we're not 'supposed' to have.

"Okay, they're pretty low on the totem pole. They've heard some rumors about a captive in the dungeon who is quite valuable, but that's the extent of their info. That must be Mina," Mav tells me, his eyes lighting up with excitement.

"Can you get a location on the dungeon?" I ask him, waiting as he continues to sift through the guard's brain.

"He's never been there, but I've got a location because every time the dumbass walks past the door that leads to it, he wonders about what it's like down there. It's tucked away out of sight, so we have to go through a couple of densely populated areas before we get to it." He takes his hand off the guy's head and waves his hand, sending them to the Collectors Division.

"Dad, can you put them in the Menagerie?" I telepath him.

"Sure can. Be careful," he responds.

Luckily, all our powers still work in the barrier; I guess if Sabboath didn't want his own, Reorniel, or Sainsiel's powers to be stifled, he couldn't put measures in place that would stifle an Archangel's skills.

But if we can use ours, why can't Mina use hers? I've got a nagging feeling that the rest of this rescue mission is not going to be as easy as it's starting off.

"Ok, let's go. We'll keep our heads down and

try not to talk to anyone. I pulled some more information out of that guy's head, so if we get questioned, let me do the talking," he cautions, and I'm happy for him to take the lead on this.

I follow him around the side of the building. Shaped like a box with very few windows that I can see, we enter through the front doors—swiping our stolen cards to allow us entry.

Keeping my head down, I discreetly look around the room. I notice the cameras that are spaced all around the entry, which doesn't seem to be guarded.

"Cameras everywhere," I warn him, and he too keeps his head down.

He leads the way through the compound. As we get further in, we start to come across more people, but nobody pays any attention to us, happy to ignore us and keep doing whatever they're doing. It's not until we get to a rowdy cafeteria that things become a problem.

Stepping through a set of double doors, we stand off to the side and look around. The smell of greasy food and beer permeates the air, and a crowded table of white-winged angels are holding court in the center of the room. Loud and obnoxious, they're catcalling and bullying other nearby tables filled with what I can sense are ABs. All of whom are trying to ignore them and just eat in peace and quiet.

"What a bunch of assholes," Mav's drawls, and I

nod my agreement. They're what I expect of a typical member of AoA, the arrogance and superiority wafting off them in an almost tangible way.

We watch as a winged female AB gets up from the table and makes her way to a dirty dishes station, carrying her tray with her empty plate. Unfortunately, she has to pass their table to get to it, and she doesn't get very far before they interfere, surrounding her like a bunch of predators.

"Fuck, what do they think this is, high school?" Mav growls, his fists clenching at his sides, but my eyes are drawn back to what's happening.

Like the bullies they are, they get in close, their words crude and demeaning. From what I can hear, there aren't as many females as males in the compound, and they think this one should accommodate the group of them.

"Does she look familiar to you?" I ask Mav, the girl's features catching my eye. She's quite pretty, with red hair and a smattering of freckles across her face. Suddenly, the situation worsens, the angels surrounding her not keeping their hands to themselves, reaching for her, their hands groping her breasts and ass.

"Yeah, I think she's one of the girls that was in Mina's year. Was chosen for Echo," he replies.

She pleads for them to stop, but they don't listen. Taking the tray from her hands, they start to herd her toward another door.

"Where does that go?" I ask Mav.

"Bedrooms," he growls in response and takes off in the group's direction.

Fuck! I should have known he wasn't going to be able to stay out of it. Mav has that real white knight complex, always rushing in to defend someone. Bar fights are a regular occurrence on a night out with Mav. Heaven help you if you harass a woman after she's said no. Always ready to defend the underdog. It's one of the things I like about him the most... at least when we're not in the middle of a likely life-threatening mission.

I hurry after him, but it's too late. He's already launched himself over the mess, pushed the girl out of the way, and started swinging at heads. They're exchanging blows, all six of them now focusing their attack on him. So, shaking my head, I join in, knowing that there's a good chance we've blown our cover. *Mina never would have been able to just watch and let it happen either*, I tell myself, knowing that's the one good thing about this. She might say that we messed up by blowing our cover, but she wouldn't regret that we tried to help the girl.

Without missing a beat, I push one or two out of the melee, making it fairer for him, but with a feral grin on his face and excitement lighting his eyes, I'd say he's actually enjoying the brawl. I try to keep it so he only has to deal with three at a time while I occupy the other three. Eventually, they start to tire, not being as combat fit as Mav and I are, and he manages to knock one or two unconscious before one of them grunts.

"Hey, I know you! You're a member of Team Alpha. Fuck, how did you get in here? I know they managed to recruit one of you, but I didn't realize they had another one." His voice is surprised, and Mav looks the same at the mention of Sam before a scowl quickly crosses his face.

Before he can put a foot in it by swearing about Sam, I step in. "Ah yeah, Team Alpha was filled with a bunch of pussies. Mav and I decided that the AoA way was more suited to our needs."

The four angels eye us with caution, but at my words, their faces perk up. One holds out a hand for a fist pump, all the fighting seemingly forgotten in that moment.

"Right on, man. Gays and demon freaks are all that remains of Alpha now since you guys have joined us. They'll be quick and easy to take care of." Mav indulges him and bumps his fist, but the scowl doesn't move off of his face. The angel talking to us starts to look a little nervous, though whether that's strictly based on Mav's expression or him now knowing our identities, I can't be sure.

"Okay, well, if you wanted first shot at the bitch, all you had to do was say so." The mouthpiece of the group gestures in the direction that the girl had fled. "We can wait for our turn."

A growl escapes Mav's mouth, and the angels all back away slightly. They move back to their table, sitting down and grabbing their forgotten about drinks. Mav and I stand there awkwardly, caught off guard that although we've been identified, the angels were too stupid to consider that we might not be telling them the truth.

"Fuck, we need to get out of here," he grunts, looking around the room for an excuse.

"Yes, we do, you moron. Next time think before you dive in," I throw back at him. Before we can make our move, one of them starts to speak again.

"Being a part of the AoA is a rush, man. We get to do whatever we want when we want it, just like with that girl there. Sabboath doesn't care what we do or who we do it to." The surrounding angels send up jeers of agreement at the asshole's words. "Seriously, none of the rule following crap here like they have at the CD. Those damn ABs get all the glory protecting Reath from realm beings even though we know they're inferior to us." He looks to Mav and me, his eyes widening before he clears his throat. "No offense intended," he grumbles, sounding like a petulant child instead of the grown ass adult he is. He quickly changes the subject.

"So... are we going to get to beat you guys too? Are you taking the same formula Samuel did?"

"What the fuck is he talking about?" Mav asks, sounding frustrated, and I know how he feels.

"I have no idea. But I do have an idea about getting out of here. Just play along."

"Well, we were looking for Sam; we were told he was going to get us up to speed on everything."

Their eyebrows all raise, looks of comprehension crossing their faces. "Oh yeah, sounds smart. I think he's still downstairs with the whore, but they'll probably drag him out of there soon. Hope she hasn't sucked and fucked the life out of him." The group erupts into riotous laughter, and my blood begins boiling. Not just because they've called Mina a whore, but because now we know that she's locked up with *Sam*, our traitorous brother who doesn't deserve to even look at her.

"I wouldn't mind having the life sucked and fucked out of me by her. Have you seen it? What a way to go," another one announces to the group, and I can feel the tension in Mav go through the roof.

"They must be talking about Mina. What do they mean about Sam being with Mina and hoping she hasn't..." He grits his teeth, and I can practically see the steam coming out of his ears. *"Sucked and fucked the life out of him."*

"Who knows? But she's been here for days now, and you know how often she needs to feed. Maybe he volunteered," I remind him while the group continues to smack talk.

"Poor bastard is really taking one for the team. If that doesn't prove he's a team player, I'm not sure what will." After that comment and our awkward silence, the group finally realizes we're not laughing, and suspicion starts to bloom on their faces.

"You must know the bitch we're talking about; she was on your team as well," one of them pushes.

"Oh, you mean the demon bitch we got stuck with because Connie had to fake her death? We had no idea she was a demon; she was just a pretty thing for me and Zeph to plow on cold nights. Can't tell you how disgusted we were when we found out," Mav jeers, the scorn in his words believable enough that the tightness leaves their shoulders, but I can tell it almost killed him to say it.

"Fuck, if Mina ever finds out I said that, I'm a dead man," he groans to me in panic, and I almost let out a chuckle at the thought of this warrior being afraid of our Mina.

"Serious groveling will be needed, but I'm pretty sure you're safe." And, as fate would have it, a noise behind me has me eating my words.

"Is that right, Mavromichali? Well, I'm sure you and Zephaniah won't mind proving yourself to our cause then." Sabboath's tone is harsh, suspicious, and *slimy* as we both turn to face him.

Smug as fuck, he's standing there. His green wings are even shaggier than usual, his skin even more sickly than the last time we saw him. *"What's wrong with him? How was this not noticed sooner?"*

"Dark magic," Mav said, the weight of those words echoing in my brain. I plaster on a blank look and shrug my shoulders.

"Whatever you need us to do, Sabboath. We're tired of bowing down to the pompous assholes on the Archangel council and working with that pathetic team they saddled us with. When we both realized Sam had defected, we wanted to know where to sign up. We wanted to join the winning side. We were the ones ordered to place Sainsiel and Reorniel in the Menagerie, but instead of doing that, we had them teleport us here. They've both gone into hiding now, but they said to call on them when you're ready for the next phase," I tell him, lying through my teeth and hoping I've choked out just enough flattery for him to not think twice about my explanation.

He doesn't look like he believes me, but he also doesn't look like he wants to pass up the chance for two strong soldiers. "Ok, here's what's going to happen. I'm going to throw you in the cell with my very hungry demons. If you manage to survive that without them draining you dry, I'll pull you out and inject you with my new formula, same as Sam, making you better than you'll ever be as a plain AB."

Thank fuck we hid our wings before we came. He has no clue of our Archangel status, and it may be all that saves us.

Bowing my head in entirely fake deference, I answer, "Absolutely, whatever we need to do to prove ourselves." His eyes move to Mav, who still hasn't said anything, and I nudge him, getting the bare minimum of a nod in return. *Well, at least Sabboath never spent enough time around us to know what he's usually like.*

"Very well." He waves his hand, and instantly, I feel a heavy weight on my neck, the sensation of something just barely keeping from choking me. Moving my hands to it, I feel a metal collar, and when I try to telepath Mav, I'm blocked. *Crap, what else can these do?* Looking to Mav, I can see he has one as well.

"What are these?" I ask through gritted teeth, not wanting to give away how angry I am.

"Just a little insurance," he assures in what I think is meant to be a calming voice, wiggling his eyebrows in a way that looks utterly ridiculous. "Get them, boys."

The angels we were talking with all pounce on us, getting in a few good hits. We try to defend ourselves, but the collar seems to be zapping my strength. They quickly overpower us, working our bodies over enough that I know I'll be sore in the morning.

"Right, let's go and see if our beasts are still hungry. You've done such a good job, you can watch on the camera if you want. I'll place one inside the curtains since they managed to avoid the other one I have in there." This is said with a grumble, and they all laugh at his words, amused that their fearless leader was outsmarted by two demons.

"Right, this is what needs to happen. Mav and

Zeph, listen up. Mina is going to be my prize mare, so to speak, and I need her to be relaxed and docile so that my pet dragon can paralyze her. I need the opportunity to harvest all those lovely little eggs she has in her womb. I can then use your seed to fertilize them, creating the army of warriors that AoA will need to turn the tide in this war. I'm going to figure out a way to accelerate their growth so we don't have to wait years to make use of them. My biggest problem, I think, is I've been relying on inferior stock. You two and Sam are the best that the academy has to offer, and combined with that demon's heritage, I think we'll create something that's unstoppable."

His gaze narrows and he pins us with one look. "But if the two of you are playing me and betray me, I will make sure your death and Mina's death, once I've harvested as many eggs and sperm as possible, are the most excruciating experience you've ever had. And I will draw it out, starting with her, so that you can watch as she pays for your treachery." His words have me shivering with their intensity, and I have no doubt that he means everything he's saying.

Sabboath's mad scientist rant makes my stomach roll, not understanding how he could talk about her, even about us, as though we're just tools to be used. *How did he get so warped?*

"Feed her and feed her well, blood *and* sex, and when she finally falls asleep completely satisfied, then we can move on to the next part of the plan. Don't worry about the other demon. He's on our side and is like you, keeping the beast fed and compliant."

Another demon? I would have thought they'd rather die than be involved in anything with Hammus ever again. Whatever could he have promised this one to get him involved in the AoA? Or maybe it's a case of what could he have threatened him with...

We've been moving through the complex and down a set of stairs the whole time he's been talking, and as I crack open an eye, I see us approach a cell filled with an opulent brocade-enclosed bed. Sounds of passion come from inside the curtain, Mina's pheromones filling the air. Everyone in the group groans with arousal, the chemicals having an immediate effect.

Sabboath opens the cell, and we get tossed on the floor as Mina cries out loudly, my dick instantly erect, but her screams of passion are soon followed by one of shock as he whips open the curtains.

"Oh, Mina, you are a hungry beast, and I see so is your friend. Well, I brought you two more to snack on. Have fun, my dear." With that, he leaves us behind.

Chapter Nineteen

Jessamina

My eyes widen in shock at the sight that greets them. *What the fuck are Mav and Zeph doing here?* Not moving, I wait until Sabboath and his goons leave the cell and walk away. As soon as they're out of sight, I hiss at Sam, "Quick, wipe that stuff off my back, damn it."

A low rumbling sound comes from him, but I ignore it because at least he does what I asked. Searching around for the clothes that I hurriedly removed, I pull them back on before scrambling off the bed.

Both are still conscious but groaning in pain as they struggle to sit up, a gasp escaping my mouth when I notice that they too have been collared.

"Oh my god, are you okay? How did you get caught?" I help them both sit up before throwing my arms around each of them in a huge hug. "Are the others here too?" They exchange a glance before Zeph shakes his head.

"No, it's just us." He returns my hug, gripping me tightly, a sigh of relief leaving his mouth as he answers the rest of my questions. "We were okay until this dickhead decided to get involved in something that was none of our business." He stabs a finger at Mav in half-hearted annoyance, but Mav doesn't shy away, looking back at Zeph with a defiant stare. I pull away and put my hands on Mav's cheeks, eyeing a nasty cut above his eyebrow, which is healing very slowly due to the collar. Before I can ask any more questions, he wraps a hand around my hair and yanks my mouth onto his, his lips searing my own with a hot, quick kiss before pulling away.

"Hi," I whisper, the desire in his eyes melting my annoyance.

He smiles slightly before snapping back at Zeph, "Please, it was only going to be moments before you jumped in too. You wouldn't have let that woman get harassed either." He turns to me, explaining, "It was a girl I recognized from your graduating class."

I snort my disgust, unable to hold in my scorn for Silas' partner. Granted, she wasn't nearly as willing to abuse me as he was, but she's complicit in all of this. "Oh yeah, Beatrice, she's here too, fucking cow."

"Actually, she's just like me," a voice above us says, and my head turns in that direction. Crap, I'd forgotten about Sam.

"What do you mean?" But then it occurs to me

what he's trying to say, and my eyes light up in understanding. Before I can ask any more questions, he nods.

"Who the fuck are you?" Zeph interrupts with a growl, finally catching sight of him too. They both jump to their feet, moving me behind them.

This time I snort with amusement. "Fuck, you're never going to believe me unless you see it," I tell him quietly, and Sam just shrugs his shoulders.

"Fine, but they have to climb up on the bed so the cameras can't see it," he replies, and Mav and Zeph exchange glances.

"We heard Sabboath say he was going to put one just above the bed since you circumnavigated his other one by leaving the curtains closed." Mav's words are flat and unimpressed as his eyes run up and down the body of the demon; he has no idea it's really his teammate, but it seems he has absolutely zero warm fuzzies for the idea of a random demon shacking up with me, even against our wills.

"Fuck!" I look around the room, wondering how we can do this, until my eye catches the bathroom door. "What about the bathroom? I wonder if there are any cameras in there..." Zeph shrugs his shoulders and moves into the bathroom, Mav quickly following him.

They're quiet for a few seconds while they must look around before Zeph calls out, "No, it looks clear."

Looking at Sam, I gesture toward the bathroom.

"Come on, might as well get this over with. At least it will be easy to clean up the blood." I snigger, anticipating Mav and Zeph's reactions to be as bad, if not worse, than mine. I mean, I'd just had an orgasm when I found out, and I'm pretty sure that was part of the reason I didn't beat the shit out of him. All those yummy endorphins still running through my system.

Or that's my excuse anyway. I watch as he moves from the bed to the bathroom, only wearing sweatpants, his gorgeous demon body on full display. I've got to say I like this version of Sam; he's ripped. I mean, normal Sam is hot, but this is like Sam squared. His tail crooks, waving me to come on, so I hurry in behind him, closing the door. Reaching over, I turn on the water in both the sink and the shower in the hope it will drown out some of the noise I expect is coming.

Turning around, I find Sam cornered by Mav and Zeph, who have both adopted the same pose. Arms crossed, legs spread, menacing looks on their faces. We don't have time for fights, so I step in between them, pushing back a little. Though this may just give them more momentum if they decide to attack him. Oh well, the blood will wash away.

Now that we're all looking at him, he shifts uncomfortably for a few seconds.

"For god's sake, just rip it off like a band-aid. They're going to be pissed at you no matter what,"

I grumble, not ready to deal with this aftermath. I'm not sure exactly how I feel about him at the moment since all that anger is blurred with all the freaking good sex. So to say I'm discombobulated is an understatement.

"Promise to hear me out before you start swinging?" he asks, and neither of them answer him, though both have confused frowns on their faces now.

A wave of magic prickles my skin, and Mav and Zeph must feel it too because they tense, waiting for what's about to happen.

The demon form fades, and he becomes the Sam we know and love. Or maybe not so much love if their reactions have anything to say about it. Both of them stand there, wide-eyed, open-mouthed, frozen to the spot, but I see the exact moment that Mav becomes aware again. Fury crosses his face, and in a blur of motion, he's launched himself at Sam, tackling him to the ground. I wince as Sam's head cracks against the tiled floor, worried that we've already reached the limit of sound that the water can cover up. Mav starts hitting him with both fists, one after the other, but Sam does nothing to defend himself, allowing Mav to work out his feelings on his face. Blood is flying, and my stomach churns with the indecision of whether or not I should jump in the middle or let them work this out in their "manly" way. The decision becomes a bit harder when the crack of Sam's jaw echoes loudly in the small space.

"You fucking traitor! You left us and chose *her*. You chose that fucking bitch over all of us. Chose to turn your back on us and take up with a racist, bigoted asshole god." A sudden stillness comes over Mav, then he stands up, his knuckles split, staring down at Sam, his face cold and blank. My heart beat speeds up and my skin covers in goosebumps at the sight of Mav so angry. I've never seen him look like this before, and honestly? It's kind of scary.

"You're dead to me," he hisses before spitting at Sam. It hits him in the face, but he doesn't move to wipe it away.

Looking down at him, I wince at the mess Mav's made of his face. "Well, I can't say you didn't deserve that," I mutter, bending down and helping him sit up before shuffling him back to lean against the wall.

"What the fuck, Mina? Why are you helping him?" Mav growls, trying to pull me away. I shake him off and lean against the wall next to Sam, his head flopping onto my shoulders, and I support him silently. I guess I'm not as angry anymore.

Mav looks at me incredulously, but Zeph has been silent the whole time, and I can see his brain running through all the possibilities. Zeph always has had the cooler head of the two, so I guess it's no surprise that he's working this all out while Mav needed to beat out the chaos in his head.

"*You're* the spy?" he asks flatly, and Sam grunts in response, licking at his bloody mouth. "You're the double agent feeding us information." At Sam's small nod, a relieved look crosses Zeph's face, but Mav's reddens with anger.

"Are you fucking kidding me? You're going to believe that shit?" he snaps at Zeph, but Zeph just nods, not looking away from Sam.

"I call bullshit." He stomps toward the door to leave, only stopping when I call his name.

"Don't, Mav, please, it's true. I know I found it hard to believe, and I'm still fucking angry at him, and it's going to take a while to forgive him, but he's suffered too. For god's sake, he's had his whole DNA changed so that he could infiltrate their organization. Please don't walk away." His back remains stiff despite my words, but he does turn around and doesn't leave. *Baby steps. That's something at least.*

Samuel explains to them both the same things he told me, and by the time he's finished, they're both quiet with thoughtful acceptance, though I have a feeling forgiveness will not come so quickly.

"So now you know where we're all at. I expect Sabboath will be here shortly due to us all hiding in here; he won't happily allow that to happen. He'll probably take me away, and he might even beat Mina again, so she needs to feed. He has plans for her, but they involve harvesting her eggs. The last time he tried, her scales were in place, and he couldn't get at them, but he's got this mad scientist dream, and I don't think he's giving it up so easily."

Mav lets out a bellow of frustration, Samuel's words confirming what they already know, and Zeph places a hand on his arm, trying to calm him down. But his eyes are wide and unseeing as he shakes with anger. It's like a silent fit, his body twitching occasionally, but his limbs are as stiff as a board.

"Fuck, Mav! Is he okay?" I've never seen him like this, but Samuel and Zeph exchange a glance that says they definitely have dealt with it before.

Zeph shakes his head, worry lining his face. "I'm afraid we've lost him to the chaos of his mind again," he says calmly, his voice not matching what his face so clearly conveys.

"Well, how can we fix him? What can we do?" I shout at them, scared. It's rare that I've ever seen the team really be vulnerable, and it's more unsettling than I thought to see one of them incapacitated. Zeph and Sam exchange another look, but this time it's distinctly uncomfortable. *What in the world could they be thinking about?*

"Oh, for fuck's sake, just spit it out!" I tell them, moving toward Mav.

"Pain usually works. Pain followed by pleasure is what's the most effective," Zeph tells me, and my mind whirls at all the possibilities and the slightest hint of a blush on his cheeks.

"So do you mean …" I trail off, not quite sure what I'm asking.

"Mav likes to use the dungeon at Eternal Damnation, and he likes to be punished," Samuel explains to me. 'Not all the time, sometimes he's the one doing the punishing, but when he gets like this, usually only Zeph can bring him around."

Zeph takes over, a resigned frown on his face. I'm guessing this isn't exactly how any of them ever planned on telling me about this part of our team dynamic. "It doesn't happen often, but Mav thrives on order and regulation. With chaos coming from all sides thanks to the Five and AoA, not being able to control what's going on around him is sending him over the edge more frequently than usual."

"Okay, so what should we do?" I look between them, but Zeph shrugs.

"I'm not sure. I don't have any of my toys here. Have you got any suggestions?" he asks Sam, and the two of them start tossing ideas back and forth, but my mind is still stuck on Zeph's words, making their comments fade into the background. *Toys! What kind of toys?* My succubus rears her head, hungry again and scenting the air for interested participants. She was already more than willing to welcome Mav and Zeph to play with us, but this revelation makes her hunger even greater. I had no idea that they were sexually fluid as well, and I can't say I'm not excited about the thought. Both Zeph and Sam groan with desire, and their eyes meet mine, lust shining in them.

"You're a naughty girl, pet," Zeph rumbles as Sam's eyes light up with an idea.

"What about if Mina and I bite him? We can make it painful to start with, not letting any of the pleasure toxin out, so he can come back to awareness and wake up a bit. Then we can flood his body with the toxin when he's finally in control, calming him down and giving us the chance to get him centered. There are still chains behind the bed that Mina was strapped into. We could put him there to restrain him."

I look at Sam in surprise, my eyes wide and my succubus nearly purring with pleasure at this plan. "Are you okay with biting him? You'll probably orgasm too," I warn him. "I'm happy to do it on my own if you'll be in any way uncomfortable." Sam's eyebrows rise in surprise, and Zeph snorts, looking between us, a little bemused.

"Sam's just as bent as the rest of us. He's just a little more discreet about it. To be honest, the only one not flexible is Dru. She's gay through and through, but the rest of us aren't fussy. We've never fully formed relationships like Trick and Sander, but when you spend so much time together, bonds form and tensions get worked out. Having you here now, I'm going to guess that the bond is possibly about to become permanent if what I'm guessing is right." Zeph's eyes are calculating, and Sam's are hopeful.

"You think you three are my mates as well?" I ask quietly, and he nods his head, looking a little worried. *Does he think I'm going to reject them? He and Mav have given me no reason to doubt them, unlike Sam, but Sam's the one I've had a crush on the longest. He's hurt me so badly, but now that I know the reasoning behind it all, I don't think I could ever reject him or any of them.*

"You could be right. Fate certainly seems to be going that way, but that's going to put me at nine mates. What could I possibly need *nine* for?"

Poor Mav is shaking quietly, a whimper occasionally escaping his mouth as we discuss everything.

"Hang on a second. Nine mates?" Zeph snaps. "How did you work that out?"

"Fuck!" I smack a hand across my mouth, blaming my succubus; she's melting my fucking brain with her neediness.

Sam starts to growl too, and I slap him across the face. "Settle down! I don't know if I'm even going to forgive you, let alone take your cock for another spin." His growl cuts off, and a wounded look crosses his face.

"Mina, stop avoiding the subject," Zeph demands, and I sigh.

"There's someone else in here who is also my mate. I was starving and beaten, and when he was put into my cell, I'm afraid I took his choice away from him." I hang my head in shame, still mortified that I had done that to Grayson. "He's one of

Sabboath's soldiers, but he's been questioning a lot of the things lately. He was given to me as punishment for his insubordination, to be fed on by the *filthy demon*. My succubus took over and coerced him into having sex with me." Tears start to run down my face as I tell them the story. I've basically been trying to block it out since it happened, but saying it all aloud now makes it real. Unfortunately, it's making all of the accompanying guilt and shame all the more present as well.

"Turns out he's my mate too, and I'm his. His dragon took over, and he bit me." I pull down the shoulder of my shirt, showing them the bite mark that's already scarred over.

"Sabboath thinks he was strong enough to refuse me and that we didn't have sex. There wasn't a camera then, and he was so proud, he let him out and was going to give him the same formula he gave Sam. Gray wasn't sure if he would survive it or not because he's already had it once. That's how he became the dragon."

"What did you say his name was?" Zeph asks, the urgency of his question surprising me. Not what I thought he'd ask at all.

"Uhh, Grayson? He told me Sabboath adopted him when he was about five, but it doesn't seem like he gets treated much better than Connie, really. Sabboath's taken both of his kids and just wants to use them as tools for AoA's plans."

"Holy shit! Tiberion's missing kid," Zeph

mumbles to himself, leaving Sam looking as confused as I feel.

He jumps to his feet, a determined look on his face, and puts out a hand to help me up. "Alright, we need to deal with Mav, and then we need to figure out a way to get us all out of here."

His team leader voice is hot, and it has me giggling like a school girl talking to her crush for the first time. Actually, not me, the stupid succubus. That's right! I'm blaming her.

"Sam, put your demon form back on, and let's get Mav on the bed. You guys can bite him, and then we'll make plans. He's useless like this, and we need him fully coherent to get out of here."

Sam transforms, and he and Zeph help Mav to his feet. Between them, they coax him out onto the bed, laying him down in the middle. I climb onto it, laying down on one side, and Samuel jumps onto the other, shuffling in behind Mav and supporting him against his chest so that he can have easy access to his neck. The sight of the two of them like that really gets my succubus excited, and I have to pull the reins, reminding her that right now this is basically a rescue mission. Maybe we can enjoy him later, but right now, we need to bring him back to us. Eagerly, I grab hold of his arm and pull it toward me.

"Okay, I'll leave you to it. Get it done quick," Zeph orders, pulling the curtains closed behind us.

"Ready?" I ask Sam, and he nods. Without

another breath, both of us lower our heads, fangs at the ready.

"Remember, no toxin until his eyes start to clear. We need him back with us before we hit him with pleasure," Sam reminds me. *Goddess, please let this work.* A moment later, I sink my fangs into Mav's wrist.

Chapter Twenty

Grayson

"Grayson, Grayson, are you listening to a word I just said?" Sabboath asks, his voice loud and grating as I shake my head. Since I left Mina in that cell, woozy from my sedation, I've thought about nothing but her.

My dragon has been riding me hard, urging me to return to her and claim her again. He keeps flashing me reminders of how she smelled and the way she felt in our arms, but all I've been able to do is listen to Sabboath ramble about world domination plans. God, I'm sick of him. It's like my eyes are finally open to everything that's wrong about what he and Hammus want to do. The reality of the demon genecide has become more pressing. Something that happened so long ago and didn't really affect me has become a whole new reality now that my mate is a demon. If he'd gotten his way, she wouldn't even exist. Now he's trying to do the same thing to the angels, again affecting my mate and her family. We just can't let them continue.

Looking up and seeing what's in his hands is a very unpleasant wake-up call.

"Are you ready?" he asks when he finally has my attention, gesturing at me with the syringe filled with what's likely his newest formula.

"Do you think this is a good idea? I mean, what if my dragon reacts badly? Also, I don't really want to be a demon. The dragon and I have gotten used to each other, and I'm just not sure how he'll handle it if we try to add another layer here for him to fight against."

"Actually, you won't be. This is a slightly different formula to the one I gave Samuel. I wouldn't want to dirty you with demon essence. I don't really care so much about him, but you, boy, *you* are my pride and joy. The one child who has never truly let me down." He smiles wide, and Connie, who is sitting on the lounge on the side of the room, whimpers quietly. Jesus, could he get any meaner? Connie and I have never really been real siblings, but there's still a part of me that feels for her. I had tried in the beginning, but she and Sabboath always made everything a competition, pitting us against one another, and when I didn't try my hardest, he would beat me. We ended up coming to resent each other fairly quickly, but I still hate to see him treat her like dirt. No one deserves that from a parent who is supposed to be kind and nurturing.

My eyes move to her bedraggled form, taking note of the way she's been deteriorating. She really isn't coping well with the original formula he injected in her, and her mind has never quite been the same. A wave of pity flows across me before I turn back to Sabboath.

"So, what's in that one?" I ask him, nodding to the needle in his hand. My outward appearance may be calm and collected, but inside, my dragon is pushing against my mind, trying to force the shift so he can eat this motherfucker.

"Oh, a bit of this and a bit of that. Unfortunately, we were never able to activate your angel blood because we don't know who your parents are, and I really don't know how your body will cope with the demon essence, unlike Sam, who has the benefit of having his blood activated. So this is the same formula minus that. You should be able to shift into anything you want as well as use all the powers that come with each form."

I want to fight him on this, but I know that to keep my mate safe I should probably go along with him. He still thinks I'm on his side, after all. But I eye the syringe like it's a venomous snake that's about to bite me. My dragon is angry, repeatedly insisting we need to rescue Jessamina instead of playing with Sabboath. *"Soon,"* I tell him. He flashes me a picture of Sam's demon form. *He was pretty beat up when they threw him in with her; she'll be okay.* I send reassuring thoughts to him, and he huffs but settles down. *"I promise, if we make it through this next formula, we will find a way to get her out."*

"Ok then, let's do this," I tell him, receiving a beaming smile in response.

"I'm sorry, but it's going to be painful," he warns as he plunges the needle into my arm, his words rendered totally insincere by the gleam of hunger that lights his eyes. He wants whatever is about to happen. Pride and joy or not, there's nothing he loves more than his experiments and mad schemes to create his perfect soldiers.

"I remember," I grumble before climbing off the examination table and lying down on the floor. He looks down at me with questions in his eyes.

"I don't want to fall off the table again when I roll around in agony; I had a headache for hours after the last time."

He nods in understanding before going back to the fridge and grabbing out another syringe. Turning, he gestures for Connie to sit on the exam table. Her eyes widen in shock, and a wary look crosses her face. He growls quietly, and she jumps to her feet, rushing toward the table.

"I've been working on your problem. Hammus gave me something that should repair your DNA, removing the first formula that attached to it. Maybe now you'll be able to be useful," he tells her, acting like it's all her fault that it went wrong, but neither of us points that out. She doesn't seem to care though. There's a hopeful glow to her face, and for the first time in a long time, she might even be *happy*.

"You're not making me a demon too, are you?" she asks carefully.

He shakes his head, eyes narrowing on her for even asking such an insipid question. "No, no, that was just for Sam. We needed him to be able to interact with Mina without her getting suspicious, and that seems to have worked. When you two finish your transition, we'll drag him out. You can sedate her again." He turns to me, lips curling up in a self-satisfied smirk. "And we will harvest all those glorious eggs."

Connie looks up at him with big wide eyes, alarm spiking through her stiff shoulders. Ever since she first started seeing Samuel, she's had it out for Mina, wanting her out of the way. Sabboath's obsession with her and decision that she'll be the lynchpin to securing AoA's success has only fanned the flames of jealousy even higher in my mentally unstable sister.

"Maybe you won't have to, Daddy. Maybe if this works, you can use mine, and then we don't need the demon slut's nasty babies. Can you take Sammy's tainted demon DNA away too?"

A frown takes over his face, and he runs a finger along his brow as though he's thinking. "You may be right; if it does work, I'll use you to breed my army too. But Mina will be a good broodmare, regardless. We can suppress those demon forms if we have to. And no, I don't think I can remove his demon form, but that doesn't matter. We'll just suppress his too. As ugly as they are, they make excellent soldiers, so I wouldn't want to do anything permanent anyway. That form seems to be a lot more resilient to outside stresses, or at least that's what our tests have shown so far." His eyes go somewhere far away, and if it were any other person, I would swear the emotion on his face was fondness. *Who am I kidding?* Of course he'd get all nostalgic and soft while remembering torture.

The light in her eyes dims a little, but she shakes her head and beams up at him. "Okay Daddy, I'm ready."

I watch as he injects her, a wave of pain starting to flow over my body. I know my transition's on its way, but hers is instantaneous. She screams silently, her mouth locked open as her body convulses, and she rolls off the table where she proceeds to twitch on the floor, frothing at the mouth.

Sabboath looks down at her. "Oops, guess she should've gotten off the table too."

As the pain takes over, I watch Connie's body stop convulsing and frothing, blood pouring from her nose and mouth, and that's the last thing I see before I blackout.

W hen my eyes open this time around, I feel clear and pain-free. This transition was easier than the last. *Maybe because I already have my dragon?* Looking within, he's quiet, but I can tell he's still there. I was worried that he would disappear in the change, but he's silently observing all that's going on. He chuffs when he notices my presence, relieved to see me awake again.

Climbing to my feet, I look around the room, searching for Connie. She's still lying in a pool of blood, but her body is still. As indifferent as I am to her these days, my heart still speeds up at the thought of her being dead. Quickly moving over to her, I stick my fingers to the pulse in her neck and sigh with surprise when I find her still breathing.

It looks like she might have made it through the transition. Stepping away from the sticky pool of blood, I take a seat on the couch, waiting for her to come around. There's nothing I can do until Sabboath returns.

While I'm waiting, I consider seeing if the formula worked. Sure, I survived it, but that doesn't mean I'm going to be able to change into anything else. I run through the realm beings I know he's stolen essence from. *Mermaid, well, I shouldn't change into that with no water around. Vampire, elf, fae. What about djinn? Yeah, I could try that. Now how does it work?* When I change into my dragon, I have to think about what it looks like in my mind. Hopefully, it works the same way. I think about the classic djinn look from the realms and pull on my magic, letting the wave wash over me.

My body sort of dissolves and reforms, until, like a traditional genie, I'm floating in a cloud of smoke, my legs gone. *Whoa, that's weird.* Looking into the mirror across the lab, I do a double take at the sight. I still look like me, but my cheekbones are sharper and my eyes more almond-shaped. My hair is long and tied in a ponytail on the top of my head, djinn-style, and I have markings all over my body. Black tattoos that look like runes but none I've ever seen before.

A groan has my head shooting up, finding Connie is awake and sitting up. I try to move over to her, but my legs don't work, of course, because I've got none. *How the fuck do I move like this?* My dragon is laughing at me, a huge toothy grin on his stupid face while puffs of smoke escape his nose as he chuckles madly. I try to wave my body back and forth in the hope that I can get some momentum, but nothing happens except my dragon rolling over with his laughter. *Asshole!*

Okay, so I can't move physically; it's got to happen with my mind then. Picturing myself over near Connie, I float forward slowly. The feeling of moving without legs is weird; there's a rolling kind of sensation like being on a boat in the ocean, an up and down motion that's hard to explain but it makes me feel kind of queasy. *There has got to be an easier way than this.* The dragon laughs even harder inside me. *What a bastard!*

I float to Connie's side and stop, thinking about the other differences I'm noticing while in this body. Unlike the dragon, I don't have another mind inside mine. I am the djinn, so I have to work this shit out on my own. Since I'm able to move my half-incorporeal body with my mind, maybe everything else needs to be directed by my mind. I know djinn have full forms. The smoke is traditional to get in and out of their lamp, which thankfully, I'm not bound to.

Just as I think this, one pops into being on the floor. *Fuck.* My eyes meet Connie's, and luckily, she's still a little confused and hasn't really noticed. I can't let anyone get hold of that; otherwise, I may be trapped. In my mind, I picture myself with legs, and within a moment, another wave of magic flows over me, and I fully form. Bending down quickly, I pick up the lamp and try out my new powers. I want to make the lamp go to my room. Blinking my eyes as I've seen on the tv, I try to make it move, but nothing happens. Then I try the crossing my arms, head bob thing. *Nope, nada.* I think if my fucking dragon was corporeal, he'd actually be wetting his pants by now, his amusement is so great.

Okay, what about a snap of the fingers? Sure enough, the lamp disappears. *Let's hope it went where I wanted it to.*

"Grayson?" Connie's voice is unsure, and I hold down a hand to help her up.

"Yep, just trying out one of my new forms. Almighty powerful djinn," I reply, helping her over to the couch, my legs working perfectly fine now that they exist. She still looks a little confused, and even though I'm worried that whatever he did to her didn't make her any better, I'm just as worried that it did. With all these powers, Connie would be a nightmare.

"Hey, Connie, can you do me a favor? Make a wish. I need to see if I got all the powers as well as the form," I request, and she nods slightly, narrowing her eyes in thought.

"Ah, okay, I wish for a cheeseburger and a glass of red wine." Well, okay, that sounds a little bit more like the normal Connie for a change.

The minute she says the word wish, it's like a compulsion. I can't help but click my fingers. On the little table next to the couch appears the two things she wished for.

"Awesome," she breathes out and reaches for the glass of wine. "It worked! You really are a djinn. I wonder if there are things you can't do?"

Instinctively, I know I can't kill anyone. Which is weird considering I couldn't even figure out how to walk. I also know if I was a bound djinn, I could only give you three wishes and that you can't wish for more wishes. But I'm not, so that doesn't count at the moment. I also know that if someone got a hold of my lamp while I'm in this form, I would be stuck like this, their slave until someone wished me free. I shudder at the thought, and my dragon finally stops laughing and tells me to shut the hell up. He's no more fond of that idea than I am, so I just shrug my shoulders in the hope that she loses interest.

Connie looks intrigued and starts to ask me something else, so I quickly imagine my usual self and let the power wash over me. I don't think I'll be using the djinn again any time soon.

Her face falls, and she seems disappointed, but she's starting to look a lot better after eating. In fact, now that I take a closer look at her, she's the healthiest I've seen her since she took the original formula. Her hair is no longer limp and stringy, her skin has lost its green pallor, and she actually looks less gaunt, like she gained some mass during the transition. "How are you feeling?" I ask carefully, and she stops eating, her nose scrunched up in thought like she's taking inventory of herself.

"Good," she stammers, eyes wide in surprise, "really fucking good." A wide smile crosses her face, and she puts the wine down before standing up. "What animal should I try?" she eagerly asks, practically vibrating with excitement.

I shrug my shoulders, not wanting to suggest something she's not ready for. "I don't know. What do you want to try?" She starts to pace back and forth, her energy building with each step.

"Something big and impressive, like your dragon. Something that could put the slutty bitch in the cells in her place."

Oh, and there it is, the jealousy didn't suddenly disappear.

"Oh, I know!" she shouts out loud, and my dragon and I go on full alert. The smile taking over her face is a bit too reminiscent of Sabboath for my liking.

"Just remember, Connie, you're still in there, so you can still be in the driver's seat. Don't let the animal take over. We have to save that for battle; your dad will be pissed if it kills a whole heap of his soldiers," I remind her, and she gives me a determined nod.

Without any more delay, a wave of magic prickles the air, and I watch as her body contorts, bones breaking and muscles reforming as she slowly changes. A scream leaves her mouth before it transforms, a mouthful of fangs growing into the open space.

The first shift to a new form is agonizing, and Connie has picked one that is *way* different from her human form. *Probably should have told her that wasn't a great idea.*

She grows in mass, but her form elongates and loses limbs. When it finally finishes, a basilisk is towering above me, fangs dripping venom.

Holy fuck. I step back a little bit, avoiding looking her in the eyes. The sounds of her scales sliding against themselves as her body curls is creepy and a little frightening. I prepare to assume my dragon form, but wild clapping by the door draws both our attention. Turning slightly but never taking my eye off Connie, I see Sabboath has returned.

"Oh, my dear, you are magnificent! Maybe there is hope for you after all," he praises, his eyes avoiding hers as well. She hisses her response but doesn't move.

"Learn how to change back, Connie. You'll need to work on a couple more forms." Her big reptile head nods, and her body slowly starts to contort again, immediately following her father's orders like the dutiful daughter she is.

"Come, Grayson, we need to get Samuel out of that cell. I just threw Mina two more snacks who are hoping to prove themselves to me just like Sam and you did. It won't be long before we can have you sedate her again. That fertility drug I gave her will be playing havoc with her demon urges, so we need to get Sam before she gets too far gone."

Now that Connie is changing, I feel comfortable putting my back to her. When we make it to the cell, a strange guy is sitting on the couch. No one else can be seen, so I'm guessing they're all inside the curtained bed. My dragon growls in anger and jealousy, but I keep a lid on the noise.

A groaning sound from inside draws my attention. But that didn't sound like pleasure; it sounded like pain.

"What's going on in there?" Sabboath snaps at the one on the chair.

He pushes his shoulder-length brown hair back before rubbing a hand across his short well-kept beard, his whiskey eyes blinking slowly as he shrugs.

"They were hungry, and they dragged him into there and left me out here." I can tell he's lying, but I don't say a word. Whatever's going on, my dragon and I are up for it if it will help Mina.

"Grayson, get the male demon," he orders, so I move over to the bed, opening the curtains. Lying on the bed are both Mina and who I'm guessing is Samuel in demon form, with another guy pinned between them. Their mouths are on his body, his open in a silent scream, and the tense lines on his face speak of agony, not pleasure.

Mina sees me, and her eyes widen slightly. She takes her mouth off the screaming guy and starts to speak, but I shake my head almost imperceptibly.

Pushing the screaming man toward Mina, I grab the dark demon and yank him off the bed. He tries to fight me, so I let a little of my sedative smoke flow from my nose, and he calms instantly. I take him by the arm and maneuver the docile demon out of the cell, Sabboath slamming the door behind us. The other man hasn't moved, likely knowing he's on probation.

"Have fun, boys. I'll be back for you in a little while!" he shouts before striding away, and I follow with the docile Sam.

We leave the cell block, and Sabboath turns to me. "Reverse that and get him back to his room. I can imagine he wants to wash all that filth off of him and change forms. He can also remove that fake collar. Once he's had some food and rest, you can go back down and sedate the others for me. I'm going to go and check on Connie and get her ready to harvest eggs too. All my beautiful soldiers in the making!" He smiles maniacally and heads back to his lab, not waiting for a response.

I guide Sam back to his rooms, and when we enter, I blow the antidote smoke in his face, and he comes around with a groan

"Man, that sucks!" He blinks a couple of times before looking at me. "You must be Grayson?" he asks, looking at me with suspicion. "That's a neat trick you've got there. Going to use it on the demon bitch downstairs?" he asks casually, letting his demon form disappear and assuming his normal one again.

A growl escapes my lips before I can stop it, and his eyes widen at my response. "Oh, so the demon bitch got to you, did she?" he pushes, and this time, my claws break through my fingertips as my dragon demands I rip him to shreds.

His eyes bug out, and he steps back, holding up his hands in defense. "Hey, settle down. I guess she was right; you *are* her mate," he says, the words almost holding a bit of jealousy.

"What did you say?" I demand, looking around

his room for cameras, pleased when I don't see any. He ignores the question.

"Is she also right that you don't find yourself aligning with the AoA way anymore?" he asks carefully, and I decide to tell him the truth. I can always kill him if he threatens to give me away.

"Yes, she is my mate, and no, I don't want to follow them anymore. I never really got a choice as a child, and it was something I always wrestled with. It was easier to give in than argue, and I stayed complacent for years. No more."

He breathes out a huge sigh of relief. "That's good to hear. You'll help me get her out of here?" he pushes, but now it's my turn to ask a question.

"You're not here because you follow the cause, are you?" He shakes his head, the grimace on his face giving a clear enough impression of what he thinks of Sabboath's plans. "And I'm guessing the two in the cell with her aren't either?" He shakes his head again.

I start to pace back and forth, my dragon echoing the movements in my mind. "But those two got caught and had to think quickly on their feet. Unfortunately, unlike you and me, he doesn't trust them because they're both collared. We need to get all three of those collars removed so that they can get out somehow."

"Don't worry about how they'll get out. They can do that; we just need those collars off," he tells me, sitting down on his bed.

I'm contemplating his words when a delicious scent hits the air, very similar to Mina's but with a more masculine tone. My eyes widen, and I stop pacing and turn to look at him.

He looks a little sheepish, a light blush taking over his cheeks as his eyes stare down at the floor. "Sorry, I'm afraid the demon side of me is still hungry, and my incubus wants to climb you like a tree."

His words take me by surprise, but I'm honestly more intrigued than offended, my cock twitching at the thought.

"I'm intrigued and flattered and definitely interested. I've always been attracted to men, but Sabboath believes being bisexual or gay is taboo, so I've learned to ignore that part of me." Even without knowing me, he seems to bristle at that information, like he's already prepared to defend me and talk me into knowing that what my "father" has tried to teach me is less than I deserve.

Something in my heart shifts, and my dragon takes notice of Sam, showing him more attention than he's given anyone beside Mina. "Can we revisit climbing me like a tree once we get Jessamina out? She'll need to agree to it. I won't go against my mate's wishes," I explain to him, not wanting to put him off but not really sure how to proceed. My experience has been limited at best, so the idea of juggling two partners is totally foreign.

"It's okay, man. I can wait, hopefully." He

winces slightly as the scent gets stronger, his demon's hunger contradicting what human politeness is demanding he say.

"Okay, we need to get Jessamina out, and you need to feed. If only we could get you back in the cell without Sabboath seeing... I also think it's the key to breaking the collar. It sparked earlier when we had sex, and she fed off of me, so I think with enough power flowing into her, she might be able to overload it."

"It didn't do anything when I had sex with her, but she didn't bite me at the same time," he mutters, sounding disappointed. "I can get down there and tell them that without anyone seeing. You just need to disable the camera above the bed," he shares, determination wiping away any of the bashfulness he had from our little pheromone situation a moment ago.

"Okay, yeah, I can do that," I tell him, wanting to question it but knowing we don't have the time. "Why don't you have a shower, and I get you some food in case Sabboath is watching?' He pulls his shirt off, and my eyes drift lower to his well-defined chest. His clearing throat has me bringing them back up, a flush warming my cheeks. He raises his eyebrow in amusement, and I desperately search for something to change the subject to, my mind latching onto something I know will distract him from my eyefucking.

"When Sabboath injected me earlier, he also

injected Connie. And whatever he did worked this time." His eyes widen at my words. "She's even more dangerous now and still hell-bent on revenge against Mina, so we have to watch her carefully."

He nods and stands up, heading for his bathroom before stopping. When he turns back to face me, there's a hard glint in his eyes and the hint of his tiger's claws peeking out from the tips of his fingers. My dragon raises its head in notice, curious about this new predator and waiting to hear what it has to say.

"Please don't let my trust in you be misplaced. I'd hate to have to kill one of Mina's mates."

Chapter Twenty-One

Jessamina

"Have fun, boys; I'll be back for you in a little while," Sabboath gleefully shouts as I hear them walk away. Giving it a moment until they're out of hearing, I roll Mav off of me and shout for Zeph.

"Get in here!" A gasp escapes Mav's mouth, breaking the silent scream that he's been stuck in since Sam and I bit him. Zeph quickly parts the curtains, climbing onto the bed next to me, looking between Mav and me in hope.

"We didn't get to the pleasure part yet, but the pain seems to have worked," I tell him, but he shakes his head.

"He'll be stuck in that sub-mode if you don't finish him off. Finish the cycle, so to speak," he explains to me, his eyes cloudy with concern as he watches his friend.

"Oh god, I'll finish the bite, shall I?" I'm feeling unsure, now that it's just me. Although I can't say I'm not curious to learn more, I'm not experienced with this kind of thing at all. *Is it possible to do this wrong?* "Do you think he would mind?"

A small smile crosses his face, and he shakes his head again. "Trust me, Mina, he won't mind at all."

Zeph lays down and manoeuvres Mav onto his side, spooning him from behind and pulling his arms tight behind his back, so he's restrained. I lick closed the holes I put in his wrist and move up to his neck, working on Sam's bite marks next. Then, moving to the other side of his neck which hasn't been chewed on yet, I bite deep, releasing the plea-sure toxins at the same time. Mav shouts, the hoarse sound bringing a smile to Zeph's lips. I swallow deep, drawn-out gulps of his blood, hoping that he can cope with how much I'm taking. His blood fills the hunger that had started to niggle at me again, making something inside me relax. He starts to squirm in between Zeph and me, his hips thrusting back and forth before finally stilling as a long low groan leaves his mouth.

As I pull away and seal the wound, his arms come up around me, and he nuzzles into my neck. "Mina, I missed you. Thank you for that," he whis-pers in my ear, my nipples pebbling and goose-bumps spreading across my skin at the husky sound of his voice.

"It worked," Zeph sighs, sounding pleased and definitely relieved. He reaches around him, pulling both of us against him in a comforting hug, just what I need after all the crap I've been through. I burst into tears, sobbing into Mav's chest as they both whisper sweet words of encouragement to me, letting me purge all the built-up emotions I hadn't known were there. Sadness and anger and guilt at my treatment of Grayson. Anger and relief in finding out Sam isn't a traitor and worry that Zeph and Mav are now just as stuck as I am.

My tears run dry, and I pull myself away from them both, Mav's chest now covered in tears and snot.

"I'm sorry," I apologize while trying to wipe it away, but all I succeed in doing is rubbing it into his shirt. It's then that I notice his uniform. In fact, both of them are dressed in what the AoA soldiers wear.

"What is this?" I ask, pointing at the offensive bit of material. Zeph snorts and rolls onto his back, moving over so we both have more room. Even with the extra space, we stay close, all of us taking comfort from the others' presence.

"That was supposed to be a disguise, but you see how well that turned out," he quietly says with an eye roll, his voice dry and his annoyance clear. Mav just shrugs his shoulders unapologetically.

"I wasn't going to allow them to rape her, and now that I know she's a spy too, I'm doubly glad I didn't," he whispers to us.

I flop onto my back, his words reminding me of what Sam said. "Maybe we should bring her when we escape, though I'm not sure how that's going to happen with both of you wearing these too." I point to the collar around my neck, the injuries around it mostly healed thanks to all the blood from Mav, but I can tell my powers are still blocked. There was always a residual current of magic flowing in my body. Not that I had ever realized until it disappeared. Now I can't help but notice it's still missing.

Zeph blows out a sigh, his fingers lightly running along the collar as though he doesn't want too much contact with it. "Yeah, we weren't expecting those; we thought we'd be able to find you, remove yours, and get the hell out of here. Evidently, we need a new plan."

My eyes get heavy, and for the first time, I realize it's been a long time since I actually got any sleep. The blinking light of the new camera above the bed becomes fuzzy, sleep coming with a vengeance. I try to fight it, but suddenly Mav's face is in front of mine. "Rest, Mina, we'll watch over you," he whispers, brushing my hair back from my face. His thumb rubs against one of my horns as he pushes it back, and my succubus rears her head, but my body is so weary she doesn't get a chance. Before I know it, I succumb to much-needed sleep, feeling safer than I have in days.

■—•••—■

I'm not sure how long it's been, but something wakes me. The blinking red light on the ceiling is missing, the camera no longer working. The bed next to me is empty, but I can hear Mav and Zeph whispering on the other side of the curtains, quietly enough that neither I nor the cameras can make out what they're saying. Sitting up, I've started to shuffle my way toward the edge when suddenly Sam, in his normal form, appears on the bed in front of me, his teleportation not restricted because he's not wearing a collar.

Before I can stop it, a small scream leaves my mouth, and he chuckles quietly, but Mav and Zeph explode into action, diving through the curtains onto the bed.

They stop when they see it's Sam, though each of them looks a little wary. Noticing their cautious glances, he barely manages to hide a wince, likely hurting because his teammates don't feel secure with him right now.

"What are you doing?" I hiss at him. "You're going to blow your cover."

"No, it's okay. Grayson took care of the camera above the bed," he reassures me. *So that's why the little light is out.*

"What do you want?" Mav gruffly asks, but Zeph doesn't look nearly as concerned.

"Grayson theorized that an overload of power

from Mina will short out the collar, and you should be able to remove them after that."

She nods, her eyes widening in realization. "Oh yeah! It sparked when we formed the mate bond."

"Well, he thinks that if you seal the mate bond with these two at the same time, that should be enough power to overload it."

His words have me freezing, a feeling of dread sinking in my stomach. "But what if these two aren't my mates?" I whisper quietly, not wanting to meet their eyes. I want so badly for them to be part of the bond. Not just so that we can overpower the collars, but because they're my family, and there'd just be something empty inside me if I couldn't have them too.

Zeph grabs my hand and squeezes it, offering a small smile as he tilts my chin up with the other hand. "We'll worry about that if it happens, but I'm willing to risk it. I have a good feeling," he reassures me, and Mav is just as quick to agree.

"I have no doubt at all; let's do this."

"Well, maybe we should be adding as many to the bond as possible to really push that overload," Zeph suggests, his eyes on Sam as he says this. A bolt of surprise hits me, my eyebrows rising without conscious thought. *That's not what I expected to come next.*

But Sam just shakes his head. "I know that none of you are completely sure that I'm on your side, and I want to prove it to you all before I attempt to bond with Mina. You wouldn't believe it for sure if we did it now, and you all deserve more than that. *She* deserves more than that."

Zeph nods, looking impressed at Sam's words, and I can't say I'm not relieved. *How do I know for sure that Connie's not going to get her hooks back into him?*

"Now, Sabboath is calling a meeting to go over his next plan, and both Grayson and I need to be there, so get the bond formed and get out of here. Everyone will be distracted for the next hour or so and hopefully won't notice the downed camera. Even if they do, Sabboath expects you to be doing this, and it's unlikely he'd think there's any ulterior motive. After the meeting, he's coming back for you, Mina. You *need* to be out before then. Grayson and I don't know how else we can save you while maintaining the illusion that we're on his side."

With a quick kiss to my cheek, Sam disappears, leaving the three of us on the bed.

I look down at my lap, feeling a little awkward, but my succubus doesn't let that slide for long before she starts to send out pheromones. Both Mav and Zeph groan, the sound almost closer to pain than desire.

"Are you sure about this?" I ask them again, but Zeph doesn't respond; he just yanks me across the bed and into his arms.

"Mina, I've been waiting for this for a long time," he growls, then kisses me like he's starving for oxygen and I'm the very air he needs. Zeph kisses like he does everything in life. He takes charge, and it's all-consuming. A weight at my back has me leaning into Mav as the two of them very effectively pin me between them, similar to what we'd done to Mav before I fell asleep. His cock is once again hard and pressing into my ass as his hands sneak between Zeph and me. Slipping his hands through the rip in the front of my shirt, he palms my breasts, rolling my nipples between his fingers and thumbs, drawing a groan from my mouth. My tail decides to get in on the action, wrapping around my body. It slips between us and rubs up and down on the bulge in the front of Zeph's pants while Mav continues to grind against my ass.

I pull my mouth away from Zeph and turn my head, searching for Mav. Finding his mouth, I pull him toward me. His kiss is more violent than Zeph's, our tongues clashing, and he catches my lip and bites down hard, punishing me for something, I'm not sure what, and I groan out loud with the force.

Pushing them back, I start to run my claw through Zeph's shirt but stop. If we need to make a getaway, they need clothes. Grabbing a tiny bit of self-control, I sheath the claw and pull the shirt over his head before quickly unbuckling his pants. With a push, he falls backward on the bed, allowing me to pull his pants off. Throwing them to the end of the bed so they're in easy reach, I run my eyes over his naked body; his broad shoulders ripple with muscle, his pecs are defined, and his washboard stomach has ridges my succubus and I want to run my tongue along. My eyes drop lower to his erect cock, standing long and thick and dripping with pre-cum, so I get on my hands and knees, crawl toward him, and lean down to take care of it for him. A moan leaves his mouth, its echo immediately coming from behind me.

As I lick and suck at Zeph's thick erection, Mav's hands are on me, removing my clothes. His hands are a light touch running over my skin like he's making sure I'm actually real.

"All this beautiful pink skin," he rumbles from behind, "and this is the best bit of it all." I feel his hot breath against my pussy before his tongue swipes through my folds, a garbled gasp escaping my mouth.

"Fuck, Mina, you taste good." I keep attacking Zeph's cock with enthusiasm as Mav runs a finger through my folds before leaning over me.

"Here, brother, taste her." He holds his finger out for Zeph, and I stop what I'm doing, hungrily watching as Zeph takes Mav's finger into his mouth, sucking on it, his eyes closed in enjoyment.

"Fuck yes, she does," he groans. He wraps my hair around one fist and guides my mouth back to his cock, the tension just tight enough to create a delicious sting that only stirs my desire even higher. As I enclose my lips around it, he says, "Mav, you must be so hungry. Why don't you fill up on

Mina?" His voice is husky, his eyes completely dilated and fixed on where my mouth closes around him.

Mav burrows his face into my pussy, sucking and licking and biting, and my inner succubus squeals with delight, though she's not completely satisfied yet.

Taking the reins, she pushes Mav away and climbs up Zeph's body, hovering my soaked entrance above his thick cock.

Just as I'm lowering myself onto it, my eyes lock with his, but a shout from behind me has me turning. My tail has wrapped around Mav's cock, gently pulling him forward while giving his cock a tail job at the same time. His eyes are just about bugging out of his head in surprise before they narrow with enjoyment, my tail undulating around his hard length as he decides to just go with it.

I laugh a little wickedly and continue my descent, my pussy enveloping Zeph's thick dick and working myself up and down until I've taken it completely. Our eyes remain locked the whole time, his breathing growing increasingly ragged the further I go. Finally, I'm flush with his hips, and I use my inner muscles to squeeze tight, drawing desperate groans of delight past his lips. Leaning down, I nip and suck at his nipple, running my tongue around each one, my hands holding his down on the bed. Creeping my mouth further up, I take his lips again, the kiss sensual and swift before my mouth moves to his neck, and I graze my fangs along his carotid.

Mav's hands on my back have me pausing and turning to look at him. Though his hands are rough as they brush over my skin, his eyes are heated with desire and longing and something so much more fragile yet powerful at the same time.

His fingers tease the tight ring of my ass, and he raises his eyebrows in question. I nod my head, a wicked little grin spreading across his face. He brings his hand forward and shoves them in my mouth.

"Suck," he commands. His words have my pussy clenching, and Zeph groans again as he watches me with Mav's fingers in my mouth.

He pushes them deep, activating my gag reflex, then drags them back out covered in lubrication before forcefully plunging them into my ass. My succubus crows her delight at the rough treatment, and I scream out loud. He stretches my tight ring, the process not taking long.

"Mina, lean forward onto Zeph for me," he coaxes, his voice low, and as I do, he takes his cock and thrusts the head of it alongside Zeph's. *Holy shit!* I didn't think I could stretch out that far, but I feel my pussy changing shape, allowing him to fit in next to Zeph.

"Fuck!" I shout as he and Zeph thrust a couple of times together, lubing up his cock, and just as I feel my body about to explode, he pulls out and lines up with my ass. He slowly pushes in past the tight ring until he's fully seated, and the three of us moan with delight.

"So fucking good," Zeph groans in front of me, nearly breathless.

"Are you ready, Mina?" Mav's husky voice is in my ear, each heated exhale another tease along my neck.

I quickly nod my head, knowing with all certainty that this needs to happen. "Yes, but I need your arm in front of me so I can bite you after I bite Zeph," I pant out in between gasps. Immediately, I feel one hand leave my hip, and it wraps around my chest in easy reach.

"Are you two ready? This is going to be quick, and it's going to hurt," I warn them, and they both grunt their okays. "'I'm sorry about the pain if we *are* mates."

Before either of them can say anything, I move on Zeph's cock, setting us back into motion again. They both get the idea and take over, alternating their thrusts. It feels so good that it only takes them a couple of thrusts to send me over the edge. As my orgasm screams its way through my body, lighting all my nerve-endings on fire, I bite down onto Zeph's neck.

Taking a couple of gulps, I switch to Mav's arm, biting down on him too. Both of them shout as the bites trigger their orgasms, their thrusts growing erratic as I drink cautiously from Mav because he's lost enough today. I seal his holes back up and return to Zeph, knowing he can afford to lose a little more.

His blood is thick, hot, and satisfying, and just as I'm swiping my tongue over the wound to close it, I feel them both stiffen. A familiar yet still searing pain erupts across my back, and I cry out along with them.

My heart just about bursts with excitement that the two of them are my mates, but another sensation soon overshadows that. As the bond forms, a wave of power flows over my body, and the collar around my neck sparks and burns red hot for what feels like minutes but is probably only a few seconds before unlatching and falling off. A wave of magic punches into me as the block is finally lifted, and I grunt with the agonizing wave of my power slamming back into my body. I look at my new mates, the same pain etched across their faces in narrowed eyes and clenched jaws.

Mav's and Zeph's collars quickly follow suit, and the three of us are left laying there, moaning in both pleasure and pain, our magic intact again. I know we haven't got time to just lay here, but I can't control myself. The overload of magic is too much for my body, so I close my eyes as darkness descends.

Chapter Twenty-Two

Mavromichali

Her eyes get heavier and heavier, Mina slowly drifting off to sleep, a small smile on her otherwise relaxed face. It's the first time I've seen her look this peaceful since maybe selection day. As her breathing deepens, a small cute whistle starts to come out of her nose, causing me to snort in amusement. A hand pushing back Mina's hair has me looking up into the whiskey brown eyes of my friend and occasional lover.

"How are you feeling, man?" His hand leaves Mina's hair and moves to mine, pushing it back from my face in a tender gesture. I don't often see those kinds of things from him; it's not the kind of relationship we've had in the past. Maybe what we have is now evolving, and I can't say I'm upset. It feels nice to be worried about and cared for, and having Mina as another reason to bring us together might give us the space and encouragement to just take our dynamic in any direction that feels natural.

Having another anchor besides Mina might help me better deal with those moments when the world seems to overwhelm my mind.

Now that I feel more settled, I realize I have a whole section of time missing. One minute I was blazing furious at Sam, and the next, I'm coming in my pants harder than I ever have, sandwiched between Zeph and Mina. With everything else that happened, this is the first time he's had to check in with me, so I guess that explains why he's so concerned. Zeph has always been the one to bring me through any episodes I've had in the past, having worked out exactly what I need and how to give it to me. I guess being here, and not being able to fix it, was also putting him out of his comfort zone.

He continues to run his hand through my hair in a gentle motion, and I snuggle into Mina a little more, taking the quick moment to feel relaxed and happy, not knowing when we're going to be able to do it again. I breathe in her unique scent, that sweet but spicy smell that is all her. She smells like sour apple candies, sweet but you know they're going to have a sharp bitter outside. If you can persevere and get to the middle, it's all sweet reward. Zeph's patient and he waits, his hand in my hair a soothing feeling, and eventually I blow out a breath.

"I'm okay right this very second, but at the same moment, I'm not." A frown crosses his brow, and I feel myself mimic it. "Right now, in this moment, everything is amazing. Mina's our mate, and I can feel our bond, and everything is awesome. But I also know we still have to get out of here. I also need to reconcile that Sam is still Sam and not a traitorous scumbag, just a lying motherfucker, and then there's everything else." He waits while I get my thoughts into some semblance of sense, not pushing me.

"The others are in a coma, we still have to fix Earth, Mina's got a new mate, not to mention the fate of the five worlds resting on her shoulders and ours through her... It's a lot, you know."

His hand moves away from my hair and drifts into Mina's while I watch him assimilate everything I've just said to him. That's what I like about Zeph and why he's such a good team leader. He thinks carefully before he talks or acts, analyzing everything. No careless words are uttered from his mouth. If he says it, he means it.

"It's a lot, you're right, but it's nothing we can't handle. We're a solid team, all of us, and with the revelation that Sammy isn't the traitor we thought he was, I think we need to move forward as quickly as possible, letting go of any animosity we might feel. All you have to do is look at it from his point of view. What would you have done if you had been asked the same thing? I know you, Mav. You would have done exactly the same, keeping that secret to protect us. And when you look at it from that point of view, all you can do is forgive him."

Zeph removes his hand, stretching his arms wide, his wings ruffling behind him, and the silvers and golds in them catch my eyes as I consider his words. He's not wrong at all, and that last bit of animosity I felt toward Sam drifts away like one of Zeph's feathers floating on the breeze. We need to be a united team to be able to achieve the impossible. His wings ruffle again, and a smile crosses my face. It's so nice to see them on a regular basis. Mine must sense my joy as they join in the celebration. The edges of my feathers shimmer with his, almost like the mating dance of a bird.

"As for her other mate," he continues, "I can imagine it will take a bit for him to fit in. Poor guy's going to have a bit of a learning curve, trying to adjust to everything, but all we can do is be supportive and help him through it. Just like we have been with Mina. If he's anywhere near half as intelligent as her, he'll get with the program quickly." Zeph's confidence is one of the reasons I originally confided in him about my mind struggles. He didn't see it as a problem, only another puzzle that needed solving, and worked out a way he could help me.

A snort from Mina has my eyes returning to her beautiful body. A wave of anxiety flows down the mate bond, and she starts to toss and turn in my arms. But I tighten them and send a wave of reassurance, feeling Zeph do the same thing until she settles once more.

"How did we get so lucky to be her mates?" I don't think he meant to say that out loud as he gazes at her, the adoration on his face plain to see.

I snort. "Fuck knows, but there's no taking it back. I'm holding onto her with my last breath if I need to." He quickly murmurs his agreement and jumps off the bed. Before long, I hear the shower running. I know we should get moving, but I'm really comfortable right where I am, so I let him shower in peace, deciding to take one when he returns. My mind drifts into that pre-sleep consciousness when you're aware but not. Flashes of us bonding with Mina return to the forefront of my mind. The sensation of sinking into her tight heat and the feel of her fangs in my arm as she swallowed mouthfuls of blood making my cock hard as rock again. I press it against her in the hope to relieve some of the pressure, but the feel of her silky soft skin just makes it worse. As she begins to quietly whimper in her sleep once more, some of that excitement dies down, replaced with a thread of concern for what she might be dreaming about.

"I'm done." Zeph's voice has me looking up. He has a towel wrapped around his waist and one in his hand drying his hair. The water still running down his torso glistens in the light of the cell, and my problem roars back to life in appreciation.

Grumbling, I roll away from Mina. "Can you

watch her while I shower? She's still restless." His eyes go straight to my erect length, and he snorts his amusement before quickly pulling on his discarded clothes and climbing on the bed next to our sleeping mate. He starts to whisper reassuring words to her as I wander toward the bathroom, my dick already in my hand as I prepare to take care of the situation.

The temperature is hot and the pressure good when I step under the running water. I've always enjoyed showers, using them as a time for reflection and a sort of meditation. The sound of the rushing water in my ears always seemed to overpower the chaos building in my mind, blocking out all other external stimuli, soothing and calming me. And this time is no different. Running my hand up and down my thick length, I think about my mate and having her come to Eternal Damnation with Zeph and me. Introducing her to the delights that submitting to us can bring. All the different toys in our cupboard that I look forward to using on her. With these thoughts, it doesn't take long before that tingling sensation at the bottom of my spine signals my impending orgasm.

Tightening my grip to almost punishing degrees, I increase the speed, my breath now leaving me in short gasps. With one last stroke, my knees nearly buckle as my cum shoots out, falling to the floor and washing down the drain. The last couple of strokes are gentle before I remove my hand altogether. That languid, freshly orgasmed feeling combined with the reassuring mate bond and the sensation deprivation of the shower have me feeling pretty damn invincible. In fact, now that I look inward, I feel the best I have in a long long time. Even after one of our sessions. I can only hope that mating with Mina is going to be a turning point for me.

Whistling, I turn off the taps and reach for a towel. Drying myself off, I return to the cell and the others. Zeph's stretched out on the bed, his hands behind his head, wings tucked in behind him and eyes closed, but they quickly fly open as I throw my towel on the bed and pull on my own discarded clothes.

"Feel better?" he asks as his brown eyes scan my naked body, appreciation shining in them. *Definitely feeling that start of something different.*

A cocky grin crosses my face, my confidence bubbling over. "Sure am."

"When you're dressed, we need to wake Mina and get out of here. Sam said we only had a short window of time, and I think we've cut far enough into it."

At these words, I hurriedly shove my feet back into my boots and sit down to do them up. "She was so tired though. It's better that she catches a quick nap than not be able to keep up when we need to hurry." Zeph sits up and reaches out a hand to me.

"I know and you're right, but we need to get going." As I finish my laces he leans over, gently waking Mina with a small shake. No matter what we have to deal with next, I'm so relieved to be alongside our pretty mate for the next part of the adventure.

Chapter Twenty-Three

Jessamina

Quiet voices and gentle shakes rouse me from a deep sleep. I'm not sure how long I've been out, but I can't imagine they let me sleep too long. I struggle to sit up, but the other two look like they've recovered quickly. Both are freshly showered and dressed, ready to get out of here. Testing my newly returned magic, I quickly clean myself and conjure clothes onto my body. Feeling really clean for the first time in a while, I wave my hand at the camera in front of the cell after I open the curtains, and it's with a smile of satisfaction on my face that I see it spark and sizzle before exploding. Climbing off the bed, I move to the bathroom and study myself in the mirror. I finally have the energy to assume my human form, and when I do, my eyes widen in surprise.

Around my neck is a scarred mess. The collar, when it got overloaded, burned a perfect ring around my neck, and instead of healing like I normally would, it's a raised pink scar, a permanent reminder of my time in captivity. Swallowing hard, I'm trying to stop the tears from forming when Mav and Zeph both appear in the mirror. They have the same ring around both their necks, just not as obvious as mine. They hadn't had to deal with days and days of it cutting into their skin.

Zeph steps up and runs a light finger over the mark before leaning in and placing a soft kiss on it. "War wounds, baby. Wear them with pride that you have survived." With those sweet words, my spirits start to rise, the first hints of real hope stirring within me.

"Come on! I just fried their cameras, but it won't be long until they notice something is wrong. Let's get out of here."

I wave my hand at the cell door, intending to unlock it and go looking for Sam and my other mate, but Zeph stops me.

"What? Let's go and find them," I insist, gesturing out of the cell. He and Mav exchange a look before he shakes his head.

"No, Mina. We need to teleport out of here. We can't risk you being caught." His eyes are soft, but his words are firm.

"We can't leave them behind, Zeph. It's not safe," I plead with him.

Mav steps closer and runs his hands up and down my arms in soothing motions, the soft contact raising goosebumps and the slightest of shivers down my back.

"At the moment, their cover is still solid, and they're in a perfect position to feed us more information. We need to allow them to do that. Sam sacrificed a lot to get in here, and we need to let him finish his job. Otherwise, this would all have been for nothing."

I push him away and cross my arms, looking at him with annoyance. "Fuck, that's a different tune to what you were singing before. You didn't even fucking trust him."

"What can I say? He's proving his loyalty. He could have quite easily jumped into that little threesome we just had and tried to seal a bond, but by waiting, he's proving to me how much he wants to make it all up to us. Got to respect the guy. You're a hard woman to turn down."

Scoffing, I look at the cell bars with longing. Now that the collar has gone, my bond with Grayson has snapped into place, and I can feel him in my soul next to Mav and Zeph, and something is pushing me to find him. Ignoring that is hard, but I finally concede to the others.

"Okay, but the minute they want out, we're coming to get them. No matter what." I hold their gazes, and they both nod their agreement.

"Let's go. Where are we going?" I ask them, and again, they exchange a mysterious look. An echo of worry flows through our mate bond. *Hmm, what could that be about?*

"We need to head to your apartment in the

demon realm castle," Mav tells me, "so we have to teleport to the ruins above and take the elevator down since none of us can teleport directly. We've got to ask your mom to fix that."

"Okay, but why there? Shouldn't we head back to the CD and regroup with the others?" I rub at the hole that is my missing mates, keenly feeling the emptiness now that the other three are there. Even though the collar is off, they're still missing, so it must have to do with the barrier.

"Ah, yeah, they're in the demon realm." Mav and Zeph exchange another look. Now I'm really worried. These mysterious looks and the whispers of unease are starting to turn into a pattern, and it's doing nothing to make me feel good about our situation. Just as I'm about to say something, Zeph steps forward and wraps his arms around me, our bond flooding with a protectiveness that is so perfectly him.

"Okay, well, let's go. I'll do it for you; you've been through a lot. Let's not push your body too far." My heart melts at the soft words and the thoughtful gesture. Leaning into his chest, I allow him to teleport the both of us to the demon realm, but it doesn't happen.

"What the fuck?" Zeph sounds incredulous and frustrated, and when he lets go and steps back, his brows draw down in worry. Running his hands through his hair, he looks at the cameras then back at Mav and me. "Shit, Sabboath must have been a little suspicious. I can't teleport out, so he's probably locked the compound down to even Archangels now."

My heart starts to race as I look between them both. "What are we going to do? We can't be caught; we won't get a chance like this again." I put a hand over my stomach, feeling a phantom pain that nearly drops me to my knees. "I will *not* let any future babies I could possibly have become fucking soldiers for that man. I'd rather die than let him harvest my eggs."

Mav puts a hand on me, the warm weight of it comforting, easing a tiny bit of the violent churning inside. "Calm down, Mina. We won't let it come to that. We'll think of something."

Zeph studies the bars of our cell, and then before our eyes, he disappears to reappear on the other side. He waves at us to join him, a contemplative look on his face. "Come on, at least we can get out of that." Mav keeps his hand on me, and in a flash, we're standing next to Zeph. *Note to self: short teleportation within the compound seem to work, but not ones that take you to another realm.*

"Can you speak to Grayson in his mind and ask him how we can get out of here?" I follow behind them, mentally reaching out.

"Gray?" I ask tentatively, hoping my end of the bond has settled within him since the spark of his bond has settled in me.

"Shit, Mina, what are you still doing here?" Concern

trickles through the bond, but it's layered, almost like both he and his dragon are telegraphing the emotion to me. *"You're going to get caught."*

"We're stuck. Sabboath has locked down teleporting out of the compound. Do you know how we can get out of here?"

"Shit, teleporting is the only way in or out." His panic is strong through the link, and I can feel him thinking. Suddenly, a wave of relief flows through him. *"When I was a kid, I found a hole in the barrier. There's a tree on the far side of the compound. In that tree is a hollow that connects to the other side. For some reason, the barrier is not present in that hollow, so you can climb through it, but it's going to be a tight squeeze for the guys,"* he warns me.

"Thank you," I reply to him, making the effort to push gratitude toward him in a delicate touch. With the boundaries I've already overstepped, I don't want to intrude on him much further. *"Don't worry, I'll cut off their arms or legs if I need to,"* I joke back, trying to ease his panic.

"Be careful, Mina. If he catches you, you'll never get away. He'll strap you to a bed and make Samuel and I rape you to keep you fed so that he can get at your eggs. He wants them so badly he's obsessing over them." After those words, he abruptly disappears, but I know better than to try and call him back. Paying attention to my surroundings, I notice we're at the steps up out of the dungeon. I can hear a few voices off to the side, likely from the guards' room. For a moment, I freeze, making the guys pause alongside me

"Okay, we just need to make it up these steps and through

the compound, out the front door, and to the tree. Piece of cake," Mav snarks, and I flip him off, but Zeph has a look in his eye that tells me he has an idea.

"Mina, what about if you shift forms into Grayson or Sam and pretend that we're handcuffed? No one will suspect anything strange of one of them walking out with the prisoners. They've both been known to others as being on Sabboath's side." Excitement rises in the bond between us, and I can't think of anything else even if I'm a little skeptical. Looking to Mav for his opinion, he shrugs. *"I can't think of anything better, and it might just work."*

Letting my magic wash over me, I shift into Grayson. *Whoa.* I feel myself grow taller and heavier in muscle mass, the heavy weight between my legs making me giggle like a twelve-year-old boy. *Seriously, when I get five minutes to spare, I want to see what the big deal about a dick is.* I wonder if one of my mates will let me fuck them in this form. At this thought, all the blood rushes south, and it hardens, the sensation strange but exhilarating at the same time. I groan in both annoyance and sexual frustration.

The guys raise their eyebrows at me, and as I adjust myself, they gain matching smirks. "Mina, we don't have time now, but later, I'd really like to know what you were thinking." The husky curiosity in Zeph's voice does nothing to solve my current problem, and if anything, I'm now even more determined to try and see this through.

With a snort, I wave them away and head toward the guards' room. Slamming open the door, I walk in like I own the place. My eyes scan the room for something I can use. A wall with shelves holding restraints and what looks like one of those buzz sticks is off to my left. The room has silenced with my entry, and as I stroll over to pick up the restraints, I spot Cheesy. It would be so easy for me to kill him now, but I'd blow our cover, and safely getting out of here with my mates is more important to me than revenge. Ignoring the want, I pick up a baton and press the button, and sure enough, it sizzles with electricity.

"Hey, Grayson, what are you doing, man?" Cheesy's voice makes me shiver internally, and I take a breath before turning around, the restraints in my hand.

"Sabboath wants the two male prisoners in with the slut demon." I almost jolt at the sound of Grayson's voice coming out of my mouth, but I manage to control it. "He wants to inject them with the new formula and see if Connie's compulsion works better on them than it did Samuel," I explain, pulling some random shit out of nowhere and holding my breath as I hope that they believe it.

"Ha ha, yeah, man, I wish Connie would use her persuasion on me," one of the other guards jokes and puts his hand up for a high five, and like morons, of course they all give him one.

Cheesy frowns slightly, showing more critical

thinking than I honestly thought him capable of. "I thought the plan was to wear the little bitch out so that you could sedate her without her armor sliding into place." I almost shiver at his words, but then my anger kicks in.

"Are you questioning me?" I bark at Cheesy, and he quickly shakes his head, visibly flinching at Grayson's anger. *Good to know.* I wish I also had the ability to blow smoke out my nose like Grayson does. I may have shifted into his body, but I don't have his dragon abilities, so selling this charade had better not come to that.

"Ah, sorry, bro. Do you need a hand?" I raise my eyebrow and stare at him, letting the weight of my gaze tell him exactly how well this will turn out for him if he continues to butt in. "Right, you got this!" He looks everywhere but at me, and as I leave the room, the silence behind me is deafening.

Quickly, I move to where I left the others. "Here, let's get these on, but we won't latch them. That way, if you need to get free to fight your way out, you can." They both let me attach the cuffs, and we make our way up the stairs. At the top, a door leads out into a little alcove, where we all stop.

"Which way now?" I ask them, and they both look a little concerned.

"We were beaten and dragged from the dining room, so I'm not actually sure," Mav tells me, and Zeph shrugs his shoulders.

"Okay, hang on." I couldn't risk pulling him

back in earlier, needing him focused on whatever he's doing with Sabboath or the others, but it's not like I have much of a choice now. *"Gray? Which way from the top of the stairs to the dining room?"*

He doesn't say anything in return but shows me a memory of the way I need to go. Sending him a wave of thanks, I push them in front of me.

"I know the way, but you need to walk in front in case we run into someone. I'm pretty sure they're all busy in a meeting, but just to be safe..."

Before we can do anything, the door behind us opens, and Cheesy comes out.

"Glad I caught you! I know you don't need my help, but I want to see you inject them with the formula. I hope you don't mind."

Fuck! Panic fills me, and I don't have any idea how to get out of this, so I give in.

"Yeah, okay, man. Why don't you lead the way to the lab? I'll even let you inject them if you want," I suggest, and he puffs up with pride. He turns and hurries off in a different direction to the one that Gray had shown me in my head, but there's nothing I can do about it now. I push at the guys, and they follow after him.

"Don't worry, I'll take care of him when we get to the lab. I don't want to draw attention to ourselves now," I whisper across their minds, and they each send a wave of warmth back at me, trusting that I can somehow make this all work out.

We make our way through a couple of winding

corridors without seeing another person before Cheesy stops at a door and opens it. We follow him in, my mind desperately reeling with ideas of how to get us out of here.

"Get on the beds," I order them, brandishing the buzz and making it crackle. They shuffle over to the beds and climb on while Cheesy heads to the fridge full of formulas.

"What are they having? The one with the demon essence like the other Alpha asshole? Or the one like yours?"

When he turns to grab them out of the fridge, I rush over, pressing the buzz bar against him, the power set possibly a *tiny* bit too high. He convulses and falls to the ground, out like a light. Bending down, I take his gun off him and shove it into the back of my pants.

"Okay, let's be quick! I'm not sure how long that will keep him out," I urge, and together, we hurry out of the lab and back the way we came.

Thankfully, the halls are still empty, but I don't know how long this will last. My heart is pounding, my mouth turning dry at the thought we're going to get caught. We make it back to the door at the top of the stairs, and I lead the others on the path that Gray had shown me. *"Get rid of those cuffs,"* I direct them. "If we come across anyone, we're going to have to fight our way out."

They quickly discard them, the restraints clanging against the floor as they land, but we don't stop to find out if anyone heard them. We get to a set of double doors, and Zeph holds up a hand. *"I know where we are now. We just have to get through the cafeteria, then it's a straight shot to the front door."* Peering through the windows, we can see that it's empty but still cautiously push them open. Quietly on swift feet, we move around the outside, seeing no point in making us a direct target.

We make it to the other side and leave the large room, Zeph taking the lead. *"The front door is just up ahead. Once we're out, we need to go left; the tree must be on the opposite side we came in on."*

We slide to a stop just before the entrance, a couple of voices escaping a little office off to the side.

Just as we're about to slide past them, a high-pitched alarm sounds out. The three of us slam our hands over our sensitive ears. It muffles it slightly, but I can still hear the announcement. *Prisoners have escaped. Detain at all costs.* Two security guards rush out of the room, and we lose any real advantage when they only startle for a moment before recovering.

Fuck! I pull the gun out of the back of my pants and hand it to Zeph, Mav standing beside us, a scalpel he must have taken from the lab in hand. I guess it's time to repay these bastards for their hospitality.

Chapter Twenty-Four

Jessamina

The guards recover quickly and rush forward, but they're no match for the shots of electricity I direct at them both. They collapse to the floor, we jump over them, and race for the front door, shouts building behind us. I smoothly shift back to my own body as we run, no longer needing to hold on to Gray's bulk when now is the time for speed.

"Hurry, Mina!" Gray's shouts, his urgency bleeding through our bond and sending another flare of adrenaline through my body.

Heading left, we sprint toward the side of the compound and round the corner, discovering the tree is definitely hard to miss. A large skeleton of a thing, there are no leaves on its branches, and it looks like it died some time ago, but I can make out the hollow Grayson was talking about. Footsteps and shouts sound out behind us as Sabboath's forces make chase. As we get to the tree, I gesture for the others to go first, and even though they look like they want to argue, I wave them off.

"Hurry up! I've got the stick to hold them off, and you're both bigger than me, so it might take you longer."

Reluctantly, they agree and disappear into the hollow. I'm just about to follow them when Sabboath flashes into the area, Samuel and Grayson by his side. He waves a hand and restraints fly toward me, but I quickly hold up my own, and they disappear. His eyes widen in shock before homing in on my neck, searching for the collar that should've rendered me helpless.

"No!" he screams, but I don't wait to see what he does. Instead, I dive into the hole and come out on the other side of the barrier surrounding the compound. Mav and Zeph are brushing themselves off, but as soon as they see me, all three of us teleport away.

In a flash, we arrive inside the throne room we'd been in previously. A wave of relief flows over my tired body, and I collapse to the floor, breathing hard and looking around. Nothing has changed; it seems the same as when we were here last. The polished floor is still littered with destroyed decorations and tattered furnishings, and that tapestry of the gods still hangs on the far wall, Hammus' piercing blue eyes looking like they could steal your soul out of your very body.

My head turns to the secret entrance behind the

tapestry, expecting Malakai to appear, and it's at that moment I realize I still can't feel them. I drop to my knees, the hole in my chest pulsing with agony. It's like it's reaching for them, but they're not there, and Grayson is gone too. The barrier is definitely blocking him, but if it's not blocking the others now that I'm outside it, where are they? A scream leaves my mouth at the thought that enters my brain.

"Dead, they're all dead." That's why Mav and Zeph hadn't said anything earlier. My agonizing wails echo around the empty chamber, bouncing off the rock walls and returning to me, the sound heartbreaking. Tears stream down my face as all of my energy disappears. It's like I'll never be happy again.

"Fuck!" This time Mav's worried voice echoes as I feel someone's arms scoop me up before they move quickly across the room.

"No, Mina, it's not what you think," Zeph tries to reassure me, but his words fall on deaf ears. I don't want to hear it; I know what I feel, and it's *nothing*. Not one of them is residing in the space that they belong. All I can feel are the two men with me.

My mind is blank, but I do notice that we are descending downward before we move quickly again. *Who let us in?* The question seems important to me, but I can't bring myself to ask it now. The sound and sights around me don't register; I feel numb, dead inside. Having survived Sabboath just to find out that more than half of my mates are dead, I'm not sure it's worth it. In fact, a part of me wishes I'd died there, no more pain, no more suffering, no more letting down the ones around me. Because why else would they be dead unless they tried to go up against Hammus and failed?

All the thoughts and chaos are too much, and I shut it all down and just breathe. Closing my eyes, I let it all go.

———•◦•———

"Mina." A voice niggles at me in the darkness where I've hidden, and I force out a groan, trying to fit all of my annoyance into that one sound.

"Mina, you need to wake up now."

That voice is annoying as fuck, and I try and bat it away, not wanting to leave the safe space of my numb void. Not wanting to face the feelings I know will overwhelm me if I open my eyes and hear the truth.

"Oh, for fuck's sake, Mina, snap out of it. Your mates are fine, and if you come back to us, you can see them." The voice is pissed off now, and with a blazing flash of light and what feels like a jolt of electricity, I sit up straight, eyes wide, blinded. When it clears, a very pissed off goddess is staring at me, hands on hips, brows creased, and mouth pursed.

"Jesus, Mina, you're supposed to be my *champion*. Having a meltdown like that is not acceptable. Get. It. Together." The last few words are thunderous and have me snapping out of my funk immediately, her words triggering memories. Memories that had been hidden, memories of speaking to Mylea before in a void-like space, much like the one I just left. Gasping in shock, I gape at her in surprise.

"I remember it all now." She has a smug smile on her lips, annoyance giving way to an all-knowing smirk. My heart races like crazy as all of it floods back in. "You want me to defeat Hammus." She nods, that smile still on her face.

"Are you fucking crazy? What the hell have you been smoking?" I shout at her, and the annoyed frown immediately comes back.

"I know you remember what I said. I put everything in motion for this to happen, Mina. *You* are the only chance this world and all the others have. Don't pussy out on me now!" Her words are like a slap across the face, easing my panic slightly and allowing me to take a couple of deep breaths. "Remember, you won't be doing it on your own. That's why I gave you so many mates."

These words are like another slap, and my worry for them returns tenfold.

"Well, where the hell are they? Why can't I feel them?" I growl back at her, not concerned with her status at all. A gasp from behind has me looking around the room. I'm on the couch in my apartment in Mom's palace. Zeph and Mav are both here as well, and so is Jophial. All three have worried looks on their faces like Mylea might smite me down at any second, but I think I'm okay. I mean, why would she make me her champion just to kill me?

Mylea spins on the spot and flounces off toward the bedroom; the pissed-off vibe is strong with her. Once she gets to the door, she pushes it open and gestures like a game show host, revealing my five mates, all laying with their beds side by side, peacefully asleep, surrounded by a golden glow.

A gasp escapes my mouth, and I hurry over to the bed Dru is in, but the glow around her stops me from making contact.

"When you were cut off from them, their bond was cut off too, and all of them suffered for it. The best thing for me to do was put them in a magical stasis, so they wouldn't suffer." My eyes move from Drusilla to Sander and Trick, who are in the next two beds further along. Then on to my Jagger and Kai, both in demon form, their blue and purple skin muted by the golden glow. There's one more bed, but it's empty.

Looking at it, I turn to Mylea with a frown. "Who was in that one?" Her grumpy look clears, and she smiles.

"That was Maggie's. She was quite beside herself when she heard about you and Sam, and we had to sedate her for a little while. Fortunately, she has recovered nicely, and Peter took her home. It did help that we confided in her that Sam was undercover and Zeph and Mav were on their way to help you escape." A pinch of guilt stabs me in my heart, but I'm relieved she's okay and Peter is looking after her.

"What about Mom? Is she okay?" A couple of snorts sound out, and Mylea shoots death stares at the two boys behind me before turning her gaze back to mine.

"I suppose it depends on what your definition of okay is." She tries to avoid the situation, so I turn to Mav, knowing he will tell me the truth. "She and your father reconnected, and things got a bit... heated."

"My father?" I feel my brow crease in a frown, and they all look surprised. *Oh shit. What bombshell did I miss on that front?*

"Oh, honey, yes. I'm sorry, I forget you still don't know. Michael is your father," Mylea says gently.

Holy fuck, Michael! Archangel Michael? Was that why he was looking at me strangely before that mission? What did that even mean? Did he seem disappointed? No, it seemed more disbelief than anything else, like he couldn't believe what he was seeing. Why didn't he say anything? Am I disappointing? Not what he expected? How do two people like Lucifer and Michael end up together? The questions whirl through my mind until the most important one slips past my lips.

"Does he know?" I ask, not sure I want to know the answer.

"He does now. Fuck, I thought we were all going to die when you were captured," Mav breathes, a weird mixture of both panic and relief in his voice at the same time.

"Where are they? Does he want to see me?" Butterflies fly in my stomach, the nerves going crazy.

"Well, it was their first interaction basically since they left you at the orphanage, so to be honest, I'm pretty sure they hate fucked each other to within an inch of their lives, and now neither of them is talking to the other." Blunt and to the point, typical Mav, his summary has me snorting with my own laughter.

"But they did want to help. Michael probably would have gone in with his big sword blazing, but he was shot down and told to get it together. In fact, it was the mention of what your succubus demon might be doing to all of Sabboath's soldiers that had him turning green and tucking tail between his legs." Another snort escapes my mouth, and this time, Mylea laughs too.

"The almighty Michael brought down with one mention of his little girl having a sex life." I sober at her words. Wow, Michael's my dad. I now have both a mom and a dad. That's going to take a little while to get used to.

Mylea reaches out, her touch gentle and warm with an otherworldly kind of comfort to it. "Everything will be okay. I promise," she reassures me, but I still have my doubts. Turning back to my mates, I bring the subject back to them.

"Can we wake them?"

She looks a little uneasy, avoiding eye contact for a moment. "We can, but it might be better to wake them one at a time. When you mate a demon, you sometimes take on a little of that demon's powers yourself. And they were all cut off from that power, so there's a good chance that they're all going to be…"

She breaks off a little awkwardly, and again, Mav's blunt words cut in. "Gagging to fuck."

Her eyebrows turn down in a frown, the expression almost reminiscent of a classic Maggie look. "Classy, Mavromichali, really classy," she drawls at him before continuing. "But he's not wrong."

"But, but, but," I stammer out, nearly dying to be having this conversation within hearing distance of Jophial. The thought of having sex with my five mates is very appealing, and my succubus is dancing a jig inside, but knowing that Samuel and Grayson are still with the AoA frightens me and dampens that desire slightly.

Before I can say anything else, Mylea holds a hand up. "But because you can't really spare the time for a 'yay we're back together orgy,' I will suppress their desires until you get a spare moment."

I snort at her words, the humor of it taking a bit of the awkwardness away. "Yay, we're back together orgy?" It sounds fun, but I'm not sure Drusilla would want in on that.

"That might be a good idea, though will it affect their performance? We need them ready to go as soon as we can. We still have to go to Minzeon and also return a cure to Earth for that plague that's affecting them so badly."

"No, it shouldn't affect anything. The bond may feel a little needy until it's been taken care of but nothing you shouldn't be able to handle. It should be much better than what you've likely been feeling in their absence," she assures me.

My eyes drift from one mate to the other, my inner succubus now sulking with that information. "No, we don't have time for an orgy, but I do need to feed her again; otherwise, she might take matters into her own hands," I explain to the group, "and Jagger and Kai could probably do with the feed too."

"That's a good idea, though they both got blood before they went under," she explains, and my heart lurches, jealousy twisting my lips into a snarl.

"Who the fuck were they feeding on?"

"Whoa." Mylea holds her hands up in defense, and Zeph and Mav both sending calming waves down the bond to me. "Trick and Sander were the donors." My jealousy dies a swift death, and my desire instantly takes over at the thought of my four mates in intimate positions. Maybe we *do* have time for a "yay, we're back together orgy."

A small smile lights up Zeph's face, Mav's choked back chuckle making me blush. "No, Mina, we don't have time." He must be able to see the lust in my eyes, or maybe I'm drooling slightly. I wipe my mouth with the back of my arm just in case.

"Okay, then let's wake up the demons and leave the others as is until you're finished." Mylea waves a hand, and Drusilla, Sander, and Trick disappear.

"Just moving them into another bedroom," she assures me before conjuring up a huge bed and moving Jagger and Kai to it before dismissing the other beds they were in. She dusts off her hands.

"There, have fun!" With that, she disappears, taking Mav and Zeph with her. Letting my human form drop, my demon flows over me, the use of my power feeling like a great stretch after the collar's deprivation of it.

While I watch, the golden glow surrounding them both slowly dissipates, so I climb up on the bed and shuffle in between, waiting for my demon lovers to wake up. Before I can even settle in, my succubus starts to give off pheromones to speed up the process. *Thirsty bitch!*

Chapter Twenty-Five

Jagger

My brain pounds and my mind is foggy as I struggle to open my eyes. *Fuck, what happened?* I try and think back to the last thing I remember. A spicy clove scent fills my mind, followed by the reminder of delicious blood and a flash of drinking from Sander. That's right; the hunger from missing Mina and the ache in our chest from the missing bond was making us sick. The video clip of Drusilla convulsing on the floor is like a movie reel on a continuous loop in my brain now that it's all coming back. Mylea offering to put us all in stasis until Mina could be rescued is the next thing that flashes. So if I'm awake, does that mean…

A sensual, exotic scent is the next thing to register, my nostrils flaring, trying to take in as much of it as I can, and as I recognize it, my eyes burst open. A vision of an angel above me has a smile reaching my lips. Her long black hair, falls down around her face like a waterfall of silk, and her red eyes are filled with desire and love. My heart skips a beat at the sight of my mate, relief flowing through me and washing away the empty ache of missing her.

"Hello, handsome." Mina's husky voice shoots straight to my cock, and my instincts take over, all rational thought gone. Growling, I pull her into me, holding her tight as I breathe in her luscious scent and just feel *her*. I'm unbelievably happy she's safe and seemingly uninjured, though there's a nasty ring of scarring around her neck, which I will be asking about later. For right now, nothing else matters.

She snuggles into my chest, her arms coming around me, and I hear her muffled voice say, "I missed you too." We're just laying there, breathing each other in, when another voice that lights my nerve-endings on fire reaches my ears.

"Mmm, that looks like fun. Can I join in?"

"Kai!" Her shout is joyous, and she squirms to get away. Reluctantly, I let go of her, and she rolls over and throws her arms around him, the two soaking in each other's presence. His arms reach around her, pulling her in tight, but they also reach for me, so between us, we make a Mina sandwich and just breathe, grateful to be alive and together once again.

Kai pulls back and starts to pepper her with questions. "What happened? How did you escape?

Are you okay?" His hand reaches up, and he runs a finger around the scarring on her neck, an angry rumble escaping his lips. Before he can say anything else, Mina silences him by putting her mouth over his in a kiss that's so hot it could start fires.

She pulls back, a blinding smile on her face and heated look in her eyes. "Less talk, more sex. I'll answer all your questions after we wake the others up so they can hear. But right now, Mama has a hunger that only you two can fix." I snort as that shuts him up instantly, his eyes becoming hooded with desire. Our mate knows how to play Kai just like a fiddle, yet that only makes her even more attractive in my eyes.

She waves her hand, and in an instant, his clothes are removed, his fit naked body on display for us both to enjoy. Mina purrs her excitement, wiggling her ass against my now aching cock, the friction doing something deliciously torturous. She reaches an arm backward, bringing my head down until our breaths mingle.

"Look at our mate, Jagger. Isn't he pretty?" she purrs before taking my mouth with hers. Her tongue tangles with mine in a sensual dance as old as time, and Kai's eyes don't leave us for even a moment. After that teasing touch, she pulls back. "Don't you think a pretty body like that deserves worshipping?" Her voice is a caress across my skin, and from the way that Kai shivers, I'd say he feels it too.

Without waiting for the answer, he grabs her and pulls her against his chest. "Mina baby, I missed you, and I'm so happy to see you. Do whatever you want to me; I won't complain. I'm just happy you're alive and safe." The solemn words from a normally not serious Kai have Mina pausing and looking between us, something heavy passing through her eyes.

"He's right, sweetheart. God, we were a mess when you were gone. I don't know what we'd do if you were actually taken from us permanently. I don't think we'd be able to survive, even for each other." Her eyes widen as Kai nods his head; the two of us need her more than just as an extra partner. There's something about her blood, her power, everything that just makes her, *her*, that we can't and don't want to live without.

"You're the glue that holds us together. Without you, we'd come apart. I really don't know how your parents survived being apart all these years; it proves how strong they are to beat the pain of a damaged soul mate bond." Her eyes shimmer with unshed tears, and her face softens.

"I know how you feel. I was so empty inside without you." She pulls us both in close, and we share a three-way kiss. It's a little messy, definitely desperate, but it's also perfect.

Kai lifts her leg, sliding it over his hip, and strokes a finger through her folds, her breath hitching at his movements. Looking over her shoulder, I watch as he feeds his cock into her pussy with one long slow thrust. A loud moan from her lips echoes through the room, and my hands brush strokes over her body, caressing her tight ass cheeks before moving higher. Reaching around, my hands find her breasts, and I rub each nipple between fingers and thumb, tweaking them as he continues to thrust in and out. Her hands are all over him, gripping him tight as they lovingly look into each other's eyes.

My heart soars with intense happiness at seeing my two mates taking their pleasure from each other. Just feeling their emotions through the bond keeps me included and part of the process even though they're physically focused on one another for the moment. Mina's tail is wrapped around my cock, softly stroking up and down. Just enough pressure and speed to keep me on edge as I watch my mates make love to each other.

Leaving one nipple, I slowly caress her soft skin as I move down to her clit, reaching between them to coat my fingers in her wetness before circling it. Kai's thrusts pick up, and both of their breathing increases. He has an intense look of concentration that causes a slight wrinkle between his eyes; he's completely in the moment. Kai pulls her even closer and leans in, giving her access to his neck at the same time he turns her head slightly. And as I watch, I can see his pupils dilate, his thrusts becoming erratic. They both groan out loud then swiftly lean in, biting down on each other's necks. Kai's throat moves rhythmically as he swallows Mina's blood, her body continuing to squirm in my arms with her prolonged orgasm.

Finally, they draw apart, both of them sweaty and breathing heavily, Kai's eyes hooded with desire. They slowly exchange more soft kisses, no words needed as they confirm their love for one another. Eventually, his eyes drift to mine, and a sly smile crosses his lips.

"I think it's time to show Jagger just how much you missed him too, love." He pulls out of her, his cock still hard and glistening with her release, and helps her roll over. When her eyes meet mine, my heart skips a beat. Her pupils are blown and her lips swollen from being loved on by Kai, and she's never looked more beautiful to me.

Looking down at her, I smile. "Hi, beautiful." A soft smile crosses her face as she wraps her arms around my neck and pulls herself into my chest.

"Hi, handsome." With those words, her mouth meets mine, her tongue slipping into it. Her tongue stroking and tangling with mine as I feel her love for me pulse deep inside our bond. It's quite amazing, and I feel my heart rate increase and my breathing pick up even more so when a hand on my cock has me looking down. Kai's purple fingers are wrapped around it, giving it slow strokes, revving my engine even higher than Mina's tail had. Mina's mouth leaves mine, and she kisses and caresses my chest. My eyes meet his over her head, and he has this relaxed, fully satisfied smile that I've only recently seen in moments with the three of us.

His hand leaves my cock, and he grabs Mina under the knee, hitching her leg over my hip this time. Looking down, I can see his release dripping out of her, and a growl of possession leaves my mouth. It's so sexy watching his cum drip out of her. Seeing where my eyes are, he runs a finger through her folds, Mina gasping from the sensation, before holding his finger up covered in their combined juices.

"Taste your mates, Jagger. Taste their desire for each other," he demands, putting his finger into my mouth. Closing my lips around it, I suck hard, removing the salty-sweet flavor off of them and running my tongue around to make sure I haven't missed any. He removes his finger and smirks at me as my eyes go to Mina, our girl now panting from the show she's been transfixed by. She grabs me by the hair, our soft sweet Mina gone and replaced by a wildcat.

"Fuck me now, Jagger, and fuck me hard," she orders, a hint of steel beneath the passion in her voice. So, sitting up, I flip her onto her hands and knees, and she squeals with surprise before shouting again.

"Yes, like this."

Before I can thrust my cock deep, Kai quickly lays down on his back and shuffles underneath Mina, giving his mouth access to her clit. Looking down at him, I raise an eyebrow, receiving nothing but his wicked grin in response. Unable to hold back any longer, I straddle his chest and thrust my cock deep into her tight wet heat. All three of us groan with the movement, but I don't wait, starting a punishing pace of thrust and retreat, Mina's pussy gripping me tight, rippling with her impending orgasm. Then I feel a warm breath on my balls, and Kai's tongue starts to caress them as I thrust in and out, his tail probing between my ass cheeks. It's covered in lube and slowly pushes in, past my tight ring, going deep. A guttural groan leaves my mouth, and my head hangs low as I adjust to the feeling. It's almost too much: my cock in Mina, his mouth on my balls, and now his tail in my ass. I'm about to tell him, but his mouth moves as Mina shouts.

"Oh my fucking god." Kai's mouth must have moved back to her clit, and without any warning, I feel her orgasm explode, her pussy clamping down hard, as I struggle to thrust through it. With the added tail, it doesn't take many more thrusts before I'm coming hard enough for my eyes to roll back into my head. Leaning forward, I bite down hard on Mina's shoulder while offering her my wrist. Her fangs slide into my skin, and my orgasm moves to the next level. My body pulses with electrical pulses, each one more powerful than the other. I continue to swallow down her sweet blood until finally pulling away and sealing the marks.

After sealing my marks in return, we both collapse to the bed, smothering Kai on the way down. His tail pulls out of my ass, and I pull out of Mina, collapsing next to them, breathing hard. Kai's muffled laughter has Mina rolling off of him.

"Wow, now that would be something, death by pussy." He chuckles, his face glistening with mine and Mina's combined release. His long demon tongue comes out, and he proceeds to lick his face like a cat, laughing the whole time.

When the three of us finally come down from our sexual bliss, Mina places a kiss on both our lips and quickly gets out of bed, conjuring clothes onto her form.

"Where are you going?" Kai's lips pout adorably, and I pull him closer to me into Mina's vacated spot, and he snuggles into my chest.

"I love you guys, and I wish we could stay and snuggle, but I have three more mates waiting to be woken and two more out there waiting for us." She points to the door, and I frown.

"Two more? *Who*?" I ask, growling and sitting up, Kai mumbling a sleepy complaint as I push him off of me. The jealousy and worry inside of me are flaring to life, and I'm fighting hard to keep myself even this calm. *What if we don't like these guys? What if they take up all her time?*

She shoots me an amused grin as she pulls her black hair up into a ponytail, not changing back into her human form, and a small smile crosses my lips. I love it when she doesn't hide her demon. She's sexy anyway, but with her horns and tail on display, she's *breathtakingly* sexy. There's a newfound confidence she's been lacking when she first transitioned. It was like watching a butterfly spread her wings for the first time and turning to face the sun. Stunning and magnificent. She catches my admiring smile and winks, quickly jumping back on the bed to give us both a kiss before hurrying out of the room.

Bemused, I suddenly realize she never answered my question, and I nudge Kai, who's snoring softly next to me. He grumbles his protest, so I get down close to him and whisper in his ear, "Mina bonded two more mates, and they're out in the other room." His purple eyes snap open instantly.

"Who? Do we like them? Shit, we'll probably hate them, and Mina will hate us." He scrambles to sit up, heaving with panic that would be adorable if I wasn't feeling my own fair share of the same thing. "We'll just kill them if that's the case." His lip juts out in a stubborn pout with those last words.

I chuckle in reply, but it cuts off when his eyes move from mine to the closed door, an insecure look on his face that I've never seen before. "I don't know. She left without answering, but we should just go and have a look."

Pulling him close, I put my hands on his cheek and place a soft kiss on those pouty lips, trying to soothe the worry from his mind. "It won't be like that. Mylea wouldn't do that to Mina *or* us. She would have made sure they were all compatible when she chose them. Otherwise, why interfere?" I stroke a loving hand down his chest and contemplate staying in bed, but he's too distracted. In any case, his roiling worries are enough to keep my own from settling, so, rolling over, I climb off and use my magic to clean us up and redress us.

With that brief use of my power, I realize one important thing: *I feel amazing*. Back to normal with the mating bond nestled deep in my chest where it's supposed to be. I'm no longer tired or achy or hungry.

Holding a hand out to Kai, I pull him out of bed and shove him forward. "Dude, what is wrong? This isn't like you. You're a take life by the balls kind of guy, and right now, you're acting like a bury-your-head-in-the-sand chicken."

I finally get some kind of reaction as his mouth drops open, so I keep going. "Stop being a pussy, you big wimp!" His eyes narrow, and he growls, a spark of the normal Kai finally peeking through.

Smiling widely, I slap him on the ass. "That's more like it. Let's get out there and give these new mates the stink eye."

I don't need to egg him on anymore because he's striding for the door, black hair streaming behind him, tail alert and ready for anything. Breathing out a sigh of relief, I quickly follow, needing to make sure he behaves enough that Mina doesn't put us on her shit list. *Not when we've just got her back.*

Chapter Twenty-Six

Malakai

Wrenching open the door, I storm through the apartment, reaching the living area quickly and looking around. The only two occupants I can see are Zeph and Mav sitting on the sofa, both looking worn out and worried. Jagger catches up to me while I'm scanning the room for these newcomers, but he pushes past and heads over to the sofa, giving them both fist bumps before dropping down next to Mav.

"Good to see you up and around," Zeph says to him, and I hear Jagger reply, but I'm too distracted.

"Kai, what are you doing? What are you looking for?" Mav's words have me looking at him, the tension of my body leaking into his. He's standing up, fists clenched, as he now gazes around the room on high alert.

"Where are Mina's two new mates? She said they were here, and I need to let them know the score."

Mav's fists unclench, his face smoothing out

before a chuckle leaves his mouth. As my eyebrow raises, he drops back down onto the sofa, completely relaxed. My eyes move from him to Jagger, who has a smile on his face too and a knowing glint in his eye that says I'm the last to have figured something out.

Then it finally hits me, the room breaking out into quiet chuckles as we're all finally on the same page. *Well, I feel stupid now.*

"You guys?" I ask, moving over to join them on the couch, and they both nod. Breathing out a sigh of relief, I push my hair back from my face.

"Thank fuck for that. I was worried it was going to be a couple of assholes who I hated. You guys, I can at least tolerate," I joke, and they exchange a look, enough of their smiles dimming to let me know there's something else we *don't* know.

"Hmm, I'm not sure that I'm liking this." I wave between them, and Jagger sits up too, the first hints of wariness traveling down the bond between us.

"What do you know that you're not telling us?" he asks firmly.

Zeph blows out a sigh. "Let's wait for Mina and the others since she's just waking them, and we can all tell you what went down while you've been asleep."

Reluctantly, I agree, and we sit there in a tense silence, but my stomach rumbles its displeasure, breaking it.

"How about I order us up some food? That way

we can all eat and be comfortable while we tell you everything." Mav stands up and heads to the tablet on the breakfast bar in the kitchen, and although I appreciate the offer, the rest of my body is telling me that what we need most is information.

"What time is it, anyway?" I ask, and Mav looks up from the tablet.

"It's nine in the morning, so I'm going to order us brunch," he replies, swiping his finger across the screen.

"And coffee," Jagger adds in, and Mav looks up, rolling his eyes.

"Of course. Any other requests?"

"Beer," I grumble, and he raises his eyebrows but quickly nods his head.

From the look they exchanged, I've got a feeling that this next conversation is going to need alcohol to soften the blow.

He finishes the order and comes back to sit down, and it's not long after that that the anticipatory silence is broken by Trick and Sander. They both look heaps better than they had before our enforced coma.

As I look them over, a small pulse of adrenaline races through my system. There was something quite... *interesting* about to begin before Mylea put us to sleep, and my body is keenly aware of what it missed out on. Both look well-rested, and they have open wounds on their necks from where Jagger and I drank from them, slightly oozing with blood. The stasis must have stopped it temporarily, and it's started again now that they're awake. I move toward Trick, intent on fixing him up and taking the opportunity to see if his body is on the same page as mine. My eyes run over his lean but strong body, an appreciative purr slipping out of my mouth. Pulling him close after inspecting the smirk that's grown with each closed inch between us, I whisper in his ear, "Thank you for helping me out before. Let me know if I can ever return the favor."

My hand brushes over his cock, making it clear just what favor I'd like to return, before I lean in and close the wounds on his neck then clean up all the dripping blood around it. He shudders as a shiver of desire runs down his back before I step away, winking at him. As I turn and head back to the sofa, I find Sander next to Jagger, doing the same thing. There's a definitive light of interest in both of their gazes, appreciation clear for the potential of what's to come between us all. We join them, me next to Jagger and Trick on the other side of Sander, but before anything can be said, Mina and Drusilla join us, their heads together as they giggle over something. Drusilla's wrapped around Mina like a cling-on, and Mina glowing with joy. It brings a smile to the lips of the rest of us on the couch. Thank goodness for all the room on the large sectional because they sit on the other end across from Mav and Zeph.

Every now and then I catch other people's feelings trickling through the bond, not just Mina and Jagger's. It feels awesome to be connected to one another and know how thrilled everyone is. It's reassuring to know there's no jealousy or resentment in any of them.

Mina looks up, her smile wide and her eyes shining with happiness before she turns to me and winks.

"I see you met my other two mates, Kai." She laughs as Drusilla, Sander, and Trick, all stand up and congratulate their teammates.

"I think we all knew it was coming but it's a relief to finally have it done." She perfectly describes how I know I'd been feeling, and I'm sure all the others were too. Hugs and back slaps are exchanged, and Dru kisses them both on the cheek, smiling, before returning quickly to Mina.

I think Mina being captured shook Dru more than we all thought, but she appears to look much better than she had before, and I'm even more relieved than I'd expected that she seems to be okay again. I like the little minx. She was the first to be friendly to me, and for that, she has my eternal gratitude.

A knock on the door has Mav leaving, his return followed by another two demons pushing carts stacked high with plates of food. He gestures to the large dining room table, and they head over there to set up. Once they have, they quickly exit as quietly as they'd entered.

"Come on, I'm starving! We can tell you everything that's happened while we eat." Mav waves us all over, running a gentle hand down Mina's arm as he passes by her like now that he *can* touch her, he doesn't want to miss the chance.

Moving over there, Dru never lets go of Mina's hand, and they find a seat next to each other while the rest of us spread out around it. The only sound that can be heard for the next few minutes is silver knocking against plates as everyone quickly attacks the food. Zeph gets up and starts pouring everyone cups of coffee from a large carafe, and Sander helps himself to one of the beers before offering everyone else one. Accepting one, I extend one of my claws, popping the top off mine before reaching over and doing it to his. He smiles gratefully, and we tap them together with a loud clink that triggers the talking.

"So, I guess we should start at the beginning," Mina mumbles around a mouthful of food, "but you go first and tell your bit, because I only ate one meal since they took me however long ago it was, and I'm starving."

"A week, I think." Dru's voice is quiet, her knuckles white as she grips her knife and fork. "I'm not sure exactly because I don't know how long we were out."

"It was only two days, " Mav reassures her, and the edge of her lips curls up in a soft, grateful smile before she keeps eating.

"Okay, so you know about the meeting, and it was after that you went into stasis," Zeph starts, and the five nod their heads, Mina continuing to shovel food into her mouth in lieu of responding. I snort but quickly blank my face as she looks up at me, eyes feral with hunger. She raises an eyebrow, but I just shake my head. I just got my mate back; I have no desire to earn her anger by coming between her and her food.

"That's what I thought," she grumbles, a forkful of scrambled eggs garbling the end of the comment.

Mav and Zeph take turns explaining all they'd been through. By the time they're finished updating us, my mind is racing. *They went on an adventure and fought a god, stopped a plague from worsening on Earth, and basically rescued Mina by themselves. Not to mention both had time to sex Mina up and become her mates.* Nothing like a magical coma to make a guy feel useless.

Zeph clears his throat and looks at Mina, who's finally slowed down her intake of food.

She shakes her head in surprise. "Jesus, sorry, I'm not sure why I was so damn hungry. I mean, I know why but that was ridiculous. It's like I was eating for five."

"Do you want to tell your part now, and then we can tell you what happened when we were together after that?" She nods, drinking down a huge gulp of coffee before leaning back in her chair and rubbing her stomach.

"Yeah, ok, I can do that. So... um..." She bites her lip, looking around the table, and the uncertainty in her eyes makes me send love down the bond. Almost immediately, some of the unease calms, as if knowing that we're standing by her no matter what she says is just what she needs to keep going forward.

"After Connie kicked me in the head, I'm not really sure what happened, but I woke up chained to a wall with cuffs around both feet and hands and a collar around my neck. I have brief flashes of before that, but it's mainly pain and misery." A growl escapes my mouth before I can stop it, and the others all mumble threats under their voices. Dru pales at Mina's words, and Mina squeezes her hand reassuringly, ever the caretaker.

My fists rhythmically clench and unclench as she shares with us how Connie and her companions treated her, my eyes narrowing when her body tenses again. *What could she possibly say that's worse than her being beaten?* Her voice hitches as she explains, "Guys, the wolf... It shifted into *Sam*." Her eyes meet all of ours, widening as she searches for panic or confusion but finds none. "You knew all this?"

"Yeah, she did the same thing after you were unconscious. It's like she wanted to shove it in our face what a fucking traitor the bastard is." Sander curls his lip up in disgust, obviously remembering what happened that day, and Trick grabs his hand, giving it a squeeze.

When no one else adds anything, she takes a deep breath and continues, probably thankful to just purge all of this as quickly as she can.

"Anyway they left, leaving behind Silas and Beatrice to torture me, but my scales clicked into place, and they couldn't do anything. By then, I was starving and weak, so my succubus decided to come out and play. I was able to siphon some energy from feeding off the lust that came from the guards who took me away to get cleaned up for Sabboath..." She pauses and looks at Drusilla. "Do you want to go and take a shower or something while I tell the next bit? It's not fun," she asks gently, but there's a stubborn set to Dru's mouth as she shakes her head.

"No, if you can live through it, then I can damn well listen to it." Mina smiles at her, but worry still flits across her eyes.

"Then they removed my clothes and started fondling me. One of them was getting ready to rape me."

"Fuck!" Trick shouts suddenly, interrupting her tale as he jumps to his feet and throws his coffee mug across the room. It shatters against a wall, leaving a big dark coffee stain behind. Sander reaches up and pulls him back down into his chair, wrapping an arm around him, while Zeph gestures at the mess, and it all disappears. *Archangel powers sure are handy.*

A chill runs down my spine as her words echo through my head on repeat. A wave of power flows through me, and I change forms to my mega demon, a bellowed roar escaping my mouth. The room drops into silence, wary eyes watching me as I pick up my chair and haul it in the same direction as Trick's mug. Before it can make contact, Mina holds up her hand, freezing it. Bringing it back to me, she lowers it into place. My breathing is erratic, and a low growling sound rumbles from deep inside my chest.

"Whoa, baby." She holds her hands up as she approaches me like you would a wild animal. Her scent fills my nose, and my breathing and heart rate calm., My body shrinks back to its normal size as she wraps her arms around me, running her hands through my hair and up and down my back in soothing motions. Her words are quiet and reassuring as I finally come to my senses.

She pulls back and looks me in the eye. "You okay?"

"Yeah, I'm sorry. It's you it happened to and here you are having to calm me. I'm so sorry."

"It's okay, Kai. I get it. I would probably be the same," she reassures me before moving me back to my seat and then sitting on my lap for the rest of the story, her close contact bringing me reassurance.

"This is where it gets good, guys." Mina's eyes now gleam with something else, and her smile turns wicked, that beautiful devilish side of her peeking out.

The table is silent as Mina finishes telling us what happened to that piece of shit angel with a bloodthirsty chuckle. A moment later, everyone explodes into cheers. She rolls her eyes but smiles anyway, the warmth she feels from our support wrapping around me like a comfortable blanket. *Our girl can take care of herself. Not that that'll stop us from trying to do it too, but I'm so lucky to have such a formidable mate.*

"But wait, there's so much more..."

By the time we've learned about Sabboath's dragon shifter son, Mina's *third* new mate, the table is silent again. *What the fuck are we going to do about him?* The first person other than me to not be a member of this relationship, and if what Mina says is true, that he's never even gone to school to get away from Sabboath, this guy's going to have a steep learning curve. I've got to say, I thought I would be pissed off, but I kind of feel a kinship to him. Team Alpha is full of great people, but if I didn't have Jagger here to anchor me, I would still be adrift. Their team has years of history together, romantic, familial, and otherwise, and it's not easy coming in as an outsider.

"There's actually a reason for him never being able to leave," Zeph says, taking over while Mina pours herself another cup of coffee. There's an excited vibe that fills the air with that dramatic pronouncement, and I'm not sure if the situation is about to become much better or much worse with whatever he shares next.

"What's that?" Jagger asks, naturally filling in what everyone wants to say.

"It's because he's Grayson, Tiberion's long lost son, and Sabboath stole him all those years ago to brainwash him and use him against his own people!"

Mina frowns, confused by his words, but the rest of us understand.

"Oh my god, he didn't die?" Drusilla asks, and Mav shakes his head.

"He says he has fuzzy memories of before, but not a lot," Mina tells us. "What's this about a Tiberion? I've never even heard of that guy."

"Grayson was the first child born to an Archangel couple, the reason that Archangels were banned from having kids. His mother was killed in an attack, and no one knew what happened to him. According to the dads, *his* dad is still broken up about losing his wife and child even now," Zeph says, compassion lacing his matter-of-fact explanation.

Mina's hand goes to the scarring I know is under the turtleneck she's currently wearing, clouds forming in her eyes.

"Tiberion, his father, who used to be a part of our fathers' circle of friends, has become a recluse, devastated by the loss of his family."

"Oh, that's all so horrible!" Mina exclaims,

genuine sorrow flooding the bond. If anyone is going to know about how much being separated from one's family can hurt, it's her. I think when she and Grayson have a chance to get to know each other, they'll realize they have a lot more in common than they might've thought.

"We have to tell someone about this," Sander urges, starting to stand up. "Who should we call? The dads? Mylea? We've got to find a way to get him out of there!"

"Hang on," Mina says quietly, stopping him by holding up a hand. "Sit back down; there's still more for me to tell."

Chapter Twenty-Seven

Jessamina

I swallow a lump in my throat. I don't know if it's there because of the information I just found out about poor Grayson, or because of what I have to tell them now. Even though Mav, Zeph, and I are on our way to forgiving Samuel, this will be the first they hear of it since they thought he'd become a traitor.

"After Grayson and I created our bond, Sabboath came back for him. Grayson then blew some kind of smoke at me that paralyzed me and carried me to the lab for Sabboath. Luckily, my armor had activated before he did this, and because of that, Sabboath wasn't able to harvest the eggs that he'd wanted to."

Again the table erupts with bellows of fury, Drusilla joining them this time. Annoyed at the continual interruptions, I wave a hand at the five of them. Instantly, they are strapped in their seats, gags around their mouths.

"If you all keep interrupting every time I say

something that upsets you, we're going to be at this all day. It was upsetting enough to live through all of this once, and I really don't want to spend my entire first day back with my mates *re*living it." My eyes move from one to the next. They can't say anything, and their eyes are all narrowed at me, but they eventually nod their heads in agreement.

So I finish the tale, speeding through Sabboath injecting me with a mystery formula and right into the part that's *really* going to make them upset.

"This time, they threw in someone new, a demon in transition that they had taken prisoner. Or so I thought." Their eyes widen, and I feel equally proud and grateful that I thought of using the gags. I can feel them pushing against my mind, trying to talk, but I've got them blocked.

"Before I could stop him, he was on me. I begged for him to stop, but he just wasn't able to. Besides that, my succubus was pretty happy to comply, so I let him fuck me." I hang my head in shame, not able to meet the other guys' eyes, a tear rolling down my cheek as I admit my second betrayal. Before the tear can hit the ground, a soft hand grabs mine, and I look up at Drusilla, her eyes imploring me to remove the restraints.

"Mina darling, you couldn't help it, and I'm sure once he was coherent again, he felt terrible. Neither of you are to blame. If anyone deserves the weight of that burden, it's Sabboath."

"He didn't bite me at the same time, so no bond

was formed, but when he finally came back to his senses, he was horrified. What was weird was that he knew my name, but we didn't get to talk again until later. Sabboath came back to visit and turned the cell into a little love nest before he would give us another chance to talk to each other."

The others have settled down, marginally, at least, so I remove their restraints as well.

"Where did he get the demon? None have been reported missing to us!" Even though his words are rough, I know there's underlying concern, so I push aside the way my back wants to bristle at his tone.

"Don't worry, it's none of the protected ones; it's one he created. He's gotten his hands on different demon essences, and he used this prisoner as a test subject to see if he could make a demon." I rub a hand across my brow, a small headache sitting behind my eyes. Everything that has happened is finally catching up with me.

"Holy shit," Trick whispers, the following silence feeling heavy as everyone is lost in this revelation. If Sabboath can create demons and shifters, what's the limit to his madness? Sander gets up and heads to the bottles of beer, handing one out to all of the guys before offering one to Dru and me, though the two of us decline with a smile. I need to be totally clear-headed to get through the rest of this.

Blowing out a breath, I continue. "Once Sabboath was gone, I helped the new demon change forms, not expecting anything, but sitting there in front of me was none other than Sam."

I hurry on before anyone can say anything, hoping the shock will keep them quiet long enough to hear the rest. "I was so fucking angry at him. I yelled and screamed and accused him of breaking my heart and all of yours too, but when I finally calmed down enough, he told me it wasn't what it looked like."

Sander scoffs but doesn't say a word as I shoot him a glare. "Yes, he said *originally,* Connie was doing something to him, a spell or something, and when he finally realized this, he went to the dads. They asked him to spy for them, and Mylea gave him divine protection and urged him to complete this task." I see Kai open his mouth to start to argue, but I hold up a finger, silencing him too.

"Don't you think if we had been told we would have all wanted to help? Are your acting skills good enough to pull that off? It had to look real! I do not like how this all came about, not at all, but it means more that he's alive and we have a chance for him to stay safe so long as his cover doesn't get blown before we're ready."

Silence reigns for what feels like the millionth time this morning, and the hints of feelings coming through our bonds really run the full range: betrayal, worry, sadness, anger, acceptance, even pity. Little tics next to the eye and twitches of hands tell the story of them trying to process all of this.

Dru is the first to break the silence. "He's not a traitor?" Her voice hitches, and she raises her eyebrows, looking at me with hope.

"No, sweetie, he's not," I tell her gently, and she bursts into tears. I put my arm around her and pull her close, her tears wetting the front of my shirt as she sobs with relief both for Sam and, I'm guessing, the fact that I'm safe again. Looking around the table, I see the wary looks on the boys' faces.

Zeph must see them too because he quickly speaks up. "Look, I know it seems impossible, I thought so too, but it's true. Sam's been feeding info to Jophial who's been passing it on to the other dads."

"I didn't want to believe it," Mav says quietly. "I wasn't going to believe it. It took me a while to see it. I even beat the shit out of him, but he really is still on our side, and I'm not going to hold a grudge because he did everything to make Mina's job easier, even if he didn't do it in a way that we liked."

"Look, I know it's hard to believe, and it may take a while for you to forgive him, but he and Grayson made it possible for the three of us to escape. Grayson worked out how to break the collar and shut down the camera, and Sam teleported into the cell and told us. They've both stayed behind for now because their cover is still solid. They want to know what he's up to next."

All cried out, Drusilla pulls back and shoots me

a watery smile. I try to smile back, but it's inter-rupted by an escaping yawn, my eyes feeling heavier than they should. "It's a lot to process, and I'm exhausted. Do you think we could table this while I have a nap? Mav and Zeph could both do with one too. None of us have been sleeping for the last two days." I laugh so they know I'm joking about them sleeping, but really, I feel like I'm about to drop.

"Go and sleep, all of you." Trick stands up and waves a hand, clearing the table of our meal. "I'm going to message Dad, let him know we're awake and okay. We should probably go and check-in at the CD, see if we can help with anything."

"Good idea." Zeph stands, coming over to me and holding out a hand. "Your dad was at the CD last we saw him. I think they were going to interro-gate all the AoA members we stunned on Minzeon. According to their source's information... which I guess means Sam, a lot of them weren't there by choice." I don't get a chance to do anything but wave goodbye to my other mates as Mav and Zeph herd me toward the bedroom I'd been in with Jagger and Kai.

The bed's a jumbled mess, but with a wave of his hand Mav has the sheets changed and tidied as Zeph helps me out of my clothes before stripping himself off. I climb into the cold, clean sheets and move into the middle, waiting for my new mates to join me. Both strip off and snuggle in, and I'm surrounded by warmth and hard bodies, but for the first time in I don't know how long, I have no interest in sex. With a whispered *I love you* echoing in each ear, the feelings in our bond only confirming that truth, I smile, comfortable, content, and safe for the first time in days. Before I can take a breath to return the sentiment, I drift off to sleep.

——— • • • ———

Waking alone has me frowning and grumpy. What's the point in having mates if you wake up and find your bed empty? Like seriously. *"Drusilla?"* I test the link, trying to find my smallest mate. The thought of her sexy body rubbing against mine is causing my hungers to explode, but there's no response. That's strange, so I quickly dress myself and head out to the living area, but there's not a soul in sight. I try to telepath again, thinking maybe they returned to our apartment on Reath, but of course we're in the underground, so I come up against the barriers of the protection spell.

A note on the table catches my eye, and I hurry over to it before I can get wrapped up in my rising irritation.

Gone back to Reath for clothes and supplies. Won't be long. Love, us. Xoxox

Not wanting to wait for my mates to return, I make my way through the palace and underground city to the elevator. A few people greet me on the way, but I make good time. Once I get topside, I quickly teleport to our apartment in the CD building.

The apartment is quiet, and a smile crosses my face as I search through the bedrooms for my mates but once again come up empty.

"Drusilla?" I push into her mind, now able to communicate with her.

"Mina, you're awake already? We expected you to sleep longer!" she exclaims, her surprise tempered by what feels like distraction.

"I got hungry and wondered where you were," I purr seductively, but she doesn't seem to notice.

"Ah yeah, we're at the CD." A feeling of worry creeps into our link, and now that I notice, I can tell that everyone else has their link shut down.

"What's going on?" I demand, but she doesn't reply right away.

"Oh, um…"

"Drusilla," I growl, resignation dropping on our bond like a weight on her shoulders.

"The guys and Michael are arguing, He's insisting on seeing you, and they're trying to convince him to wait until you've rested. He's having a bit of a tantrum. Lucifer says he's very volatile at the moment because he's kept all his emotions bottled up for twenty years, but the way he's behaving isn't making the guys feel any more comfortable with him visiting you right now. Unfortunately, they're presenting like a toddler having a tantrum. The other dads are trying to

calm him, but it's not working, and Lucifer is just laughing at him, which I'm afraid is making it worse. It's a shit show."

Surprise hits me with another hint of adrenaline. Siffa and I got along well right from the beginning even though I didn't know she was my mom. Michael and I didn't really have a chance to even talk since we were thrown into the mission. What I had seen of Michael had made me assume that he was a very controlled man. This doesn't seem normal, and I'm not sure how I feel about it.

"Should I come there? Do you think that will help?" I ask her. She's silent for a moment before a wave of relief flows down her link.

"Your mom says yes. He's not going to be happy until he can meet you properly and see for himself that you're okay. She says to come in demon form. He needs to reconcile with the thought that you're a demon as well as an angel and that you have demon needs, hence the eight mates. I guess part of the freakout is automatically having an adult daughter with a very healthy sex life."

I wince, the warmth of a blush racing over my face and neck. *"He knows?"* I get it, eight's a lot, but I *do* get very hungry, and really, it's Mylea's fault.

"Yeah, but your mom says he'll get over it eventually. It's not like they don't fuck like animals when they're together. Before you yell at me for scarring you for life, that is a direct quote from her." I cringe, wrinkling my nose. That's *not* cool; they're my parents. Nobody wants to hear about their parents fucking. Amusement trickles

into the bond, its lightness helping me recover from some of the embarrassment.

"*Okay, demon form. I can do that. I'll be there in a moment.*" A wave of love and reassurance is what I get in return; she must feel how nervous I am.

Taking a deep breath, I let my demon form take over, wings and all, then change my outfit from long sleeves and pants to shorts, keeping the turtleneck. Eight mates is what we need to fix right now, not throwing the permanent scars into the ring just yet.

I stretch my wings out, groaning with the relief. *Oh god, that feels good.* I can't imagine what the others must have gone through, hiding their true forms all the time. No wonder they didn't want to have to worry about hiding them at home.

Looking around my room, I search for my magic wand, but then a feeling of dread floods my stomach. Fuck, that was in my hair when I was captured on Minzeon. *Did Connie or one of the others take it? Shit, I have to ask Sam. My mind continues to race for a minute before I'm forced to confront the truth of what I'm doing right now: stalling. Is my wand important? Yes. Is it more important than keeping my all-powerful, tantrum-having Archangel father from fighting with my mates? No.*

Time to put on my big girl panties and get out of here. Bringing a picture of the portal room at the CD into my mind, I focus on it. When it's clear, I imagine myself there, and in a flash of light, I am.

I look around the room, taking advantage of the flashing light to scope out the scene while they're all shielding their eyes and waiting. *Wow, this portaling thing is cool. My light isn't white like the Archangels' usually is. Mine is a pink haze, an exact match to my skin. It's pretty!*

The light clears, but they all stay frozen with their hands over their eyes.

"Mina, you need to dim yourself," my mom tells me, still shielding like the others.

"Okay, well, how do I do that?" I ask, beginning to feel slightly hysterical as I watch people start to drop to the floor, screaming, their eyes bleeding. *Holy crap!* "And why am I lit up like this? Archdemons don't glow!" I scream, the panic in my voice and my body affecting my power, the light around me doing the exact opposite of what I want: flaring brighter.

"Well... when we activated your demon blood, I snuck Michael's in at the same time and activated your angel side too. It's why you're so damn powerful and have the feather wings and the angelic glow." The sheepishness in Raphael's voice is obvious even beneath the volume of the groans and screams filling the room.

I'm about to portal out again, unable to control the light, until I can see another, this bright and golden, walking toward me. Michael has a gentle smile on his face as he reaches out his hands to me.

I take them, and he steps into my space, showing none of the signs of pain that are hitting the others. "Just breathe with me," he says softly, so

I match my breathing to his, and as I do, it's like his magic also holds on to mine. I can feel what he's doing, and he dims his light bit by bit, his magic showing mine how it's done. Keeping my breaths aligned with his, I make my light do the same. Before too long, it disappears, and I'm standing there holding my dad's hands, his smile lighting up the room.

"That was great, Mina. You just have to remember to do that every time. Other than Archangels and demons, that light is debilitating to others. For us, it's a bit uncomfortable, but as you can see, its effect is much harder for an AB to withstand." My mates and their dads are positioned around the room, helping the people who were blinded. Their injuries disappear, but they're still a little wide-eyed when looking at me, their apprehension almost tinged with an edge of fear.

My eyes move back to the man in front of me, still holding my hands. His gaze is running the length of me, stopping on my horns and then my wings. His smile gets a little crooked as he gets to my tail, but he quickly gets rid of it.

Eww, I'm not sure I want to know what that *smile was about.*

A worry deep inside has my stomach eating itself. *What does he think? Do I meet his expectations, or is he disappointed?*

Eventually, his gaze comes back to mine, and he pulls me into his arms, his touch reverent and his words genuine. "You are every bit as beautiful as I knew you would be. I am so sorry that your mother and I did what we did, and if we had to go through it again, I would never have given in to pressure. I would have kept you and shouted from the top of the mountains about both you and your mother." He sounds angry, but at himself, not at me.

A hand on my back has me looking up, and my mom joins our hug, my heart feeling like it's going to explode with joy. Out of the corner of my eye, I can see we're surrounded by a privacy bubble—this special moment just for the three of us. Mom has tears rolling down her cheek, and when Michael pulls back, he has misty eyes too.

"God, I missed you so much." He takes Mom's hand before he continues. "*Both* of you so very much. Don't be surprised if I don't let you out of my sight for the next hundred years or so," he tells me, chuckling slightly, and I look to my mom with worry. She must be able to see what's wrong in my eyes. I mean, I get it, but I'm a grown woman with a life. That's going to take him a little bit to get used to, and I hope he doesn't resent me for it, but he *is* going to have to get used to it.

She smiles at him, giving his hand a gentle squeeze. "You mean when she's not working with the CD or with her mates. Don't forget she's a grown woman." Her words practically echo my thoughts, and I'm definitely glad I've got the both of them here. I think Michael's going to need

Mom's help to keep himself balanced as far as my life is concerned.

A frown crosses his face, and he grumbles, "She doesn't need to work. I can take care of her financially. I missed out on so much, and I just want to look after her. It's not fair that we just found her, and now she's going to be taken away from us again!" With that last sentence I hear what Dru was talking about; there's a tinge of hurt to his words, almost hidden beneath the defiant petulance that probably led to earliers tantrum. His words break my heart. Oh my god, Archangel Michael is a huge softie. I pull him into another hug.

"We can still get to know each other; I'll spend plenty of time with you." I change the subject slightly. *Sorry, Mom, about to throw you under the bridge.* "I'm assuming you two will live together again. I'll come and visit all the time."

She glares at me briefly, and I shrug in apology as Michael answers, "Of course we will. I have my house on Amilles." Before he can go any further, she interrupts.

"Well, I have my business on Reath, and I can't very well up and leave it. Not to mention the demon sanctuary on Habbalea."

"Your business?" Dad looks at her, questions in his eyes. Interesting that he's focusing on that part. From the look on his face, the demon sanctuary isn't a surprise. One of the others must have told him about it even if they didn't say she was running it.

Holy fuck, she hasn't told him. I step away from both of them. Thankfully, they seem to have lost interest in me as they face off with one another.

"Yes, I own Eternal Damnation," she tells him, and a look of thunder crosses his face immediately.

"The sex club!"

Not waiting for her response, I turn and quickly exit the privacy bubble, leaving what could possibly be a violent and messy conversation. But hey, at least the attention is off me.

Chapter Twenty-Eight

Jessamina

When I exit the bubble, I notice that the room is a lot quieter with only my mates, the dads, and Clementine remaining.

Drusilla watches me hurry toward them, her eyebrow raising in question. "What's wrong?"

"Ah, we might want to move somewhere else. Mom just told Dad about owning Eternal Damnation."

"Oh, fuck." Zadkiel, Zeph's dad, blanches. "Okay, let's meet back in the conference room upstairs."

One by one, everyone teleports out until just Uriel and I remain. He doesn't look to be in a hurry to leave. In fact, he's creeping closer and closer to the privacy bubble.

"What are you doing?" He jumps and turns to look at me sheepishly.

"Oh, I thought you left when everyone else did." I cross my arms and wait for him to give me an explanation.

"Fine, I wanted to watch Lucifer hand Michael his ass. It's happened once before, and it was the best fight ever." His eyes sparkle, and his grin is gleeful as he looks between me and where my parents are.

Silently, I just raise an eyebrow until his grin drops.

"Fuck, Mina, you're no fun," he grumbles and disappears. Worrying whether I should leave or stay and mediate my parents' fight, I stare at the bubble. Damn it, I wish I could see if they're physically fighting. I don't really want them kicking each other's asses like Uriel said. Deciding to do the right thing, I walk back into the bubble... and immediately regret it.

Holy fuck, I've never made such a bad decision. Slamming my eyes closed at the sight of my parents no longer fighting, I quickly teleport to the conference room, remembering to automatically dim my light.

Jesus, now I need to bleach my eyes. I gag a little, and when I look around, Uriel has a shit-eating grin on his face.

"They weren't fighting anymore, were they?" I just flip him the finger, and he and the other dads chuckle.

Looking around the table, I find a seat open between Sander and Trick, my stomach rumbling with the sight of them. The thought of how their blood tasted has my hunger rising and my core pulsing with thoughts of their naked bodies. Damn it, I'm going to have to feed, and soon. For now, I shake off the feeling and take the seat between them, giving both a kiss on the cheek while trying to ignore the succubus in my head who's screaming at me.

"Okay, this is where we're at," Clementine starts, standing up. "The CD is now clear of all those involved with the AoA, and teams have been restructured and changed. We lost Echo and Bravo. From what we understand, Brock had the rest of his teammates killed, and he was definitely *not* there under compulsion." Jagger's eyes harden at the mention of his previous team leader, and a growl escapes his lips, but he stays quiet.

"Nasty piece of work, that one." Chamuel shudders, a dramatic grimace twisting his face. "His mind was a mess, and he will rot in the Menagerie for the rest of his life."

"Echo have disappeared. They must have gotten away before we could round everyone up.

"Actually, I think they were tipped off," Zeph cuts in, sharing the information about Silas and Beatrice. "I think Mylea needed her to be in the compound, so I think she must have dropped a hint. And, well, Silas is no longer a problem. We didn't see any of the others, but I'm sure they're there somewhere."

"Okay, so Teams Charlie and Delta have now become Bravo and Charlie respectively, and we've cut our losses. We're not replacing Echo. We've got

Team Dragon, and once they get the dragon population sorted, they can take Echo's place."

My heart warms at the mention of Team Dragon at the same time that I'm hit with probably irrational guilt. I have been such a bad friend. I really need to reach out to Livie and see how they're doing. God, my life has changed so quickly in such a short amount of time. I hope she forgives me.

"All of the captured AoA members have been interrogated, and your source was right, just under half of them were not there by their own choices. We've moved them to the hospital wing to be kept under observation and tested to see if we can fix what Sabboath has done to them or at least stabilize it. As of now, they're no longer under any compulsion and not a danger to us. The rest will join Brock in prison."

Raphael stands up, looking at me, and Clementine takes a seat. "Mav and Zeph have shared with us what happened while they were in the compound, so you won't have to go over it again, Mina." I smile gratefully at them, glad I can work on moving forward instead of being dragged back into the memories for the second time today.

"I can't believe the information about Grayson. That's great news, seeing as we thought he was dead. We need to reach out to Tiberion. It will be such an immense relief to him after so many years with no closure." The other fathers quickly murmur their agreement.

"We will have to figure out a way to get him out of there, and I'm sure he will want to be involved all the way. But first, we have to deal with something else. Unfortunately, Jophial also had a telepathic visit from Samuel again. He's informed us that Sabboath is planning an attack on the water supply for Amilles. He's hoping to drop some kind of chemical in it which will make the angels aggressive, short-tempered, and volatile in the hope to spark another civil war. It seems he wants the angels to go the way of the demons, and we cannot let this happen."

Wow, that would be a disaster. Everyone else must be lost in similar thoughts because the table is quiet.

"Of course, we're not going to let that happen. Everyone suit up and meet back here in twenty minutes. We're going there to defend the water supply and protect the people of Amilles, so they don't suffer the same fate as the people of Habbalea."

"Will we be enough? Are we bringing in other teams?" Drusilla's voice breaks the tense silence, and Uriel stands up, smiling wickedly at his daughter.

"I think that five Archdemons, ten Archangels, and an Archdemon/Archangel hybrid will make any army think twice."

He flexes his wings and conjures up his big sword. She still looks worried, but her frown does ease slightly.

I stand up, hating to draw attention to myself, but there's not much I can do about it. "I need to feed before we leave." I look down at the table, not meeting anyone's eyes. "I'm sorry, I know this is a problem." Not only were my mates risked by having to launch a rescue mission to get me home, but the rest of them were put in a magical coma so that their bond to me didn't kill them! I'm feeling a bit less of a badass lately and more of a burden.

"Rubbish!" Azrael, Mav's normally reserved father waves his hand at me. "Don't you dare apologize. You are what you are, and you need to do what you have to. None of us will ever hold that against you." I shoot him a grateful smile, feeling a little more comfortable with his reassurance.

"No, and we still have to let Michael and Lucifer know what's going on." Zadkiel grimaces again, looking at the other dads out of the corner of his eye.

"Dibs, not me," I grumble, and it's echoed by the rest of Team Alpha around the table.

"I'll do it." Chamuel closes his eyes in concentration, telepathing my father, but it doesn't last long before his eyes pop wide in shock. "Ah, well, yes, I told him, but he may be a little longer." His cheeks turn a little red, and Uriel starts to chuckle again, the wicked grin he gave Dru only growing wider.

"Dude, you should know better than to try and telepath him while they're on their own. I thought you'd learned that years ago."

Chamuel runs a hand through his hair and stands up. "Yeah, it's been so long that I'd forgotten... won't be making *that* mistake again."

"Okay, hopefully twenty minutes is enough," Raphael says. "Otherwise, we'll go without them, and they'll just have to get over it."

"Bah, just tell him that Mina is in danger. That will have him there in an instant," Zadkiel suggests, a rather ruthless smile on his face, and the other dads grin with delight at his words.

Raphael clears his throat, looking at the other dads like they're misbehaving children who need to focus. "Drusilla, you and Jophial will be on comms again. She'll meet you in the Communications room when you're ready."

She looks at me, a gentle smile on her face. "I think you need more than what I can give you at the moment." I have to sheepishly nod my head, not wanting to meet her eyes, but she leaves her seat and comes over to me, lifting my head so I can look into her beautiful green gaze. "Mina, it's like Azrael said, never be ashamed of what you need. I'm looking forward to getting you alone, but that can wait for now. I'm not upset." Her words aren't quiet, and I hear a gagging sound. Both of us turn to where it came from, and it's Uriel looking slightly green, his sword having lost its glow. *Ha, payback's a bitch.* We both ignore him, knowing he can teleport out of the room if he really can't handle his daughter taking a moment with her mate. She places her soft lips to mine and pulls me in close, our breasts rubbing. Her hands drift down to squeeze my ass, her tongue twisting with mine like it does on other parts of my body, and when we break apart, I'm panting for air. Before I can say anything, she smiles and walks out of the room, heading to Communications.

"Take Trick and Sander." Zeph's voice has me looking around, and I find that only my teammates are left, so the rest must have portaled out while Dru was kissing me. "Mav and I'll make sure Jagger and Kai get some blood if they need it." I look at my team leader, his assertive command making me tingle all over, and I must start to produce pheromones because a wicked smile comes to his face.

"You like it when I tell you what to do, don't you?" He stalks over to me and hauls me up his body, placing a fast, fierce kiss on my lips before pulling away. "When this is all over, Mav and I will take you to our room at Eternal Damnation, and you'll learn what it's like to please your master," he whispers in my ear, causing me to groan aloud and chase his lips with my own as he pulls away. I'm a panting, sweaty ball of desire, and if Sander and Trick don't do something, I'm likely to jump any one of my six remaining mates right here and now.

Looking around, the guys all have heated eyes, missing no part of my reaction to Zeph. Before I can say anything, Sander and Trick crowd in close, wrapping their wings around my body so I'm trapped by a cocoon of feathers. Within a blink, someone teleports us, and when they step back, I'm in a room I've never been in before. I take a deep breath, the scent that reaches my nose telling me it's Trick's. That citrus smell with a hint of sage is familiar and has goosebumps breaking out across my skin, my nipples tightening even further. His bed is as large as Sander's and is piled high with green and gray throw pillows atop a gray comforter with darker gray accents.

Before I can look around any further, my clothes disappear. Gasping with surprise, I spin around and find Sander, naked with his arms pinned above his head, against the wall next to the door. He's held there by an unseen force, and Trick is on his knees, fully clothed still, lapping at his thick cock. Never putting his mouth over it, just running his tongue up and down, moving down to his balls and then back again. Sander's head is thrashing back and forth, and he's begging him for more. The sight has my thighs immediately slicking with my desire as Trick steps back, leaving Sander, his cock dribbling pre-cum, pupils blown wide.

He looks at me with a sinful grin. "I figured we didn't have a lot of time, so I got him started for you." Trick's dominant side is such a turn on from the usually quiet and reserved man. As much as my succubus likes to take the reins when she's hungry, she practically rolls over and shows her belly when he takes charge.

"Would you like to help him out, Mina?" Trick's voice is low and sexy, his citrus scent heady in the air. He's as turned on as I am. Stalking forward, I get down on my knees. Looking up at Sander from under my lashes, I can see him panting, wide-eyed and open-mouthed, and I feel sexy and strong. Sticking out my tongue, I run it the length of his fat cock, swirling it around the head before sticking it into the eye, licking out all of his juices. Swallowing them down, I groan at the taste of him, and he echoes it above.

"Please, Mina, *please*," he gasps, so I give him what he needs. Engulfing his head with my mouth, I take him into the back of my throat and swallow. My muscles contract around him, and his shouts sound out through the room. I continue to do this over and over again until he's a heaving mess.

Suddenly, I feel hands on my horns. My head is yanked back before I'm spun around and shoved back on my knees, Trick thrusting his cock deep into my mouth. I just about orgasm on the spot, his dominance almost pushing me over the edge. Sander's groan matches Trick's as he thrusts in and out forcefully, controlling his pace with my horns, his hands on them sending pulses of electricity straight to my clit. My eyes water as I breathe through my nose, his pace punishing, but all of a sudden he stops again and pulls out. He lets me go, and I sag on my knees slightly, my breathing slowly calming.

Before I can recover too much, I find myself lifted, levitating off the ground. Looking up, I see Trick studying me in concentration as he maneuvers me so I'm laying on my belly and my mouth is once again at Sander's cock. This is a new trick, and while it's one I wasn't expecting, I am *definitely* not opposed.

"Suck him off while I fuck your sweet pussy," he orders, pushing my mouth onto Sander's cock. I groan around it, and he echoes my sounds. Before I've even started to suck, Trick thrusts deep into my wet cunt, the sounds loud in the otherwise quiet room. He doesn't pause before setting a furious pace, pounding me just like I need. He's so demanding that it's hard for me to concentrate on Sander's cock, and of course he notices. He smacks my ass, the sting a biting contrast to the pleasure he's wringing out of my pussy.

"Now, now, Mina, you can't be greedy and keep all the pleasure to yourself. Poor Sander." He maneuvers me again, pulling out then putting me in a sitting position, still facing our partner. I watch as Sander moves away from the wall, no longer frozen.

"Sorry, I wouldn't want you to miss out because Mina can't multitask." His words are said close to my ear, and Sander grins wide as he steps up to me.

"You teased me before, Mina. That wasn't very nice."

Oh gods, now they're both dominating me. *I'm not going to last at all.* Sander pulls me closer, and I wrap my arms around his neck. Trick's arms come around me and cup my breasts as Sander lines his cock up with my weeping pussy. As he thrusts deep, Trick pinches both my nipples hard, and I detonate, a scream leaving my mouth as my orgasm explodes, rolling waves of pleasure flowing through all my limbs.

He continues to drive into me as I lean forward and bite down into his neck, sucking hard, and his movements become frantic before he's moaning, a guttural sound. His head is thrown back, eyes closed, pleasure causing his body to lock tight as he comes. Trick continues to pinch at my nipples, prolonging my orgasm. Finally, I stop drinking, still not sure how much I can take from my non-demon mates. I don't want to put him in any danger before the upcoming mission.

I slump against his chest, and he holds me tight, Trick's muscular naked chest leaning against my back as he wipes sweaty tendrils of black hair out of my face, peppering my neck with kisses and words of praise.

"Such a good girl, taking care of your mate like that. Now it's my turn to take care of you." He pulls me off Sander's still hard cock and carries me over to his bed, laying me down gently. As I watch him, my eyes still heavy with desire, he climbs up onto the bed. He kisses my ankle and then slowly places kisses all the way up my calf to my knee and then along the inside of my thighs, alternating side to side until I feel his warm breath on my still throbbing core. Placing a gentle kiss to my clit, he then sticks his tongue as deep as he can into my pussy, licking and sucking mine and Sander's combined release.

Sander appears next to me and starts to lavish my tender nipples with attention, his tongue a gentle contrast to Trick's pinching from before. The wet slurping sounds as Trick continues to use his tongue have me groaning out loud. Finally, he's eaten his fill and pulls away, moving up my body and placing kisses until he gets to Sander. They exchange a wet passionate kiss right in front of me as I pant with want. My tail must get impatient because it gets in between them, forcing their mouths apart, causing them both to laugh before Trick slides his dick into my aching channel. Face to face, he rolls his hips in a motion that has him hitting all the right spots inside, and my orgasm builds in a slow, delicious climb. Not a moment later, Sander appears behind him with a devilish grin on his face and a bottle of lube in his hand. Quickly, he squeezes some into it, rubbing it onto his cock, and he must be prepping Trick if his glazed over eyes are anything to go by.

"All aboard the Mina train," he quips, and

Trick's eyes widen slightly as Sander slides his dick deep into his ass. With Trick sandwiched between us, Sander works us both deep and hard until we're all tumbling over the edge into oblivion, and I bite down into Trick's neck, sucking deep and sending him over again.

Finally, the three of us come down and pull apart just in time for Jagger's voice to slide into my mind.

"You just about done in there? Time's up." He sounds amused as he fades away, not waiting for an answer.

"Asshole," Sander grumbles, so he must have projected it into all our heads. We take an extra couple of minutes to recover our breathing—the two boys on either side of me, our hearts beating in time with each other.

Chapter Twenty-Nine

Jessamina

When we make it to the portal room, I don't get very far before a blur is running toward me in a flurry of wings and leather. Worried that Sabboath has found me, my heart pounds, and I throw my hands up, stopping my attacker with telekinesis, freezing them on the spot.

As they stop, unable to move, the room explodes into chuckles and laughter as the wide eyes of my best friend meet me, a look of shock frozen on her face. *Oops.*

I release her, and she doesn't even hesitate at my new look; she just continues on the same path, throwing her leather-clad arms around me, her white wings brushing my face as she hugs me tight. Guess her blood's been activated since I last saw her.

Surprise shoots through me at her easy accep-tance, but then I shake myself out of it. This girl has been through everything with me; of course, she's not going to judge me even though I've changed... *a lot*. Livie's familiar scent fills my senses, and my eyes prickle with tears as I feel her shudder with emotion.

"Fucking hell, Mina, you gave us a scare." She pulls back, and her eyes rake up and down my body. "And look at you, are you fucking hot, or what?! And eight sexy as fuck mates. Girl, you need to invest in some industrial-strength lube so that your vagina doesn't catch on fire."

Livie's blunt words have me snorting before the two of us collapse in laughter against one another, a piece of myself clicking back into place now that my bestie is here with me. Behind her, a shadow looms. Looking up, the cheeky, grinning face of her boyfriend James is a sight for sore eyes. I reach out and pull him into a hug, and of course he can't help but add his own two cents.

"I always knew you were a succubus in disguise; it was the only excuse for that ever-revolving bedroom door." His arms are big enough to wrap around both of us as I embrace my friends for the first time in what feels like months.

Growls start filling the room from behind us, the jealous fools, but Livie and James don't sweat it, instead falling into another round of laughter that has me giggling along with them even as I roll my eyes at my mates.

"What are you guys doing here?" I ask, pushing

one of James' feathers out of my mouth and ignoring the little shiver that runs through me as Livie and James play with mine.

"Mina, has anyone told you, you look like a stripper demon?" James' wide-eyed innocent look doesn't fool me, so I punch him in the shoulder. He grunts in pain and quickly removes his hands, still chuckling. Asshole.

"I was thinking more demon Barbie," Livie teases, getting in her own dig, but I just turn around and flounce toward the others instead of taking the bait. *Some friends they are.* I hear their snorts of amusement as they follow behind me.

"We're here just for a little more back up," Janet tells me, also pulling me into a quick hug while Brace gives me a fist bump over her shoulder.

"Looking good, Mina! Glad to see you're okay." I smile at them both, but my hand subconsciously wanders up to my neck. A big hand on mine stops it, pulling it away. Zeph places a kiss on the back of it before he drops it down, his eyes reassuring and safe.

"It's so great to see you all," I tell them, smiling at the rest of Team Dragon.

"Alright, take a look around, memorize who is on your side, and only trust the people here. You may see old friends, team members, or acquaintances, but that doesn't mean they are to be trusted." Raphael's voice projects over the noise of the gathered people, his seriousness easy to pick up on. I scan the crowd, looking for my parents, but I can't see either of them. Although I do see Kai and Jagger's dads in full demon form, talking with Zadkiel.

Frowning, I look for Uriel. I find Sander's dad standing off to the side, tapping his foot impatiently, so I move over to him, brushing against Kai and Jagger as I pass. I can't help but touch my mates whenever I'm near them. Sidling up to Uriel, he raises his eyebrows in question.

"Where are Mom and Dad?" I whisper while Raphael keeps talking, and he rolls his eyes. "They'll be here soon; if not, they can catch up. You and your mates are much better with time frames than they are. I guess they're making up for a lot of lost time."

Damn it, and now I have that mental picture again, and by the look on his face, he knows it. I flip off Dru and Sander's father without shame and walk away to the sounds of his chuckles. I swear he's more demon than angel.

Everyone is geared up and brandishing weapons as Raphael finishes his directions. I've missed the speech, but I'm sure one of the others will catch me up. Moving toward my mates, I stand next to Zeph.

"I haven't got a weapon, so I'm just going to run up to the storeroom and grab something. I lost my magic wand on Minzeon," I explain, the barest hitch in my breath. I've had that since I was an infant and am devastated by its loss, finally having to accept the reality. I've avoided thinking about it too much up until now.

Zeph doesn't say anything, so I look at him, and he has a smile on his face. I'm not sure what there's to smile about, and annoyance grows quickly. Before I can say anything, he does. "Yeah, you did, but I found it and picked it up. I've been keeping it safe for you. He waves his hand, and my magic wand appears in his grip. It flashes blue and gold before settling down, the sparks almost like it's welcoming me back. I take it and throw my arms around him, being careful not to stab him with it.

"Oh my god! I felt like a limb was missing. You don't understand how much this means to me. I'm not sure how I can thank you enough."

His eyes narrow and heat as he whispers across my mind, *"I'm sure I can think of something."* My core clenches at his husky words, but we don't have time for me to show him how much I appreciate it. Finally, Mom and Dad arrive, and we're ready to head out on our mission.

"Ok, everyone, you have your instructions. Fan out and surround the facility. Once we know where the enemy is coming from, we can proceed from there. Oh, and remember Samuel and Grayson, who may be in animal form, are on our side. *Do not* kill them. If you have to knock them out, that's fine, but non-lethal response, please." Raphael looks at me. "Mina will be pissed if you kill her mate and friend, and there's no one who wants to see what an angry hybrid could do to us all. Alright, let's head out. Cloak yourselves when you get there. Sabboath will still be able to feel us through it when he arrives, but it should give us a small element of surprise."

Everyone starts to pop out, but I haven't been to Amilles, so I have no point of reference. My dad approaches me before I can ask anyone else for help, his eyes darting down to the magic wand still in my hand.

"You've still got it." He points to it, picking it up and turning it over. "Mylea gave this to us as a birthing gift, said that it was your birthright. I guess she's known all along you were destined for greatness. Glad to see you still have it, and I can't wait to see it in action. The blasted thing would never work for me." Mom joins us and laughs at my Dad.

"He had an epic tantrum when he tried and failed too." He passes it back to me, and I shove it into my ponytail. Dad winces at that but doesn't say a word, but Mom just snorts. Even in our few interactions as a family, it's become pretty obvious who's the "fun parent."

She holds out her hand, inviting me to take it. "I know you haven't been to Amilles before; you can come with me."

I grab her hand, which is warm and soft in mine, giving her a grateful smile. In a flash, she has us there, and after I settle my light, I open my eyes. Amilles is much like Reath, but the air feels cleaner and smells fresher, and the colors are brighter and more vivid. It feels like the world is in high-definition.

The main water supply is a huge dam that catches the runoff from the mountain behind via a waterfall. The crystal blue water is sparkling in the morning light. It wouldn't be hard to contaminate it since it seems to be completely unprotected, and I shudder to think what will happen if we fail. We're spread out around the shoreline, but there are still large gaps between us.

"Good luck, babe." Dru's loving warmth is a bright presence in my mind, and I make a note to find some quality time with my more delicate mate.

"Mina?" I nearly jump when Sam suddenly broadcasts in my head. I look around, but I can't see him. The lake's surrounded by a planted forest used to encourage people to stay away.

"Where are you?" I ask, scanning the forest.

"Hidden in the woods. But you're too late; it's already happened. This was a trap. Beatrice has been discovered, and Sabboath gave us false information for her to pass on. He doesn't know it was me that did. He's gone and has left the rest of us behind in the hope that we can kill a few of you. I think he knows that's not going to happen, but he seems to hope it will slow you down from finding an antidote."

"But none of the ABs can teleport. How did he think they were going to escape?" What he's done today basically proves that Sabboath finds his forces to be disposable. As if I needed any more convincing that he was an all-around vile person.

"There's a portal behind the waterfall, but it's only going to be open for a period of time before it closes. Basically, he left them here to be captured. He knows I can teleport now that the demon in me has been activated, and a lot of the angels can too, and well, Grayson and Connie can change into whatever form they want, so I'm sure he figured they could just fly away or use the magic at their disposal."

"Connie can what?*"* I ask, all his other words diminishing against this bit of information.

"Watch out, Mina! He's changed her again, and it's not good. The crazy is gone, but she is still hell-bent on killing you. Her favorite form is a giant snake. Don't look her directly in the eyes. Warn everyone!"

He stops talking, and I fill everyone else in on the information through the group link we'd opened when we arrived.

"Okay, then that changes things," Dad says, taking over and projecting into everyone's minds. *"If it's already in the water, we now need the antidote for that as well. Time to call on our friends on Minzeon again. Team Dragon, you secure a sample and take it there, please."* Brace and Janet nod their response, and their team heads to the water's edge, conjuring up small flasks and filling them before Janet opens a portal they funnel through. Well, at least I know they're out of

the way and safe now. I won't have to worry about them in the upcoming fight.

"Alright, look alive, people. We don't want to kill them when they attack. We don't know if they're here voluntarily or not. Let's just knock them out, and we can sort it all out later. Remember, you heard what Mina said, don't look directly in the eyes of the snake."

Before he can say anything else, Sabboath's forces come streaming out of the forest. There are a lot more in normal form this time around, likely those angels who were unwilling to take the "common" formula. Our dads and my mom soon engage them in battle. It actually looks like our side is toying with them; none are making much of an effort. The animals are left to us, and the boys get rid of their swords and conjure up the light guns. It's like shooting fish in a barrel, and they pick them off one by one, stunning them all.

Suddenly, a rustling sound has me turning back toward the forest, my mouth dropping open at what I'm seeing. The rustling sound is the snake's scales sliding against one another as she slowly undulates out of the trees. When he said she was a big snake, I was thinking anaconda, but this thing is as tall as a house, her head raised up high. Her double set of fangs must each be the length of my forearm, and they're dripping with venom that melts the grass it lands on. Her scales are dark green in color, lightening to white around her belly.

"Fuck me!" Kai calls out from not far behind me, his voice filled with awe and trepidation.

Not wanting to meet her eyes, I look anywhere but at her head, my gaze flicking to either side of her. Samuel flanks her in his demon form, and Gray lands next to them with a rush of air, the ground shuddering with his dragon's weight.

I send a wave of love and relief through our mate bond now that I can feel it again, hoping that he knows whatever happens next is because we have to keep up appearances.

"Be careful, Mina." His voice is funny in my head, not quite sounding like him, almost like his voice has merged with another- his dragon's? *"She won't stop until she recaptures you. She is under strict instructions from Sabboath, and she won't dare leave without accomplishing her only task."*

Before I can reply, her scales rustle even louder and she moves, her tail curling around her body. Clasped in the end is a very unconscious Beatrice. My heart sinks, not knowing how we can get out of this without losing at least one life or my freedom.

Her huge head moves, her mouth starting to open as drops of venom fall around Beatrice.

"If you come with usss, I will let your friend go," she hisses at me, and I blink in shock. *That's the last thing I was expecting. A giant snake, sure. A giant TALKING snake? Well, that's a whole other problem.*

"Don't you dare move, Mina," my dad shouts from across the clearing.

My hackles rise, my tail whipping back and forth as if it's just as agitated as the rest of me. "Don't tell me what to do!" I shout back, rather childish I know, but I guess we've got my teenage years to make up for.

Someone snorts next to me, but I don't dare take my eyes off of Beatrice's still form.

"Your dad's right, Mina," Mav argues, a vulnerable and obvious panic coming at me with his words. *"Don't you dare give yourself up."*

"I have to; I can't let Beatrice suffer. It couldn't have been easy being a double agent, and who knows how long she's been doing it. Besides, Samuel and Grayson are still good. They'll protect me. I'll just go with them until we get clear, and then the three of us will overwhelm her." The worry from all of my mates is almost overwhelming, but I don't wait for them to argue. I've never been one to let someone else suffer if they didn't have to. Stepping forward, I raise my hands and go to remove the magic wand from my hair, but it's shrunk down so small I don't think she'll notice it, so I leave it there. Leaving my hands in the air, I continue to walk forward to the protests of my mates and the orders of my father. They all stop when Connie waves Beatrice's body around violently.

The snake smirks, such a weird look to see on an inhuman face. "Yesss, that'sss what I thought. Not susso tough now."

"Give the demon the girl and let him bring her forward." I demand, not going any further. "And I'll wait for him here; he can restrain me."

She's so giddy with her victory that she throws Beatrice at Sam, but he stays standing, only the grunt that leaves him indicating how hard and carelessly Connie threw her. He walks forward and places her on the ground next to me then grabs me by the arm, marching me forward and into the trees away from the group.

"If any of you come after usss, I will bite Mina, and sssshe will be dead within ssssecondsss." The ground vibrates, and a rush of wind blows through the trees, meaning Grayson must have taken off again. Looking up, I can see the shadow of his dragon through the leaves, but I don't say anything because Connie slithers after us.

"Quickly, they won't take long! We need to go."

We are running now, her large body knocking down trees that Samuel and I have to dodge.

"Fucking hell, Connie, change back!" he shouts at her as she almost kills both of us with a tree. We reach another clearing and Grayson lands, changing in a smooth, practiced motion, Samuel conjuring clothes onto his body. He's still hanging onto my arm for show, but his touch is gentle.

The sound of shouts reaches us, and Connie whips her big reptilian head around, peering through the trees. "Quick, demon, teleport ussss out of here," she orders, and I feel a wave of magic, but nothing happens.

"What are you waiting for?" She moves her head back and forth in an agitated motion, the venom starting to build up and drip from her fangs once more.

"I'm not sure! I tried, but nothing happened," he tells her, panic in his voice. Her lidless eyes narrow on me, and I watch from the corner of my eyes, still mindful to avoid direct eye contact.

"What did you do?"

"Hey, don't blame me if your demon is useless," I snap back at her, and Sam's hand twitches on my arm.

"Okay, let's change form, and I can fly us out of here then." Grayson's trying to pacify Connie, but I feel another wave of magic as they unsuccessfully try to shift, nothing happening.

"Arggg!" Connie's snake is getting more and more agitated, her head weaving back and forth like she's preparing to strike. I take a step back. I'm not sure if those fangs will be able to pierce my scales or not, but when I try to will them over my body, nothing happens.

Oh fuck.

The shouting is getting closer, and we can see movement through the bushes. Up in the sky, I note one or two angels, but I can't make out the color of their wings.

"We're trapped," Samuel rumbles at Connie.

"No, we're not. As long as we've got that bitch, we'll be fine. We jussst have to work out what issss blocking the magic."

I have a fair idea, but I don't plan on sharing that with her. Not at all.

Chapter Thirty

Jessamina

Everything seems to be going to hell. Something is blocking us from using magic, the rest of them have just about caught up to us, which is going to have Connie striking out, and I will *definitely* be her target.

"Fucking hell, Zeph! You have to stop. Mina's in danger," Sam screams through our team link, his panic all too real, but he's too late. Dad comes crashing out of the woods, sword blazing, followed by Mom carrying a whip in each hand. I guess neither were going to see me kidnapped again if they could help it. This was a stupid plan, but I guess Sabboath's arrogance knows no bounds, and his obsession with me and my possible future babies has grown to ridiculous proportions.

I watch in horror and what feels like slow motion as Connie's snake can't take being cornered anymore. With the speed of a cobra, she strikes at me, but I manage to move out of the way, my extra speed helping. Unfortunately, my speed does nothing for my clumsiness, and I trip over a root and stumble. By the time I right myself, she's turned and is in mid-strike again. There's nothing I can do to escape, and I watch helplessly, closing my eyes. My body tenses, waiting for the inevitable pain, but it never comes.

Cracking my eyes open, I look around in amazement. Everything and everyone around me is frozen. I stumble to my feet and quickly move out of the way of her fangs, but I don't get far before a golden glow appears in the clearing, and Mylea steps out of it.

"That was very dramatic," I say to her sarcastically, but she just smiles serenely, her eyes sad.

"What is it? What's wrong?" My heart skips a beat as her smile drops.

"I'm sorry, Mina, but I can't stop what happens next. I've interfered too much already and can't change the next event. It *needs* to happen." My eyes go back to the dripping fangs of Connie's snake. Despite everything else around us being frozen, they continue to drip acidic venom onto the ground. My heart sinks when I understand what she's telling me.

Glancing around the clearing, I take a good look at the people who have become family to me. My mom and dad, only newly found, and my mate's fathers, all of whom I had wanted to get to know.

My gaze then moves to my mates, eyes wide and mouths open in horror and dismay as they watch

Connie's snake strike at me. My mates who have carved such a space in my soul and heart. My gaze falls on Sam, sadness welling at the fact that we never got to see if he, too, was one of my mates. A tear rolls down my cheek at this thought, its hot trail nearly burning in the tension of the moment. I'm almost one hundred percent sure he would have been. It would have been a cruel joke for him not to have been part of our group, especially when he'd worked so hard to help us all.

Mylea clears her throat, and I turn, wiping away the tears that have been falling.

"Although I cannot stop what is to happen, I can at least grant you that last wish." A gasp leaves my mouth in shock.

"You mean Sam and me?" She nods her head again, serene goddess smile back in place, though its brightness had been dimmed.

"Yes, if you bond with Sam, your mating circle will be complete. This means that when you die, your nine mates should survive as they will have each other to lean on. The only reason the others got sick when you were cut off from them was that the bond wasn't fully complete."

"So, Sam is my mate, and if I make this final bond, then they will survive what is to come?" My voice hitches with pent-up frustration, fear, and all the things I'll never get to say to my eight other mates, but I've already come to accept what will happen, and the knowledge that they will survive is *everything*.

She nods once more.

"Okay, then unfreeze him," I demand, and she laughs, a tinkling sound echoing through the still clearing.

"Oh no, I'm afraid I can't unfreeze just one. They are all frozen together, and if I unfreeze one, well, everyone unfreezes. We're going to have to go back to a moment in time from before. Don't worry, it will be fine. Samuel's transition is still riding him hard when I plan for you to go, and you will have no trouble convincing him of it. Fog his mind a little with your pheromones," she advises, and I grimace with guilt, but she goes on. "This *needs* to happen, Mina, so you're going to have to leave the guilt behind, and whatever you do, you can't tell him anything that goes on here. Tell him that Grayson got you out of the cell to help out with his needs. That should be all Sam needs to hear. I mean, it's not like you two haven't fucked already. You just need to bite him, but keep in mind he'll probably bite you back in that form."

I take a deep breath and look around at the others for possibly the last time. "Okay, let's do this."

She holds out a hand, and I grip it tight. Before we move, she waves at my neck, returning the collar I had on, and I gasp with fear, but she quickly reassures me. "That one is all for looks. He'd expect you to still have it."

Whirling, dizzying motion happens, and I find myself suddenly in a very sterile dorm room with Mylea's words in my mind. "Remember, Grayson put you there, so he needs to think you're the Mina from that time. I'll come back for you when it's done."

Looking around, Sam's nowhere to be seen, but I can hear a shower running. I quickly strip off my uniform so that he doesn't suspect anything and push the door open, stepping into the bathroom, naked. Steam fills the room, and through it, I can see Sam standing under the hot water.

"Grayson, is that you? Change your mind about feeding me?" His words are husky, and as he turns around, I can see him stroking his long thick cock, his shimmery black demon form glistening in the light. My mouth waters at the sight of it, and my pheromones fill the room with my scent.

I jolt when my mind finally comprehends his words, and I can't say I'm not intrigued to see my dragon mate and my newest demon mate writhing against one another. But for now, Sam's all mine. His eyes widen in surprise as he catches sight of me.

"Mina! How did you get in here?" He goes to step out of the shower, but I stop him, pushing him back against the wall and crowding him.

"Grayson told me you still needed help with your transition, and he's needed elsewhere at the moment, so he broke me out." I step under the steaming hot water and pull him toward me, silencing his questions with my mouth. He groans and gives in, wrapping his arms around me, his rock hard cock hard against my stomach.

I pull away. "We have to be quick. He said we only had a few minutes but that you needed to feed before the meeting." My pheromones continue to fill the air, and his eyes glaze over and hood with desire.

With no more words, he swings me around, pushing my back against the shower wall, a waterfall cascading over his back. His eyes devour the sight of my body, and my skin prickles with awareness. His is the last mate bond to form, and I'm excited but also sad with the knowledge that I won't ever be able to spend my life with them. That I've failed my task set forward by Mylea and that Hammus will continue to terrify the worlds.

Hopefully, once bonded, my mates will be strong enough to help hold him back. That they will thwart him at every turn. That they will go on and stay strong together, living their lives to the fullest.

Tears trickle down my face, but Sam doesn't notice because of the shower. He puts his forehead against mine, and he says the words that I've been longing to hear for so long—before Connie ever appeared on the scene. I've been a little bit in love with this man for as long as I can remember.

"I'm so sorry I ever hurt you. I *never* wanted to

do that. I love you, Mina." With those last three words, he thrusts deep. We groan in unison from the feeling, both a lot more aware this time than the last. We pause, savoring the feeling before I look up into his eyes.

"You need to bite me this time, Sam. Drink from my blood and become one with your brothers and me." The words feel somewhat ceremonial, and I guess they are since he is the final link. I'm not sure where they came from, but it feels right to say them.

He pulls back, quickly building me to a peak, my limbs and tongue tingling with the impending implosion. Lifting me up, I wrap my legs around his waist as he powers into me. Building me higher and higher, suddenly a sucking motion on my clit has me gasping aloud. I had forgotten that about his demon dick, and my eyes widen as his meet mine with a quick wink. Not willing to be outdone, my tail fondles his balls, his thrusts becoming erratic, and just as I know he's about to go over the edge, I sink my fangs into his neck. He shouts out loudly before shoving his cock as deep as he can, his fangs matching the movement, both sending me over the cliff. Lights explode before my eyes like fireworks going off as my orgasm slams into me. I struggle to swallow through the sensation, but I'm determined to drink from my mate, his blood like a fine whiskey, smooth with a kick.

Pulling back, I unwrap my feet and lower

myself to the ground, preparing for the pain I know is coming. And sure enough, the minute they touch the wet floor, a searing sensation flows through my back as my mark expands, spreading out further. Samuel grunts and falls to his knees in the shower as he silently deals with the pain, his head against my stomach while I stroke his hair in an attempt to soothe him through the process. I watch as his mate mark forms on his shoulder. He, like the others, has the heart in the middle with the infinity symbol through it, but the rest of his pattern around it is different. Nine different mates with nine different designs, all making one complete mark on my back.

No sooner does it finish than the room freezes again. This must be my cue to leave. I step away from Sam, running my fingers through his hair one last time. Bending down, I whisper in his ear, "I love you too."

Grabbing a towel, I quickly dry off and head out to the bedroom to put my clothes back on. Once dressed, Mylea appears.

"I'll have to take all his memories. No one can know that this has occurred. I will delay the pain of the mark on the others until after. All of them will be none the wiser, for now. I guarantee that he will remember it eventually; he'll have the memory of this moment to comfort him."

She puts her hand on my arm, her touch soft. "When everyone unfreezes and realizes what has happened, no one will be able to get to you in time.

If it's any consolation, you'll not remember any of it." The sadness in her tone is heartbreaking, but I put on a brave face and give her a smile.

"What do you mean, I won't remember any of it? Do you mean Sam?" She shakes her head, her own eyes growing as glassy as I'm sure mine are becoming.

"No, Mina, the pain of dying." My stomach lurches at her confirmation of what I knew all along, but I swallow the lump in my throat.

"Thank you for this. For giving me these last moments with Sam and allowing me to fulfill this final bond. You don't know how much I appreciate it."

She takes my hand, but just before I expect the whirling sensation, she stops and slowly runs her other hand over my body, swirling it around my chest and stomach until a glowing shimmery ball coalesces in her hand. It pulses like it's breathing. "Just something to give to Drusilla to remind her of you. She will be affected the most because she is not mated to any of the others like they all are."

"You mated all the boys as well?" I ask, disappointed that I'll never get to see that.

"Yes, it was needed," is all she replies as the golden orb disappears. She leans in and kisses me on both cheeks.

The swirling sensation happens then blinding pain as Connie's basilisk fangs pierce my body. A violent scream escapes my mouth as I feel her tearing my chest open. The world has unfrozen around me, the others' shouts and screams of horror becoming the soundtrack to my final moments, and there's nothing I can do as I sink to my knees. Just before I close my eyes, I watch Samuel, massive sword blazing, propel himself into the air, wings thrusting hard as he brings down the blade just behind Connie's head, severing it in one go. But it's too late for me. Her blank-eyed head drops down next to me as my heart starts to slow, my eyes closing for the last time.

Chapter Thirty-One

Samuel

Everything happens so fast, horror piercing my heart as Connie strikes at Mina. My instincts kick in, my sword appearing in my hand, blazing with light. Leaping into the air, I raise it high above my head, my pulse racing and breathing rough. I veer toward them, my wings thrusting hard, but I don't get there in time.

Connie's fangs pierce Mina's chest, a crack resounding when those venomous daggers break clear through bone. With a scream, I slash down with my sword and sever the snake's head before landing next to Mina. It thuds to the ground with an open-eyed stare, no longer able to hurt anyone, but I failed to keep the one person I love safe. Dropping to my knees, I pull Mina against my chest, my hands trying to stem the flow of blood coming from the impossibly big hole, but it's useless. Her heart stops beating, and she takes her last breath in my arms.

"Mina, noooo!" My anguished cry fills the air,

echoed by those around me. Tears stream down my face as I rock back and forth, holding the one woman who meant the world to me. I've been robbed of the chance to become her mate, of telling her I love her.

A shrill scream has me grimacing before my eyes move to where Drusilla has just teleported in. Her face is a picture of agony as she collapses against her brother and Trick, sobbing uncontrollably.

A hand on my shoulder has me looking up at Raphael, whose misty eyes hold such sadness. "Let go, Sam. I need to see if I can do anything." By the sound of his voice, he knows like I do that it's too late.

Lying her gently on the ground, I shuffle backward, making room for Raphael and her parents. Michael's face is pale, while Lucifer sobs inconsolably into his arms. When he gets a close look at the daughter he never had the chance to know, he throws his head back and screams, the pain of his anguished scream having as big of a presence as his power.

"How could you?" Thunder rumbles as lightning cracks across the sky, a reflection of his mood.

Glancing around, I notice my teammates on the ground, clutching at their chests. Their bond with Mina is gone once again. Each of them is leaning on another, except for one solitary figure. Grayson is on his knees, clutching at his chest, but unlike the others, he's struggling to breath. I stand up to make my way over to him, knowing he'll need someone to support him over the next few weeks, but before I can take a step, he falls face-first to the ground and starts convulsing.

Picking up the pace, I rush over to him, calling for Raphael, who rushes over.

"What's wrong with him?" I ask, afraid to touch him.

"I'm not sure. This is similar to what happened to Drusilla when she was cut off from Mina, but it's definitely more violent."

A golden glow fills the clearing, and when it disappears, Mylea is standing beside Michael and Lucifer, her hand on his shoulder.

"I'm sorry. There was nothing I could do. This was how it was meant to be," she says quietly, her apology just barely loud enough for our advanced hearing to detect. Her gaze moves from one mate to the next, all of whom have struggled to their feet and made their way over to Grayson, providing strong silent support for a brother in need.

"You'll all need each other over the coming days, especially Grayson. He's reacting so violently because his Archangel blood has never been activated. To fix him, you need to track down Tiberion."

Michael scoffs in anger at her words, but she just gently shakes her head. "Do this for your daughter's mate. She would not want him to suffer and follow her to where she is. Because that is what will happen if you don't do this." Her gaze turns to me, softening even more.

"And Samuel, I have some memories to return to you. It will make it so that everyone's pain is not so great. Well, after the initial bit."

Waving her hand, my mind is filled with the scent of Mina, the feel of her luscious body as I pound into her, and the taste of her blood as it runs down my throat.

Of the pain in my arm as our mate bond forms. Of those whispered words, "I love you." *Fuck, Mina and I completed a mate bond.* I look up at the goddess in shock, but all around me, Mina's other mates shout out in pain as they feel my mate bond form. It seems to go on forever yet ends abruptly at the same time. The eight of us surround Grayson in a circle, a gentle heat sitting inside my chest as I feel these men and woman deep in my soul.

"Although Mina is no longer with you, you still have each other. This will keep you from getting sick like last time. Lean on one another, use each other to sustain the demons in the group, and take comfort in one another. I promise you, things will get better."

She moves over to Drusilla and helps her to her feet. Drusilla's face is tear-stained and red from sobbing, her hair a mess of black around her face. Mylea tugs her closer for a gentle hug before pulling back again.

"I have something for you. You, most of all, will need comfort. You will feel left out at times, through no one's fault, but I have something for you. A task to keep you occupied until you, too, are ready to find love elsewhere." She produces a glowing golden orb of light in her hand. It pulses in and out, the glow getting brighter before fading in a pulsing rhythm.

"Look after this. It was a part of Mina, part of her soul, and it needs to be loved and cherished and protected. This is your job now. Keep it safe, and when you are feeling low, focus on sending all your love for Mina to it, taking comfort in the knowledge that you are sharing your love with her."

With that, she hands Drusilla the glowing orb and moves over to Mina's body. With a wave of her hand, Mina is surrounded in a golden light, much like the orb Dru was given, and with a sad smile of goodbye, they disappear together.

We don't have any time to grieve, Grayson's incoherent shouts drawing our attention to him as he starts bleeding from his nose and mouth. Scooping him into his arms, Raphael shouts at Michael, "I need you to get Tiberion! I know you know where he is. Please, do it for Mina but do it for him too. Let something positive come out of this."

Michael still looks devastated, but he takes a deep breath and nods his head. He waves Uriel over and gently passes Lucifer to him.

"Look after her for me. I may be a while. He moves around a lot, so I have a few places to look."

"Of course I will, my friend." Uriel wraps an arm around her and pulls her to his chest as she continues to sob quietly. It's almost like she doesn't have the energy to keep going, and something in me twists at seeing such a formidable woman so distraught.

My heart is heavy in my chest as I stagger to my feet, my teammates following suit around me. Raphael disappears with Grayson after telling us he's taking him to the CD hospital wing, leaving the rest of us behind. We all look at each other, none of us really knowing what to say. Zeph runs a hand through his hair and blows out a deep breath.

"I guess we should head to the CD too. Grayson needs us." His voice is flat, his grief obvious by his red-rimmed eyes and the lack of his usual authoritative demeanor. The rest of us start to shift, getting ready to go, but Drusilla is just standing there, looking at the orb in her hand.

Sander tries to poke a finger at it, but she slaps it away. The look on her face has changed from devastation to a sort of wonder.

"What does it feel like?" I ask, curious as to what she holds as well as kind of jealous that she gets it, while all of us get nothing. *Why her? Why did she get chosen?* But then I shake my head, Mylea's comment becoming clear. All of us can find comfort in one another if we eventually decide to. Drusilla has no one unless she moves on to someone outside of the team.

"It feels like Mina. Like the same feeling I had whenever I was around her, excitement and a sense of rightness like I'd found my home. I also have this huge need to protect it. Sander poking at it made me feel like I had to cut his head off." I snort as Sander's eyes widen, but at least her comment brings a smile to most of their faces, Mav the only exception. He's lost and defeated, a shadow of his former self. He'll need to be watched; the poor guy just barely got his head straightened out before losing part of his anchor again almost immediately after.

The orb continues to flash in and out, having a slightly mesmerizing quality to it. Eventually, Trick comes to his senses. "We can't all go to the hospital; we'll just get in the way."

"How about we take shifts? I'll go first," I tell them, needing something to distract myself from the whole situation. My heart is heavy, but if I keep myself busy, I may be able to avoid thinking about what happened. Even though the likelihood is slim thanks to the ache in my chest. Everyone agrees, the rest deciding to return to our apartment, which really isn't going to be big enough for all of us anymore, but I guess we'll work something out when a crazy Archangel isn't trying to launch another genocide.

One by one, they leave without a backward glance.

I look around the almost empty clearing. Michael left shortly after Raphael had pleaded with him, as did the rest of the dads, so now the only one remaining is mine. He strides toward me, arms wide open, and I collapse into them, eager for the comfort that only he can provide. The utter devastation I'd been holding inside bursts out of me, and I wail against his chest, his arms holding me tight as I fall apart. He says nothing, knowing no words can make this any better, just holding me and letting me be.

I'm not sure how long we stand there, but when I finally pull back, I feel wrung out, an empty shell. His eyes scan up and down my body, taking in my demon form, but he doesn't look disgusted, just sad.

"I am so sorry, my boy. This was not what I wanted for you. Had I known this would happen, we'd never have asked for you to go undercover. Not only did Sabboath do this to you, you missed precious time with her."

I shake my head, knowing that this burden rests on no one other than Sabboath. "It's okay, Dad. I rather like my new form and new powers. You should see what else I can do." My smile is shaky and feels forced when I tell him this, but I keep going, hoping that eventually it'll become a bit more genuine. "We sealed the mate bond while she was in captivity. I'm not sure why my memories were taken away though."

"Mylea would have interfered only if she had no other option. Maybe one day we'll find out why she did it." His voice is gentle but really no comfort right now.

"I need to go and check on Grayson. What are you doing now?" I ask, my eyes zooming in on the puddle of blood that Mina left behind. *I wouldn't want anyone using that for something nefarious.* A moment later, my heart clenches, realizing that really, there's no risk to her anymore. Who can hurt the dead?

"I'm going to go and tell your mother what happened," he says, but I pay no attention. I march over to the stained patch of grass like a man possessed and wave my hand, setting the puddle of blood on fire. As it sizzles and smokes, burning brightly, all traces of Mina are now gone.

My eyes then swing to the severed head of the snake, its massive body sprawled on the ground. Magic subtly fills the clearing, surrounding us like a soft breeze that you barely notice until it's built up strength. Dad and I both jolt in surprise as another golden glow appears, this one is brighter and deeper than the one that accompanied Mylea, and when it clears, three gods stand there.

Dad gets down on one knee, bowing his head, and I follow suit. I know from my lessons that these are Mylea's remaining mates: Azeyr, Eagi, and Matoz. The three of them walk over to Connie's remains and surround her, all holding out hands. Suddenly, the head floats over to the body and knits itself back on, the now whole serpent slowly shifting from snake back into Connie's human form. Once that's complete, the rise and fall of her chest becomes obvious.

"What the fuck are you doing?!" I scream, jumping to my feet, but I'm blocked by a wall. While I watch, Connie's features change slightly, her hair lightening before becoming a dirty blonde, her eyes changing to green, and a smattering of freckles covering her face. Her skinny body fills out, and when they step back, I have to really stare closely to see what she used to look like.

Azeyr turns to my father and me, a stern expression firmly in place. "Connie has suffered greatly for the sins of her father. She was never really given a choice in this battle, and Mylea decided she did not need to continue to suffer. She will be given a new identity, memories, and another chance to make better choices in a new life. Please find it in your heart to forgive her. You yourself know how easy it is to be swayed by a bit of magic."

Shame flushes my cheeks, and I lower my head in acknowledgment. *They're not wrong.* The fight drained out of me, I step back and let them do their thing. In a flash, they and Connie are gone, leaving the clearing empty. With all signs of both women, Connie and Mina, gone, I glance back, reminded of the reason we'd come here in the first place.

"The water supply? What's going to happen with that?" I ask my dad.

"Well, Team Dragon has gone to Minzeon to have an antidote formulated, and Zadkiel and Azrael were going to warn the cities not to drink the water supply until further notice. They're going to ship as much bottled water as possible from the other worlds. The people of Amilles are safe, and it should take Sabboath a little while to figure this out since he has no living informants to tell him what happened. We have some time to come up with a plan to try and catch him."

"I could go back in. My cover's not blown yet, and, well, someone needs to tell him about his daughter. I'll tell him Grayson was captured. If you rough me up a little, it will make it look like I managed to escape."

Dad narrows his eyes at me, the weight of his stare making it clear how he feels about this particular plan. "Are you sure? You've suffered a huge loss, son. Is your mind really in the right space?"

A sense of rightness fills my being, and I instinctively stand a little taller and straighter. "Yes, for Mina I will do this. We still need to know what they have planned, and who knows how long it will take Mylea to come up with another way to get rid of Hammus. For now, all we can do is damage control," I reason, feeling more sure of this decision than I have anything else over the last few days.

He looks resigned when he nods his head.

"Okay, be careful and make sure you hide your mate mark. You don't want anyone seeing that." I nod my head and telepath Zeph telling him what I'm going to do. He tries to argue, but in the end, I win. I think he's too tired to put up much of a fight, but I ask him to look after Grayson, and he quickly agrees. His first instinct is always to lead and care for the rest of our team, so giving him a job has almost the same effect it has on Mav. A mission always helps focus and calm those two.

"Can you hit me a couple of times?" I ask, trying not to focus on the way he shifts uncomfortably, definitely not liking the request. But a moment later, a hit to the jaw has me seeing stars, but I hold my ground. He gets out a knife and slashes lightly at my shirt, the material ripping to reveal welling blood where he's broken the skin. To finish it off, his fist sails into my stomach, and I double over as the breath whooshes out of my lungs, a pained groan echoing through the empty space.

My dad chuckles, and though I'm not a fan of being laughed at, I'm glad he's seeing some lightness in the situation. "I can still kick your ass," he gloats.

I just grunt. "I mean, sure, Dad. I'm not even defending myself, but I'll let you think that." His grin drops as I lift a hand to wave goodbye, and with a flash, I teleport out.

Chapter Thirty-Two

Zephaniah

When Samuel had spoken into my mind to tell me he was going back into Sabboath's lair, I tried to talk him out of it, but he'd been adamant.

So I agreed to look after Grayson for him and he returned to the enemy. I just hope we're not doing the wrong thing. Even though we've only just reconciled, losing Samuel so quickly after losing Mina would probably break us.

Grayson's hospital room is silent, except for the beeping machines keeping him alive. I feel a wicked sense of déjà vu, and my mind flashes back, super-imposing Mina's body over Grayson's, my heart aching.

I can't believe she's gone. My mind refuses to face the fact that I won't be seeing her ever again, but I need to focus on keeping our team together. I left Mav under the watchful eye of the others. He seems to be doing okay, or as okay as he can be, but that could change at any moment. I didn't want to leave

420

him, but I made a promise to Sam. If he can make the sacrifice to go back and be our spy once more, then the least I can do is keep a watch over Mina's new mate who's in need of a lifeline.

My eyes scan his body. He has dark skin, is tall, probably taller than all of us, with shoulder-length dark hair. I can't believe Sabboath had kept him hidden after all this time. If Tiberion doesn't kill the asshole, I'll be surprised. He must know he's on borrowed time, and hopefully he'll panic and slip up. As of right now, the plan is for Sam to tell Sabboath that Gray's been captured. Just to be safe, we've kicked all the medical staff out of the hospital since they still haven't been checked for AoA influence.

The smell of antiseptic tickles my nose as I imagine what our life would have been like if Mina hadn't died. If she'd defeated Hammus and the worlds were safe from his tyranny once and for all.

Would we all still have continued with the CD? I can imagine that Kai would continue to help rebuild the demon underground. But with Hammus gone, they could have tried to find a way to bring them out from the cavern they've been hiding in. Grayson and his dad, like Mina, Michael, and Lucifer, could have built a relationship with each other. Well, I guess they still can. I just hope that Siffa and Michael lean on one another during this time instead of falling apart like they did last time.

My mind moves to Drusilla and her mysterious

ball of light, needing to fill the quiet in this sterile room. Just before I'd left, I poked my head into her room and found her fast asleep, curled around the gold orb. A small serene smile graced her face, and I thanked Mylea for whatever it is and the small amount of relief it's giving to her during this time.

The room lights up with the arrival of an Archangel, breaking me from my mind's rambling, and when it clears, Michael is standing there with whom I assume is Grayson's father. A tall, dark, and imposing man with close-cropped black hair and skin the color of obsidian. The only color to be seen is his piercing blue eyes. He takes one look at the figure in the bed and staggers, Michael reaching out to steady him.

"It's him. It's my boy." His voice cracks on the last word, and tears start to run down his cheeks, leaving glistening tracks against the dark backdrop. Sobbing, he steps forward, and I quickly leave my chair, offering it to him before stepping back. Michael grabs hold of me and pulls me into a hug. His emotions are so easily felt, his devastation clear, but he's offering me a shoulder to lean on. I accept his hug, clapping him on the shoulder, and when we step back, we watch as father and son reunite. Something I'd only just witnessed happening between the man next to me and his daughter. For it to be ripped so easily away from him and me is a bitter pill to swallow.

Tiberion collapses into my vacated chair like his

legs can no longer support his body or emotions. He reaches out and grasps Grayson's hand, running his other over his son's face and pushing his hair back. His eyes are wide with wonder as the tears continue to flow.

Raphael enters the room, the tools needed for the blood activation in his hands. He's going to do it directly from father to son to save time.

Tiberion looks up as he enters. "Raph! It's my boy."

Raphael's face immediately holds a gentle smile for his old friend. "I know, T. I'm so happy for you. I'm assuming Michael explained the basics of what's happening. Shall we do this?" He waves the medical supplies in his hands, and Tiberion eagerly nods his head.

Their quiet murmuring takes a backseat as I turn to Michael. "Did you explain where he was or what has happened?"

Michael shakes his head. "Not yet. Tiberion is a bit of a hot head, ruled by his emotions." I snort inwardly at the pot calling the kettle black, but I'm not brave or foolish enough to let the sound escape. "If I told him what had happened, he would be after Sabboath within moments. We'll get to that once Grayson is up and about again."

I nod, unable to argue with his logic.

"I'm going to go and find my wife. Grayson will be okay now. Why don't you return to your family and grieve? With no body, there's no point in having a funeral. We'll have a little wake in a few days' time. Her mother will want that. I also need to go and tell Maggie and Peter."

I hold up a hand, a furious wave of grief and guilt flowing through my body. "Can we not do that yet? Can we keep this all on the downlow for now?"

He raises an eyebrow in question and frowns. "Why would we do that?"

"Because Sam went back in."

Lightning flashes outside of the window. "Why on earth would he do that?" Michael demands loudly. Raphael and Tiberion turn to look at the commotion, but I wave them off and walk Michael out of the room.

"He realizes this isn't finished yet, and he didn't want us caught unaware. He's doing a brave thing considering he can't mourn like the rest of us. He doesn't want Mina's death to have been meaningless, and if we lose all our inside information, then that's what it will become."

Michael paces back and forth, his anger and grief palpable in the air as he mulls over my words, but the emotions wane quickly as he calms down. "Yes, you're right. He is, and we'll be ready whenever he needs us," he reassures me, but I actually have a thought about that.

"Why do we have to wait until he strikes? Why don't we make a move against him? If we take out his forces, then surely Hammus will be forced to rethink his tactics. If he can't infect people or terrorize like what's happening on Minzeon, then he really is a god with no followers. No one to do his dirty work."

Michael's eyes gleam at the thought of going after Sabboath, something akin to hunger flashing in his gaze. "Yes, you may be right. Let's take a day or two just to mourn my daughter, and then we'll talk about destroying that vile man."

He says his goodbyes and leaves to comfort Lucifer, but I stay a little longer, watching as Raphael carefully places a needle into Tiberion's vein connected to clear tubing. The other end of the tube has a needle which is placed into Grayson's arm.

"Why are we doing this? If he was born from two Archangel parents, that makes him an Archangel. Isn't that why you all had to hide us?" All this information occurs to me suddenly, and the two Archangels exchange side glances, immediately drawing my attention deeper.

"Yes, you're born Archangels, but when Grayson was born, Mylea told us you'd need an infusion of blood from one parent at five years old. We had to figure out a way to covertly get each of you what you needed."

I think back to when I got my wings, and he's right. Just before they erupted, I'd had a blood transfusion, but I hadn't thought anything about it when I was a kid. My foster parents had told me I needed more iron. I feel a little stupid now, scoffing at myself for believing that an angel would need a blood transfusion, but I guess they didn't want to risk us giving anything away. I mean, we were already keeping a pretty big secret.

"Grayson was taken before he could have his infusion, which means his blood wasn't fully activated. That's why he doesn't have all his Archangel magic or wings."

"How do you think this is going to react with the other stuff that Sabboath injected into his system?" I ask Raphael telepathically, not wanting to cause his father more undue stress.

"Well, Sam seems to be okay, but he did have some divine protection. If Grayson has problems, we'll ask one of the gods to step in. It's the least they can do," Raphael finishes, the statement almost in a growl. He shakes off his frustration and gestures to the next bed. "Zeph, roll that over here and jack it a little higher, please. Tiberion, climb on up. We need you higher so the blood will flow downward." I do as he says, and Tiberion makes himself comfortable, his eyes fixed on his son like Gray will disappear if he looks away too long.

"I'm going to head home for a little while and check on the others," I tell Raphael, the weight of everything that's happened today sitting heavily on my shoulders. "Let me know if anything happens with Grayson?" Raphael nods his head, but

Tiberion frowns, taking a look at me for really the first time since he arrived.

"Who are you, and what do you have to do with Grayson?" His tone is abrupt and suspicious, his forehead furrowed as he looks at me.

"It's okay, T. I'll tell you everything later, but this is Zadkiel's son, Zephaniah." Raphael keeps himself calm and collected, his tone soothing in order to comfort his skittish friend. His frown eases a little, but I can't blame the guy. Trust must be fairly thin for him at the moment.

Nodding my thanks to Trick's dad, I teleport home. The house is quiet when I arrive, and I find the boys on the couch, all with drinks in hand, the silence sad and heavy. Going to the fridge, I grab out a beer for myself and join them. Trick and Sander have Mav sandwiched between them, but his eyes are still fairly clear, so I breathe out a sigh of relief.

"How's Grayson?" Trick asks.

"Good. Michael found his dad, and when I left, your dad had just hooked them together for the transfer."

"What happened to Sam?" Jagger sits up from where Kai had his arm around him, more worry on his face than I would've expected. "I want to thank him for dispatching Connie for us."

Blowing out a big sigh, I put my bottle down and rest my head in my hands.

"What aren't you telling us?" Mav growls, and I look up to see them all watching me.

"Fuck, Sam went back in." They all erupt into noise, but I hold my hand up, stopping them. Quickly, I explain his reasons and what he and Chamuel witnessed in the clearing, seeing frustration, anger, and acceptance crossing each of their faces as they all take in the news in their own way.

"I can't believe they gave that bitch another chance!" Kai spits out, his anger mirrored by the others, but before I can say anything, Sander does.

"I can. Mylea is all about redemption. Look at how many chances she's given Hammus. He almost destroyed a whole race, but she forgave him. And to be honest, she's right. Connie is a product of a horrific upbringing, and I just hope she chooses to be better with this next chance she's been given." *Sander*, the voice of reason, who would have thought it? Equally as surprised but listening to him nonetheless, his words do have the others settling down.

"I don't know about any of you guys, but I just want to drink myself stupid and go to bed, putting an end to today and everything that has happened. I'll deal with it in the morning."

My friends, old and new, all make their agreements, and we spend the rest of the evening entertaining Jagger and Kai with tales of what Mina had been like when we were at the academy, the pranks she would pull on Sam, and the fierce way she would fight.

When it's time to say goodnight, I insist on Mav coming to bed with me so that he's not alone. Before I do, I check in on Drusilla, finding her still sleeping peacefully, the orb curled up in her arms. One can only hope that Mav and I can both find the same relief.

——•·•·•——

The next couple of days are much the same. Drusilla carries around the golden orb wherever she goes, finding comfort in it that none of us have been able to give her. At least she's allowing others to hold it when she needs to go to the toilet or shower.

Like now, she hands it to Mav, and it's almost like the orb gets excited, the light pulsing faster. He looks to Dru for help as a panicked look crosses his face, but she just smiles and pats him on the shoulder. "It's really happy to see you, Mav. It likes you." She leaves him standing there with that look, but the panic soon gives way to something almost peaceful.

"What did it feel like?" Sander asks once Dru returns and takes it back.

Mav's eyes are wide, staring after it with longing as Dru sits down with it in her lap. "It's hard to explain. While I was holding it, it felt like Mina was still here." A pang of grief strikes into my heart, wishing for nothing other than to be close to her again, to feel her in my arms once more.

"Dru, honey, I'm not sure that when Mylea gave it to you she meant for you to hang onto it all the time. What if you drop it?"

Worry crosses her face, and her smile drops. "I know you're right, but just give me a few more days, and then I'll store it in my safe space," she reluctantly agrees, and I give it to her.

Our safe space is a secret pocket that an Archangel can create to store things. It's where our weapons are kept so we don't have to carry them around all the time, a little pocket dimension that only we can access. I'd been meaning to show Mina how to create one for her magic wand so she didn't have to keep putting it in her hair, but I'd just never made the time. A wave of regret rolls over me, sadness directly on its heels. I think that's the way things are going to be for a little while.

A knock at the door has us all jolting with surprise. Exchanging surprised looks with each other, Trick gets up to see who it is.

When he opens it, his dad is standing there, quickly coming in and giving him a tight hug before he focuses on the rest of us. "Hey, kids. How are you doing?" We all mumble some sort of response, and a wry smile crosses his mouth. "Stupid question, I guess. I just wanted to let you know that Grayson is doing really well. The blood transfusion kicked in his Archangel powers and brought out his wings. I was happy to discharge him and was going to bring him here, but his dad's reluctant to let Grayson out of his sight until he's mastered a few skills. So Tiberion's gone away with him for now, back to wherever he'd been hiding. I imagine you could probably reach him if you needed to." He taps the side of his head, reminding us that Grayson is part of our circle too.

"I'm headed into the CD if any of you want to join me. Sometimes, keeping busy is the best thing."

Dru shakes her head immediately. "No, my mom is coming over, and I have this." She shows Raphael, his eyes widening just enough for us to notice.

"Is that Mina's soul?" he asks, his voice tinged with awe.

"I'm not all that sure? I think it might be a memory of her soul. I thought about it all night. Why would Mylea not let her soul rest? Though as much as I wouldn't want Mina to be kept from the rest she's earned, this is the only thing that brings me any comfort lately..." She trails off, a small bit of guilt darkening the peaceful ease that was on her face moments earlier.

He looks a little disappointed. If I know him, he'd love to get his hands on it to study it, but there's no way Dru would ever let that happen. Knowing a losing battle when he sees one, he turns to us.

"What about it, guys? I think Michael is going

to make a plan to storm Ferijen and take out Sabboath's operations there. We also need to go check on the progress of both the antidote for Earth and Amilles. I know you're all hurting right now, but you could make a big difference in what happens next and whether Sabboath pays for what he's done."

Sander stands up, Kai not far behind him. "I'm in."

Kai stands beside Sander, clapping his hand on his shoulder. "Mina wouldn't want us standing around, missing her. We need to finish all the things we started. I, for one, want to kick Sabboath's ass. In fact, I think it would be therapeutic."

Mav, Trick, and Jagger all join the two, and I look to Raphael, standing a little taller now that I feel a sense of purpose filling me again. "I guess we're all in."

Chapter Thirty-Three

Grayson

The place that my father has brought me to is a little wooden cabin hidden in a vast forest on the other side of Reath. Isolated and solitary, the cabin is surrounded by snow-clad pine trees. The air is clear and cold, and the sweet scent of the tree needles fills the air. Currently, we're in a clearing testing out my new wings.

Unlike my father's angel wings, mine are not feathered, nor are they like Samuel's leathery demon wings. Mine look exactly like they did when in dragon form. Red and silver scales cover the large things, just like my dragon, and they've retained the same shape as well. Not as large vertically as an angel or demon but they have a much larger span than either of them.

Dad's been giving me instructions for a while now. He seems nervous about letting me try, so I block him out and launch myself into the air like I would as a dragon. Large up and down thrusts have me away from the ground in seconds, leaving my

433

dad behind, mouth open in surprise. I do a couple of laps of the clearing before landing again.

"You forget that I've flown before, albeit in dragon form, so this wasn't very different," I tell him, and he runs a hand over his chin, his eyes dropping.

"I know. I'm sorry, it's taking a little bit of adjustment," he immediately apologizes, and I put my hand on his shoulder, liking the connection despite how weird it feels. We're in a strange in-between kind of place, him and me. The idea of having real family right in front of me, especially someone who never forgot me, fills me up in a way I've never experienced before. But... we're still strangers to each other, and there's a bit of uncertainty about how we should interact in this very new relationship of ours.

"Don't be... Dad." That word is weird in my mouth, but I find I like it. "It's an adjustment for us both, not to mention I have this ache in my chest from Mina and the rest." To say he wasn't pleased when he had heard I'd been pulled into Mina's mating circle is putting it lightly. He ranted and raved and broke some things, shouted about having my choices taken from me again. It wasn't until he said he was glad she was dead that I got angry.

Smoke billowed out of my nose, and I'd had to struggle not to shift. Up until then, my dragon had been in mourning for his mate, but right then and there he was ready to rip my dad to shreds. He didn't care who he was. Luckily, I was able to settle him, and Dad hasn't said another word, but I know he's waiting to.

From the minute we got here, he's been teaching me all the Archangel tricks. To say that I'm feeling overwhelmed is an understatement.

What with these new powers combined with the ones that Sabboath infused onto my DNA, I feel all out of control. Couple that with the knowledge that Mina passed, and I'm struggling to find any sense.

The last thing I need to learn is teleporting, and as my father explains it, I pay close attention. So far he hasn't let me leave this place, and I'm feeling as trapped as I had when I was with Sabboath. I know he means well, but he's going to have to let loose on the reins a little more. I'm a grown adult, and he's just going to have to get used to it. We spend the next hour with him teleporting me places and having me return to the clearing. It's hard when I haven't been anywhere else since I don't have anywhere to picture, but every time he takes me somewhere, it's one more new place to add to my mind. Freedom surges within me as the list continues to grow, both my dragon and I wanting to stretch our wings and have a taste of what life is supposed to be like.

Once we're finished to his satisfaction, we walk back to the cabin. Although I don't feel the change of temperature all that much, it's nice to be back in the fire-warmed cabin.

"That was great," my father says as he goes to the fridge and grabs us both a beer. "You picked everything up really quickly." He hands me one of the bottles, and I take a long sip.

Throwing myself down on the couch, I stretch out my legs. "So I was thinking now that I can do all that, I might head back to the CD, see if I can catch up with Team Alpha."

A frown forms on his face, his tension clear in the way his fingers clench about the bottle in his hand. "Why would you want to do that?"

"Mostly, I want to see how they're all coping with Mina's death." My heart aches at these words. Raphael had explained what had happened, why I had been in the hospital, but I'm having trouble wrapping my head around it. My dragon's been practically non-existent since I woke up, only reacting when my father says nasty things about his mate. I'm not sure if he'll recover. I didn't know her very well, but that bond was there and filled a spot in my heart, and although it's still there, it feels incomplete. But I don't say anything; Dad gets furious every time I mention her. "I also want to see if they were able to fix the water supply on Amilles."

Dad stands up and throws his bottle of beer across the room, smashing it against a wall in a big mess of flying foam and glass. He whirls on me.

"Why the fuck would you care? Those fucking angels are the reason I missed the last twenty or so years of your life! The Collectors Division isn't much better." His words are harsh and his anger crackles across my skin, the electricity in the air causing my hair to rise as it fills the room. But I have seen so many temper tantrums from Sabboath over the years that this is nothing, and I continue to drink my beer calmly. He doesn't like that I don't fight back, so he keeps going. "You will not have anything to do with any of them. I forbid it."

A puff of smoke drifts out of my nose as my dragon shows his displeasure, and I hold him back from the much more dramatic response he desires. I get it. I mean, he has every right to be bitter and angry, but that's him and not me. But the other unignorable fact is that he was very careful not to teleport me anywhere near Reath's capital city and the Collectors Division. Even if I overlooked his attitude, that one decision shows he's trying to keep me locked away, and I won't be a prisoner again. He waves his hand, clearing his mess, unhappy with my lack of reaction, and storms back out of the cabin.

Well, I'm afraid that he's going to be disappointed. He forgets that I'm not limited to teleporting. I mean, we're on the same world, so I could very well shift and fly until I find it, but I think he's also forgotten about the other skills I have now. That thought has me sitting up straight. My djinn lamp is at the compound. Fuck! I hope no one finds it. No one would know what it was, hopefully, and I'm not sure whether they could summon me if I wasn't in my djinn form. Or if now that I've taken it once, it's like my dragon and a part of me permanently. Shit. There are too many possible loopholes to what Sabboath has done, and unfortunately, I don't have the time to figure them all out.

Standing up, I pace back and forth; I need that lamp. I think about reaching out to Sam, but before I can, a voice in my head has me stopping on the spot.

"Grayson?" The voice is familiar. The guy from the cell, the one on the couch. Zephaniah, Sam had told me his name.

"Yeah, Zeph, isn't it?" I send back cautiously, not sure how to act. Up until recently, I was on the wrong side of this fight. It would be safe to assume that they're wary of me.

"We could do with your help if you're interested."

I jump on the olive branch. *"Yeah, absolutely, what do you need?"*

"How about you head back here, and I can let you in on what we're planning?" he suggests. I take a moment to think about his words, almost testing the bond for any feelings of distrust, but he seems genuine. I guess there's only one way to find out.

"I have a problem. I wasn't fully conscious when I left the CD, and Dad explained I need a picture in my head to be able to teleport. He hasn't taken me anywhere close to the city,

I don't think. I'm not confident enough to just think it and will it to happen."

"Yeah it's only demons who can think it and it will happen, angels need a picture in their mind. I'm not sure why that's the way it is." He says to me and I'm not surprised Dad didn't tell me about the differences.

"And I'm reluctant to change into djinn form. In the spirit of full disclosure, my lamp is still at Sabboath's compound, and I'm not sure if anyone's found it or not. I'm actually not sure if I have to be in djinn form to be controlled, or if I can be controlled like this too."

Surprise trickles down the link followed by determination.

"Wow, a djinn. Sabboath gave you guys some interesting powers." He doesn't sound disgusted, just interested, unlike my father who was horrified when I'd explained what happened. *"Well, we need to make that a priority to get it back. I'm going to send a picture of where we are into your mind, and then you should be able to just come on over."* The picture he sends is of a conference room with a larger table surrounded by beings that I recognize from the clearing the day Mina died. Along with that connection, my guilt rears its vicious head again, my dragon shifting uncomfortably in my mind. Everything happened so fast, and I wasn't able to stop Connie, and now everyone is suffering because of it.

With that picture in my mind, I draw my magic into myself, and within seconds, I appear in the same room.

Walking over toward me is a familiar man. This is the guy that was in the cell that day, Zeph. Tall, with long brown hair, tired eyes, and a welcoming smile that looks a little strained. Can't say I blame him. He holds out a hand, and I reach for it.

"Hey, man, you're looking a lot better than last time we saw you." We shake hands and slap each other on the back before stepping apart.

"Yeah, I feel a lot better too, though there is still this empty feeling inside..." Just like that, he reaches up to rub the same spot I always do, and I instantly feel a part of something.

"I know how you feel." His eyes blank for a moment as if he's thinking about why we all feel like that, and I take a moment to look around the room. Coming back to himself, he sees it.

"Come on, I'll introduce you to everyone." I nod and follow him over to the table, but the one person I'm looking for is missing.

"Where's Samuel?" I ask him, a tinge of worry breaking through all the sadness inside. Zeph runs a hand over his bearded chin and grimaces.

"Sam went back in. His cover wasn't blown, and he decided he'd be more help if he returned to get more intel."

"Shit! What about the girl? Did she survive? I know Connie had held onto her pretty damn tight and was flinging her around, last I can remember"

"Beatrice will be okay. She had some broken ribs and a concussion, but those will heal with time," one of the Archangels says to me. This one has emerald green wings, with dirty blond hair cut short.

"Raphael, this is Grayson." At the mention of his name, a flash of a memory from before Sabboath flashes into my mind, of being swung up on this man's shoulders for a ride. A feeling of warmth and love flows through me at it.

My eyes must widen in surprise because he smiles at me. "Grayson, it is so good to see you again. You don't know how happy it made me and the others when we found out you were alive."

My eyes scan the group, and I start to recognize others. These are all my father's friends from before, and a sense of familiarity washes over me as more memories of these men come back. Like uncles, they doted on me as a kid, taking me fishing and camping and throwing the ball. I remember having so much fun with all of them.

"Let me introduce you to our sons." He goes around the room pointing out each of the guys, as well as the four demons in the room.

Once introductions are done, we all sit down, but before they can start on their plan, I jump in.

"Listen, I think that I should go back in too. Samuel needs back up, and I have something I need to retrieve that's vital." Saying it again, I realize how true this feels; in fact, something is *urging* me to return. A primal fear for Sam, that he's all alone.

They all start to argue, but Uriel's voice is the

loudest. "What are you going to tell them?" He doesn't seem opposed to the idea, but the calculating glint to his eyes tells me that he won't back me up unless I have a smart way to do this.

"Just that I was captured and escaped."

"The Menagerie is very heavily warded, making it fairly impossible to get out of without help. Sabboath knows this. He's the only reason the Five were able to escape in the first place," Zadkiel warns me, but I have an idea.

I nod my head. "Yes, but he's now given me all these other powers. If I shift into my djinn form, I can tell him it was that magic that allowed me to escape. He wouldn't be able to question it because it's never been tried before. Beings like Sam and I have never existed before now."

I can see them all mulling it over in their heads, but I can tell I'm winning.

"Look, we just got Sam back, and I'd feel more comfortable if he had back up," Lysander adds in his two cents, and I nod my head in thanks.

"We've just lost Mina, and I'm reluctant to lose any more of my friends. I think he should go in." Patrick quietly adds his approval, Lysander moving closer to him and putting a hand on his back. One by one they agree until it's unanimous.

"First sign of trouble between now and when we breach the compound, you get Sam and yourself out of there," Raphael directs, and I agree.

"It shouldn't be long; we just need a sense of

how many he still has working for him and if we need to add extra man power," Azrael explains.

"I'll use my djinn powers to message you. Sabboath locked that place down tight once these two breached it. The only way in or out is if he specifically opens a portal. But if this works, and I can get in or out, then I will help you bring everyone in."

"I'm sure he's covered that hole in the tree now," Zeph points out. We can't mind speak with Sam to get him to help us, so this is starting to feel like it would've been our only option even if they hadn't all agreed. I stand up and let the magic wash over me, becoming that floating mix of vapor and substance that I first experienced in the lab.

"Holy shit," a voice says off to the side as my body changes, and when I open my eyes, I know I'm once again suspended above the floor.

Everyone gathers around, their eyes wide with amazement. Lysander steps forward and runs a hand through where the lower half of my body should be. It feels weird, like a tickling sensation, like when you drop from a great height really quickly.

"Huh, that's weird," he says stepping back. "Do you know what you can do?"

"Pretty much anything you can wish for. But I'm not bound to obey because I'm not bound to my lamp, and you're not my master, or I hope that's how it works," I tell him waiting for my dragon to slap me again, but he's still subdued, like he recognizes these guys for who they are. Mates of his mate and he trusts them.

"Mina would've gotten a kick out of this." Jagger smiles slightly, his eyes still sad, and all the others speak up with agreement. Despite the small smiles and the almost undetectable lightening in their eyes, their grief still weighs heavy, almost a physical presence in the room

"Can I wish her back?" The words have me looking up. Standing there are who I now know are Mina's parents, both looking wrecked with grief, though there's a spark of hope in Lucifer's eyes that it kills me to have to snuff.

Shaking my head, her face falls. "No, I'm sorry. I can't kill anyone, nor can I bring anyone back from the dead. Those are two of the most important rules. If I could, I would have already."

Michael wraps an arm around his mate's shoulders, pulling her closer, and my dragon scratches against my mind, his pain at seeing what we could have had making him restless. "Az just messaged us and told us what you are doing." He and his mate exchange a glance. "We thank you from the bottoms of our hearts, but we're both sure Mina wouldn't want you risking your lives. You should wait for us to figure another way in."

"Seriously, Michael?" Uriel's growls in equal parts disbelief and frustration. "Don't let your flame die with your daughter! Where's the almighty

Archangel warrior?" He looks at Lucifer, sparing her none of the aggravation he's feeling right now. "And you, the demon's champion? Have the two of you turned soft?"

Uriel's words have the right effect, fire flashing in both of their eyes.

"Fuck off," Lucifer growls, but he keeps poking.

"No, don't let your daughter's death be in vain! Let's put a stop to the AoA, cut off Sabboath's little worker bees, and then we can strike at the person who is really responsible.

"Hammus!" growls Michael, and Uriel nods while Lucifer steps forward and grabs my hands.

"Be careful." I nod my head and wave goodbye to everyone before I click my fingers and disappear.

Samuel

After Dad hit me a few times, I teleported behind the waterfall on Amilles where Sabboath had opened a portal to the compound. Thanks to his paranoia, he'd locked down the compound, making it so teleportation in and out of it was impossible. Right now, the portal behind the waterfall is the only way in and out of it, and that's only for the few hours he's willing to risk leaving it open. When Mav, Mina, and Zeph escaped, he'd been furious and had obliterated the tree with one wave of his hand. Even his more "obedient" soldiers like Grayson and me weren't made exceptions to his teleportation restriction.

Fuck. The thought of Grayson has my demon hungers rising, my incubus entirely too interested in the dark dragon. My inner demon is insisting that Grayson can feed us now that Mina is gone. Even though he's sad that we've lost our mate, his instincts are pushing him to take care of his hungers despite his grief.

Both of my inner animals have been very quiet since Mina died too. I can feel their sorrow and anguish even though they never established that bond with her.

A wave of grief stabs at me, so strong it almost knocks me to my knees. Staggering, I put my hand out to steady myself, the rock wet with moss underneath my hand. Closing my eyes, I take a cleansing breath. The waterfall is thunderous in my ears, and the smell of dampness wafts out of the cave, helping me focus on where I am right now. Exhaling, I continue into the cave, water splashing me as it thunders into the pool below.

Shining bright like a beacon in the night is the portal. Bracing myself, I run through, acting like I'm escaping for my life.

"Quick, quick, close it!" I scream, stumbling and falling to my knees. With a rush of power, the portal closes behind me.

"Samuel! What the hell happened?" I look up to see Sabboath staring down at me with a few bloodied angels behind him. Panting, I pretend to catch my breath, finalizing the story I want to share. He looks from me back to where the portal had been.

"Where are Connie and Grayson?" There's a wrinkle between his eyes, almost like he's concerned. *As if the asshole actually cares about his children. Probably just worried that he's lost some of his research subjects.*

"Grayson was captured, and Connie..." I break off and look up at him, one hand rising to my chest as though the beating pain I feel in it is for her and not Mina. "I'm sorry, man, but she's dead." His face pales and his eyebrow twitches, but these are the only reactions that I can see. "She attacked and killed Mina. There was no protecting Connie from the wrath of her mother and father and friends after that." I keep my voice low and flat, needing it to be steady so he has no reason to doubt me.

It's at this news, not the knowledge that his daughter is dead, that he blows his top. "She fucking did *what?* Killed her?! Well, then the stupid bitch deserved all she got. Been next to useless all her life. The only good thing she ever did for me was bring you in." There's no hint of remorse behind his words; one would think he was talking of an enemy rather than his daughter, and I'm sort of glad now that Connie got a second chance. I wouldn't wish this man on anyone.

"And Grayson got captured?" he asks. Without missing a beat, I nod, that much closer to pulling this whole thing off. Should've known he wouldn't dig too deep into what had happened to Connie.

"Yes. I only just managed to escape while they trapped him in dragon form; they were so distracted by the fight he was putting up. Remember, he has a whole heap of new tricks up his sleeve, so I'm sure he'll try to figure out a way to get back to the compound. I thought you'd rather have one of us back than none."

Sabboath runs a hand across his weak chin and nods thoughtfully. "You may be right. Grayson has always been a smart boy. I'm sure he'll make it back to us."

He waves his hands, sending the remaining angels away, and helps me to my feet. "Alright, Samuel, we won't have Mina now, so we'll have to find a way to get us some new breeding stock. It's a good thing I included incubus in that demon essence. It'll be up to you now to lure us in some new female. Preferable pure angel, but ABs will do in a pinch. Actually, that other girl that's on Team Alpha would be a perfect specimen. That would give me the chance to see if there's something special in the biology of your group of elites. We'll have to sort out a plan to get her here as soon as possible."

We're walking back toward the living areas as he talks, the compound eerily quiet now that he's lost most of his soldiers to the Collectors Division. The ones that are still left are quiet, avoiding Sabboath's eye in the hope he will keep walking.

"How is the transition going, anyway? Sorry about triggering that but I needed Mina to react to you. That's all down the drain now, I guess."

His words are suspiciously casual and make me want to punch him in his dick. Fuck, people's lives obviously mean nothing to him in his bid for greatness. My teeth grind together in the struggle to not tell him where to shove it, and my animals send a wave of their grief toward me, as if reminding me why I need to keep my cool. *Do this for Mina. Don't let her death be meaningless.*

"Why don't you rest up and regroup? Do you need me to send some girls to your room? We've still got a few that you can make use of. Now that Grayson's temporarily away and Connie and Mina are dead, you're one of my prized soldiers." He slaps me on the back with affection, the urge to shower nearly making me twitch at the contact.

Do not kill this man just yet, Sam. "I'll be fine. I'm not really feeling it at the moment," I lie since there's no way I'm forcing one of those girls to feed me.

He frowns, looking concerned. "Are you sure?" Jesus, this guy's priorities are mixed up. His only daughter was slaughtered, yet he's worried about whether I need to fuck someone or not.

"Maybe a little while later I'll make use of them." He smiles at these words, and when I stop at my room, he keeps going.

"Make sure you're in peak condition, Samuel. I need to go and meet with our overlord and advise him of the situation. Now that the CD and the damn Archangel council has interfered with my plans for Amilles and Reath, we may need to step up our operation in Minzeon." He continues to mutter as he walks off, but I store that information away, and as soon as I can, I'll share it with one of the others.

Opening and closing my door, I look around my room, noting its stark lack of personality. I hadn't wanted to do anything with it when Connie tried to convince me to make it nicer. Really, all it has is a functional bed, with a chest of drawers for my clothes. What was the point of putting anything personal up when the only things I wanted would have shown my ties to team Alpha?

My mind goes back to the new memories that Mylea returned to me. Of filling Mina with my cock and of the flow of her blood down my throat, and my cock throbs with need.

Fuck, this need is still riding me hard, and without Mina, I'm going to have to find someone else to take care of it. My stomach lurches at the thought, my heart aching. Sitting down on my bed, I let all the emotions free. Everything that I had kept bottled in since I watched Connie attack Mina. Anger, helplessness, and even fear come flooding back. Followed by my utter devastation at the loss of her and what might have been had we had the chance.

Tears stream down my cheeks as I throw myself backward, smothering my face in my pillow before I scream, hoping that the sound is muffled.

After a while, pure exhaustion smothers me and I try to remember the last time I actually slept. Unless you count the blackout from my transition, it was a while ago. Maybe if I get some sleep, every-thing won't feel so desperate. Somehow, I doubt it, but I'm going to give it a try anyway. Blocking out everything that's happening around me, I close my eyes and pray for oblivion to take me away from all the bad memories.

——— • ◆ • ———

When I wake, I have no idea how long I've been asleep but my need is riding me even harder than before. The knowledge that we're on lockdown basically taunting me. I'm going to have to suck it up and ask one of the girls here to help me, but the likelihood that anyone will volunteer is pretty dismal. They're all anti-demon; that's part of the reason they're in the AoA to start with. Sabboath will have to order it, or I'll have to overwhelm them with pheromones, and I'm not prepared to do that. I'd rather starve than take away someone's right to consent to sharing any part of their body. Mind made up, I decide I'll grab a shower and go down to the lab. At least I should be able to get some blood from there. The other hunger will just have to wait.

My shower is quick, and the memories of Mina are punishing me, so when I get out to dry off, I'm hard as a rock. Wrapped in a towel, I walk out into my bedroom, coming to an abrupt stop and dropping my towel in shock. Standing, or should I say floating, three feet above the ground is a fucking djinn. Flames that don't seem to burn take up the space where his legs should be, and he has a muscled, naked chest that's covered in black markings. Heart beating fast, I glance around my room, looking for something to use as a weapon but finding nothing.

Moving my face back to the djinn, it drifts higher, over-plump lips and defined cheekbones to almond-shaped silver eyes. A sexy flaming package that has my incubus ready to lick his lips in anticipation. *I'd like to see what's below the flames.*

Frowning, I look closer, trying to figure out the niggle of familiarity that's teasing me until it hits me.

"Fuck, Grayson! How did you get in here?" I relax a little now that I know I'm not in danger, but that also gives my hungers the opportunity to come back to the forefront. Bending down, I pick up my towel, but when he doesn't respond to my question, my eyes go back to his.

His gaze is locked on my hard cock, his stare holding undisguised desire, and he licks his lips before swallowing and shaking his head.

"Sorry," he apologizes, the hint of color that graces those beautiful cheeks giving away his embarrassment at being caught. That look in his eyes and the blush in his cheeks are all my incubus needs to take over. He's hungry, and here's someone we both want to feed from.

"Don't be," I purr, my incubus dropping our towel again before strutting over to him. The flames surrounding Grayson have a gentle heat, but they tickle more than burn against my legs, so I crowd closer to him. Honestly, the sensation just fans my own flame higher. Leaning in, I grab hold of his ponytail and hold his head where I want it. Stepping even closer so that my chest is pushed against his, I lean in and taste his lips, running my tongue along the seam.

"Before my incubus takes over completely," I force out, wrestling back control and looking him in the eye, "are you okay with this? If not, you need to leave. *Now*."

Instead of shying away, his hands run up my naked back and he nods his head, his breath coming more rapidly now. With that show of consent, all pretense of being in control leaves me, and my incubus firmly grips our body in his control. "Open for me, Grayson," I command, a push of compulsion on my lips, and as he obeys I dip my tongue, tasting and teasing his mouth. His flavor is fresh and spicy, and it doesn't take long before his tongue joins in tangling with mine.

My fangs drop into my mouth, one cutting his plump lip and drawing a gasp from him that goes straight to my cock, but I ignore it as his blood hits my taste buds.

Groaning, I pull myself flush with him, trying to grind my pelvis into his, but it hits no resistance.

Looking down, I realize the problem. "We're going to need the rest of your body for this, Grayson," I tell him, and he snorts his amusement before the flames coalesce and his lower half solidifies. *Thank god.* This makes him taller than me now, kissing him becoming a little difficult.

Eager to fix that little problem, I take him over to the bed and climb on, pulling him up after me. Lying down, I pat the bed, inviting him to join me. He lays down facing me, our bodies flush against one another, my naked erection rubbing against him, pre-cum dribbling from the top.

Once again, I check with him, my need to respect him and his body greater than any influence from my incubus. "Are you sure you want this? I don't want my incubus taking your decision out of your hands."

With my words, his eyes smolder and harden, and he puts his hand around my head. "Shut up and kiss me," he orders, a bit of a growl behind the words. Barely a second later, his mouth is pressed against mine, sending a pulse of excitement through me.

I'm not sure how long we lay there kissing, our hands fondling each other's bodies, but eventually, Grayson pulls back and stands up. When his body reformed, his legs were covered by billowing loose pants, his erect cock causing them to tent. He now removes these, leaving him naked and hard, a feast for my senses. Looking a little nervous, he climbs back onto the bed, avoiding meeting my eyes. I don't want him nervous; I want him frantic with need, so as he lays down next to me, I shuffle my body down the bed until my mouth reaches his thick length. The dark skin glistens with pre-cum, and I run my tongue around it, licking it all up. He groans and grabs hold of the bedsheets with his hands, his body taut with tension.

Chuckling at his reactions, I repeat the action and jump in surprise when his hand leaves the sheets and finds my horns. Moaning with the sensation of his hands on them, it's my turn to grip the bedsheets in my clenched hands. "Watch out for the ends. They're very sharp," I warn him before turning back to my task. My tongue runs up and down his shaft, his taste both sweet and salty against my tongue.

He grunts and pants what he says next. "They actually changed shape as soon as I grabbed them; they're blunted round ends now."

Concentrating on giving him the best blow job he's ever had, I engulf the head of his cock, taking him deep into my mouth, sucking and swallowing with every up and down movement.

His moans are getting louder, and I just hope no one walks in; that would be very bad. I know he told me to feed, but the masculine noises are bound to draw someone's attention. He must have the same idea because he pushes me off him and sits up.

With a snap of his fingers, a lamp appears in his hand. Gold with silver markings and studded with rubies, it glows in the light.

"How about we take this somewhere we won't be disturbed?" He waves a hand at the door, and a bar appears across it. After that, he places the lamp down on the chest of drawers and holds out his hand to me. Happy to accept it, he pulls me off the bed and wraps his arms around me. A weird sensation crosses my body, and it's like we dissolve into nothing but pure matter, our essence whisking away from the compound and all the ugliness it contains.

Chapter Thirty-Five

Samuel

Still wrapped in Grayson's arms, I look around the room we've reformed in. In the middle is a huge round bed, low to the ground and covered in colorful scattered pillows. Billowy drapes hang from the ceiling, giving the room the feel of a Bedouin tent, and the floor is covered with vibrant multi-colored mats. There's a light smell of some exotic incense in the air, but it's heady, not overwhelming.

"Are we inside your lamp?" I ask, looking back at Grayson.

"Yeah, we are. I think I can change it to however I want it to look, but I kind of like this. What do you think?" There's an adorable wrinkle between his brows like he's worried about how I'm going to react, but I'm so turned on now that the design of the room is the furthest thing from my mind. The thought of being alone with him and not being interrupted is sexy as fuck, but another thought unexpectedly comes to mind, bringing with it a wave of sadness that has me sighing.

"Mina would have gotten a kick out of this. You're lucky she never knew about this or got her hand on your lamp. She'd never have let you go." I smile with soft affection at the thought of our missing mate.

His eyes cloud with sadness, and something in me wants to wrap him in my arms as though that would protect him from the pain of what we've lost. "I would have given my lamp to her without hesitation," he tells me, serious as ever. "Even though I only just met her, I couldn't wait to get to know her, pheromones be damned. My dragon has been inconsolable, and that alone tells me that we've missed out on someone very special. Not to mention the way the rest of her mates are mourning her... Only someone amazing could inspire so many others to care for her so deeply."

My incubus is not happy with where the mood has gone, the inconsiderate dick, and pumps more pheromones into the air, wanting us panting instead of crying. Pupils dilating, Grayson pulls me in for another kiss. This one starts off softer, tempered by the sadness we were feeling a moment ago, but it soon turns fierce as my lure does its job. We crash down onto the low bed, a tangle of limbs, cocks rubbing as we both thrust against the other.

Pulling away, I go back to what I was doing before we moved, his hands gripping my horns once more, but as I push his pleasure higher with my tongue, my tail decides to get in on the act, starting to probe at his ring. He gasps and tenses a little, so I push it away. Conjuring up a bottle of lube, I pour some into my palm, coating the fingers of one hand with it. As my mouth goes back to his dick, I run a finger around the pucker of his ass, massaging in the lube before pushing one finger in. He groans, his cock twitching in my mouth, so I ease back a little, cupping his balls with my free hand. His breathing is coming harder and faster as I push another finger in next to the other.

Slowly, I thrust them in and out, and Grayson's head tosses back and forth in pleasure, cries bursting from his mouth. "Fuck, Sam." Easing back, I add in one more finger, stretching him

"Is this still okay?" I ask, and he groans, nodding his head with a bit of desperation that confirms he's enjoying himself.

"Yes," he sighs, the sexy sound almost pained, and my own cock leaks with pre-cum once more. Pulling out, I run my hand over my hard length, coating it with lube, and climb back up the bed. Running my tongue around each of his nipples before I loom over him and lean in, giving him a kiss. His hands go to my hair, and he pulls me back, an animal-like glint in his eye that says his dragon might be as close to the surface as my incubus.

"Just fuck me already," he growls, and isn't that a fucking turn on. Moving his knees back, I line up with his hole and slowly push my way in, pulling back then pushing in until I'm fully seated. His channel grips me tightly in a way I haven't experienced in a long time, partly through Connie's influence to start with, and that carried over once she had disappeared. She would have never been okay with me taking a male lover, and the more distance I get from her, the more I question why I was ever with her.

His hands grip my upper arms hard, that tiny twist of pleasure/pain bringing my focus entirely back to him. We're both panting, and I take a moment to catch my breath, leaning in and kissing him some more until he relaxes again.

"I'm going to bite you too, okay?"

His body is now vibrating, but he manages a short nod, so without waiting any longer, I pull back and thrust in hard, over and over. His cock rubs against my stomach with every movement, our balls slapping together, and the sounds coming from us both are raw and primal. My tail pushes between us and wraps around his cock, milking it with each of my thrusts, and he shouts with surprise, followed by another desperate moan.

"Going to come," he grunts out, so I lean down, and just as I feel my balls tighten, I bite down into his neck. He shouts out loudly as I draw in large gulps of his rich, almost fiery blood, and I can feel his cum painting my stomach as I fill him with my own. Breathing hard, I seal the holes in his neck and pull out, collapsing next to him.

Suddenly, the skin around Mina's mate mark

starts to burn. Breathing through the pain, I look down, realizing my mark has another section to it. Grayson's face is contorted in pain too, and when I look at his groin, his mark now has my pattern around it too. My eyes widen in shock, a sense of rightness and fulfillment quickly on its heels. I might've lost one mate, and Grayson won't replace Mina in my heart, but something in me is shifting to create room for him too.

He's staring at the ceiling, eyes wide and his breathing ragged. "My dragon is riding me so hard to bite you," he says quietly. "It's the most animated I've seen him since Mina left us."

Waving a hand, I conjure up a cloth and wipe over his stomach before cleaning mine, getting rid of it once we're both taken care of.

My skin is buzzing from all the energy I absorbed from him, and I snuggle into his side, waiting for him to say something else. I just popped his cherry, and I'm worried that he's upset. I'm actually a little thrilled about all this, but I wish Mina was here between us. That would be perfect.

"Ah, fuck it." He rolls over and wraps me in his arms, his mouth taking mine in a punishing tangle of tongues and teeth, a growl escaping his lips as he pulls back. My eyes widen as I watch his mouth change, my now satisfied incubus peeking out in curiosity, wondering what kind of fun we can get up to with this new surprise. Gray's teeth elongate, both bottom and top, and he yanks my neck to the side and bites down hard, drawing blood. Just like that, I orgasm, once again painting his stomach with cum. Growling, he licks at the marks he's made, all the time thrusting his cock against mine until he too is covering my stomach with his seed.

He finishes tending to the wound and pulls back, snapping his fingers. Instantly, we're both clean. Once again, he wraps his arms back around me and snuggles close, nuzzling at my neck, a sort of purring sound coming out of his mouth. My animals are going nuts inside me, wanting me to claim him that way too, but it's going to have to wait for now. *Super endurance or not, I think I need a break. And we need to talk now that my hunger isn't pushing me to ravage him.*

The fog of my need has cleared, and I can finally think clearly, realizing that I haven't even asked him the most important question. "What are you doing here?"

He's still nibbling at my neck and purring when he replies, "When Zeph said you'd returned, I just couldn't let you come back alone. Everything inside me was overwhelmed with the need to follow you and make sure that you were safe. I'll just stay in djinn form. Sabboath will believe I escaped, no problem. He only likes to see what's in front of him." As he speaks, he breaks up his words with little licks and nips, taking his time worshipping at my throat and around his mark. The mix of sensations is almost enough to make me throw any kind of common sense to the wind, so I pull back, looking him in the eye so he doesn't keep getting distracted.

"You did that for *me*?" I'm a little overwhelmed; it's been a while since anyone had my back like that. I mean, I've really only ever had my adoptive parents and my team as those constants in my life. Well, them, Dad, and Mina. And just recently I've been an asshole to all of them because of Connie. It warms my heart to have him say it, especially since, mate bond or not, we don't know each other much at all yet, and it would be easy for him to think the worst of me rather than seeing me as someone worth saving.

"So you met everyone? How are they all? Mina's death must be sending them all reeling. I wish I could be there for them, but I'm probably the last person they want to see at the moment. I wasn't even quick enough to save Mina." My guilt rolls through me, destroying all the good feelings that Grayson had conjured with his words.

"Stop that, Sam." Grayson raises his head and grabs me by the chin, forcing me to meet his eyes. "Yes, they are all devastated, but they don't blame you at all. This was not your fault, and they've decided to stop waiting around for his next move. Mina's death has pushed them all over the edge. They want to storm the compound, so I need to be in here when they're ready to go. Find a way to get them in."

Before I can say anything, a bell sounds out through the lamp. "What is that?"

The silver pupil in his eye expands until there's a sheen over the whole thing, his eyes totally whited out. A frown crosses his face, and then the silver shrinks down once again until his eyes are back to normal.

"The lamp says there's someone banging on your door, pushing against my magic. We need to leave." He snaps his fingers, clothing us both in AoA uniforms. Before we dematerialize into that dizzying matter again, he wraps his arms around me, placing another fierce kiss on my mouth. I barely have the chance to register our disappearance before we reform in my room at the compound, the lamp still sitting safely on top of the dresser.

"Damn it, Samuel, wake up! What are you doing?" Sabboath calls through the door, his voice wrapped in so much of his usual haughty impatience that I honestly have no idea how long he's been out there.

"Shit! He can't see my lamp," Grayson hisses, so I grab it and thrust it into my safe space, the little pocket of reality where I keep all my valuables.

"If he asks about a lamp, tell him you don't have one," I whisper back, and he nods his head. "Now leave here. He'll want to know why you're in my room. Pop back in after I see what he wants."

He waves his hand at the bar on my door, and it

disappears. Before Sabboath even opens it, Grayson disappears as well. Hurriedly, I pull off my shirt and pants and pull on a pair of sweats. My hair is already mussed from sex with Grayson, so I look like I just got out of bed.

Cracking open the door, I peer out at Sabboath, a thunderous look on his face.

"Sorry, man, I was sleeping. It's been a hard couple of days." He looks slightly mollified but is still abrupt when he says his next words.

"Well, get up. I have our next orders. Get dressed and come to the meeting room and we'll discuss it." He storms off down the corridor, and I close the door, breathing out a sigh of relief as I follow the orders and hurry after him.

⎯ • ◆ • ⎯

Sabboath has been ranting for a good thirty minutes by the time Grayson decides to pop in. He's back in his half-djinn form, flames crackling high, an imperious look on his face. Sabboath's mouth drops open in shock, a greedy glint immediately filling his eyes. I almost snort in laughter as I've never seen him look so surprised, but he quickly recovers.

"Grayson! What happened?" he demands.

"I escaped, obviously. They couldn't keep me in this form." Power rolls off of him, his voice deep and alluring, and my dick gets hard with the sound. Fuck, that's not good. I shuffle a little further under the table so that the asshole angel next to me doesn't see. I think I'm alright since they're all fairly gobsmacked at his appearance, but this wouldn't be a good time for an accidental hard-on to blow our cover.

A smug look crosses Sabboath's face at the confirmation of Gray's power, and I just know he's giving himself a pat on the back. "Good boy, now sit down. You'll come in handy for the next phase. I was just telling everyone that we need to kidnap a few higher level angels and some strong ABs to create my new soldiers."

"He's still on the breeding program rant?"

Gray's voice whispering across my mind is a welcome surprise, and thankfully, I'm so used to my team dropping in whenever they feel like it that I don't visibly startle. *"Yes, and you and I are his prize studs,"* I tell him wryly. His internal shudder telegraphs down our bond, letting me know he feels just as happy about that fact as I do.

"While I was gone, I tested the compound's barrier a little, and I'm pretty sure I can bring it down to let the others in. I passed word to them, and they're in the process of transferring teams into Ferijen. It shouldn't take them too long to get into place. They'll let us know when they are ready." My heart skips a beat, a combination of nervousness for my team and excitement at this all being almost over blending in a tumultuous mix.

"Thank god, because I've had enough of this. He'd already told me we're to ramp up the assault on Minzeon. With the goddess Pele already working there for his aims, he's managed to convince Rūaumoko, a Maori volcano god, to help out. If we don't get to Minzeon soon and stop them, their realm will be overrun by exploding volcanoes. All Hammus will have to do is offer to help, and the people will agree to be his servants just for the sake of saving their lives."

"But my main priority is setting up a new base. This one is now compromised, and although they can't get in, we still need to get out, and I cannot be always opening portals like a damn taxi driver. I've got more important things to be doing. Grayson and Samuel, you'll come with me to Habbalea. I want to check out some of the cave systems there. What better place to keep a secret base than a planet that's uninhabitable?"

Grayson and I nod our agreement, and he dismisses everyone else with a wave of his hand. There aren't as many upper level angels left since a lot were captured in Amilles before Mina was killed, and there aren't many normal troops either. Sabboath's numbers are getting low, but in his megalomania he doesn't see the truth that his madness will soon be ended.

Once the room is clear, he looks at us. "Samuel, now that you're an Archdemon, you won't need a breathing apparatus on Habbalea, and Grayson, I suggest you stay in djinn form. You probably won't need one either, but be prepared to conjure up some BA gear."

With a wave of his hand, he creates a portal, and we follow him into the barren desert realm, Grayson floating on flames behind me.

We're in a ruined city that sits nestled into a cliff face. The ridge runs further than I can see, but the boundary where the city stops and the barren land continues is clearly demarcated.

"The palace is on the other side of the city." Sabboath points in the opposite direction to where we are. "But there are a few temples left standing on this side, and if there were ever some hidden doorways into the cliff, it will probably be in there. Hammus' priest weren't stupid men; they'd have had an escape route. Demons were always such volatile creatures, ruled by their appetites, so having an escape route planned for if things ever went sideways or got out of control was just common sense." He tuts and starts walking forward.

"You two check that one out over there, and I'll check on this one." He walks off in the direction of a temple that still looks fairly intact, directing us to one that's crumbling and barely standing.

I walk over to the temple and duck under the collapsing door frame. Grayson is right on my heels, his arms crossed in djinn style. Floating over the ground, he's basically silent, the only detectable sign of his presence a soft tingle that is likely more related to our mate bond than anything else. I raise an amused eyebrow at him, and he shrugs. "It's really weird. I don't know what to do with my arms since I have no legs. This pose is the most comfortable... I get it now."

His eyes turn silver again, and I go on high alert. When they clear, he talks into my mind. *"That was Zeph. They're almost in place. Once I lower the barrier, Sabboath's going to know who it was, and he'll know I'm not with him anymore. I'm not going to be able to stay and protect you,"* he warns, his eyes darkening with concern as a wrinkle crosses his brow.

His words bring a warmth to my soul, but before I can say anything, Sabboath shouts from outside the temple, "Sam, Grayson, get out here quick." We hurry out to see what he wants, finding him standing before a portal, his mouth thinned in a furious grimace. "The base is under attack. We need to return." We race through his portal, coming out in front of the compound. Through the golden barrier we can see the Archangel council, the three Archdemons, Team Alpha, and an array of CD agents behind them.

"Fuck!" Sabboath screams, but despite his exclamation, he doesn't look too concerned about them getting in. I can hear the alarm going off inside the compound, and suddenly, people are pouring out the door until we're surrounded by AoA soldiers, so few as there are left anyway.

"We need to evacuate," Sabboath instructs, but

before he can open a portal, Grayson snaps his fingers and the barrier falls.

Sabboath blinks at Grayson in disbelief before extending his wings and jumping into the sky, brandishing a sword. "You little cunt. That's the thanks I get for taking you in and raising you!" His voice is venomous as he lunges for Grayson. A replay of Mina's death comes to mind, and I materialize my sword and dive between them. Before I can strike out at Sabboath, a large black man with snowy white feathers, with baby blue and gray streaks, flies between us and the vengeance-seeking Archangel.

"Sabboath!" he growls, and the slimy Archangel pulls back, looking at him with horror.

"Tiberion, they found you?"

"Yes, they did, and I look forward to giving you the death you deserve for stealing away my child!" He rushes at him, a loud clanging sound ringing out as their swords meet.

All around us, there's fighting, but it's clear that the AoA soldiers are no match for the CD and friends. Within half an hour, everyone is rounded up. The only fight still taking place is between Sabboath and Tiberion, and I really think Gray's dad is just toying with his food.

He gets another slash in, hitting Sabboath's wing, and he falls to the ground in a heap. Before Tiberion can land and deal out a killing blow, there's a flash of light, revealing another Archangel standing above Sabboath. He quickly puts a hand on him and turns to wink at the rest of us.

"Lesterial," Uriel bellows, "don't do it!" The angel laughs and shrugs right before he and Sabboath disappear.

"Fuck." Tiberion's roar of disappointment echoes around us, but there's nothing that can be done. Sabboath has slipped our trap for now.

Chapter Thirty-Six

Jessamina

My death was excruciating. I could feel the basilisk's venom pumping through my veins as my blood poured out of the hole in my chest, its path like liquid fire. And when darkness finally came, it was no relief. The pain continued to burn, memories of how the spider's venom had done the same plaguing me. How is it that both times she tried to kill me it's been with venom? *Fuck, how unoriginal.* Though I guess I'm not in any position to argue its effectiveness.

It's like my whole body and soul is being reshaped. I'd always thought death was supposed to be nirvana, a place where all your dreams and wishes came true. That one day, once they had decided they'd had enough of life, my mates would join me.

The thought of my mates brings me such sadness, its depth threatening to overpower the agony that just won't quit. I had such a short time with them, but I'm greedy, and I wanted *more.* I

473

wanted to love and live with them, to have adventures, and later on, babies. Babies who'd love us all equally, and it wouldn't matter which one was their father or mother. Round chubby cheeks and legs with smiles that would light up a room.

But I guess that won't happen now. Maybe I did something wrong in life, maybe the nuns were right and I was a wicked child. Now I'm paying my penance.

"Oh, for fuck's sake, Mina. I can't stand your morose inner monologuing anymore. You need to wake up and stop feeling sorry for yourself. You're not dead... well, not in a traditional sense."

Opening my eyes, I find myself on a comfortable bed in a tastefully appointed bedroom. *What the fuck?* Mind you, the bed could fit a college basketball team. It's so big I think it could fit me and all my mates on it.

"Where am I?" I ask the amused goddess, already feeling a little irritated at the repeat situation. *Why is she always loitering around when I'm in pain and nearly dying? Or I guess sort of dead if she's to be believed.*

"At my place, of course. You didn't think that I just existed, did you?"

"Well, I hadn't really thought about it," I admit. "But where exactly is it?"

"You know how you see the boys pull their weapons out of thin air occasionally?" My mind drifts to my boys' weapons, though it's not their metal ones I'm thinking about. My fangs slip into place, and great hunger flows through me, just the thought sending my succubus into a near frenzy.

"Oh, for crying out loud, get your mind out of the gutter. Damn succubus demons always thinking with their pussies," Mylea grumbles, holding up a hand. "Come on, I'll explain it to you as I show you around."

Taking her hand, I allow her to pull me out of bed, following her out of the bedroom and through a gorgeous large house. Every room we go through is homey and comfortable, the atmosphere like a real family house.

"Can you have children?" I ask out of the blue. She flinches, and I mentally kick myself for my lack of tact. "I'm sorry, it's none of my business."

She pushes open a set of double doors, and we exit the house to a large veranda with some comfy-looking chairs. She gestures to one, and I sit down as she blows out a deep breath of air.

"No, it's okay. You need to know this, so I'm happy to explain. It's just a little painful. I can have children, but it takes every one of my mates participating at once or having sexual relations with all of them within a short window of time to fertilize the egg," she tells me, not looking the least bit embarrassed.

"Hammus has always been selfish and never interested in group sex. Frankly, he also was never interested in having sex with me so quickly after I'd been with the others. I actually always wondered why we'd been fated to mate. Anyway, it wasn't important enough for me to push the situation, so for many years we were happy just the five of us. Then once I'd decided I was ready, he turned on everyone and distanced himself, and without him, no children. Once you destroy him, it should become possible for me to have one with my remaining mates." By the end of her explanation, her eyes are glistening, tears threatening to spill over. Blinking rapidly, she seems to push those emotions back.

"Is that why you want me to destroy him?" I ask, feeling suspicious all of a sudden. Her head snaps up in shock, and she shakes it almost violently.

"No! I won't say I won't be happy at the chance, but he can't go on like this, constantly stirring up trouble. The worlds used to be such happy places, and now they are always on the verge of one crisis or another because he keeps messing with the natural order of things."

My suspicion settles, her reasoning making enough sense that I have no choice but to trust her at this point. Unsure what to say next, I look around. We're sitting on the edge of a crystal blue ocean, gentle waves lapping at the edge of the house. Gulls are screaming, and I can see a fish jumping further out to sea. The salty smell of the sea and the warm sun on my face is relaxing, and I breathe deeply before letting it back out.

"Where exactly are we?" I ask again.

"Well, like I was trying to tell you, like the boys' safe spaces where they store their weapons, this is our own pocket of reality. Originally, once the worlds were created and they were in balance, there wasn't much for us to do except to watch over them, so we created this space for us to just be." Her smile grows warm, some of the earlier upset melting away, but there's still a fragile edge that tells me we've got more serious topics ahead of us. "But more and more, we were needed out there, and this place doesn't get used as much as it used to. I'm hoping that will change."

"So, explain to me what happened," I tell her, gesturing to myself. "I'm not really dead, you said? That seems like an important place to start."

"You died, but your death activated the little piece of myself that I added to you when your parents conceived you, thus activating your goddess genes and making you viable for resurrection. I couldn't let the others see it since events needed to happen in a certain way, and I needed time to talk to you about what will happen next." Her face is apologetic as she continues, though I've got the stirrings of anger coming to life inside me. The fate of the worlds is more important than my feelings, sure, but I'm a little tired of these surprises that wind up with my mates heartbroken and my body in agony.

Some of my growing irritation must start showing on my face because she softly says, "You were always going to have to die to ascend, and I'm sorry for that."

Then she claps her hands together and bounces in her chair. "But let's talk about what's changed. Physically, you look the same. You'll just have the ethereal glow we all have, and you can tamp that down. It'll give you a headache if it's always on," she grumbles but continues. "The red streaks from your mother have gone, and your eyes will no longer glow red; they'll look like all of ours." She points to her multicolored, ever-shifting eye color. "Now, a bit of the goddess power was already poking its little head out; that's how you were able to turn invisible and shapeshift your human form," she explains, answering a few of the questions I'd been wondering.

She waves a hand, and a couple of cocktails appear in front of us. Picking one up, she takes a sip and gestures at me to take the other.

"Originally, you were just going to replace Hammus as the goddess of demons, but Eagi and I are going to have to restore the balance between Reath and Earth. We need to bring basic magic to the people of Reath and stop it from colliding with the creativity of Earth. The realm beings will not continue to exist." With that dramatic pronouncement delivered as casually as a weather report, I basically choke on my cocktail, my eyes watering as I cough and sputter until I can get words out.

"But all those people!" I argue, and she shakes her head, her lips pressed together in a thin line.

"Many of those creatures are just the product of someone's imagination, and specific character creations and mythological beings, such as Cinderella or Frankenstein's monster and even all of the gods from Earth mythology, will disappear. Creatures such as vampires, weres, the fae, mermaids, and so on will be allowed to survive and breed. We didn't think it was necessary to erase whole species, as we would be no better than Hammus with his demons. We will form the realms into one just for these creatures and attach it to Habbalea. They'll be your responsibility along with the demons. It will be a big job, as that many species are bound to be volatile, but you'll have nine mates to help you out. I'm sure you can handle it, and frankly, the four of us deserve a vacation after all this time."

My mouth drops open in shock, and the cocktail glass just about falls out of my hand. She lunges for it before it manages to drop and puts it on the little table between us, the corner of her mouth turning down as though she's not satisfied with my reaction. *Oh, sorry, how is one supposed to act when magical godhood is revealed along with the giant pile of responsibility being dropped on your shoulders at the same time?*

"Because you'll be the goddess of all these

different creatures, you'll be able to shift into any of them as you wish, with all their powers at your fingertips. You will still have your demon side, which will continue to need to be fed, and everything that makes you angel. Basically, you're one powerful mixed basket, but I knew you'd have to be in order to give the worlds what they need."

My mind stumbles over all of this information, not sure what question to ask next. She doesn't seem too concerned because she plows on, showing no awareness that my mind is basically imploding right now.

"We need you to rest here for a little while longer until you build your new strength up. Ideally, we'd have your mates here to help you, but that is not possible at the moment as they have their own task that needs to be taken care of." She finishes sipping her cocktail, her nonchalant manner rubbing on fraying nerves. Everything seems like it's no big deal to her, but this is fucking *huge* to me.

"But my mates... they all think I'm dead. Why can't I see them or speak to them?" She ignores my question and keeps going, giving a basic play-by-play.

"As we speak, the council and the CD are storming the compound you were kept on in Ferijen, and then they will be taking care of some problems in Minzeon and returning the two cures to both Earth and Amilles. Once that is all taken care of, we will need to draw out Hammus so you can take care of him."

"But how the fuck am I supposed to do that?" I yell at her, jumping to my feet. Everything is finally taking its toll, and I lash out in anger that I honestly don't care to rein in. Thunder rumbles across the sky, and in front of us the sea has grown dark, the waves picking up as the wind begins to blow. Instead of showing signs of alarm like a normal person would, she claps her hand in glee, a bright excitement widening her eyes.

"Oh yes, my baby goddess, I can feel that power starting to build! You're going to be impressive, possibly even more powerful than me." She sounds thrilled at the idea and not the least bit concerned that a giant wave is now heading toward us, cresting just in front of the house.

Lightning crackles across the sky, but just as I expect the waves to break over us, it hits a barrier and disappears.

Breathing a sigh of relief at the near miss, I'm still waiting for an answer from Mylea, and she sighs, rolling her eyes before holding out her hand. All levity disappears from her face as my magic wand appears in it, flashing colors like my new eyes.

"This weapon has always been in my possession. No one else knows the real purpose of it, but it was intended to be a god killer in case anyone needed to be stopped. The beings that made us always knew there was a chance that this might happen and entrusted me, as their first creation, to keep it safe until it was needed one day. The runes are not angel runes; in fact, I'm not sure what they are, but if you pierce Hammus' skin with this, it will unmake him. You needed to become a goddess to actually work the sword in that way, and since I can't stop him, I had to let you follow down this path regardless of its dangers or pain."

She stands up, her body starting to glow as her own power leaks out, unable to be contained with the seriousness of the conversation. "I'm trusting you with this, and *no one* can ever know it was this that destroyed him. Once the deed has been done, you must keep it safe. I don't think it will work against us in other people's hands, but it pays to be careful, especially with your own godhood being so new and fragile. It has a spell on it now to always return to you. I didn't think about that last time, and, well, you've needed it a few times." She snorts a little, breaking the tension. *I guess even goddesses fuck up sometimes.* I take it from her, and it lights up so brightly I have to close my eyes against it, almost like it's showing its joy in being reunited with me, but it dims moments later. As I look it over, I realize there are new runes on it that weren't there before.

"Huh," Mylea grunts, as surprised as I am. "Well, I wasn't expecting that, but I guess that's a good thing, or I hope it is."

"Anyway," she says airily, waving her hand around, "rest and recover because the last thing we need to do is repair Habbalea, but the guys and I can help you with that one. It's a pretty big job, but I think the demons are ready to move top side again, don't you? And I daresay they'll be thrilled to have a new goddess." She picks up the glasses and strolls back inside, leaving me with the steaming pile of information she's just given me.

Goddamn it! Left to my thoughts, they return to the inevitable, the distance between my mates and me. My soul aches from the missing bonds, and an extreme longing fills my very being.

"Bring more booze," I yell to her, and she laughs, the sound both regretful and genuinely amused.

"Sorry, it won't work for you anymore. Well, it might if you drink blood from an inebriated mate. I don't know... you'll have to experiment. There are lots of things that won't affect you now, but I just like the way they taste," she replies, and I groan in frustration. Curling my feet into my lap, I wave my hand and a blanket appears. *I think I'm just going to nap right here for a little while longer.* I'm suddenly feeling exhausted, though whether that's from the new goddess powers, all of this information, the shitload of responsibility coming my way, or all of the above, I don't know. All I can do for now is close my eyes and let my body regain its strength.

━ •◆• ━

I'm not sure how long I slept, but when I wake, I feel better about everything. Determination fills me to master these skills in the shortest amount of time possible so that my mates and I no longer have to suffer. At least I know they're alive, but that's a cold comfort when they're all in the process of mourning me. I can't imagine what they're going through. Maybe they won't even be happy to see me when the crazy goddess finally lets me return...

I'm resigned to what must happen to Hammus but okay with everything else. The only thing I'm going to have to work out is how I'm going to draw him out of the woodwork. With Hammus having his own pocket reality to hide in, one that his mates have never been able to reach, the odds are not in our favor. Our best bet right now, Mylea assures me, is to use his greatest weakness against him: his ego.

Time works differently in this little pocket of reality, and I'm not sure how long I spend there, circling through thoughts of what's to come. It feels like weeks, practicing shifting into all the species that will be living in the newly combined realm, working on figuring out their different magics and needs. I don't know much, if anything, about being a goddess, but I do know that I don't want to be like Hammus. This'll be one of the biggest challenges I've ever faced, but I'm going to give the realm beings and the demons the goddess they deserve.

It's not until I shift into a vampire that I start to

think about my own needs and how I haven't felt hungry for blood or sex since I've been here, asking Mylea about it the next time she comes to check on my progress. "On this plane, you don't need anything to survive. You're sustained by your goddess essence. It doesn't mean we don't like to eat or drink or have sex here, but we don't need it. When you return to the world, that's when your needs will come back. But if you try, you can allow it to trickle back in slowly so that you're not jonesing for a bloody orgy the minute you see your mates again. Wouldn't that be a disaster?"

I continue working on my shifts, and as fun as they are, it's a little lonely and boring not having anyone to share it with. Mylea doesn't have the same capabilities, so she can only watch and comment, not experience this new life with me. Though she's quick to dispel my worries that I won't be able to reconnect with my mates when they discover just how different I am from the Mina they knew.

"Yes, but two of your mates can now do the same things. You won't always be alone, and you have the powers to give the rest of your mates the options too." My heart races at the thoughts of Grayson and Sam. I've been very careful not to think too much about any of them. Each time, my magic would get out of control, and then it would rain for hours. This time, I try to center myself, focusing on my excitement to see them again instead of the pain of missing them, and my magic steadies, the ocean in front of the house staying calm and blue.

"Woo hoo!" Mylea shouts, throwing her arm around me. "You're finally ready to return. You have excellent control of your powers, and your emotions don't affect them anymore." She pulls back, eyebrows turned down in a frown that's at odds with her whoops of excitement from moments before. "Are you ready for this?"

Swallowing hard, I nod my head. "You bet your ass, I am."

"Good. Then there's one last thing you need to do in order to reach the pinnacle of your power. You must have sex with all of your mates at the same time."

"Dru's not going to be keen on that," I tell her, biting my lip, and she shakes her head, waving her hand at me to hold that thought.

"Sorry, all of your *male* mates. Finish that mating bond between all eight of them so they will then be able to access all of their own power and feed it to you if needed. Just make sure that you have sex with Dru within a short time frame, say an hour." She winks at me, the dirty bitch. "Maybe Dru first and then the others. You'll probably be too tired after all that to do anything else, and that girl deserves a good time. They've all been missing you, but I'm afraid your absence has hit her the hardest, the poor thing."

My heart twinges at the mention of Dru being so distraught, but for the moment, my vagina speaks louder than my heart. "How the fuck am I supposed to have sex with eight men at the same time? I've got skills, but that's ridiculous."

Peals of laughter sound out around us as she doubles over, her amusement nearly bringing her to tears. "As long as you're all connected somehow, it doesn't matter. They don't all need to be connected to *you*. Woo woo, all aboard the Mina train," she calls out, miming pulling a train horn. *Dear goddess, there are some things you can never unsee.*

"Bitch." I flip her off while she continues to giggle for a few moments before calming down. Once she's gotten herself together, she stands a bit taller, the aura of her power seeping into the atmosphere around us. When she looks into my eyes, it feels like she's reading my soul. "So, Mina, are you ready for the next chapter in your life?" A twinge of nerves is quickly pushed out of the way by the need to see my mates. For them, I will pull up my big girl panties and embrace my destiny.

"Let's go."

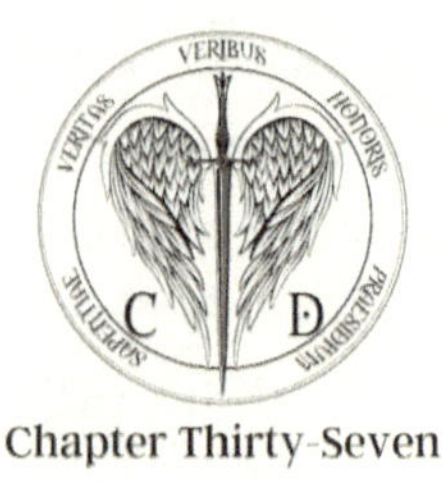

Chapter Thirty-Seven

Mavromichali

Following Mina's death, having something to keep me busy is helping my mind stay focused and not descend into its normal chaos. I've been throwing myself at everything I can to stay occupied, so when they need volunteers to stay behind at Sabboath's compound and sweep it clean, I'm one of the first that volunteers.

Together with Grayson, Mina's new dragon/djinn mate, I'm combing through Sabboath's lab, confiscating his research on genetic modification.

Now back in his normal form, Grayson explains to me how it all came about. "Sabboath was always obsessed with becoming better. I'm sure you noticed that he wasn't anywhere near as strong or as handsome as any of your fathers, and he was *obsessed* with becoming better than or, at the very least, equal to them. I have no idea where that stemmed from, but I believe he was dabbling in dark blood magic even as an angel. I don't think his ascension was natural, and using dark magic to give himself Archangel status could very well be the biggest reason he became what he is now." I pause what I'm doing, putting down the vials that I was about to pack into our styrofoam carriers.

"Did you ever suspect anything was wrong?" I ask, my curiosity getting the better of me. For some reason, the answer to this question feels important somehow. Grayson seems like a nice guy, but I guess that I just need to know that he has the sharpness that members of Team Alpha need. Now that Mina's gone, we need to protect each other at all costs. We can't afford to lose more family.

"All the damn time, but what was I to do? I lived here in the compound with no way of getting in or out. Sabboath obviously had none of my dad's blood to activate my Archangel powers, and getting the boost from that would have been the only way I could get out without his help. So I made the best of a bad situation. Yes, I picked up some bad habits and attitudes along the way, but deep down I always knew that they were wrong and a reflection of him and not how *I* felt. From my attraction to men to sympathizing with the demons, I was never free to share how I really felt. Growing up here was stifling, and sometimes I wondered if I should just give in and become his perfect little soldier like Connie."

For a moment, his eyes seem to be faraway, and my curiosity pokes at me to ask about what he's thinking, but I force myself to wait for him to finish.

"But now, looking back, I realize that wouldn't have done any good. It's not like he loved her anymore because she sacrificed everything for him. I was better off staying true to myself in all the small ways I could, biding my time until the day that I found Mina and got my first real taste of freedom." He's quite worked up by the end of his little rant, and I reach out, putting a hand on him. I allow a wave of reassurance to flow through me into him, reminding him that he's not alone. He breathes deeply, and the tension leaves his shoulders.

"No one blames you. You were dealt a terrible blow, and you coped with it the best you could," I assure him, and he nods his head in thanks before looking back into the fridge. Thinking it's probably better for the both of us if we take a break from the heavy topics, I let him get back to work.

"Ah, Mav, can you just look into that one over there?" He points to the other refrigerator containing a few blood bags. "Some of the vials are missing. They're filled with a golden liquid; they have to be here somewhere." There's worry almost surrounding him like an aura, and when I open the fridge, there are one or two vials laying on their side like they were dumped out in a rush, but nothing else apart from the bags of blood.

"No, there's nothing here," I reply, and he paints the air blue with his words.

"Fucking hell! That bastard must have popped back in here while we were all out front and grabbed them. It didn't even occur to me to protect what was *inside* the compound."

"What's wrong?" I ask, his reaction starting to stir my own worry.

He picks up a clear vial of liquid. "This is the newest formula, the one that he gave me. No one else had received this one except Connie." He pulls up a black vial. "This is the one that most of the others received, and it only gives them the ability to shift into one creature." Next, he grabs one of the red ones. "This is Sam's. His has the demon essence, and there's only a couple of those. I think you and Zeph were going to get one of these too. The most important thing is that there were a few vials of gold, and they were filled with a formula that I think contained god essence."

"Where did he get god essence from?" I ask, surprised until a moment of realization hits me. "When they got Matoz on Minzeon, right?"

"Yes, and there weren't many of those, only two or three, but they're missing!" He slams his fist against the glass door, and it shatters to the ground. Waving his hands at the nearby computers, they disappear back to the CD. He hands me one of the cases of formula and then picks up the other for himself, his motions hurried.

"Come on, there's nothing else here that we need. They can burn this place down for all I care." He storms off toward the front of the complex, and I follow after him, the thought of Sabboath with some god essence formula making my heart race. Once we reach the front, we discover my dad is there, overseeing the exploration of the compound.

"Hi, boys," he greets, but his smile doesn't quite meet his eyes, and I know he's as tired and worried as us all. After Grayson updates him on what we found, he disappears, teleporting back to the CD. Before I can follow, Dad claps a hand on my shoulder.

"Are you okay? Your mom would like to see you when you get a chance." I nod my head, not surprised. I haven't seen her in a while, and like most of the other moms, they stay away from Collectors Division business for the sake of their relationships.

Jophial, the only one who gets involved, has always been pretty easy-going and stays mostly in the Menagerie to avoid any serious fights with Zadkiel, but Lucifer and Michael are the perfect example of what would happen if both our mothers and fathers worked together. It's just easier if they don't; too much power and potential ego in one place, and we'd just never get anything done. Last I heard, the other mothers were busy helping with the rebuild of the orphanage Mina had grown up in, monitoring the reconstruction and finding new people to staff the place.

"I think we're headed to Minzeon next, but I'll try and get to see her after that," I assure him. After a tight hug that threatens to crumble some of my carefully held resolve, I return to the CD. When I arrive, Grayson is talking to Jophial in the Menagerie, and she has the case of vials in her hand.

"I'll put these in the vault and let Michael know what you told me about the missing ones." I over-hear as I walk over and hand off my case too. "Things have escalated in Minzeon, and the rest of Alpha is waiting for you in the portal room."

"Damn it, I thought that losing his compound would slow down his plans, but I guess he just went straight there after Lesterial dropped in and grabbed him." Grayson sounds defeated. Like the rest of us, Mina's missing bond is weighing on him, and it really is a struggle to keep going sometimes.

I pull him into a quick tight hug, knowing it always makes me feel better. He stiffens in surprise but relaxes after a moment, his arms coming around me. We stand there for a couple of breaths, just taking comfort in each other, before he pulls away.

"Thanks, man, I needed that." His eyes have a slight sheen to them, and I blink away the tears that threaten to give mine the same look.

"You and me both," I tell him. "Keeping busy is helping, but Mina never leaves the back of my mind. I think it's like that for all of us. Sometimes you just need to stop and breathe."

Jophial's been quiet during our exchange, but she now interrupts, probably realizing that we need to keep moving. If not, we might get lost in everything we're dealing with.

"I'm sorry, boys. I know it's tough on all of you, but you need to get going. Do this and return the two antidotes to Amilles and Earth, and I will make sure you all get some much needed time off as soon as that's done," she promises us, sympathy shining in her eyes. With that, we say goodbye and pop to the portal room.

When we get there, Sam, Kai, and Jagger are all in demon form. It's weird seeing Sam like that because unlike Jagger and Kai who still look like themselves, Sam really doesn't. I guess because he's a man-made demon as opposed to a born demon. In any case, now that we have him back home and with us, I'm sure we're all going to get used to this new Sam pretty fast.

As we approach, the tension in his face drains away at the sight of Grayson. None of us were very surprised when we found out the two of them were mates; Mylea *did* say that all of us males were linked and should take comfort in one another. I'm glad the two of them have found some tiny sliver of peace in one another, but at the moment, I can't even fathom anything like that. Though from the looks on Kai and Jagger's faces, they're going to need some feeding soon even though they're not still dealing with their transition like Sam is. Throwing aside the thought that it'll be my and Zeph's turns to step up and help with that next, I focus my mind on the mission ahead of us.

"Oh good, you're both here." Zeph smiles at us, but it's only relieved on the surface. "So, us storming the compound didn't really stop Sabboath like we'd hoped, and there are now two volcano gods stirring up trouble on Minzeon. The planet has a significant amount of what were previously extinct volcanoes, but that is no longer the case. The gods are causing widespread destruction and pollution, and the people are starting to panic. Air quality is at its lowest, even with their advanced tech, and all of their transport has been grounded because of it."

I guess hovertech becomes pretty unsafe when you can't tell whether you're about to hover into a building or another vehicle.

"They're becoming desperate, and it's just a matter of time before Sabboath or even Hammus approaches them with a solution in exchange for their devotion. Matoz can't do anything because of the whole freewill thing and that godawful non-interference issue," Zeph summarizes, the exasperation in his voice echoing what each of us is feeling. Our bond is practically vibrating with the frustration and complete astonishment we feel at the reminder that it's the gods own fault they can't help us right now.

"Oh, for fuck's sake, you'd think that that would be irrelevant now," Sander snaps, and Trick gently rubs his arm in a likely useless attempt to soothe away some of his annoyance.

"Yes, but *technically*, it's being caused by realm beings, and that's the job of the CD," Jagger points out, and though his calm explanation does nothing to fix the scowl on Sander's face, our irritated teammate nods his head.

"Okay, so we're dealing with Pele and Rūaumoko, both mythical volcano gods, and they need to be taken to the Menagerie to serve their time. There's a specific area where the volcanoes are located, so we think that's where we'll find them. Grayson and Mav, suit up with the fire retardant gear we use for dealing with the dragons. We'll leave when you're ready."

Zeph gives us instructions, and I lead Grayson to the same room that Mina had found so fascinating before our last mission to Minzeon. In no time, we're both dressed and ready to go, and Zeph has a tech open a portal to the right area since not all of us have been before.

"God, please be careful," Dru pleads. She's still too delicate to leave the apartment. *"I just can't lose any of you. I'm not sure if I would survive."*

She hasn't returned to work yet, staying holed up with the golden orb all day every day. We're not worried yet because we know she will start to heal eventually, but it does mean that we have to deal with an unfamiliar tech working with us. Hopefully, that person is as good at their job as Dru. We need a win right now.

We all send her reassuring words, Gray included, even though the two of them haven't officially met yet.

"When this is done, we need to look at getting a new place," I say to Zeph as the portal flares to life before us. "There's just not enough room for all of us at the apartment, and now that our Archangel status is out there, we can live anywhere and teleport in and out as needed."

"I was thinking the same thing the other day," he replies. "Let's give that job to Dru. She needs something to keep occupied, and it might make her feel better to move to a new place that she's decided could really feel like home."

With that, we step through the portal, ready to face this latest challenge as a team, albeit one that's still a bit broken. No matter what jagged edges we might have, we'll protect each other at all costs, volcano gods be damned.

Zeph waves his hand, and we all step through on high alert. When we do step through, we're directly in the path of a lava flow. Jagger, Kai, and Sam immediately take to the sky, the rest of us releasing our wings and following soon after them. The air is thick with ash and smoke from the volcano, making it difficult to breathe. The ground is covered with rivers of lava, destroying everything in their path. I can see hundreds of animals running away from the flow of the lava, but they can't run non-stop.

"Let's split up, four teams of two. Each going in a different direction. If you see them, let us know, and we will back you up."

I follow Zeph as the others all split up into their usual twosomes. We head up above the dirty air, flying fast and far until we get to the end of the ridge of volcanoes before turning around, keeping an eye out for the troublesome gods. The ash in my feather is uncomfortable, and the occasional spark keeps landing in my wings, creating a brief sharp burn before flickering out.

"This sucks," I shout over to Zeph, and he grimaces and nods his agreement.

"It sure does. We're not going to be able to do this for too long. Even with our healing abilities, our lungs aren't going to be able to handle it."

He's right; my breathing is already heavier, and I don't feel like I'm getting enough oxygen. A shout in my head has us paying attention, wiping away my distraction with the discomfort I'm going through right now.

"Shit, we've found Pele. She's just north of where the portal was. She's playing in a river of lava and hasn't noticed us yet. The sound from all the eruptions is blocking any noise we might make, and the shitty visibility is actually working in our favor." Trick sounds like he's struggling with the breathing too, even his mental voice becoming a little labored. *"Guys, we need to do this*

quickly. Sander is struggling big time, and I'm not much better."

"Okay, let's round her up, and the two of you can go back to the Menagerie," Zeph directs as we both speed to where they are.

When we arrive, the four of us circle the god, who still hasn't noticed us. She seems to be drunk on all the sensations, too wrapped up in her fiery playground to pay attention to much else, and we quickly wrap a net around her. Finally, this has her screaming in surprise, but before she can lash out any power at the volcano, Trick and Sander fly down and pick her up, both disappearing back to the Menagerie.

"Well, that was quick. Let's head the opposite way now. The other one must be here somewhere." Zeph leads and I follow, looking around at what the world has become. The minute that the god left, all the active volcanoes in her vicinity stopped. The lava that was already running is drying up and disappearing, with no more to replace it. The air is still smoky, but it's becoming easier to breathe with the closest volcanoes now dormant again.

Heading back in the opposite direction, we come across more active volcanoes and the air thickens once again. *At least we know we're going the right way.* A cough forces its way out of my lungs. I struggle to stop, my body shaking with the force of the coughing, and I struggle to fly straight. Zeph looks at me with worry in his eyes, excited voices clamoring in our heads before he can check in with me.

"Quick, there he is! Oh, fuck, he's seen us."

"Watch out! Shit, he's throwing lava balls."

Kai and Jagger's exclamations go back and forth, a combination of stress and breathlessness urging us to fly faster.

"Grayson and I aren't far; we can see you. Hang on! We'll be there shortly," Sam chimes in, and relief hits me with the knowledge that we're that much closer to having most of our team together to tackle the second god. Zeph and I flap our wings harder and put on a burst of speed. It's hard to see anything through the cloud of debris, but I know we must be getting close when a lava ball comes out of the smoke, narrowly missing me.

"Fuck, that was close." Zeph is almost breathless with surprise. Suddenly, the smoke clears slightly and I can see Jagger, Kai, and Sam ahead of us all, dodging flying lava balls.

When we get to them, I shout to Sam, "Where's Grayson?" I'm worried that my new friend has been hit, and I search the ground for him, trying to look for a sense of him in our team bond.

"He's shifting into his dragon. We're covering him." Sure enough, as he finishes telling me this, a massive and familiar silver and red dragon flies through the air between us and them, diving at where the lava balls are coming from. One hits him, but it doesn't even faze him as he breathes a stream of fire in the direction of the god before peeling off and coming around.

We continue to try and make our way closer, but every time we do, more lava is thrown at us. Kind of unsurprisingly, Gray's dragon isn't having much luck with using his fire against the volcano god, but at least he's diverted some attention away from us for a few minutes.

"Gray, you're going to need to try something else. Try your paralytic smoke," Sam shouts at him, but before he can, a wave of what looks like fire pixies streams toward us. They attack all of us, the force of their attack forcing us closer to the sea of lava beneath us. Even Grayson's dragon is affected if the loud roars are any indication. I can see him snapping at them, his jaw crunching down, but there's just too many of them.

A shout of horror has me looking up. Kai's wings are on fire, and he's falling toward the ground. This distraction is enough for them to over-whelm me, and I'm joining him before I can even orient myself, the boiling lava becoming all too close for comfort.

Fuck! Looking down, my heart beat races as I try to get them off of me. Plummeting toward the ground, the wind is rushing through my ears bringing the smell of sulfur as a choking reminder of how close I am to possibly the end of my life.

My eyes look for Kai but he's no better. Finally, when we're nearly about to hit the ground, there's a golden glow and everything freezes. I'm suspended in mid-air, an unexpected feeling that's better than burning alive but still entirely disorienting.

I look around, trying to see through the smoke, but it's no use. I'm about to start calling out to the team, trying to figure out what the fuck is going on, when a voice nearby has me thinking I must have actually died.

"Hello, boys! Phew, that was fucking close."

Chapter Thirty-Eight

Malakai

I must be hearing things because I could have sworn that was Mina's voice. Looking around, I can see everything and everyone around us is suspended like time has stopped, but I'm somehow still aware. My eyes go to where I last saw Mav, and he's the same. Jagger, Zeph, Samuel, and Grayson's dragon are also suspended in mid-air, the dragon roaring his frustration at not being able to move. A glowing golden figure nearby draws my attention, and when I turn, I expect to see Mylea, but I couldn't be more wrong.

An ethereal beauty stands before me, bringing tears to my eyes, her sudden appearance sucking whatever remaining air I have out of my lungs.

Hovering in mid-air with no wings, dressed in a flowing pink dress the same color as her demon form, golden blonde hair free of those bold ruby streaks, is my mate.

The same mate that I watched have her chest ripped open by that snake. The same mate who

503

bled out before our very eyes. The same mate whose missing bond has had my body and soul aching with despair since the tie was severed.

"Mina!" Mav's shout of disbelief has me coming to my senses, shocking me out of my open-mouthed stare.

"*You're alive?*" The words are breathless as they leave my mouth, followed by hacking coughs. She might have stopped us from falling and my wings may not be burning, but I'm still in trouble. A small wrinkle creases her brow as she looks between me and Mav and then up to the other three, concern shining in her eyes.

"Shit, that was close." She waves her hand, and Mav and I are both instantly transported onto the back of the red and silver dragon. Our wings are healed, my lungs feel clearer, and my eyes aren't stinging anymore.

"Holy shit." Mav's hands are on my waist as we both straddle the giant lizard's neck, nestled between a couple of thorny ridges. His scales are smooth and slippery, but we seem to be secure where we are.

"Is that Mylea?" Zeph asks, peering down toward the golden figure who's not so clear now that we're up here.

"Can't be. Mylea has silver hair," Jagger chimes in. We watch as giant pink fluffy wings explode out of her back. Giving them a strong flap, she flies toward us.

"No fucking way," Sam swears, and I know how he feels. Literally. The skepticism from the rest of the team is overwhelming our bond, making it hard to create room for other emotions. Soon, she reaches us and smiles shyly at the others, her hand rubbing Grayson between the eyes.

"Hi." Her voice now has the same musical quality that Mylea has, but other than that, this is definitely Mina. *Our Mina.* Their mouths drop open in shock, Grayson purring his delight at her hand on him.

"Just let me wrap this up and we'll talk, yeah? I'll explain everything. I'm just going to leave you here out of the way." She starts to fly off, a small smile on her lips.

"Mina," Zeph shouts, "you get back here and let us go!" She just waves a hand, shushing him, and he roars.

"Mina, don't think I won't punish you for this!" She turns and flies back to us, his face calming a little until she stops, still too far away to reach. *Well, if we could even move, that is.*

"Promise?" she asks, shooting him a cheeky little wink before flying away again.

Grayson joins him in roaring this time, but Sam just starts to chuckle as do Jagger and Mav behind me.

"That cheeky minx." I join in the laughter, which I think is more hysterical relief at seeing her alive than anything else. The smoke clears all around us, and we drift slowly to the ground. As we watch, she waves a hand. Instantly, the volcanoes are put out and the Maori god is immobilized. Lava disappears, the scorched ground repairing itself before our eyes. Once we finally make it to the ground, landing gently, Mina is there waiting for us, Rūaumoko wrapped in glowing chains, ready to be transported.

My eyes rake over my sexy mate's figure, my fangs dropping with the scent of her and the memory of what her body feels like between mine and Jagger's. The power drifting off her is immense, and I can't wait to see what that feels like against my naked body. The pull toward her makes my soul ache, and I know the minute I can move, I'll be all over her.

She turns her attention back to us, and with a pulse of power, we're unfrozen. The minute this happens, I hop off Grayson's back and race toward my mate, but I don't get there quickly enough.

Zeph beats us all, and he has her by the arms, shaking her furiously. "That was reckless! That's why you keep getting into trouble, Mina. You make reckless decisions!"

"Hey, man, ease off." I grab hold of his shoulder, but he shrugs me off.

Mina doesn't seem too upset. Honestly, she's showing much more patience than I would have expected. She lifts her hands, cupping his cheeks and resting her forehead against his. With a soft kiss on the lips, she pulls back, barely leaving space between them, and whispers, "I missed you too, baby." Those words seem to trigger something, and before I know it, he has her wrapped in his arms, kissing her like it's the last time. Relief floods my system at her words, and my knees threaten to buckle with the emotions overcoming me. Jagger reaches out a hand to steady me before wrapping his arm around my shoulders and drawing me closer. His relief and worry flood our link as well as his love for me and our resurrected mate.

A groaning sound is heard as Grayson changes form and joins the circle of men surrounding Mina, all who still look like I feel. A little unsure if this is real or not and terrified that she might just disappear from in front of us again.

"Hey, bro, do you think one of you could untie me?" The hopeful, unexpected words from the Maori god have them breaking apart. But none of us pay attention, and I can't wait any longer. Pushing Zeph out of the way, I muscle in. Wrapping my arms around her, I study her face. Her eyes are no longer lavender; instead, they have the same color-changing effect that the gods' do, her skin is soft and supple under my palms, and she buzzes with power.

"Looks like someone got another upgrade," I say quietly, and she winks before I lean in and devour her mouth. She returns the kiss with the same enthusiasm, her fangs dropping into place and drawing blood from my lip, which she sucks at to get more. A groan escapes my mouth, my dick hardening instantly, but I know my brothers are waiting for their turn, so I pull away.

One by one, they all take a turn to look her over, assuring themselves that this is real. But eventually, they all have kissed her hard, and as Grayson steps back, she looks around. "Where are Sander and Trick?"

"They returned to the Menagerie with Pele, which we also need to do with this one. Both of them weren't doing well with the smoke," Jagger explains, and another little frown crosses her face.

"Well, let's go then," she pushes, but before she can do anything, Mav holds up his hand.

"Hang on, we still need to get the antidotes and return them to Amilles and Earth."

"Okay, Grayson, Samuel, Kai, and Jagger, you take our bad god back to the CD, and Mav, Mina, and I will go to Minzeon and get the antidotes. I've been there before, so I know where we're going." Zeph takes charge, but his eyes don't leave Mina. None of their eyes do. It's like if they blink or look away, she'll disappear.

"No. I don't think we should split up," Mav interrupts our team leader. "We've only just got Mina back, and I, for one, don't want to let her out of my sight, and I'm sure the others feel the same way." He has a stubborn set to his lips, but his words have a huge grin crossing Mina's. She throws her arms around him, kissing him soundly again.

"I agree. I don't care to let you leave my sight for the next ten years," she laughs, placing lots of little kisses all over his face. He looks pleased with her reaction, but before anyone else can say something, she breaks away.

"Don't worry, I got this," she assures us all. She waves her hands, and Rūaumoko disappears.

"Where did he go?" Samuel asks, and she smiles at him.

"Straight to a cell in the Menagerie, of course. Alright, guys, I think human form is required for this little jaunt." With another wave of her hand, magic flows over Sam, Jagger, and me, and I'm instantly in my other form, clean and wearing a new uniform. A moment later, everyone, including her, is cleaned up and ready to be seen by the general public.

Looking around at the group, she nods her head, happy with the results. With a wave of her hand, Trick and Sander appear in front of her, their backs to us. They're both wearing hospital gowns, their butts hanging out in the breeze. A snort of laughter escapes my mouth, and within seconds, the rest of us are laughing a little hysterically as poor Trick and Sander yelp and pull the gowns closed.

"What the fuck?" Trick shouts, but Sander's next words have us silent instantly.

"Oh my god. We died." A sob escapes his

mouth, and I can see tears shining in Mina's eyes. "We fucking died, but I'm so freaking happy about it." He throws himself at Mina, wrapping his arms around her, sobbing. "God, I missed you so much." Trick joins their hug, and he too is sobbing, their voices raspy and their bodies still coated in the lingering smell of smoke.

"You're not dead," Samuel tells them gently, putting a hand on each of their shoulders. "We're not quite sure what is going on, but I'm assuming Mina brought you both here so we could all find out together."

Mina untangles herself and releases a pulse of power. Sander and Trick are clothed and cleaned and healed just like the rest of us. Smiling, she nods her head.

"Yes, I will explain everything, but I want to do it somewhere comfortable. Let's get this done, and then we can return home so Drusilla can listen too."

None of us want to let her out of our sight, so we all readily agree, and with a flash, we arrive at a high-rise building in the middle of Minzeon's capital city.

"This is where Azeyr brought the plague sample and where Team Dragon were tasked to bring the water sample," Mina tells us. She must see my frown of confusion because she explains, "He told me while I was going through my ascension at

Mylea's place." *That's definitely something we're digging into later.*

"Let's head upstairs and see what they've come up with. Matoz had let Clementine know that they were ready for us." Zeph takes point, and we all let him, settling comfortably into following his lead as per usual. Sander has yet to drop Mina's hand, and she doesn't look unhappy about it at all. In fact, I don't think any of us are going to be far from her over the next few weeks, if not longer, so I hope she's ready to re-evaluate her definition of personal space.

As much as I understand, I feel the over-whelming need for skin to skin contact with her as well. My inner demon is rumbling, and my fangs keep clicking into my mouth as I struggle to hold form. I shift closer to Jagger, my arm brushing against his for comfort, and he grabs my hand, squeezing it reassuringly.

"Don't worry. Our turn will come."

Mina turns back toward me, frowning then whispering something to Sander who nods and moves ahead with Trick, Mav, Zeph, and Grayson, leaving behind the three of us demons.

She gestures to a nearby closet, and the four of us crowd in there.

"I'm sorry, I know this is hard for the three of you. If your inner demon is anything like mine, they're screaming at you to fix our bond, but we can't just yet. I'm going to put them in a kind of stasis just so we can get through these next couple of hours or however long it takes us. That way you guys won't struggle to hold your form. Is that okay? Mylea taught me how to do this, and it'll just give us the time we need to get things sorted out, I promise."

Relief flows through me, and I can feel that Sam and Jagger are experiencing the same.

"Yeah, that would be great, actually," Sam says with a sigh. "It's really riding me hard, and even mating with Grayson hasn't fixed it."

A range of emotions crosses Mina's face. First surprise then a little jealousy followed by a whole heaping of lust as her demon starts to perfume the little area with her pheromones. Groans escape all three of our mouths, my fangs nearly piercing through my lip from the tension that's escalated all too quickly.

"I want to hear all about that later, but for now..." She starts to glow, a soft golden light that seems familiar, and she lays her hand on each of us, one after the other, ending with me. A wave of powerful magic slams into my body, and I grunt with the force.

"Sorry," she apologizes, "I'm still getting used to all of this, and it's not like Mylea had demons for me to practice on." I can't actually say anything, but I wait for her to finish, and when the magic eases off, I'm one hundred percent in control, like I've just fed, and fed well.

"Better?" She raises a questioning eyebrow, and I smile, letting out a sigh that the others echo. "Good, let's catch up with the others."

With the ease of blinking her eyes, we arrive in the elevator with the others, just in time for it to open and let us out on a floor containing a sophisticated lab. A man wearing glasses looks up as we enter and comes rushing over to us, hand out enthusiastically.

"You must be Team Alpha! We've been expecting you. Are you also the ones responsible for the disappearance of all the volcanoes?" His enthusiasm is a bit over the top, but Zeph nods his head, an amused smile on his face.

"Yes, that was us."

"Thank you *so* very much. As far as our intelligence and technology has gotten us, I'm afraid that was all beyond our scope."

"We're glad that we could help," Zeph assures him.

The scientist gestures to us to follow him, briskly leading us deeper into the lab. "If you just head this way, I can give you the antidotes and return the sample to you."

We all exchange glances with each other, Mav asking the question that the rest of us are itching to. "Uhm, that's great about the antidotes, but why would you want to return the sample?"

He leads his way into a hospital room where a young woman sleeps on a bed. "Well, she can't very well stay here, can she? She needs to be returned to wherever Lord Azeyr got her."

There's a moment of stunned silence before Mina steps forward and whispers, "Are you telling me that instead of just finding medical samples of the virus, he brought you a whole person?"

"Yes, he did, and it was actually the best course. We were able to study its effect on the human body and how it worked and then develop a cure from there! Miss Smith has made a full recovery, and the antidote and a vaccine were successfully formulated. The antidote just needs to be added to the world's water supplies. This is the same as what needs to happen on Amilles." He stops and fidgets a little like he doesn't want to tell us the rest even though he must.

"Oh, just spit it out already." Mina seems to be losing her cool as she keeps studying the girl in the bed. She steps away from the group so the doctor can't see her eyes as they start to kaleidoscope, changing color. She studies the girl, eyes narrowed in a stare, until they widen in surprise.

"Holy shit," she whispers as the doctor continues.

"I'm afraid something has happened to the girl. The virus has... changed her. I'm assuming because it was originally magic that created it, and, well, the girl now has some magical abilities. In fact, I wouldn't hesitate to say that everyone on Earth who had been infected by the virus will start to exhibit some form of magical ability. Mostly mental things like telekinesis, telepathy, and possibly control over the elements."

"Fucking hell!" The curse slips from my mouth louder than I had intended, but I think the moment calls for it.

"Try seeing it from my point of view." A sweet southern drawl has us all turning to face the now awake girl. She's sitting up in bed, and we can get a better look at her now without feeling like total creeps. She's pretty, with dark chestnut hair down past her shoulders, clear blue eyes, and a pert nose with a smattering of freckles. "That big dude just grabbed me from out of the hospital and brought me here with no explanation! I was literally on death's door; the doctors had told me there was nothing else they could do because it was a wait and see game." Her voice hitches with these words, but she gets herself together much quicker than I'd expect. "To then be not only cured but told about all these other worlds and races and beings that are like something out of fiction! Well, it's safe to say that I thought I'd died and gone to heaven."

"That seems to be going around." Sander chuckles but soon shuts up when Mina frowns at him.

"But I'm okay now and excited about what I can do." She holds out her hand, and the glass of water on the table next to her comes floating shakily toward her, finally making it to her hand, and she grins with joy. "It's hard work, but I'm getting there."

"Jesus, Eagi and the Archangel council need to be told about this, and shit, Earth is going to need training schools and new rules..." The words come tumbling out of Trick's mouth, panic starting to build in his eyes. I'm not sure if he's more afraid of telling them or of what duties might get thrown onto Team Alpha's shoulders to help out.

"Clementine is going to have a cow. We're going to need to have a branch of the Collectors Division on Earth, I think."

Mina paces back and forth across the room, running her hands through her hair in frustration, muttering, but we can all hear what she's saying.

"No, this is *not* fair. This is my first day on the job! You don't get to drop this in my lap like this. I have a bigger fucking task that you've already given me, so you can get your asses here and help me," she snaps in a loud shout, and no sooner has she finished than the golden glow you'd expect from a god appears in the room. Mylea and Azeyr appear, accompanied by two more gods that I recognize from the tapestry back at the Habbalea compound.

Matoz is the epitome of sexy geek. Long lean body that you know has sculpted muscles under his clothes, with sexy black-rimmed glasses and tousled hair that could just as easily be thanks to sex or forgetting to brush it. Eagi looks like your basic college jock, fit and tanned with tousled hair that's shaved on the sides, and he's dressed in jeans and a t-shirt. Throw in the warrior, Azeyr, and Mylea's men are smoking hot.

"You bellowed," Mylea snarks, her words sarcastic as she crosses her arms and taps her foot. Mina is busy checking out Matoz and Eagi, totally oblivious, so I clear my throat not so subtly, and she blinks, shaking her before looking at Mylea.

"Yep! Tag! You're it. This is above my paygrade, so it's all yours. If I have to take care of your problem, you can take care of this. No more sitting on your asses and allowing freewill." She points to Eagi. A lazy grin crosses his face, and he winks, momentarily rendering her speechless.

"You got this, baby," I whisper into her head. She doesn't say anything, but a wave of love flows back down the link. "I'm not saying take over and rule like a dictator, but you need to get involved in your creations' lives. Maybe then you won't get bored and end up like the other one."

There's a tense silence as the gods consider what Mina has said. Power crackles around the room, and I brace myself for the possible smiting that may be coming her way. The four gods hold a silent conversation, their multicolored eyes hiding any emotion that they may be feeling. Eventually, they finish, and Mylea smiles at Mina indulgently like she's her favorite younger sister. The others also look at her fondly, amused by her little temper tantrum.

"Yes, maybe you are right..." Matoz says thoughtfully, the words ringing with power. "Maybe it is time for us to get involved. Very well, young goddess. I can see now that Mylea did the right thing. We will do this for you."

"Thank you," Mina breathes out in a rush of gratitude. "I'm going to take my mates home and fix this bond, and then I'm going to need your help in drawing Hammus out. I'll leave you to deal with all of this and will let you know when I'm ready."

The four gods incline their heads, and within seconds, we're back on Reath in our apartment.

Chapter Thirty-Nine

Drusilla

It's been a few days since Jessamina's death, and I'm in this weird numb space. I can't reconcile my mind and heart with what I'd seen. Yes, I watched with my own two eyes as that snake punctured her chest and crimson rivers of blood poured out, soaking the ground below her, but in my heart it feels like it was all a nightmare. Although dulled, our bond is still there, and I think the glowing orb of light that Mylea gave me has something to do with it.

Today, all of the others have gone back to work, needing a distraction from the reality of everything, but I was entrusted with this thing, and I plan on following the task to the letter, so I stayed home. Making myself comfortable on the couch, I place the ball of light next to me. I know Mylea told me to keep it safe and my safe space would be the perfect spot for it, but I don't feel like I can let it out of my sight just yet. I feel the need to be touching it constantly, nurturing it, caring for it. Its pulsing

519

light, almost like a heartbeat, is soothing and calming for when my negative emotions push to the forefront of my mind.

The flashing ball before me makes me feel like Mina is still with us. I'm pretty sure that's its purpose, why Mylea gave it to me. To ease my acceptance of her death, and one day when I'm ready, I will have no need for it anymore. I will be ready to put it in my safe space, and there it will stay until a time when I'm feeling particularly lonely or nostalgic and I'll pull it out and remember the wonderful memories I have of her.

While I sit there staring into air, contemplating getting up and making some lunch, I can feel some currents of concern, anger, and surprise coming from the muted link I share with the boys. They all promised to lock it down for my sanity; I couldn't cope with worrying about them at the moment, but they still leak through occasionally. I'm considering telepathing my brother to check on him when a movement by the window has me on high alert.

Snatching the ball from where it's sitting, I bundle it under my arm, preparing to defend it with my life if need be, but it's only Mylea. She's standing by our window, a serene if somewhat melancholy look on her face that oozes power. It practically crackles around her. She breathes out a large sigh and spins to face me.

"We're almost there," she tells me, smiling sadly, "almost at the reason that I brought Jessamina into this world and created a mate bond between you all."

Ah, I guess that explains why she's upset. I would be too if I knew and was actively helping my mate be destroyed. Though it doesn't explain why she's here right now. I wait it out, not saying anything, figuring she'll fill the silence and maybe explain what she's doing at our apartment.

"You know, I never thought it would come to this. I have no idea where I went wrong. Where it *all* went wrong. We were so happy for years, and I just don't know..." She sounds so defeated. I tuck my orb back on the cushioned sofa and make my way to the sorrowful goddess, wrapping my arms around her and holding her tight.

"I'm sorry, I can't imagine what you must be going through," I say gently, and she shudders in my arms, sobbing quietly.

I'm not sure how long we stand there like that, but by the time she pulls away, both our faces are streaked with tears. Waving her hand, she conjures a box of tissues out of the air and offers me one. Taking it, I dry my eyes and blow my nose. She gets herself together, and with another deep sigh, she smiles.

"Thank you, I really needed that. Now we need to talk." Like a switch has been flipped, she's all business-like as she leads me back to the sofa and my orb. Picking it up, she sits down with it in her lap and pats the seat for me to join her.

"Some things are going to happen over the next day or so, big things, and no, I cannot tell you about them, but you need to promise me something." The seriousness of her words has me frozen, wondering what could be more serious than our mate dying in front of us. All I can do is nod, waiting for her to explain what she needs me to do now.

"Do not give this orb to anyone, and I mean *anyone*. This is not the right time for it to be given away. There will come a right time, but until then, it is not to leave your possession." The cryptic nature of her words has me frowning, confusion rising to the top of everything else I've been feeling for days.

"Oh, sweetheart, I know that's confusing, but that's all I can tell you right now. Put it away and only pull it out when you're on your own. This is very important. Can you do that, Drusilla?"

"Of course I can, Mylea. I won't let you down." Concern joins my confusion, the two feelings like weights pressing down on my chest, but I make the promise anyway. Just to prove it to her, I wave my hand and place the orb in my safe space. As soon as I close the little pocket of reality, my instincts scream at me to get it and protect it, but I clench my fist, trying to tamp down the urge to do what they say.

"It probably won't get easier, but I'm proud of you." She leans in and gives me a kiss on the cheek. "Pretty soon you're going to be distracted anyway." She steps back and looks me up and down. "Oh, honey, why don't you go and have a shower and pamper yourself? Shave and wash your hair and just do all the things you did before Mina. She won't be upset that you're taking care of yourself." Her nose wrinkles a little as she waves her hand at me, and I take a subtle sniff of my arm pits. Yeah, she's right. I've let myself go a little in the last few days. But what's the point?

"Trust me, she'll thank you for it," she mutters and then stands up, clapping her hands together. I frown at that last comment, but she stalks toward the front door, a not so subtle hint that our conversation is over for now. "Well, I must be off. Have fun!" She winks, and with her next step, she disappears.

Well, that was a little strange. Ignoring the urge to get out the orb and hug it, I take her advice, heading to the bathroom to take some time for much-needed self-care.

—— • • • ——

A good time later, I've showered and washed my hair and shaved all the important bits. I'm just sitting on my bed, putting moisturizer on, when Sander's voice makes me jump.

"Drusilla, where are you?" he asks, sounding quite urgent and surprisingly serious.

"In my bedroom. Is everything okay? His urgency has my heart racing a little faster.

"Yeah, but don't be scared. I promise it's all real."

"Sander, what the fuck are you..." My words break off as a flash of golden light appears in my room. *What could Mylea be coming back for?* When that light dies down, standing before me with the glow of a goddess, is Jessamina.

"Hey, baby." She smiles at me, and it's like my heart doesn't know if it can take the leap and believe what it's seeing, or if it can't withstand the risk. "I missed you so much."

My mind struggles to make sense of what I'm seeing, and I stand up, letting the towel wrapped around me drop to the floor.

Her eyebrows raise as an adorable giggle sneaks out. "Now this is what I call a welcome home present." Putting out my hand, I walk over to her, unable to speak. I grab hold of her arm, amazed to find it's solid.

Without taking a breath, I run my hands all over her body, a desperate sob escaping my mouth. "You're here, and you're *you*. I mean, you're not broken. You're not dead. You're alive." Nonsense flows out of my mouth unbidden as tears stream down my cheeks. All she does is wrap her arms around me and pull me close. The warmth and power radiating off of her body pulses into me, soothing and stimulating at the same time. A sigh of relief escapes my mouth before I start to sob in her arms, my body shaking violently.

"Yes, baby, I'm sorry for everything you've been

through. I tried to get back as quickly as I possibly could. I know how hard it must have been." She's cooing sweet words into my ear and rubbing my back, trying to soothe me. "But I'm here now. I missed you so much." The last little words are purred, and her hands slip lower toward my naked ass, but she shakes her head slightly. "Sorry, I'm a little hungry, but I can wait until you're ready." She eases back a bit on the pressure, but I grip her tight and rub my body against hers, needing that closeness.

"Let me feed you," I beg. "Let me show you how much I missed you and how much I love you." After thinking I'd lost her, I'm so reluctant to let her go or even let her out of my sight that it's painful. There's a desperate craving inside of me for the intimacy I've been missing the last week. The orb has been comforting, but I've been craving my mate too, and this is exactly what I need. I wave my hand and her clothes disappear, leaving her body naked and on display, a feast for my eyes. Leaning down, I wrap my mouth around one of her rosy nipples, placing gentle kisses before using my tongue and teeth to tease it into a tight bud. Switching to her other side, I do the same thing. She moans, a husky sound from deep inside that sends a pulse of plea-sure right to my core, and I push her backward toward the bed.

She falls back onto the mattress, bouncing slightly, her eyes hooded with desire. As I climb up next to her, I run one finger from her mound to her breast bone, teasing her. "This body is delightful, but I want to see the real Mina, my pretty pink demon," I purr, and with a wave of magic, Mina's demon form appears, minus the wings.

Climbing up on the bed, I straddle her hips, my already soaked folds rubbing against her mound. I grab her wrists, placing her hands above her head. "Keep them there," I order, and she nods in agreement, her breath coming faster as her pheromones scent the air. I can feel her tail nudging my ass, trying to get beneath me, but I won't let it have access yet. My gaze runs the length of my mate, my hands following the path of my eyes. Starting with her horns, I caress them with my hands before bending down and licking them with my tongue. While I'm lavishing them with attention. Mina slips one of my nipples into her mouth. The wet heat causes a delicious shivering sensation which washes over me before she uses a fang to scrape at them. The pain is an exquisite contrast that's already driving me into a frenzy. My tongue continues lashing her horn, and she moans, pulling away and breathing even harder. Mina writhes underneath me, her mound rubbing deliciously against my clit at this angle.

"Fuck, that feels amazing. It's almost like you have your tongue on my clit," she pants.

"Not yet, I don't," I tease as I move away from her horns and down her body, placing small kisses all the way along, until I get to her soaking folds. I inhale deeply, taking in the sweet scent of my mate, my mouth watering. Pushing her legs apart, I swipe my tongue through her folds and savor the flavor of her as it hits my taste buds.

A deep guttural moan escapes her mouth, and as I continue to alternate between flicking my tongue around her clit to sucking on her folds and dipping my tongue inside of her, she makes the most delicious sounds of enjoyment. But suddenly, a flurry of motions has me disoriented, and when I finally come back to myself, I discover Mina has positioned me on my back with her head between my legs and her hot cunt hovering over my face. She swipes a tongue through my folds and moans with delight. "Now, *this* is better." She proceeds to feast on my pussy like it's her very last meal, making it difficult for me to do the same. Eventually, I coordinate my movements, and she grinds down onto my face, writhing with enjoyment.

My face is soaked from her fluids and I'm in this blissful state, but I don't want her to orgasm like this. Pushing her off, I conjure a dildo into my hand. This one has an end for me to slip into my pussy, so I flip her onto her back and slip the end into me before parting her legs and impaling her with the other end.

"Fuck, Drusilla," she shouts out loud. It's usually her tail fucking me, but I wanted my turn to fuck my mate. Leaning in, I kiss her, and with languid thrusts, I build her orgasm back up again, sucking at her nipples before tweaking them with both my hands. My clit bumps against her every time I thrust, my orgasm building as well.

"I'm going to come," she pants, and just before she goes over the edge, I lean in.

"Bite me, Mina," I demand, and when her teeth sink into my neck, I scream, the orgasm rushing over me like a bolt of lightning. I try to keep thrusting, wanting to make hers last longer and wishing that I could bite my mate and give her the same kind of pleasure.

She finishes drinking from me as both our orgasms subside, but little pulses keep my clit tingling as I remove the dildo from her and then me. Waving a hand, I send it to the bathroom sink to be cleaned later.

Rolling toward her, I eagerly find her mouth, my hunger for her no less diminished after our reunion. The coppery taste of my blood lingers, but it's not off putting. I kiss her long and scissor my legs between hers, getting as close as I can, our breasts pushing against one another.

"God, that was hot," she moans, grinding her pussy against my leg. I pull her chin up, finding her pupils are blown and she has that well-fucked glaze to her eyes.

"Mina honey, be a good girl and tell me all about where you've been. Maybe I'll let you do it to me next time."

"Oh," she blurts out, suddenly sitting upright. "I wonder if I can change my body now that I'm an almighty goddess? I could grow a temporary dick to fuck you with?" Her eyes are wide, and she must be a little bit sex drunk because she turns to me and asks, "Would that be something you'd go for? I wonder how that would feel or work..." Her gaze becomes distant, her mind seemingly rolling all sorts of scenarios around, and I laugh out loud, completely amused and ecstatic to have her back in my arms.

"What made you think about that?" I ask, still laughing. There are bigger things to worry about, like the goddess comment, but I've got to let her try and explain this first. A smile breaks out across my face, one of the first in days, and I want just a tiny bit more time before I have to confront reality again. Even if it's just a minute or two.

"Oh, I had to shift into Grayson while we were trapped, to help Mav and Zeph and me escape. Anyway, I had a dick, of course, and it was a nice dick, and I was thinking about whether one of them would let me fuck them with it. I also plan on shape-shifting and jerking off too, maybe convince one of them to give me a blowjob. I want to know what it feels like, but now that I'm a goddess, maybe I don't need to shift into one of them. I could grow my own. I'll have to ask Mylea."

Still blown away by this ridiculous conversation, I can't say I'm not a little intrigued, but I hold my hand up before we go further down this dick-filled rabbit hole.

"Stop, just stop. We can talk about that later. Now I want to hear all about this goddess thing." She lays back down and pulls me into her arms, telling me about everything that's happened since the day she died.

Chapter Forty

Lysander

I shudder at the thought of what's happening in my sister's room, double checking that our bond is locked down. I'm so glad that my sister has Mina too, but I'll be happy if I never get a front row seat to just how much they love each other in the bedroom.

Trick wraps his arms around me, snorting with laughter. "You're a good brother and mate." He places a kiss on my mouth before shouting, "Who wants pizza? I don't know about everyone else, but I need food and beer, and I am *not* cooking." After a round of agreements, he goes in search of the household tablet to place the order.

The rest of us crowd in on the oversized sofas which really aren't that big anymore with all of us.

Things are still a little awkward with Grayson and Sam, but they've come a long way from where we were on the day Mina died. Or didn't die, as the case may be. It hasn't been that long, but there's nothing like a vicious case of grief to make you set aside your baggage.

"Is anyone dying to know what happened?" I put it out there, drawing everyone's attention to me. They'd all been chatting quietly, mostly the others throwing questions at Sam and Grayson about their changes. Everyone seems strangely fascinated by their new abilities and downright amazed that they haven't explored more.

But my words now have them looking thoughtful. Finally, Zeph speaks up. "I have a fair idea, but until Mina fills us in, I'm not going to speculate anymore."

"And what about that glowing orb of light that Dru has? What do you think that is to Mina?"

There's a flash of light, and Mylea appears in the room just as Trick returns with the tablet. "Oh good, you're all here and Mina and Dru aren't. I need to be quick, sorry, but I need to remove the memory of the orb from all of you. You'll get it back eventually." She waves her hand, and I'm hit with a moment of mental fog before we continue our questions.

"So you've got both a tiger and wolf form, plus you can turn into a demon?" There's a weird sense of déjà vu hitting me, but I can't figure out why. Shaking my head, I follow the conversation.

"And you now have a dragon and djinn form?" He points to Grayson as Trick returns with the tablet.

"Yes, apparently we can access more, but I haven't really had a chance to try it out yet," Grayson says, his voice deep and a bit raspy. His eyes flick back and forth from human to reptile, like his dragon is trying to peek out. He's sexy as fuck, and I smile with amusement as Samuel snuggles into his chest. Well, how the mighty have fallen. Out of all of us, Sam was the one least wanting to be tied down, but they seem fairly smitten with each other.

"That is wicked cool." Kai leans forward, his eyes wide with excitement, riveted by every word that comes out of Grayson's mouth. *Looks like Grayson's won over another.*

Scanning my group of friends, I'm thrilled that we can finally be who we are meant to be and that we have our mate back. Life is pretty fucking perfect right now apart from the whole Hammus thing hanging over us, and I've got a feeling that's about to come to a head too.

A little while later, the pizzas and beer arrive and we're all digging in when a very relaxed-looking Mina and Drusilla make their way out from the bedroom. We've all had a few beers by now, and when Kai raises his glass and cheers, everyone else joins in. Drusilla blushes pink to the roots of her hair, but Mina just shoots us a saucy wink before dropping into the last remaining spot and pulling Dru onto her lap.

"Food for my wench," she orders with a snap of

her fingers. Everyone laughs as Dru smacks Mina on the arm before joining in. Mina smacks a kiss on her lips in return and makes a plate of pizza and a cocktail appear out of air in front of Dru. She glows slightly as she does, and the noise drops off, the sudden show of power reminding us that we have some big things to discuss.

Rolling her eyes, she helps Dru stand before letting her take her spot.

"I guess I better get it all out there; otherwise, you lot will start nagging." She walks over to stand near the large picture window. Looking out over the city, she sighs.

"Dying sucked," she starts, and my heart skips a beat, Mav choking on his beer at her dry pronouncement. Zeph pats him absently while waiting for Mina to continue. "But according to Mylea, it needed to happen, which is why none of you were able to stop it. I knew it was coming. Before she struck, Mylea had done this whole time freezing thing, and that was when she filled me in. It's also when she took me through time to seal my bond with Sam. If we hadn't done that, none of you would have survived my death."

Her words are shocking to say the least. She goes on to explain why she needed to die, something about activating the goddess inside, and then needing to master her powers. That was what took her so long to return to us. We're all pretty quiet through the whole tale until she gets to the part about needing her full potential to defeat Hammus.

"Hang on a second. Are you saying we need to have a "yay, we're back together" orgy to help all our powers reach their full potential?" The words rush out of my mouth, and I hope I don't sound too eager, but my cock has already decided that he's all in.

She snorts at my words, and Drusilla wrinkles her nose. "Eww, no thanks." Again, Mina laughs.

"Actually, Drusilla, what we did just then was enough for you to activate your part, but I still need to fix the bond with all of the others to make it count."

My sister stands up, picking up her plate and glass as she goes. "Say no more. I'm going to take this to bed and put on a movie and my headphones. Come get me when it's done." She waves goodbye and hurries away.

Mina rushes after her, stopping her before she leaves. They have a quietly whispered conversation that ends in smiles on both ladies' behalf. Mina kisses Dru before she leaves then comes back over, throwing herself in the vacated space.

"So, are you all up for it?" My eyes move from one teammate to the next, and there isn't an ounce of hesitation in any of them. In fact, Kai and Jagger quickly morph to demon form, and Samuel isn't long after them.

Mina's smile turns wicked, and I feel a wisp of her magic before our room disappears. What replaces it is nothing short of a sexual playroom. The couch has changed, and the floor is now covered in large sumptuous cushions; there's a sex swing hanging from the ceiling and a table covered with all kinds of toys and lubrication. *Damn.*

"Still okay?" she checks, and a chorus of yesses has her waving her hands until we're all standing around in nothing but our underwear, some not even having that. Mina stands before us, the first hints of nervousness showing in the almost blush that graces her cheeks.

"I'm not sure how this is all going to work being that there are eight of you and only one of me, but I guess we'll just make it work. Let me know if you're feeling left out. I think my succubus is going to take charge once we get started, so... this will be fun." She sounds a little breathless, but it could easily be from lust or nerves. Almost bouncing on her toes, she looks around at all of us, and I can almost hear her trying to figure out where to start.

"Let's help her out a little," I say to Trick, and the two of us make our way toward her. She smiles up at me as I move to her front, Trick walking around to her back. Her demon tail wraps around my leg with a light squeeze, like it's trying to make sure I don't forget it's here too. Bending down, I drop a gentle kiss on her lips as Trick places them on her

neck, little pecks that let him explore. She melts into my arms with the contact, her hands locking around my waist. Her tongue slips into my mouth, and we tangle them together.

I feel Trick's hands between us, caressing her breast through the sheer fabric, and she moans when he pinches her nipples. Eager to keep this moving forward, I pull back.

"How about we get you into that swing, baby? Then you can let the eight of us do all the work." Her eyes flash through colors faster at my suggestion, and she bites her lip before nodding her head. This is an interesting side of Mina I haven't seen before. One that's nervous about sex. Nothing usually fazes her, but I guess working out the logistics of eight mates *is* a little tricky.

Mav and Zeph come forward and take her by the hand. They have the most experience with those sorts of things, so I step back, pulling Trick into my arms and smashing my mouth against his. My cock is rock hard, and I can feel it leaking at the thought of what's about to happen, so I need to be careful not to bust a nut before we even get going. I can't help but rub my cock into his, his familiar taste lighting up my senses and driving me insane.

Both of us are breathing hard as I pull away. Dropping to my knees, I pull his briefs down with the movement, and his long thick length springs free. A dribble of pre-cum glistens on the end, so I use my tongue to scoop it up, and Trick groans, grabbing hold of my hair. I shuffle us around so I can watch Mav and Zeph strap Mina into the harness before wrapping my lips around his head and lashing my tongue around it. His knees buckle slightly, but he stays upright, gripping my hair tighter. Taking him to the back of my throat, I swallow, and he moans again before I drag my lips back up.

He pushes me away and pulls me to my feet. Spinning me, he brings me over to a now suspended Mina. "I think you need to put your oral skills to good use. Get down on your knees and lick her pussy," he commands, and my cock twitches at both his words and the sight before me.

Zeph and Mav have rigged it so she's suspended on her belly, legs spread wide. As I approach her, I listen to Zeph order her to suck Mav's cock. He approaches her, his fat length angry and red, and she groans, licking her lips before opening her mouth and taking it deep.

I climb under her and run my tongue along her now dripping slit, her flavor exploding on my tongue as her juices fill my mouth.

"We all need to be connected, right?" Trick asks, and Mina pulls back from Mav's cock and nods, her breath coming in pants.

"Yes, as long as we're all connected somehow, the power will seal."

"Alright, let's think about this." Trick starts to issue instructions in his hot Dom voice, and my dick weeps even more as I add two fingers to Mina's wet heat. I'm going to keep her on the edge until he's got everyone situated.

Chapter Forty-One

Patrick

Watching Mina strung up in that swing makes my balls ache. Add in her mouth on Mav and Sander's mouth on her pussy, and well, I don't think I'm going to last very long. Teasing my cock with light tortuous strokes, I consider where everyone needs to start, thinking about how we can do this so everyone is connected.

"Mina only has so many holes and hands, so this is how it's going to work. Zeph, you get her pussy." He nods and moves over to where she's dangling, stroking his hands along her back before swinging her back and forth on Mav's cock, making her take it deep, choking her slightly.

"That's a good girl," he tells her, still stroking her back with one hand as he grabs his cock with the other and then lines himself up. "Watch out, Sander," he warns, but Sander only stops teasing Mina long enough to grin.

"I'm good as long as you are."

Zeph pushes in, everyone groaning as their eyes

lock on what's happening. He thrusts a couple more times, taking his time. Sander's tongue still flicks her clit, but he also swipes it across Zeph's balls every time he bottoms out.

"Fuck," Kai moans as he strokes his hand along Jagger's cock. "Where do you want us? Please," he begs. I shudder, finding his pleading desperation sexy as fuck. I've gotten used to taking control with Sander, and having more people under my orders is sending a thrill through me.

"Come here," I demand, and he and Jagger walk over, their eyes glazed with lust. Mina's pumping so many pheromones into the air that the guys have become complacent and easy to command. It's a fucking dream for me, and knowing that we're all fluid and open to being with one another, not just Mina, gives me so many options that my mind is nearly spinning with how to make this all play out.

"Get down and suck my cock while I think about it." They both drop to their knees in front of me and start to lick and suck in between exchanging kisses. A shiver runs through my body. Mina turns her head slightly, Mav's cock still in her mouth, and her eyes widen at the new view.

"Kai, I want you to fuck Jagger's ass while Mina gives him a hand job." Kai and Jagger nod, moving away from my cock. With just a thought, two more sex swings are hanging from the roof on either side of Mina, keeping her as the focal point. Kai helps

seat Jagger in one, unlike Mina's belly-down position, before lubing up his ass and sliding in. Jagger's
eyes close and his mouth opens with the pleasure,
his fangs glistening in the light, as Kai seats himself.
His tail wiggles itself out of the harness and waves
with enthusiasm before wrapping around Kai and
caressing him all over.

He grunts, looking over at me with impatience
and almost pain etched across his face with the
effort to hold still. "Hurry up, I'm not sure I can last
long." I turn to the other two, not entirely sure how
they're going to be reacting, but Sam's already
down on his knees, sucking on Grayson's cock while
his tail rails his mate's ass. Both seem to be lost in
the moment.

"Samuel!" I snap, and he pulls back, blinking in
surprise. "The other swing is for you guys. Get
Grayson in it." Still a little dazed, he nods and
removes his tail before dragging Grayson over and
helping him into the swing. The power pulsing
through me with the thrill of controlling everyone is
allowing me to keep a clear head amongst the overload of pheromones in the air.

A fine sheen of sweat covers Mina's body,
accenting every beautiful curve as she's teased and
fucked to the point that only nonsensical sighs and
moans burst from her lips. The smell of sex is in the
air, blending with her pheromones and promising
that this will be a reunion we all remember, the
guys' grunts and groans joining Mina's. I move

closer to them all, taking one of Mina's hands and placing it on Jagger's cock, then walking over to her other side and doing the same with Grayson's.

"What about you, Trick?" Zeph grunts as he keeps a slow but steady pace in Mina's pussy. I get down on my knees and crawl toward Sander.

"Okay, are you all ready?" I ask as I run my tongue along Sander's cock, drinking in his dribbling pre-cum. There's so much the whole thing is coated. He moans but continues to suck and lick at Mina and Zeph.

"Let's do this." Everyone really lets go as I take Sander's cock deep into the back of my throat, swallowing and sucking and milking him. His hand reaches for mine, and he strokes it as he continues to feast.

Suddenly, the power in the room starts to build until I can feel it crackling through my body. Mina's moans around Mav's cock grow louder, and the power ripples as though it's mimicking the cresting of her pleasure. The electricity in the air prickles and caresses and builds until it's almost painful, and then, like a shockwave, it explodes outward. The sound of people coming fills the room, my hearing almost growing fuzzy as I struggle to stay conscious amid the cascade of overwhelming sensation. Power burns through my body like it's molding and shaping my very soul, touching so deep within me that I know I'm changing in some permanent way. With a grunt, Sander's cum hits the back of my throat, and I swallow furiously while thrusting into his hand as I come. Then, just as quickly as it arrived, the power recedes, taking with it all my energy, and as I watch Zeph pull out of Mina and collapse to the ground, everything turns black.

——•◦•——

Jessamina

I'm not sure how much later it is when I wake, but the picture window is dark and stars twinkle across the sky. I'm still suspended in this contraption, and worse, I'm still sticky. Not to mention I'm getting cold, and the combination of all these things is really freaking uncomfortable. Using my powers, I transport out of the swing and clean myself, putting on some sweats. Looking around the room, the boys are still as thoroughly knocked out as if they'd been hit with a sleeping spell, including Jagger and Grayson in swings to match the contraption I was trapped in.

Poor things, I can't leave them all like this. Stretching my power once more, everyone disappears back to the beds in the apartment, all coupled up and clean. By the time the next few minutes have passed, the room is entirely pristine, all traces of an orgy cleared away.

Once everything is back to normal, I reach out for Drusilla.

"Hey, babe, it's safe if you want to come out." When I'm met with only silence, I reach out to her mind, finding the same blissed out blankness that took over the guys. She must've gotten a burst of power too.

Feeling a little disappointed, I look around the room, reacquainting myself with the home I've gotten to spend so little time in. *We're going to have to look at making this place bigger. This place is not big enough for the ten of us.* A tingle of excitement runs through me at the thought of us creating a home and eventually, my recent conversation with Mylea on my mind, a family. *Speaking of family... I've probably got some ridiculously upset parents to check in on.* Cringing at the thought of the waterworks that will most certainly be Maggie's "welcome back from the dead" gift, I decide to try my luck with my biological parents first.

Using my new powers, I reach out, feeling for Lucifer and Michael. I get the sense that they're downstairs in the CD portal room, so I teleport. When my glow clears, the room, apart from the other four gods, is on high alert, weapons brandished and waiting for an attack. The room is as silent as a tomb.

"Oh, thank fuck, I thought it was Hammus," Uriel sighs, breaking the silence as his flaming sword disappears. "I knew you couldn't be dead. Good to see you, sweetheart." He sits back down and casually throws his feet up on the table, waiting for the inevitable fall out. I raise my eyebrow at him, but he just winks at me, content to stay out of it. *Shit stirring bastard.*

The room explodes into noise as my mother screams and throws herself at me, my father not far behind. There's a babble of questions and it's all a little too much, but thankfully, Azeyr steps in.

"SILENCE!" he roars, and the chaos stops just as quickly as it started. "Now give Mina a bit of room, and we'll explain everything." At his use of the word *we* both Lucifer and Michael look at him with narrowed eyes that would definitely have me thinking carefully about what I was going to say next. Apparently not intimidated in the least, Azeyr doesn't even flinch.

I give him a grateful smile as Mom tugs me over to a chair and sits down next to me, Dad on the other side, neither wanting to let go of my hands.

I get a few minutes of peace to myself as Mylea gives everyone the summary of what happened, making her apologies for the grief that she had to let them go through. I'm not sure Mom and Dad are quite over that part, but we've got bigger things to worry about than their anger at how the goddess handled all of this. When she finally finishes, I snort at the ridiculousness of the whole situation.

"So, if you have any ideas on luring out a mega maniacal god, could you share with the group, please?" My words are thick with a sarcastic bite that doesn't hide my nervousness, and my dad squeezes my hand.

"Don't be scared, baby. I'm pretty sure you're going to find he doesn't live up to your expectations at all."

A frown crosses my face, considering this is the first time anyone's ever told me something like that. "What do you mean?"

"All these gods in the room, power oozes off of them, but they have something Hammus doesn't: devoted followers. In the height of his power, Hammus had demons who were loyal to him, who were dedicated to caring for his temples and worshipping his existence. Now? What does he have? The loyalty of a sadistic Archangel with a black blood magic addiction and the surviving members of AoA. It's no wonder he's hiding away like a coward, using his secret spot to protect himself from the people with real power."

My head turns to Mylea, and she winks at me. *So that's the whole reason for the orgy. Makes sense now. Let's* not *talk to Dad about how his newly discovered daughter just got her own dose of worship right before our little family reunion.* For the first time, confidence starts to build within me and I'm actually thinking that I might just be able to do this, achieve the all-important destiny that Mylea insists I was made for.

"Those demons are going to love you though." My mom pulls me in for a quick hug before pulling away. "If you can fix Habbalea so it's habitable again and they can leave the caves, I'm sure they will kiss the ground you walk on."

I shrug, a little uncomfortable at the idea of that degree of devotion. "Yeah, maybe just a muffin basket is all the thanks I need."

Everyone around the table laughs, but it's with a lightness that doesn't touch me. I still have a big list of jobs to do, and they're big ones, which is a heavy burden to bear. On one hand, I'm fixing a whole race, and on another, I'm destroying millions by restoring the balance to Earth and Reath. Thankfully, the other four will help me with that just like they helped with Earth and Amilles.

Blowing out a deep breath, I stand up. "Alright, let's do this before my mates wake up. They would just be a liability if I took them now, and he could use them as a weapon against me. They won't be happy about it, but I'm a lot safer now than I was before."

The gods nod and stand up, followed by the angels and demons around the table.

Matoz frowns, his eyes narrowing behind his glasses as he shakes his head. "Nope, sorry, you guys need to sit this one out too." They burst into loud protests, but Eagi holds up a hand and their mouths snap shut.

"Same reason that Mina doesn't want her mates there. You are a weakness for her, and this long-awaited confrontation is too important to risk on a possible hostage situation that we can easily avoid.

It will just be the five of us. Mylea is going to draw him out with the premise that he needs to meet the new goddess, one who is more powerful than all of us."

She snorts, rolling her eyes as she starts to explain. "It's practically guaranteed to work. His ego has always been huge, and he won't even consider it's a trap. In fact, I'm sure he won't even believe it. In the end, no matter what he believes, he'll take the bait, if only for the chance to rub it in my face if he thinks he can prove me wrong."

Lucifer shakes her head. "I will not stand by while that evil man…." She breaks off as Michael wraps his arm around her, shaking his head.

"No, love, I feel the same way, but we need to trust in the five of them. They will not let anything happen to her." I cast a suspicious eye his way. What the hell? My father is normally not that rational, or at least what I've seen of him so far. What the fuck is going on?

"Siffa, you have to realize, your little girl is more powerful than all of you at the moment. When the demons and remaining realm beings become aware of her, she will be the most powerful of us all." Mylea takes her by the hand, and as she speaks, there's a soft whisper of power that flows with her words. She's not bespelling my mom, but she's definitely doing something to help calm her down and make her a little bit more agreeable. *Ahh, that must explain Dad's actions too.*

Mom looks between me and Dad and then nods her agreement, her brows still drawn together in worry.

"Excellent." Mylea drops her hands and backs away, that whisper of power easing with each step. "And to ensure you do as told..." She waves her hand and freezes everyone in the room.

Azeyr snorts. "They're going to kick your ass when you wake them up."

"Yes, but they will be alive and safe to do that, so I'll be glad that they have the opportunity to try," she replies before clapping her hands together. "Alright, let's head to Habbalea!"

Chapter Forty-Two

Jessamina

The air is dry and dusty, lightning crackling across the horizon when we reach Habbalea. The smell of ozone burns my nostrils, and the wind whips tiny particles of sand through the air, the particles stinging when they hit my face.

As a group, we look around the barren and desolate planet. Unlike the last time I was here, there isn't any sign of civilization. Only an occasional fallen down dead tree and a few tufts of dry grass.

"We've chosen a spot far away from any settlement just in case there is widespread destruction," Matoz says, striding away from the group, Eagi and Azeyr following quickly behind.

"Where are they going?" I ask Mylea as we watch them spread out in a semicircle around us before they disappear.

"Element of surprise," she tells me, her voice flatter than I've ever heard it. When I turn to look at her, tears are streaming down her face.

Fuck, of course this is hard for her. I gather her in my arms and pull her in for a hug, allowing her to purge her sadness before we get this thing started. No words are needed. I have no idea how she's feeling right now, but at least I can be there for her. Eventually, she pulls back and conjures a tissue to wipe her face, blowing her nose before it disappears again.

"Thank you," she says quietly, and I nod my head in acknowledgement. Stepping back, she allows her godly glow to infuse her being.

"Hammus, I call on you. You are required to come and meet our new brethren, one who is most powerful. Possibly the most powerful of us all." Her divine voices echoes across the land, my body shuddering with the power it holds. We're waiting patiently when I realize I haven't got my magic wand. At just the thought of it, it appears, tucked into my ponytail where it belongs. Reaching a hand up to check on it, I discover it's small enough to not be noticed. *Good, I'll leave it there until I need it.* According to Mylea, I only need to pierce his skin with it, and it should do the rest. I cross my toes in my boots, just to be on the safe side.

The air around us crackles even more as lightning continues to split the sky, touching down between the two of us. It's blinding, and I put my hand up to shield my eyes. When I remove it, the light dissipates, and standing there before us is a being oozing power.

I blink twice, trying to reconcile my mind with what I see. This man looks nothing like the virile, handsome god depicted in the tapestry in the ruined throne room. This guy reminds me of the traitorous Archangels. Withered and shriveled, he is stooped over, his back bent at an odd angle, his hair long and graying, clutching a staff that appears to actually be needed to hold him up. It looks like a gnarled tree branch, its woven branches twisted up into a cradle for a black rock that pulses with an insidious power.

Mylea gasps in surprise before putting her hand over her mouth. Meanwhile, a twisted grin stretches the sallow face of the being before us, a hair-raising cackle flying free from his mouth.

"It's been a while, now hasn't it?" There's an ugliness to even that simple statement, the same insidiousness that pulses from the stone underlying his words. In no way, shape, or form can I understand how this is her *mate* who is looking at her with such blatant disdain.

"What happened to you?" she cries, looking at him with disbelief. The tears from before threaten to fall again, her eyes immediately glistening with the held back pain of seeing someone she loved, and likely still loves, twisted into such unrecogniz-able sickness.

"This is what happens when everyone you love turns against you," he spits out, sneering at her. "Don't think I don't know that you've been conspiring against me! I still have one or two loyal followers, and they have told me much of recent happenings. Of the way that you and yours are working to ruin the only foothold of power I have left in this world!" His eyes are becoming crazed, darting around as though he can't stay focused on one thing for too long.

"Don't underestimate me, because I will not go easy on you, nor will I forgive. If you make this move, Mylea, you will undoubtedly regret it. When you lose, I will punish you, as well as those other three fools, for all eternity." He waves his hand, and the other three tumble out of their little pockets of reality, looking equally shocked that Hammus could manipulate them in his broken state.

Mylea's mouth drops open at his show of power, her three mates gathering around her in stumbling steps as they regain their equilibrium. "How?"

He shrugs, unconcerned despite being vastly outnumbered. "A little sacrifice and magic makes a powerful god. Sabboath discovered a way to funnel the power of sacrificed realm beings to me."

"The missing realm creatures," I gasp, and his attention shoots to me. That must account for his appearance as well.

"So this is the little upstart bitch," he jeers, circling me like a predator around his prey. You'd think my heart would be racing, but it's not. I'm calm and collected because I instinctively know that

I'm more powerful than this guy. He might have better fighting skills, but I don't have to win. I just have to draw blood.

He sneers again and starts to ramble on about betrayal and being the best and blah, blah, blah. Honestly, it's such a cliche bad guy monologue that I lose interest. Reaching up into my hair, I pull out the magic wand, and it instantly forms into a sword, the spelled runes bursting with light and power.

That gets his attention, and he stops mid-sentence, his eyes narrowing on me with an awareness and precision that he's lacked since the moment he appeared.

"Dude, has anyone ever told you that you're an ass?" I ask, and he sputters, no nasty replies at the ready this time. For a disgraced god, you'd think that he'd be a little more used to people treating him like the trash that he is.

Leaping forward, I strike at him, but he brings his staff up quickly and blocks it. Thunder rumbles all around us and lighting touches down in five different strikes as our weapons collide against one another, a shockwave of power knocking us both backward. I tumble ass over tit through the air but finally manage to stop myself before I hit the ground. Hovering just above it, I watch as Hammus rights himself. He brushes some dust off his shirt and looks up at me, his eyes that were similar to mine now bleeding to darkness as insidious black veins appear under his skin. Man, that is some ugly shit. He makes Sabboath look like he's just returned from a spa retreat.

He chuckles, a smile that he in no way deserves to have spreading across his face. "Is that all you've got?" I roll my eyes in response.

"Hardly." We run at each other and collide in a flurry of stabbing and hacking movements, each one blocking the other, neither getting the upper hand.

Back and forth, we parry, attacking and defending. My heart is pounding, and I'm sucking in huge gulps of air as we fight for supremacy, but I'm not the only one. He seems to be slowing down, not used to fighting and certainly not against someone who is at least his equal. Just as I go to draw first blood, he launches himself into the air like a rocket, his staff pointing at the other gods who have been watching on in silence.

I can just tell by the feel of the blast that it will have some deadly consequences, and ice runs through my veins at the realization that Mylea might not be the only one with a weapon that can unmake a god. Willing to risk it all, I throw myself in front of the blast.

I close my eyes as the power hits my chest, hoping that Mylea's theory about my power level is correct. My mates will be so pissed if they lose me so soon after getting me back. The wave of power hits me like a runaway train, burying deep into my soul, the pain worse than when I died at Connie's feet. Gritting my teeth to hold in the scream that is threatening to escape, I hold my ground as the insidious invasion tries to eat away at my very being. But it has no effect. My goddess glow intensifies, and my own power fights back, devouring the curse like it was nothing. When my eyes meet Hammus', his mouth has dropped open in shock, and that smug look has finally disappeared.

Taking half a second, I put a bubble around the others, throwing their own words back at them. "Sorry, guys, you're my weakness at the moment!" When I spin back around, Hammus is staring at me, fury flashing in his eyes.

"That should have killed you. Why didn't that kill you?!" he screams, the petulance in his voice making the angry god sound more like a child throwing a tantrum than an all-powerful being who should be feared.

"I guess I'm just more badass than you," I goad cheerfully, and he screams his frustration to the sky. Just then the clouds open and a deluge of rain falls to the ground, though whether nature is trying to mimic his emotions or drown him out, I'm not entirely sure. I mean, I've barely spoken to the god and I'd totally be into anything that will shut him up at this point.

For a moment, I can't see him, but a flash of

lightning illuminates the god coming straight at me so that I have just enough time to hold up my hand, flinging a conjured fire ball at him. It hits him and sets his cloak on fire while I drop down to the ground.

The ground rumbles and undulates, causing me to stumble, and I lose sight of Hammus. I send out my senses, searching for him, but all I can feel is his closeness, unlike when I detected Mom and Dad's exact location. It's like he's gone into stealth mode, much like I've done before. I scan my surroundings, looking for that almost indistinguishable ripple in the air or a break in the rain, and I barely catch movement out of the corner of my eye before his staff is flying toward me.

I thrust up my sword, my arms aching with the collison. The force of the blow sends vibrations down my arms, and I almost drop my weapon, convinced that my wrist bones might be splintered. I grit my teeth and push through the excruciating pain. Never has it been more important to ignore it than now. I stumble onto one knee as I try to keep the staff from touching me. Unable to remove either hand from my sword, I use my mind to imagine him flying backward. Thankfully, he does, right onto the branch of an overturned dead tree. It spears him right through the shoulder, and he groans with the impact.

Struggling to my feet, I move over to the now

impaled god, watching as he struggles and fails to remove the branch from his shoulder. A small pulse of power escapes him, but I throw up a block on it. Now that he's injured and distracted, I can better hold off his magic than I could before.

"Damn you!" he shrieks. "This shouldn't be possible."

Even though every part of me is exhausted and aching, I answer, needing him to know that all of this, everything that's about to happen to him, has been through his own making.

"Dude, you've been a very naughty boy, and these are the consequences. People like you are too arrogant to consider anything possibly going wrong or having to pay for what you've done. You're a prime example of what is wrong with the human psyche, but today, at least, you will be stopped. I hope you enjoy your afterlife more than you've enjoyed and squandered this one." With those words I shove my sword deep into his heart. It lights up, a bolt of lightning striking me at the same time, running through me and into the sword. Once the power leaves my hands, I get thrown clean back across the clearing, landing at the bottom of the bubble encasing the others. The bubble dissolves, and Mylea scoops me up, pulling me out of the way.

The sight that greets my eyes when I make it to my feet is breathtaking. Hammus is surrounded by a tornado of light, tiny rainbow-colored molecules circling him at great speeds. The colors seem to be drawing all the power out of him, his body starting to flake away like feathers on the wind. As quickly as it arrived, it disappears, sucked back into the sword before it clatters to the ground, flashing all the same rainbow colors as the vortex.

Just like that, the god is gone.

"Holy shit." Eagi walks over to look down at the sword as Matoz and Azeyr comfort Mylea. "Remind me to never piss you off while you're using that." I snort, trying to help him out and appreciating his mostly unsuccessful attempt to lighten the mood. "I'm pretty sure I'm taking a few years off after that."

He picks up the sword and tries to hand it to me, but I shake my head, holding up my wrists. "Can you just hang onto it for now?" I ask.

He screws up his face, looking at the sword with all the interest that he'd give a rotting corpse. *Got it. Gods don't like touching the sword.* "Fuck no, I can't. I'll just put it out of the way, and you can grab it from the house when you need it again." He shoves it into the pocket of reality their house is in, willing it to return to my room there.

A gentle hand on my shoulder has me turning, the movement making me grimace in pain. Mylea's sad eyes shine with pride, and I can't blame her for feeling conflicted. What Hammus became was terrible, and even if tonight was essentially euthanizing an animal that had gone rabid, it hurts to mourn the loss of what you once had.

"I knew you could do it. Thank you, Mina. You'll never know how much this means to me." She reaches for my hands, hers glowing gold, and as she touches me, I feel the bones knitting back together.

"There, much quicker than waiting for it to happen and a lot less painful." She smiles, but it doesn't quite reach her eyes.

Holding out my hands, I test the movement, noting that my wrists feel strong once again. I take stock of the rest of my body, and apart from slight fatigue, I'm already starting to feel better.

"While we're here, shall we fix this world?" I ask them, the urge to do something positive riding me hard after something so negative.

"Yes, let's." She tucks her arm through mine, and we arrive in the large square in the demon city belowground. There's no one around, and the quiet atmosphere is a relief after all of the noise aboveground. I'm not quite ready to meet the demons as their new goddess. I think I'll need some support to deal with that experience.

"But first, I think you should rest, eat, and recover while I make a few arrangements. The power we're going to use needs to come from the demons themselves. We're going to need every one of them to fuel this thing, and they all need to be on the planet to do it," she says, walking me toward the palace. "Go and rest in your rooms, and when everything is done, I will call for you. Your mates will have woken with that power surge too, and I'm sure they'll be here shortly. I'm sorry, but I put a cover on your bond so that you weren't distracted by them during the fight. When I take it off, you're going to find they're very, *very* angry."

With these words the minx disappears, and sure enough, my bond comes back online. Anger and worry hit me, the force and depth of it all enough to make me stagger, the weight of their panic bringing tears to my eyes. I'm so sorry for doing this to them *again*, no matter how necessary it was.

"Mina, for fuck's sake answer one of us," Jagger snarls in a tone I've never heard from him before. Now that Hammus has been destroyed, the barrier has been dropped, and teleporting and mind communication are now possible once more.

"I'm so sorry."

"Where are you? All our parents just arrived, and you were gone. They told us you were with Mylea, but no one knew where."

Damn, that's a lot of people in our apartment.

"I'm in the demon settlement on Habbalea. You better all come here. Make sure your and Kai's dads come too, please. It's time to fix this world." The feelings that return to me after those words change from worry and annoyance to complete wonder, but his reply is still gruffer than I'd like.

"We'll be there soon," he tells me, and his presence cuts off.

Blowing out a sigh, I continue my trudge to my room, waves of exhaustion beating me almost as hard as the knowledge that I'm going to have to do some *major* sucking up once again.

Chapter Forty-Three

Jagger

After speaking with Mina, I update everyone, their silent stares and furrowed brows showing how lost we all feel right now. Angry expletives escape Zeph's mouth, conveying our annoyance that our mate had left us behind once again. When will she learn we're stronger together than apart?

"What happens now?" Dru's voice is quiet but easily heard in the heavy silence, asking the question that we all need an answer to.

"What you do now is reassure Mina that, no matter what or how it happened, she has done the right thing. Comfort her whenever guilt strikes at her, because it will. I can guarantee it. You don't take a life, whether the death was sanctioned or not, without feeling some kind of remorse." Raphael's profound words give me something to focus on, and right now, I'll cling to that guidance as our best way to move forward.

"Good advice, Raphael, but there is something

else we need you to do." Mylea's voice and golden glow precede her entrance into the room, and when the powerful haze clears, she looks tired and worn. It's the first time I've seen the goddess look anything less than perfect.

Both Drusilla and Lucifer approach the woman, hugging her as they whisper what must be words of condolences. Of course... Hammus was her mate. I'd forgotten he was anything but an evil overlord and the destroyer of my race. I guess he wasn't always like that, and this must be difficult for her.

When they pull away, she looks a little brighter. "We still have a few tasks to achieve, and the next one involves all demons returning to Habbalea."

"Is Mina okay?" Mav interrupts, but she just smiles at him. Thank fuck, he asked. I was ready to scream at her. Those quick few sentences from Mina weren't nearly enough to soothe the panic still flowing through me.

"Mina is just fine; she sustained a couple of injuries, but she's all healed up."

"And Hammus?" Uriel asks.

Her eyes drop to the ground as she sighs. "He is gone." With those words it's like the room lets out a collective sigh of relief, but no one is insensitive enough to cheer aloud.

"Why do we need to gather the demons?" Kai asks, sounding a little unsure and a bit worried.

She smiles, though it's softened by her mourning. "It's time to fix your world." My heartbeat races, and I look to my demon partner to find his eyes are wide with shock and anticipation.

"I need you to gather all demons who don't currently reside in the hidden refuge and bring them back so that we can make this happen," she instructs Kai, Siffa, our fathers, and me.

Turning to the Archangel council, she adds, "Can you guys help round them up?" Then she turns to the rest of Team Alpha. "Mina is at the palace, resting. You guys can go and keep her company, making sure she eats and rests because it's her that needs to do most of the work next."

Zeph nods, answering as representative for our team. "Drusilla, you and Grayson go and keep Mina company. The rest of us will help gather the remaining demons to Habbalea."

"Excellent." Mylea rubs her hands together, anticipation bringing a sharper glint to her eyes. "We will all return to the demon underground as soon as possible and finally make amends for Hammus."

"Hang on." I put my hand up, thinking of how I can say my next point while not disrespecting the goddess. "I have no problems helping out, but can we all just pop in and check on Mina first? I have this itch that's telling me I need to make sure she's alright for myself, and I don't think I can really focus on anything else until I *know* that my mate is okay."

"I don't want to hear about any damn itch,"

Michael grumbles, and everyone laughs when Siffa shoves her elbow into his side.

"No, not *that* kind of itch. I just need to see her with my own eyes and maybe wrap my arms around her for a moment." My words are quiet, but I feel a warmth of gratitude coming from a few of Mina's other mates, including Kai and Samuel. Team Alpha has been regarded as the elite team that can do everything for so long, I think that sometimes it's forgotten that they have their own needs too. Right now, our family needs to come before our team duties. Even just for a few minutes.

The girls in the room all smile even though the dads roll their eyes.

"Thank fuck you said something," Trick calls out. "I feel exactly the same." Dru and the other guys all chime in with their agreements, and Zeph holds up his hands.

"Okay, okay, I know when I'm outvoted. Mina first, demons second." Relief flows over me when he gives in, and if I'm not mistaken, some of his own relief flows down the bonds in return.

"My animals were pushing me to go and find her. I've been struggling to hold my form with all of their pushing." Sam's admission has Grayson nodding in agreement.

"My dragon wanted to burst out of my skin too," he admits. "And I don't think anyone wants to see what happens if that guy just bursts free."

One by one, people start to leave.

"I'm heading to Eternal Damnation. I have a whole heap of demons that work there," Siffa says, "and I know of quite a few more who hide in plain sight and don't take their demon form. It will be such a relief for them not to have to hide."

"You're not going to that club without me," Michael grumbles, grabbing hold of her hand. She looks down at it and raises her eyebrows, unimpressed, and he stumbles over his next words. "Ah, I mean... what I mean is, would it be alright if I accompanied you on that task?" He shuffles his feet like a high school boy waiting to know if his crush will go on a date with him, and humor unfurls inside me at seeing this powerful Archangel reduced to a nervous child.

The people remaining in the room smother smiles behind hands or snort quietly in amusement.

"Don't forget, my darling mate, I own that club just like I own your ass," Lucifer retorts, the words laced with affection despite the growl that accompanies them.

"Guys, I think we should leave," Kai projects to us all, an uncomfortable urgency flowing down the bond like he knows something we all haven't figured out yet.

A growl leaves Michael's mouth, and now it's all of our turns to shift awkwardly.

"Damn, yep, let's go." One by one, we all leave the apartment and arrive at Mina's apartment on Habbalea.

"Fuck, I hope they don't destroy the place," Drusilla mutters, sounding worried, a little frown marring her forehead.

"Who do you hope doesn't destroy what?" Mina's voice reaches us from the huge sectional as her head pops over the top, looking tired but unmarked. Ignoring the question, I take a leap and land on her outstretched body. Pulling her into my arms, I hold her tightly and just breathe. Taking in the scent of my mate and feeling stable and content for the first time in an hour.

In fact, I think it's the first time since she died.

— • —

Jessamina

The weight of Jagger's body on mine is comforting and reassuring. We both lie there, basking in each other's presence. His sweet cinnamon scent soothes my frazzled mind and senses. Ever since I got back to my apartment, the confrontation with Hammus has been running a never-ending loop through my head. Had I done the right thing? Should we have looked for another solution? Deep down, I know it was the only choice possible, but Jagger's warmth and comfort are a balm on my frayed soul nonetheless.

"Hi," I whisper in his ear, and he nuzzles at my neck.

"Hi," he whispers in return before pulling back and placing a gentle kiss on my lips.

"Are you hungry?" I ask, but he shakes his head.

"I am, but it can wait." He moves off of me, and the little bubble we were in immediately pops. One by one, my mates join me on the couch for a snuggle, all giving me sweet kisses and comforting hugs until only Drusilla and Grayson remain. They both pile onto the couch with me, Grayson dragging me up his body and Dru grabbing hold of my feet, pushing her thumb into the arches of one. A groan escapes my mouth, and Sander adjusts his cock inside his pants.

"Damn, baby girl, when you start making those kinds of noises? It makes it difficult to leave again."

Frowning, I ask, "Where are you going?"

Dru waves them away, snuggling closer despite talking to them. "Go and get it done, come back as soon as you can. I'll explain to her." The seven of them disappear, and the noise in the room drops.

Grayson is breathing deeply, inhaling my scent, and a purring sound comes out of his mouth. When I turn to look at him, his eyes are reptilian, his dragon peeking out once more. There's a warmth in his eyes that has nothing to do with his other form's ability to breathe fire. This is an affectionate, possessive flame that says only one word: *mate*.

"Did you know that I can shapeshift now?" I start conversationally. "Any form I want." A rumbling growl comes from deep inside his chest, and his cock hardens underneath my ass. "Maybe you'll have to teach me to shift, and we can go flying together." Immediately, a picture of us is thrust into my mind. Two dragons, one silver and red and one the same pink and gold as my scales, are flying together. Once they land, his dragon bares his teeth and playfully lunges, holding the other dragon down as he mounts her and ruts ferociously.

"Oh my." The words escape as another growl rumbles from Grayson. "Yes, well, we will keep that in mind." My breathing has increased, and my panties are now damp. Who knew that would be such a turn on?

Drusilla clears her throat, the noise shaking me out of the lusty fog that started to creep in.

When I look up, I'm expecting her to scold me, but instead, heat flares in her eyes and a question I was not expecting comes out of her mouth. "So... did you ask Mylea about the whole shapeshifting penis thing?"

A cough explodes from Grayson in surprise, and I grin at his response and her question. "No, I haven't, but I promise I will."

Before we can get too deep into that much too distracting conversation, they explain to me where the guys have disappeared to and have some food delivered to our room. The whole time none of us move from the couch, the thought of being separated from them making me anxious. In between bites of food, we both use the time to get to know Grayson a little better. I may know his body intimately and I can feel his soul, but I want to know all the little things about him. A bonus is that I also find out a lot more about Drusilla.

When I think back to my gauntlet run and the chain of events that sprang from that day, I'm stunned to realize it hasn't been all that long since it happened.

The brightest news is that although Maggie and Peter are eager to see me, they were never told of my supposed death, which takes a gigantic weight off my chest. Knowing they've only been dealing with the regular amount of crazy parent worry is so much better than thinking Maggie's had to deal with the thought that I was gone forever.

Finally, Mylea's voice rings out in my head, making me sit upright. "Alright, Mina, it's time to meet one lot of responsibility." Her voice sounds amused, and I feel a wave of magic wash over me. No longer am I wearing my battle clothes. I'm wrapped in a black goddess-style dress, fastened over one shoulder and draped to accentuate my body. Golden circlets wrap around each arm, and I feel one settle on my head around my horns, but my feet are left bare.

When I look up from my perusal of myself, Grayson and Drusilla are gone. Figuring Mylea was responsible for that little surprise, I shake my head and push away the nerves that threaten to rise at being alone.

"How come you all only have one race of people to look after, but you dump me with two?" I grumble back to the woman. I know the others might gasp at my overfamiliarity with the goddess, but in the time we've spent together during our little chats and power practice sessions, she's become a bit of the big sister I never had.

"Just lucky, I guess," she giggles, and her magic flows over me once again as my apartment disappears, bringing me to somewhere new.

——•◆•——

The main square of the underground demon city is filled to capacity. Casting my gaze around, I find there's a rainbow of colors and shapes. Immediately upon my arrival, the noise ceases, and it's so quiet you could hear a pin drop.

From my position, I can see my family, mates, and their families off to one side, all smiling wide. On the raised platform with me, I'm flanked by the other gods, but still no one makes a sound.

"What the fuck did you tell them?" I whisper out the side of my mouth as I awkwardly wave.

"Only that you had defeated Hammus and were now preparing to heal their world," Mylea says, not keeping her voice down. *Oh, that's all? No fucking pressure.*

"Well, they don't seem too thrilled about it," I snap back and quickly make a backup plan in my head for if this all goes ass up.

Before I can execute any of it, a small voice in the crowd shouts out, "Oh, look, Mommy! It's that girl, the one that looks like a Barbie doll. I love her."

And that's all it takes to erupt the crowd into thunderous applause and cheers. All around me people are shouting out their thanks and blessing me. Demons are hugging and dancing and celebrating the end of an era and welcoming a new and hopefully better one.

I wave my hand, and tables filled with food and drinks appear all around the square. "Please enjoy. Make this a day of celebration. Celebrate the death of a tyrant and a return to your old way of life. When I am done here, you may all leave and never have to look back if you so choose."

The five of us rise into the air, the joy and wonder of the demons pulsing through me until the power becomes so great that if I don't do something with it, I feel like I may just explode into a million pieces.

I grunt with the continual influx, and Azeyr grabs my hand. "Hold it a little longer, Jessamina," he urges as we continue to float upward, through the ground, until we finally reach the surface, but we don't stop. Instead, we keep floating into the atmosphere. The higher we get and the smaller the world beneath us becomes, the more I start to panic. I can't breathe in space, but Matoz just grabs my other hand and laughs.

"You can do anything now," he tells me, reading my mind.

"Just hold it a *little* longer," Mylea urges, repeating Azeyr's words, as she and Azeyr finish our circle. The force pulsing through me is excruciating, and it keeps building as the others pump their own power into me. Tears stream down my face, and I grind my teeth against the onslaught until I just can't hold it anymore.

The power bursts out of me like a wave of atomic energy, washing over the planet, but instead of wreaking destruction in its path, it heals everything it touches. The ground turns green, trees and plants sprouting everywhere. Water fills into empty lakes and oceans and rivers, and buildings in cities rebuild and repair. The atmosphere itself becomes normal again, the air breathable and clean.

I'm not sure how long the power pulses out of me, wave after wave after wave, but by the time it finally subsides, Habbalea is a lush tropical planet that doesn't show a single battle scar from its past. Smiling with sheer joy at the sight, my mind shuts down and I start to fall.

Chapter Forty-Four

Jessamina

For the past week, we've spent hours moving the demons back into the habitable cities of Habbalea, every single one of them thrilled with the way the world shaped itself. There were a few squabbles here and there as people selected where they wished to live and what they wanted to do with their lives. Many of them continued to do what they had done in the past, but there were quite a few career changes as well.

The native animal species that they'd been protecting were released back into the wild. I declared that they were to be protected until their numbers could flourish, no killing animals unless in self-defense. Mom and Dad took the castle up above as their new home, on my insistence. I was going to have to split my time between a number of different places, and it didn't make sense for them not to have it. Mom and Asmodeus and Belphegor were appointed as Archdemon council and made respon-sible for the day to day running of demon life.

Dad's pleased because it means Mom doesn't have time for Eternal Damnation anymore. She still owns it, but against my will, she told me he doesn't mind so much now that she's taken him there and made use of one of the rooms a few times. There's no brain bleach that can get rid of *that* knowledge. My mates and I claimed the underground palace as our home, and I blocked all access in and out via the elevator, desperately hoping for some quiet time to just get reacquainted with each other. Unfortunately, most of our families can teleport in anyway, so it's not much of a deterrent.

Definitely not soon enough, we're finally getting some down time, and I'm planning to sex up my mates, when Mylea comes for another visit.

"Oh, fuck me," I groan as her golden glow diminishes. "Seriously, I thought you'd leave me alone for a little while," I complain, throwing my hands over my eyes. I'm on the couch with Jagger and Kai and had just convinced the both of them to sneak off to my bedroom with me. I was going to shift shape into their favorite movie star fantasy, and then they were going to allow me to fuck them with the actor's cock, or mine, or whoever's. Anyway, I was looking forward to my first blowjob too, and now she's ruined it.

She snorts as she reads the information out of my brain. *Yeah, I forgot about that particular trick of hers.*

"Damn it, stay out of my head." I flip her off, but she just snorts again.

"Sorry to put a cramp in your very interesting evening activities, but we've got to fix this imbalance. It's time to return magic to Reath and dissolve all the realms bar one for the remaining species to live on. Have you thought about what you're going to name it?"

"Yes, I have, actually." I pull away from Kai and climb off of his lap, leaving him and Jagger extremely frustrated. Both look at Mylea with annoyance on their faces, but she just ignores them. Apparently, my new closeness with the goddess has given the rest of them enough bravery to be a little more themselves in her presence. "I'm going to call it Unity."

Mylea nods, a bright smile on her face. "Yeah, that's actually not bad. Okay, let's go get it done, then you can have some time for your... experiments." Jagger and Kai stand up to come with me, but she shakes her head. "Sorry, guys, gods only." With a wink, she transports us to Reath.

"Fuck, you just love pissing my mates off, don't you?" I grumble at her, but she laughs, not a care in the world for what they do or don't mind.

"Don't act like you don't love the angry sex that you'll get when you get home," she teases, and I smile to myself at her words. *She's not fucking wrong.*

"So, what we need to do is draw the magical creatures out of the realms and reshape them so that the specific myths and creations from Earth cease to exist and the remaining species become real. We then need to funnel that magic back into Reath." I give her a *what the fuck* look, and she responds in the way she normally does, with a laugh. "Don't worry, I'll do all the heavy lifting this time. You just have to be the battery."

I'm relieved and feeling much calmer about it as her three sidekicks arrive to help out. All three of them give me a hug and a kiss while teasing me about the situation I'd just left behind. Mylea had obviously filled them in, but her next comment sure shuts them up. "Excuse me, I know that each and every one of you has had a test run in a female's body during sex as well, so I don't think any of you have room to throw stones." Laughter bubbles up out of my chest, my turn this time, but I smother it with a cough as they all look anywhere other than at me.

"Okay, *that* subject is officially out of bounds," Matoz declares, and everyone agrees. Who knew gods could blush?

Once again, we join hands, but this time we stay grounded. The realms are on a parallel plane to Reath, so it's the best place to drain their magic from.

Unlike when I had to push power into Habbalea, we now have to draw the power out of the realms, reshaping and reforming it before evenly distributing it over Reath and its people. This draw of power is a gentle trickle unlike the tidal wave needed for the demon planet.

Realm by realm, I can feel the beings from Earth's imagination fading. Santa Claus, Halloween creatures, fairy-tale princesses, and religious constructs all disappearing, only to be remembered in the books and TV shows in the Earth realm. The remaining energy trickles through, touching each of the remaining races, solidifying them into real beings. Vampires, mermaids, fae, shifters, and djinn, as well as the creatures like unicorns and phoenixes and dragons. Many a weird and wonderful creature chosen and protected by Mylea's spell.

Eventually, the draw stops and she triggers the release. The power steadily flows outward over Reath, reconnecting the people with their magic. Magic which is very similar to the power that the Earth plague survivors now possess.

When it's done and we've dropped our hands, I ask them a question that's been on my mind.

"What happened to the girl, the one that genius, here," I say, pointing to Azeyr with my thumb, "stole. Did she settle back in on Earth okay?"

Azeyr grumbles at me, "Isn't it lucky that I did steal her, or we may not have found out about the change before numerous worldwide disasters had occurred?"

Yeah, I guess he's right about that.

"Madeline is just fine. It turns out that only young people between the ages of eighteen and twenty-five are showing signs of magic, and as such, we have set up a number of academies across the world to allow them to learn how to use it from experienced instructors in a safe environment. We will do much the same here to re-teach those who have been without their magic for too long. There's a possibility one will be needed in Unity as well, though they may have a handle on their own magic."

"What a great idea." Maybe now that magic is out there and they know about the other worlds, we can create some kind of interplanetary travel that Earthlings, Minzeons, Reathians, and demons can participate in. Angels have had all the advantages in the past, and now it's time to even the playing field."

"I couldn't agree more," Eagi says, hip bumping me, "and maybe you and your mates can spend a little time lecturing every now and again."

Damn it, I walked straight into that. "Um, I'm not sure how much time I'll have, but I'll keep it in mind," I force out, the smile on my face likely as insincere to them as I know it is.

"Now, how about we check out your new realm?" Myela says with a wave of her hand. A large ornate double door appears before me, the magic she used carrying a familiar signature.

"That's my magic!" I exclaim, walking closer and expecting it.

"Yes, this is the only way in and out of the realm unless they have permission from you to enter or exit. That way no one can escape, and no one can get in uninvited. No accidental wandering into a realm with bloodthirsty creatures for the rest of the planets' populations. You will be able to access it from anywhere, as well as people you give permission to. Think very carefully about who you allow this to because they can then take in and bring out whatever and whoever they wish," she warns.

The decorative gold handles glow with excitement as I approach, but just before I pull them open, a voice behind me has me pausing.

"You didn't think we were going to let you check out our new home on your own, did you?" Zeph's question has me smiling, and when I turn, all nine of my mates are there, dressed in CD uniforms with smiles on their faces.

"Would I do something like that?" I ask them.

Their smiles turn disgruntled as each and every one of them replies "Yes" in unison.

Shrugging, I wave them forward and push open the doors. We all enter and find a realm much like Reath. Sending out my magic, I learn what I can, cataloguing that it has different climates and habitats, all personalized to the different beings that have created their own pockets of communities.

"The people of this world intrinsically know that you are their goddess, but I would suggest you appoint a council like the demons did. It will save you many headaches over time, and you'll only need to mediate if they cannot come to an agreement." Noting her valuable advice, I promise that I'll sit down and figure that out as soon as I can.

Once again, she waves her hand, and what shimmers to solidity in front of us is nothing short of my dream house.

"This is our gift to you, a welcome to the family thing," she explains, "a space for you and your mates to live and love and be a family. It also has the impressive ability of being able to appear anywhere in the realm you want it. All you need to do is think of where you want it to be, and it will appear there."

"Though make sure everyone is in the house when you move or at least let them know where you've gone." Azeyr sounds like he speaks from experience, and Mylea blushes slightly, though she ignores him.

"Before I let you go to enjoy your downtime, there are a few things we need to discuss. Sabboath is still out there, and from what Grayson has said, he has another formula that contains god essence." Gray mumbles his confirmation, and my heart starts to pound. Fuck, I'd forgotten about him and Lesterial escaping. "Eventually, we will have to deal with him, but I don't think that needs to be done straight away." My heart rate eases a little, relieved that I'll have some time to get a handle on this goddess thing before we're called to active Sabboath hunting duty.

"We've put out an all world APB kind of thing,"

Zeph tells the goddess. "He'll make a mistake eventually, and when he does, there will be worlds of people looking to catch him in the act."

A pleased smile crossed Mylea's face, impressed that he's already making plans. Her gaze moves to Drusilla.

"Drusilla, come here," she requests, gesturing to my softest mate.

"Drusilla here has been hanging on to something that I took from you. Something that would have died with you when you did." I frown in confusion. *I don't remember her doing that.*

"Remember when I told you that to have a child I needed to have sex with each of my partners within a short period of time?" I nod, still not sure where she's going with this.

"Well, when you were in the prison, you had sex with the four there, and when you got out, you had sex with the remaining four." My heart starts to pound for a completely different reason now, and Dru gasps, her hand going to her mouth.

"Can you get the orb, please?" Mylea asks her gently, and Dru reaches into her safe space and pulls out the pulsing orb, handing it to Mylea. She takes the orb and holds it out toward my stomach, a flow of magic washing over me as the orb disappears, but when I look down, my stomach has a small bump to it.

Drusilla gasps, her face losing nearly all color. "The pulsing was a heartbeat!" Tears well in her eyes, her bottom lip trembling. "We're going to have a baby?"

A thud like something hitting the ground draws my attention, and when I turn to look at the other guys, Sander is flat on his back, lights out. The others look just as shocked, mouths open and eyes wide with surprise.

"Congratulations! I'm going to be honest, I get the feeling there is more than one in there, but I couldn't tell you exactly how many. Even at this stage in development, they're blocking me. I'm not sure how they're managing that, but you're going to have fun raising such powerful beings."

I put my hand over my stomach, and a rolling feeling goes through it as if they're moving. Tears fill my eyes as my mates all step closer.

"A baby?"

"No, babies," Samuel says as they all crowd in, leaving a shell-shocked but now conscious Sander sitting on the ground. Their hands reach out to touch my belly as my face is smothered with kisses, joy filling the air around us.

"Okay, okay, back off! You can all celebrate in a moment. Let me finish, and we will leave you be." Mylea shoos them out of the way, but I can still hear them congratulating each other like they did all the hard work.

Turning to me, she grabs my hands, her face beaming with pride. "Now, you have well and truly fulfilled all you were destined to, my sweet girl. I believe it's time that you and your mates got a vacation." The guys and Dru whoop and cheer with excitement. "Go and explore your new home, and I'll make sure no one will bother you for at least a month. Don't worry, I'll let them know where you all are, but because they are unable to access the realm, you will be left alone."

Drusilla doesn't need to be told twice, and she rushes off to inspect our new digs, the guys following behind once they've helped Sander to his feet.

"Thank you, Jessamina Michaels. You've exceeded all my expectations, and I couldn't be prouder." Mylea places a kiss on my forehead before she and her mates all disappear.

A tear rolls down my cheeks as I think about all that has happened and realize that I couldn't be any happier than I am today. Looking around the clearing in front of our house, I watch as a unicorn trots by, not concerned in the least by my presence, and decide that no matter what life throws at me, I can get through it with the support of family and my wonderful mates.

"Hey, are you coming?" Sander steps out of the front door and waves to me, and it's with love in my heart and light in my soul that I follow after them, ready to start the next phase of my life.

<u>THE MOTHER FUCKING END</u>

Thank you for reading!
I hope you enjoyed the book. It would be super awesome if you could leave a review wherever you bought it, because I love to hear what you thought of the story

That's it for Mina and the gang but as you probably noticed I left a thread or two open that could allow me to come back to it one day.

For now sign up to my newsletter for an occasional extra scene from Mina and the boys.

Sign up to my newsletter here
https://landing.mailerlite.com/webforms/ landing/s7a8a6

Another way to do that is to join me Facebook group. I drop teasers and giveaways in there all the time. Here's the link

https://www.facebook.com/ groups/1068846123323085

ACKNOWLEDGMENTS

It has almost been one year since I first published Guardian and Guardian Ascending marks my seventh book in that year. It has been one hell of a ride and I can't wait to bring to life all the other stories in my head.

Thank you to Claire Bosman and Lisa Whitman who allowed me to use their angel names in my book. Sorry they're assholes.

To Christy Dow thank you for your suggestion of the name Grayson, I think it was perfect I'd like to know what you thought.

Again thank you to Ashley at Infinity Book covers for the fabulous cover and dealing with me reformatting and needing the paperbacks adjusted.

Thank you to Michelle from Inked Imaginations for the editing. This was a beast of a book to quote you and I can't thank you enough for all your hard work on it.

Lastly to the girls who keep me sane on a day to day basis. Emma Cole, Grace McGinty and Hope Brown. Without you I'm sure I would be bald and rocking in a corner. Love your faces.

If you want a taste of what I'm working on, turn the page to read the first chapter of my new contemporary adult bully reverse harem that is out now with book two coming, fingers crossed before the end of the year.

Lexie

Neighpalm Industries Collective

Chapter One

"Harlow! Are you up here?" My best friend Maxine's husky voice carries up the stairs to my apartment above the barn. She claims it's from all the dust and hay from working with the horses everyday, but she's had it for as long as I've known her, and that's from before both of us could talk.

"Yeah, come on up," I call back, my eyes glued to the TV in front of me, the noise of her feet on the stairs getting louder the closer she gets. She bursts into the room, and I can see and smell that she's showered. Unlike the smell of horses and hay, which my apartment and I both usually smell like, she smells spicy and sweet. Probably some expensive designer fragrance that costs a gazillion dollars a bottle.

Looking her up and down, I can tell she's here

to harass me to join her for a night on the town. She's wearing a black bodycon dress that hugs her curves in all the right ways. Her dark blue eyes are accentuated by her smoky eyeshadow, and her burgundy lipstick and perfectly tousled pixie cut make her look like Tinkerbell gone wild. Her short frame is boosted by the five inch heels she's wearing. You would never know this girl wears boots and jeans most days and handles horses that could easily kill her if things go wrong.

"What are you doing? You want to hit a club?" she asks, going to my fridge and grabbing a bottle of beer for herself. Flipping the bottle top onto the counter, she takes a long pull before heading back over to the couch.

Taking a sip of my own beer, I watch, smiling, as her nose wrinkles when she looks for a clean place to sit. Not that my apartment is *dirty*, but I'm not great at picking up after myself, and there are books and magazines lying all over every surface.

She glances at the TV. "You're not watching those damn abandoned videos again, are you?" she asks in disgust.

"Check this out," I say to her, pointing at the television. "They're visiting this abandoned zoo in Detroit!"

"Huh?" She looks at me, confused, while finally moving some of my vet journals out of the way and taking a seat.

I take another sip of my beer. "I don't get it.

Why do they leave all these buildings abandoned? Why don't they repurpose them? The zoo would make a great animal sanctuary for the animals that idiots buy but can't manage. Like big cats and huge ass snakes and things." Shaking my head, I take another sip of my beer. "All these places in the world, houses and hospitals and shit, that people have just picked up and left abandoned for various reasons. It's fascinating. And these guys go around checking them out and filming them, discovering all the history. How cool is that?"

The incredulous look on Max's face almost makes me snort my beer through my nose. "Fucking hell, Harlow, you need to get laid. Your obsession with abandoned things is disturbing. Isn't your little menagerie downstairs enough?" Her tone is disgusted. "We're going out, and I won't take no for an answer. How long do you need to get ready?'

Looking down at my dirty jeans and fuzzy wool socks that I haven't bothered getting changed out of, I shrug my shoulders. "Nah, it's been a long day. You go and have fun; I'm going to stick to my abandoned, lonely buildings."

The look she gives me is borderline homicidal. "Is that supposed to be some kind of metaphor for your life, because, bitch, I've got no sympathy." She chugs her beer down in one go. "You're no more abandoned and unloved than I am. My parents think you walk on water, and I would pick you over my own siblings every time."

I roll my eyes at her dramatics. "You have no siblings, you spoiled, rich princess. So there *is* no competition."

"Who cares? It's the thought, right?" She waves her hand. "I'm giving you half an hour and then calling the car around. If you're not ready, I'll tell Mom that you're up here crying."

I shudder and quickly stand up, flicking off the television. "Damn, you don't play fair," I snap at her and stomp off to the bathroom to have a quick shower. "You better be buying the drinks. You know I hate spending money in those pretentious fucking clubs you drag me to with all those damn stuck up people you call friends."

Maxine is what you would call uber-wealthy. She comes from old, established money and probably has every right to be as stuck up as the rest of the patrons, but her parents raised her to be down to earth and to work hard. There isn't a snobby bone in her body. Well, not too many, anyway.

"Bah, if you didn't keep giving money to that crack whore who gave birth to you, you wouldn't have a problem. You know she's just going to snort it or shoot it up."

Closing the door to my bathroom, a bone weariness crosses my body at the thought of my mother. Never has she been responsible or even partly concerned about my welfare, but I still make sure she has a roof over her head, her bills are paid, and she has money for food. Though

Maxine is right, most of the food money goes on drugs.

I peel off my dirty work clothes, leaving them where they fall, and turn on the shower. Hot steam fills the small bathroom, and I step under the sharp spray, groaning when the heat hits my body. Standing there, I give myself five minutes to wallow in sadness.

My mother used to be a personal assistant for Maxine's parents, and they were beyond thrilled when she announced her pregnancy at the same time as Melinda, Maxine's mom. I was an instant playmate for their daughter, and we lived on the estate, so we've been inseparable since birth.

Unfortunately, while pregnant with me, Mom fell in with the wrong crowd. Maxine's parents kept her on for as long as they could after I was born, but by the time I turned two, she was doing hard drugs and not turning up for work. On the occasion she did, she stole from them to feed her habit. They let her go but allowed her to continue to drop me off to be looked after by the same nanny who looked after Maxine while she tried to keep one crummy job after the other. By the time I was five she was permanently unemployed.

Moving from couch to couch of one sleazy boyfriend to the next or begging her druggie friends to give us a room for the night had child protective services stepping in when Melinda demanded enough was enough. I was promptly removed from my mother's care and moved directly into Maxine's bedroom, a perfectly pretty princess bed to call my own, and welcomed like I was one of them.

Melinda and Charles were everything a girl could want in foster parents, but the children at the schools they sent me to never let me forget where and what I came from. Maxine was my staunchest supporter and still is, but deep down, a simmering resentment brewed toward the one who should love me above all else. It wasn't until my late teens when I did some lashing out of my own and Melinda and Chuck sent me to a therapist, that I came to realize that none of it was my fault. My mother had her own deep seeded issues and was way too selfish to be putting the wellbeing of a child before her own. That's on her, not me.

The one thing I will always hold against her though is the fact that she would never tell me about my father. She would use it as a way to manipulate me, promising to tell me things, and one day I realized that every story was different every time, so nothing ever added up. That was when I decided she probably didn't know who he was and let go of the thought of ever being rescued. It wasn't long after that that I went to stay with Maxine permanently and tucked that dream down into the recesses of my soul. Mom's always been a stain on my life; on visitation rights, she would drag me down to whichever bar or strip club she was working in at the time, and I would sit in the corner coloring while she tried to find her next fix. Later on, I discovered she was also finding her nightly meal ticket.

I never told Melinda or Chuck where we went; Diane took care of that by threatening Maxine with harm if I ever told anyone. It wasn't until I was about fifteen and the men she was trying to score with started to hit on me that she finally declared our fortnightly visits done with. I didn't see her for three years after that until I had finally graduated high school and was awarded a scholarship to the local university. By then I was working for Melinda and Chuck on their horse farm and had been for years, being paid decent money. That's when the guilt trip came raining down, and I started paying her money to keep her away from Maxine and her family.

"Hey, what are you doing in there? You didn't fall asleep, did you?" A thump on the doors made me jump. Maxine's patience had never lasted long.

Grabbing the soap, I shout back, "Sorry, I was daydreaming! I'll be fast." Making quick work of cleaning myself and my hair, I'm out and drying off when I hear her shout through the door again.

"I've put a dress on the bed. Wear it," she demands, and I groan to myself but she must hear it. "No, don't complain! I know if I leave you to it, you'll throw on a pair of ripped jeans and a fitted shirt or something. We're clubbing, not heading down to the local pub." Sniggering to myself, I wipe the condensation away from the mirror and study my reflection. My skin is sunkissed from all the time I spend outside, but, as yet, there are no fine lines developing. I'm careful to religiously apply sunscreen if I'm going to be outside for any length of time. Using my towel, I rub at my natural sun streaked blonde hair to stop it from dripping before wrapping it around my body. I grab out the blow drier and blast the long length until it's almost dry before running a brush through it. It has the windswept tousled look, and I figure that's good enough. I put a hair tie around my wrist in case it gets too hot in the club and I need to tie the whole lot up.

Unlike Maxine, I apply minimal makeup. Just some shadow, liner to my eyes to make the hazel stand out, and mascara to darken the blonde lashes. A bit of lipstick to my full lips and I'm good to go. Blowing myself a kiss in the mirror and rolling my eyes when Maxine shouts at me again to hurry up, I leave the bathroom in search of what horror she's placed out for me to wear.

Her text notification sounds while I'm stuffing myself into the tight blue number, and it's lucky my work is physical and I'm in great shape because there isn't an inch of my silhouette that this dress doesn't show off. But once it's on, the stretchy fabric allows easy movement, and I don't feel uncomfortable at all.

"That's the car," she tells me, looking up from

her screen and giving me a wolf whistle. "Girl, you clean up hot."

Rolling my eyes again, I grab my phone and hold it and my wallet up. "Where exactly am I supposed to put these?" I ask her sarcastically. "The dress doesn't exactly have pockets. Why don't they make dresses with pockets? Designers really are letting the female species down."

This time she rolls her eyes. "Put the wallet down, you won't need it, and the phone just shove into the top of your dress. Lord knows those things are big enough to keep it safe." She points at my breasts which are looking fabulous in the dress, though she's exaggerating about the size. Really, they're just a little more than a handful for a man with average-sized hands.

Doing what she says, we head down the stairs to the waiting car. "Good evening, ladies," William's elderly voice greets us as we climb in. He's been the Bostons' driver for as long as I can remember and is in his late sixties.

I shoot Maxine a dirty look before replying to him, "William, what are you doing driving us this late? We could have called a cab."

Maxine scoffs at me before he can answer. "Bitch, don't get your nonexistent panties in a twist." My heart in my throat, I look down at my dress to make sure nothing is showing, and she laughs, winking at me before continuing. " I tried to but he insisted on driving us. When we get there, he's going to return and go to bed, and we'll get a cab or an uber home." She growls, looking at him in the rearview mirror.

He just nods and smiles. "Of course, Miss Maxine."

He points the car in the direction of Hartford, and we get moving. Maxine has her phone in hand, and her fingers are moving furiously across the screen. "The gang's all there already," she tells me without looking up. "They can't wait to see us." I scoff and sit quietly as I watch the rural area roll by and slowly build up until we're traveling through the city. 'The Gang' are all kids we went to school with. Snobby rich kids who always treated me no better than the dirt at the bottom of their shoe, but Maxine protected me from the worst of their petty bullying.

William pulls the car up in front of a building glittering with spotlights and a line that stretches back around the block. A neon sign of a horse head and palm trees with martini glass in the middle is lit up with the words Club Neighpalm splashed across the front. I groan at the sight of that line and look down at the heels that Max made me wear. Unlike her five-inch, mine are slightly lower at about three inches, but I'm naturally taller than Max. I'm also not used to wearing them like she is. She spends an equal amount of time in boots or heels, whereas I try to go barefoot whenever I don't have on my boots. Either that or flip flops.

We climb out of the car, thanking William, and he smiles and waves goodbye before driving back into traffic. I start to head toward the back of the line, but Max grabs me. "Where are you going?" she asks, looking confused.

"To the back of the line." I tell her, gesturing down the block.

She just shakes her head and mumbles, "It's like you don't even know me." Then she pulls me toward the door, giving our names to the big beefy bouncer who eyes us appreciatively before stepping aside to let us in.

"Ok," I concede, "I should have known better. How did you get us on the list?"

"You know my grandparents' besties Grace and Howard?" she says as we walk through the quiet foyer.

"Nanna and Poppy Summers?" I reply in confusion, thinking about the kind elderly couple that visit Nana and Grandpa Boston a couple a times a year.

Nana and Grandpa Boston, Chuck's parents, are an older, refined couple who I've always felt didn't agree with Melinda and Chuck taking on a stray junkie's daughter. They were never outwardly hostile, but they never went out of their way to make me feel like I was wanted.

Nanna and Poppy Summers were the complete opposite. They filled a much needed void when they visited the house. My mother's parents died before I was born, so I had no grandparent figures in my life, but every time they visited they treated me as one of their own. Nanna would bake with me or take me on excursions to museums and the zoo and things. Poppy would slip me candy and chocolate, and when I fell off my pony for the first time, he was the one who picked me up, brushed me off, dried my tears, and made me get back on. "You're not a successful horseman until you've fallen off at least a hundred times," he reassured me. They would always invite me to come and stay with them at their place in California, but that was the one thing I was never allowed to do. When Mom gave me up to Melinda and Chuck, she made them promise I was never allowed to leave the state. Just another way to control and manipulate me throughout the year

"Yeah, this is one of their clubs. You know Neighplam Industries is a huge family corporation, and they have an airline, hotels, record and movie studios, even an energy drink. This is the latest club to open, and they put us on the list when I asked them too. We also get to drink for free tonight. VIPs all night long." She does a little happy dance as we walk, and I shake my head at her, but a smile crosses my lips, amused at her antics.

We approach the large wooden doors that also have the horse head and palm trees on them. The thud of the music can only just be heard through them, the soundproofing doing what it's supposed to. We stop, and Maxine turns to me, eyebrow raised, putting her hand up on the door. "You ready for this?" I just add my hands to hers, and together we push open the heavy club doors and step into a pounding, hedonistic delight.

Want more? Get Abandoned Girl here https:// books2read.com/AbandonedGirl